PENGUII

The Love Child

Fran Cusworth is a journalist with the *Herald Sun*. She lives in Melbourne's north with her husband and two children. This is her first novel.

Love
the

Child

FRAN CUSWORTH

PENGUIN BOOKS

PENGUIN BOOKS

Published by the Penguin Group
Penguin Group (Australia)
250 Camberwell Road, Camberwell, Victoria 3124, Australia
(a division of Pearson Australia Group Pty Ltd)
Penguin Group (USA) Inc.
375 Hudson Street, New York, New York 10014, USA
Penguin Group (Canada)
90 Eglinton Avenue East, Suite 700, Toronto ON M4P 2Y3, Canada
(a division of Pearson Penguin Canada Inc.)
Penguin Books Ltd
80 Strand, London WC2R 0RL, England
Penguin Ireland
25 St Stephen's Green, Dublin 2, Ireland
(a division of Penguin Books Ltd)
Penguin Books India Pvt Ltd
11 Community Centre, Panchsheel Park, New Delhi – 110 017, India
Penguin Group (NZ)
Cnr Airborne and Rosedale Roads, Albany, Auckland, New Zealand
(a division of Pearson New Zealand Ltd)
Penguin Books (South Africa) (Pty) Ltd
24 Sturdee Avenue, Rosebank, Johannesburg 2196, South Africa

Penguin Books Ltd, Registered Offices: 80 Strand, London WC2R 0RL, England

First published by Penguin Group (Australia), a division of Pearson Australia Group Pty
Ltd, 2006

1 3 5 7 9 10 8 6 4 2

Cover design and artwork by Liz Seymour © Penguin Group (Australia)
Text design by Cathy Larsen © Penguin Group (Australia)
Typeset in 12/14.5pt Granjon by Post Pre-press Group, Brisbane, Queensland
Printed and bound in Australia by McPherson's Printing Group, Maryborough, Victoria

National Library of Australia
Cataloguing-in-Publication data:

Cusworth, Frances Ann.
The love child.

ISBN-13: 978 0 14 300418 9
ISBN-10: 0 14 300418 2

1. Friendship – Fiction 2. Orphans – Fiction. I. Title

A823.4

www.penguin.com.au

For Simon

1

'Gloves,' insisted Cooper.

He thrust the blue woollen gloves towards Serena and she closed her eyes, gathering strength.

Here they finally were: pusher on the doorstep, bag packed, everyone fed and dressed. Sandals buckled, sunscreen applied, hats on. It was like wading through mud in concrete boots, trying to escape the house some days. And now, when all she wanted was Cate and a coffee, the prospect of laboriously guiding sweaty little fingers into tiny woollen sleeves.

'It's thirty-six degrees, Coop. Too hot. We're not wearing gloves today.'

Cooper shrieked, the horror-movie howl of someone shot in the back.

'Daddy does it! I want Daddy.'

Ah. The D-word. Guaranteed to make her lose it. She lost it.

'Cooper McAllister! Stop being such a bloody brat!'

They finally set off, Serena pushing baby Angus in the stroller with one hand. Cooper trailed from her other hand, still grizzling. She was minding Finn this morning too, and he was hitching a ride on the stroller at Angus's feet. The footpath radiated heat and a train clacked past, visible in gaps between the renovated Federation homes. She would be a better mother when she went back to work. Michael was going to call towards the end of the week, had hinted they might be able to give her a part-time job, although part time at MRA would mean something horrendous like working four days with one from home, or seven days crammed into three, or donating half a kidney instead of all her vital organs.

Cooper fell to the footpath, his head lolling on concrete.

'It's too hot.'

'Come *on*.'

Lately, it just seemed to be getting harder. There were days when Dave didn't get home until after midnight, days when she felt she was in some Lilliputian prison camp, stepping high to get over the safety fences that separated the kitchen from the back room; the back room from the toilet. Days when Angus crawled into a near-death experience every ten minutes, and when the only pretend games three-year-old Cooper wanted to play were ones where he was the predator (crocodile, dinosaur, Fat Controller) and she was the prey.

'I'm tired.' Cooper glared at the stroller where Finn perched on the step and Angus nestled inside. 'That's *my* seat.'

An elderly couple smiled fondly and stepped off the footpath to move past them.

Serena crouched to look Cooper in the eye. 'Well, today you're sharing it with Finn. He's your friend.' And what *had* happened to Priya and Richard? They were meant to collect Finn straight after the meeting with the real-estate agent, but that was an hour ago. Serena had left a note on the door asking them to come up to the local community centre. They weren't missing out on playgroup just because Priya and Richard had raced off to check out some hot property tip without calling.

'Finny's just a *little* boy. You're not *his* mummy. You're *my* mummy.'

Cooper frowned at dark-haired, dark-eyed Finn, who noticed the pause in movement and climbed down from the stroller. He staggered towards the road hopefully, Serena snatching him back just as a four-wheel drive surged past. Shit. Eighteen months was the worst age of all.

She took Angus out, sat him on her hip and ordered Cooper into the seat.

'Never learn to talk,' she told Angus, and kissed his cool fat cheek. He blinked at her. She helped Finn back on the step and pushed off quickly, hoping speed would silence them.

In the playgroup room, Cate stood staring at the noticeboard. Behind her, her son Matthew tottered with the strain of tugging a yellow wheelbarrow from the high cavity of the toy cupboard. Serena hastily took the barrow and put it on the ground before it could smash down on Matty's fair head. Cate was her comrade on the frontline, her best mum's group mate, but she could be a little vague.

'Can you believe someone would call their child Destiny?' she asked Serena now. 'What if they grow up to be a checkout chick?'

'Coo-ah!' shouted Matty.

'Mah-ee!' cried Cooper. He pulled down his shorts to

reveal Buzz Lightyear underpants. Matty lowered his own pants in greeting.

'Well, I guess checkout chick is a destiny, like any other.' Serena dragged out a garbage bin of sandpit toys and two ride-on dozers. She found a toy pram with a baby doll in a nappy and wheeled that out too.

'But you know what I mean, *Destiny*, it sort of implies they're going to create world peace or something.' Cate shook her head. 'Our generation,' she tsked.

Cate was very down on her own generation. Caesarean rates too high, telly watching too prevalent, meat-eating rampant, no instinctive knowledge of child-rearing. She admitted guilt to all these crimes herself, but there was a sense they had been inflicted on her by the unstoppable tide of shoddy mainstream parenting.

'But every generation has names of hope. You know, Faith, Honour. Hope even. My mum had an Aunty Hope.'

The boys hurled themselves at the ride-on dozers and clattered wildly around the room.

'Hope. Jesus, that name went out of fashion.' Cate nodded meaningfully. 'Says a lot about our generation, doesn't it?'

'Can we fix it? Yes we can! Can we . . .' The boys were working up to a hysterical chant now. Cate looked sheepish.

'Bloody Bob the Builder. Matt's hooked on it.'

'Well, listen to that positive affirmation it's given them. A message of empowerment in today's world . . .'

Serena checked on Angus, who was falling asleep in the stroller. Finn, with his jerky walk, brought Serena a tambourine and handed it up to her.

'He's very comfortable with you.' Cate watched Finn as he tapped the tambourine against Serena's knee.

'He should be. He's known me all his life.'

Serena remembered Finn's birth in more detail than the births of her own two children; able to watch the heartstopping miracle of a baby emerging while someone else bore the pain. She had applied the hot compresses and urged Priya to breathe all the way out. She had watched Richard bite his lip until it bled at the sound of Priya's screams, but she had known Priya would survive.

She went to the window and checked for them. No sign of their car. She had been deeply touched when Priya asked her to come to the birth, proud that their friendship, begun as uni students, had blossomed to such trust. Ana came to Finn's birth too, but she sat with her head between her knees for most of it.

Serena retreated to the noticeboard.

'Why do these people put up reports of what they do in playgroup every week? What are they trying to prove?'

'I think it's a schedule. And the names mean who brings morning tea.'

Serena read aloud. '"Wednesday Feb 3. Baby massage lecture. Di. Wednesday Feb 10. Art and craft therapist from St Ives. Rachel (macrobiotic delights!!!) Feb 17. First-aid course. Need a volunteer for MT. Feb 24. Every child brings favourite book to share. Group video and scrapbooking. Bindy." God, what do we do? Throw the kids some toys and ignore them for two hours.'

'I think it's very Steiner, what *we* do.'

'What, ignore them?'

'Let them have their own space, discover appropriate objects of play as they need.'

'Oh. Is that what we're doing?' Serena went into the kitchen, locking the safety gate behind her. She switched on the kettle and took out some cups. 'Who's coming?'

'Mel's got a meeting with some retailer about her new business . . .'

'Still the postnatal yoga classes?'

They were all in awe of Mel, who had left her job as human resources chief of the nation's largest telco to inflict her organisational genius on her son.

'No, the baby sling. She's outsourced the piecework, done her marketing plan, now she's getting onto the retail outlets.'

Serena shook her head. 'Well, Sharon rang this morning and she said Dhakota had a touch of a cold – he was coughing like a ninety-year-old – but she was *pretty sure* Shakylah was over her chicken pox . . .'

'. . . and let me guess, she was going to bring them along to make our kids sick too . . .'

'Exactly, only she was just picking up a family block of chocolate and some Coke for them to share at playgroup . . .' Serena reached for her mobile phone, ringing somewhere in the bottom of her nappy bag.

'Nooooo . . .' Cate's container of chopped carrots and celery already sat on the kitchen bench. She had been a sports dietitian, and her son was weaned onto a diet of biodynamic sea plants, vegetable juice and mashed tofu. She looked frantic. 'Can we leave? Now?'

'Ah, what's a bit of chocolate?'

Serena paddled around her bag, digging through used tissues and the sticky folds of a plastic change mat until the ringing grew more shrill. 'This is why I hate mobiles. Hello?'

'Sorry? Detective Constable who?'

A minute later she sat abruptly on the cold linoleum floor, the phone clattering down beside her, her eyes fixed on Finn's frowning face as he banged the tambourine. She heard the child gate slam as if it was underwater, and Cate called her name. Words swam in her head senselessly: '. . . *a car accident* . . .' and '. . . *dead instantly* . . .' and '. . . *understand in your care* . . .'. Then Cooper's fingers were like birds' feet on her hair as tears streamed down her cheeks and she struggled to breathe.

'Mummy? Mummy? What's the matter, Mummy?'

2

Ana sat back and tapped her pen on the table.

'I'm thinking,' she held up an imaginary headline, '*Ease Up On Stockers*. Aren't we all being a bit hard on him?'

She often thought that being junior columnist for the *Morning Star* would be great training for a career in sales. In the news conference room at half past ten every morning, here she was, selling her ideas to eight men. When that was done, she had to sit at a computer and sell them to her readers. Somewhere along the line, she also had to convince herself to buy her own arguments.

She leaned forward over the table's polished surface. Around her was the usual phalanx of male attire: jacket; jacket, shirt and tie; shirt and loosened tie (managing editor); shirt no tie; shirt no tie (sports editors); tie being stroked lovingly (senior columnist) and tie tucked goofily away between shirt buttons (picture editor). Beyond the soundproof glass windows of this room, reporters typed at computers, while the windows to the other side offered a twenty-fifth floor, ceiling-to-carpet panorama of West Melbourne and Port Phillip Bay.

Ana sought eye contact where she could. She opened her hands and beseeched. She feigned scorn, outrage. She sold.

'It's like, if you adopt a child, you practically have to

do a masters degree to prove you're a fit parent. And then when your marriage breaks down, like Terry Stockman's, you get every man and his dog passing judgement on your parenting . . .' Stockman was a once-popular local business identity who had, in a moment of hysteria, kidnapped his children after he lost a family court custody dispute. The children had been recovered but Stockers' financial backers were vanishing even faster than his visiting rights.

'He didn't adopt. They're from his sperm,' said Zac Banks, senior columnist. He sat sideways in his chair, staring out to the bay, and spoke resentfully, as if he had been interrupted from some extended period of Buddhist meditation. He made a lethargic wanking gesture with one fist over his groin as he spoke.

Ana blinked hard to stop herself rolling her eyes at him. *Congratulations, Zac, on that groundbreaking scoop. And you got to say the word sperm and gesture to your penis in front of me – ten points to Slytherin.*

'I know, but the issue is still there: who has the right to be a parent? And who has the right to judge that?'

The police scanner hissed and muttered in the corner. 'Ccchhhh . . . Head-on in Northcote. Double fatal, High Street blocked on city outbound side, TOG present . . . cchhhhh . . . over . . .'

Zac, of course, would never mention his own two teenagers in any discussion about parenting. It was like he was some celebrity spunk who felt it best to hide the fact he had a girlfriend, so as not to break the hearts of any fans.

Crazy, that nature let some people reproduce at all

while others missed out. Or nearly missed out. Like Priya and Richard – three years of trying before they had Finn. No alcohol, all those tests.

'I still think they should arrest pregnant women who smoke,' said Pete Pryor, editor of the Gotcha gossip section. Happily married, grown children.

'I think Ana's got a point about Stockers. As a society, we are pretty hard on fathers,' said Morrie Lumiere, features. Divorcee who took his kids to the footy every second weekend. Ana nodded at him gratefully.

'What about IVF?' said Jason Lowenthal, managing editor. Married three times, with adult children older than his new wife. 'Ban it for single women. And women over forty. There's a column for you.' He nodded at Ana and she bent her head and wrote on her notepad in shorthand, *Jesus Christ get me out of here*. Lowenthal watched her approvingly. He couldn't do shorthand but he liked his people using it.

'Mate, I think all new parents should do a certified parenting course before they're allowed to give birth,' said Daniel Rizzo, sport. Married, no kids.

Lowenthal nodded emphatically, flickering his fingers towards her notepad as if he were feeding goldfish. 'Another great idea for you, Ana. Lots of op-ed ideas flying around today!'

Well, yeah, for other people's opinions, Ana reflected, as she resentfully noted them. *Cert parent course. Ban IVF single. Pick up drycleaning.* She could usually rely on Lowenthal forgetting his ideas, although occasionally he would fall in love with his own genius and nag until she followed through. She, however, held stubbornly to the apparently outdated notion that opinion pieces were meant to reflect opinions held by the writer, not by her boss. Funny how *Zac* wasn't expected to be the editor's mouthpiece.

'Yes, they're duly noted. So, for today I'll push ahead with Stockers,' she said, scribbling assertively on her notepad to avoid meeting anyone's eye. She had already half-written this column and she was hoping to get away at a reasonable hour for her weekly dinner with Priya and Richard. It was her turn to choose the takeaway and she had found a great new Thai restaurant. Lowenthal flicked furiously through his diary, and answered a call on his mobile. Morrie Lumiere picked his teeth and Ana briskly slapped her pen down on her notepad to indicate closure of the subject. Only Zac watched her every move, as if highly amused.

'Well, I guess that's it.' She stood.

'I think they should keep a record of people who've had abortions, and they should never be allowed to do IVF,' said Pete Pryor thoughtfully. He winked at her.

'By people, you mean women,' said Ana.

'Meow.' Zac made a clawing motion.

'No! Men, too!' Pryor protested. 'Fathers, you know. It's not just *women* who make babies, Ana!' He stared at her in mock hurt and she rolled her eyes at him.

'Dickhead.' She said it with mild affection. The gossip writer was her favourite of all the suits, having a conspiratorial sense of humour.

Zac tilted his head at her. 'Is it hard for you to write these pieces, about having children?'

'No. I do research.' Zac was her least favourite. She slammed her notebook shut. 'Like with any subject.'

She knew how they saw her: Ana Haverfield, unmarried, no kids, desperately clinging to her youth, motherhood gene defective. They were practically leaning down to listen at her womb for the ticking clock some days.

'Well, Ana,' said Lowenthal, closing his mobile and scribbling on a piece of paper. Only the bald spot on the top of his head pointed towards her, like a shiny, featureless face. 'I look forward to reading that one.'

Which one? She didn't dare ask. She would follow her usual technique of listening carefully to the wisdom of her fellow editors, and then writing whatever she wanted.

It had worked for her so far.

Back at her desk she checked her phone messages. Three from her mother, sounding increasingly frail. The first one said that she'd run out of cigarettes, but had read something about how chewing on sunflower seeds helped the cravings, and it was true, she didn't need extra cigarettes, although she would love a visit from Ana whenever she could spare the time. The second said she had eaten all her sunflower seeds and could Ana drop by with a new packet, and maybe some cigarettes as well, just in case? The third said she had decided to write her autobiography, and maybe Ana could help her. And the cigarettes?

'Only if you've got the time. I know you're very, very busy,' Lily finished sadly. There was a long pause and some sniffing and she hung up.

Ana flicked back through her diary. It was two weeks since she had visited her mother and she knew the phone calls would increase in frequency now until she drove out there. She sighed. She wished she weren't the only child left, that Nick had lived, and grown into a nice normal brother, and they could call each other at times like these and say, 'Oh dear, she's starting up, I'll go and visit her.' 'No, you're too busy, let me.' 'No, really, let me . . .' She went out to the shops for sunflower seeds and cigarettes and then took a work car out to the hostel, a fifteen-minute drive away.

Lily was tearily grateful, as thin and dry as if smoking had fossilised her. She still trembled, but the weeping and temper had eased these days, as if the bland pastels of the nursing home had finally dissipated her once-toxic griefs. Ana stayed for a carefully timed twenty minutes, promising to return the following evening, and then raced back to work, grabbing a sandwich on the way and mentally planning her afternoon. She would write the Stockman column by two, then spend an hour updating her ideas file. Do some research on a government tip off she'd had about the Hammer Hill project and have a quick coffee with a PR consultant who was trying to sell her a story. Give a talk to the cadets at five, and then race out for dinner with Priya and Richard.

Back at her desk again, Ana checked her emails. Beyond her corral walls, the newsroom buzzed. Keyboards clicked like knitting needles, phones rang, a voice on a radio talkback show whined, '. . . they should all go back home if they don't like it here . . .' A bank of televisions screened silently talking heads, and clocks showed times from Amsterdam to Zurich.

She opened an email from her friend and colleague

Marnie, newly back from maternity leave. Marnie had once had the prime window seat next to Ana's but that had been snapped up during her absence by the industrial reporter. Marnie was now seated at a temporary desk squeezed in between the cadet and the work experience student at the furthest leg of the L-shaped office, where the broken chairs were herded.

From: Marnie Atkinson

To: Ana Haverfield

> Just pumped 190 mL of breastmilk, PB for late morning. News want to me to do pic story on two lesbians parenting a child from donor sperm, must make good visuals, ie spiky hair, pet dog. Know anyone? Must go pump milk again at one, so fretting.

From: Ana Haverfield

To: Marnie Atkinson

> Great job with the milk. I don't know how you fit in pumping three times a day. How is Lucy?
> When are they going to stop giving you mummy stories? Is it driving you mad?

From: Marnie Atkinson

To: Ana Haverfield

> What's driving me mad is the fridge. When did journos become health freaks? The fridge is chockers with organic yoghurts and lunch boxes the size of small cars. Daniel Rizzo just cracked the sads because I took his six pack of Gatorade out to make room for my three-month-old baby's expressed breast milk, I mean sorreeeee!!
> Mummy stories, is that what they are? I hadn't noticed. Whatever.

It doesn't worry me. I don't think. Not until you mentioned it.

Got a lesbian for me?

Ana emailed Marnie some names and numbers before turning back to her own work. She spent the next hour trawling through parenting websites.

'Infertility may seem a curse, but maybe it's nature's way of healthy population control,' said one writer to a Christian website. *'And, sad as it is to consider, maybe some parents simply should not have children . . . IVF can only be against God's will . . .'*

She picked up the phone and dialled Priya's number. Priya would find this stuff hilarious. But as the phone rang out, Ana remembered one of Priya's bad days after the birth, when she couldn't seem to get out of bed for crying.

'Maybe I wasn't meant to have Finn,' she wept, Finn swaddled and asleep in a white Moses basket beside her. 'Maybe this is why it took us so long.'

'What do you mean?' Ana said, putting down a cup of tea and sitting on the edge of the mattress.

'I'm not coping,' Priya wiped her eyes. 'I shouldn't have had a baby. I wasn't meant to.'

It did all seem to come hard to Priya. The years of waiting, that horrendous birth, the mastitis that forced an end to breastfeeding, and an underweight baby who seemed to scream off any extra fat his parents could get onto him.

So different from Serena. Serena had delivered one fat, happy baby, shortly followed by another, and dropped her geology career like a hot potato to become a pillar of the local mothers' group.

Ana picked up her ringing phone.

'It's me.'

It was Serena, who rarely called her at work. Funny how bad news, big news, came with only a heartbeat of warning, a change of habit, the tickle in your mind from a police scanner. A friend's shaking voice.

Funny that, but she would only think it much later.

'Priya and Richard are dead. They were killed in a car accident today.' Serena's breathing was hoarse and rattly. Ana realised Serena's teeth were chattering.

Dead. Dead. Had she really said that?

'What?'

'Dead. Car accident. Both killed instantly.'

'*Dead*?' Ana inhaled so hard her chest hurt. The world around her became a blur, broken by objects in strangely sharp focus. Zac Banks emerged from the fog, stopped at her desk and stared at her. She turned away and pressed Serena's voice to her ear.

'The police just rang.'

'What . . . but where?'

'Northcote. They were going to see a real-estate agent. A truck slammed into their car. They died instantly.'

'And Finn?' Ana's voice grew higher and louder with each word. People around her fell silent, watching. 'Was Finn in the car too?'

Serena was sobbing now. 'No. He's . . . with me. I was . . . minding him . . . for them.'

Ana dropped the phone into its cradle. She momentarily thought, *Is this a joke?* But she had known Serena for almost twenty years, as long as she had known Priya. Serena had held Ana's hand at Nick's funeral; they had gone together to Priya's mother's funeral. Serena wouldn't joke about death.

She stood, surrounded by some deep, faint, whooshing noise. For a befuddled second she thought of Finn's special windy-day sound, the way he waved his arms and blew out his cheeks. Zac held her shoulder and called for someone to bring a glass of water, and to go and get Marnie. Ana reached out her shaking hand and found it like trying to manoeuvre a flapping fish.

She had a picture of Finn on her desk, which the newspaper had just used to illustrate a story on child water safety. Priya had been delighted; she pre-ordered ten copies from her local newsagent. Finn was sitting in the bath, his black curls wet, silver ripples ringing his round tummy. Face-up like a flower, an open-mouthed smile. Those ripples, that moment, this moment, would never come again and for a wild second Ana knew that the rushing in her ears had always been there; not the sound of Finn's windy day but the rush and clamour of time, of life, thundering by way too fast.

3

Serena emptied the paste out of the saucepan onto the bench. The saucepan fell on the floor and she jumped back to dodge its hot weight.

'Fuck,' she said. Her tears started again. Finn and Cooper watched from their little table, eyes wide.

'Fuh,' breathed Finn.

'Don't say that!' said Cooper.

'Stop bossing him, Coop.'

'It's a naughty word.'

'He's just a baby. Babies don't know what they're saying.'

'*You're* not a baby.'

Serena took a chef's knife and axed the playdough into four chunks. She pressed a thumb-hole into each. She took down the food colouring and poured in blue, green, red, yellow.

Through the window, it rained. The house was still warm from the heatwave of the past few days, and out to the north, thunder rolled. The washing on the line had been there for three days. Cooper and Angus would have nothing to wear. Or Finn. Orphan; was there a lonelier word in the world? Finn had been the centre of his parents' universe. Quite whose problem he was now, was yet to be determined. Richard had hated his father but the old man was flying in for the funeral and as the last remaining grandparent, he would need to help decide Finn's future. He had already rung from Scotland, his voice frail but curt, and indicated he would see Finn at the funeral, a veiled instruction that made Serena bristle. Funeral my arse. She had rung her mother and asked her to babysit, firmly of the opinion that funerals were not for children. How did you dress an eighteen-month-old for his parents' funeral? Did you take photographs, carry toys for him to play with? She knew the first wail from Finn at the funeral, be it from fatigue or frustration or hunger, would make people distraught. Best avoid the whole thing.

The funeral. At least she might get to spend some time with Dave. He said he would take a day off. She leaned her face back so the tears would stop falling in the playdough.

The answering machine flashed with a message she had already played twice.

'Serena, Michael here from MRA. I've spoken to Alex about taking you back part time and it's looking good. Just got to argue the case with Sydney. It might be June before we get a decision, these things move slowly, but I'm confident. Give me a call.'

She hadn't called.

Finn screamed. Cooper stepped away from him, his face a picture of aggrieved innocence. He held a Spiderman doll. Finn roared, his eyes cupped with tears.

'Cooper McAllister, was Finn playing with Spiderman?'

'His my Spi-man.'

Serena pried the doll out of her son's chubby fingers.

She scooped up Finn, gave him some playdough and pointed Spiderman head-first up the hall.

'Go to your room. Time out. Right now. I've asked you to be extra nice to Finn, haven't I? No, you're not having Spiderman. Spiderman's going on a holiday in my wardrobe.'

Cooper stared up at her, heartbroken, his mouth opening in horror.

'And not Cooper?'

'No. Spiderman's shocked at you, being mean to Finn.'

'No, he's not! He's *my* Spi-man.' Tears.

'MOVE!'

Finn wailed for his playdough, which he had dropped on the floor. Serena stepped in it with her bare foot.

'I want Spi-man!'

Finn howled.

Damn. They had woken Angus. She held Finn with one arm and kneaded playdough with the other. Violent red streaked and bubbled through the white dough. She pushed it and pounded it until it turned an even pink.

'Mumma?' said Finn. He had been asking for three days, tugging at her hand and leading her to the front door. She gave him the pink ball and put him down. 'Ah,' he said appreciatively. God, but he was easily distracted.

Serena scraped the muck off her foot with a tissue. She stepped out the back door and let the fat raindrops fall in her hair, and slide down her neck. The timber of the deck was still warm under her feet. The ripe gooseberries had fallen onto the concrete and cooked slowly in crimson crusts. Finn saw her leaving and toddled after her.

'Cooper,' she shouted. 'Come and play with Finn. And play nicely.'

She shut the door on them all. She ran to the boys' cubby and swung up in two moves. Inside, the wooden floor was dry and her rocks were stacked in a corner with a Thomas the Tank Engine that had no wheels. She picked up a rock and turned it over. Coarse grained ignimbrite with prominent spherulites. Dogwood; thickly timbered forests, sun breaking through to the Tambo River. She had loved that field trip, her last one. Priya had been there too. They sat under the moon and drank Poss's home-brew to the sound of the banjo frogs, until Priya became giggly and lay down on the moonlit grass.

Priya. Dead. It was impossible.

And now that Priya was gone, the biggest secret of Finn's short life rested with Serena. A secret also linked to the world of rocks and forests; of four-wheel drives and core samples and drill rigs in a clearing, and sunsets from the balconies of country pubs.

Another woman's secret, that weighed almost as heavy as her own.

She pressed her palm against the jagged edges of ignimbrite until it hurt and she placed the other hand on her belly. She prodded her own flesh for what she feared, beneath the soft surface.

Resistance.

She sucked in a breath. She had still told no one.

'Priya always said she wanted to be buried,' said Ana later, in Serena's kitchen. She had Finn on her lap and was feeding him a bowl of spaghetti. Finn plunged his fingers into the pasta; dropped the spirals on the floor. 'Should I stop him doing that?'

'Yes!' said Serena. Did she have to mother everybody, even bloody Ms big time Columnist here? But she knew she was being unbearable; cranky, sick, unfair to her old and dear friend. Premenstrual, maybe? Her heart lurched with hope.

She cradled Angus on her lap and watched him feed. Three feeds a day at what was he, ten, nearly eleven months? She should get a bloody medal. She had almost coaxed him off the breast, she had just about done it. But since she'd been crying every day, Angus demanded the breast with fresh vigour, eyeing her jealously over the pale curve as he sucked, holding on long after she knew he'd finished. His tiny teeth grazed her nipple and she clenched her jaw. She shifted her stomach under Angus's hip and the dread rose in her again, tasting like metal in her mouth.

She looked up. Ana wept silently over Finn's head, as the little boy turned the pages of a book. Serena stared. She wanted to ask Ana something, a question so stupid and insecure it would strip her naked. Did Priya like me, she wanted to ask? Did she think I was a good mother?

But she said nothing, just leaned over to stroke Ana's shoulder.

'I can't believe she's gone.' Ana wiped away tears.

'I know. We're going to miss her so much.'

They had been saying the same thing, back and forward, for three days now. It was like a chant. And she still couldn't believe it. All those crazy times at uni, the three of them sharing the house in St Kilda, when all the big questions of their lives were ahead of them, waiting to be answered. Would they marry? Who would they marry? Would they get the jobs they wanted – doctor, geologist, journalist? Would they have children? Would anyone get famous, or rich, or sleep with someone famous or rich? But, would one of them die before the age of forty, leaving a small child orphaned? That had never been a question. That was never on the list of possibilities. She felt like she had to go back and sift through her memories of Priya. The night the three of them got so drunk at a club that Ana was sick in Priya's handbag and Serena tore a hole in the pool table's green felt with some wild handling of the cue, and Priya became friendly with the chef, and ended up shagging him out the back on a delivery of freshly laundered napkins. Priya at her wedding to Richard, a vision in a deep purple sari with gold flashing at every extremity. At her mother's funeral, when she sat expressionless in the front row throughout, Melbourne's medical fraternity filling the seats behind. All her memories of Priya had to be redrawn now, with her tragic ending up ahead.

It started to rain again. Cooper appeared at the back screen door, in yellow raincoat and matching boots.

'Mummy,' he wailed. 'The cubby's wet.'

'Well, open the door and come in, quick.'

'It's locked.'

'It's not.'

'It is.'

'It is not. Just hold the handle down.'

Jesus, her every waking hour was full of these utterly tedious exchanges. *Must return Michael's call.*

'Finn didn't have godparents, did he?' Serena switched Angus to the other breast.

'Priya said if she was going to have anyone it would have been us.' Ana sipped her coffee and looked about her at the kitchen with toys strewn everywhere. 'Would you think about adopting him? He knows you so well.'

Serena flinched. 'I'm planning on going back to work soon. In June, maybe. At MRA.' But her low-level nausea suddenly peaked, as if to remind her that this could be complicated.

'Really?'

'What about you? He knows you pretty well too.'

'Oh God,' said Ana, stretching out her legs and crossing them at the ankles. 'I'd be hopeless.'

Serena studied her friend thoughtfully. Ana wore expensively casual charcoal work pants and a pink shirt with sharp creases down the arms. Serena couldn't remember the last time she herself had ironed anything. Ana wore crimson patent-leather boots with square toes and block heels, and at her throat she wore an incredibly detailed necklace of tiny interlocked gold cats, which Cooper yearned to own. Ana lived in an inner-city flat with floor-to-ceiling windows and she went to book groups and yoga weekends and meetings in Canberra and she had four newspapers delivered every morning and read them all by breakfast. It was impossible to imagine Ana as a mother.

But Serena had once found it impossible to imagine Priya as a mother. She could be so fey, so remote. She remembered Priya as she had last seen her, in the doorway, all puff-parka and black curls, and a tiny Bart Simpson backpack, dropping Finn off for a play. *Thanks, Sreny. You're a mate. We'll just be an hour or two.*

Serena had taken the bag. Taken the little boy, like plucking a blossom of parka and black curls off the tree of Priya, for what would be, as it turned out, the very last time. You made me feel confident, she told her dead friend. You made me feel good about myself.

She wept. Angus, dislodged by her hiccupping, rolled off her breast and stared up at her. He was flushed and shiny eyed, his chubby skin like white chocolate, and he reached for her wet lips and smiled.

4

'So, Ana, what have you got for us today?'

Ana blinked. Morrie Lumiere guffawed and Rizzo clicked his fingers in front of her eyes.

'Wakey wakey.'

'Sorry.'

It was Ana's first day back since Priya's death, and a week since the funeral. She had spent the time sitting around at Serena's, drinking cups of iced tea and crying and reading stories to the boys. On the hot days, she and Serena took the boys swimming at the Northcote Y, dangling their ankles in the toddlers' pool, sipping icy poles and taking it in turns to cry while Cooper and Finn ran in and out of the water. When it got too crazy at Serena's, she made her excuses and left, going home to her apartment on Brunswick Street, in Fitzroy. By morning most days, a stale misery sent her reeling back out to Serena's. Now, sitting in the *Morning Star*'s conference room, she felt light and fragile, as though the first agony of grief had moved into something more meditative and fractionally easier to bear.

However, having fingers snapped in her face during morning conference could be all it took to shatter her.

She consulted her list.

'The ACTU's living wage case, that's running at the moment. I thought I'd write something comparing average wages of women in 2005 with men in 1995, arguing that women are ten years behind, and should be . . .' she trailed off lamely, aware that Lowenthal was looking at her in disbelief.

'You mean the living wage case that was resolved last Thursday?'

Ouch.

'Ah . . . yes.' She thought quickly. 'A sort of post-outcome commentary on the . . . er . . . outcome.' Please, no one ask me what the outcome was, she prayed.

Lowenthal glared.

'When you're a journalist it helps to actually *read* the newspaper, Ana.'

Ow. Truly horrible. Why had she come to work today? She felt her delicate state of balance teetering, her face flushing. Zac leaned forward.

'Actually, Jason, if I'm going to Sydney next week there's a few columns I'd like to use up in the paper over the next few days, if Ana doesn't mind giving me the space.'

Typical Zac, jumping in on any weakness.

'And I've got that Fred Simons one I'd like to get run tomorrow if possible,' interjected Pete Pryor.

'Done. Well, that's it, lads. Hop to it.'

Lowenthal left. Ana bitterly noted the 'lads', as if she weren't there. She stacked her notebooks slowly, while the others filed out.

Pete Pryor stopped beside her. 'How was your friend's funeral?'

'Oh, you know. Crap. And now Lowenthal thinks I've completely lost the plot. Luckily Zac's there to capitalise on my stupidity.' She glared after the senior columnist, now weaving his way towards the far side of the office.

Pryor batted his eyelids.

'Goodness. I imagine he thought he was helping you out.'

'Really?' She considered it. 'Maybe he was. Don't tell him I said that, Pete. I'm not myself at the moment.'

'I'd say you're more yourself than ever, Ms Haverfield. Chip on shoulder present and accounted for.' Pryor put his finger beside his nose and grinned at her in a camp manner. 'And trust me, I'm . . .'

'. . . a journalist,' she finished for him. 'Yeah, right.'

'But seriously, Ana. There are more important things in the world than who writes yet another column in yet another newspaper.'

'I know that.' She bristled. First she got told off for being slack, then she got jumped on for being some sort of heartless work obsessive. But Pryor put his hand on her arm.

'In fact, there are a lot of things.'

Oh, piss off.

Back at her desk there were flowers and a card from Marnie. *Welcome back. Be kind to yourself.* She pictured Marnie's morning; get herself ready, feed and dress baby Lucy and pack her bag, drop Lucy off at childcare with three packets of frozen breast milk, drive to the station and catch the train in to work. When did Marnie buy flowers and write on a card, how did she have the energy to be so thoughtful? The gesture brought Ana more guilt than comfort.

She worked her way through twenty-eight phone messages, deleting as she went, noting names and numbers on a pad. Then she went through ninety-six emails, deleting most, saving the ones that needed answers.

She went back to her phone list. A man called Elijah Moyal, who said he was a lawyer, had left three messages. On the third message, he clarified further – he was Priya and Richard's lawyer.

She rang Serena. 'Did a guy called Elijah Moyal call you? Priya and Richard's lawyer?'

'No. Their lawyer? I didn't even know they had one. Get down off that chair now! Let go of it. What does he want?'

'I don't know. I haven't called him back yet. What could it be, do you think?'

'If you can't share it, then it goes into Mummy's wardrobe and she locks the door. Maybe it's to do with their will?'

'Did they have one?'

'I don't know. She never said. But probably. Ouch! Go to your room! Right now!'

'Are you sure he hasn't rung you?' A new dread was creeping up Ana's throat. 'Serena, I'm scared.'

'Finny, Cooper's sorry. It was an accident. Sorry, Ana, what did you say?'

'Nothing. Don't worry.' She hung up.

She sat and stared at the lawyer's number, lost in thought. She had left for the funeral from Serena's house, following Dave and Serena's car in her own. The funeral was big on friends and people their own age, but short on family. Richard's father had flown in from

Edinburgh that morning, a man who even leaned on his walking frame as though trying to subjugate it to his will. Ana and Serena helped him to a seat in the front row of the half-full church, where he jabbed combatively at the cushion before lowering his fragile rump onto it. Ana and Serena exchanged glances. They had been hearing about Richard's dad for years, a man so disgusted by his son's screenwriting aspirations that he had taken back the car that had been a gift for his son's eighteenth birthday and sold it, upon which Richard took a holiday to Australia, met Priya and stayed.

He cleared his throat at Serena. 'So, Finn's staying with you?'

'He is for now . . .'

'Very kind of you. Is he a good boy?'

Serena raised her eyebrows. 'Ah . . . well at eighteen months of age it's hard to . . .'

'Still a baby. Right. But when they get older . . .' He shook his head and frowned, eyes bright.

Serena leaned forward. 'Well, we are thinking about what's best for him in the long term. Richard . . .'

The old rogue dragged out a handkerchief and slapped at his eyes as if trying to kill an insect.

'Best he stays where he was born, I think.'

'But . . .'

'I'm too old, I can't possibly care for him now. And anyway,' he squeezed his handkerchief in enormous knuckles and spoke surprisingly softly, 'I would be no good at it. Richard wouldn't want it. But if it's all right, I'd like to see the child before I go home.'

Later, at the wake, Ana cornered Serena by the cheesecake.

'How is it going, having Finn?' Privately, she thought it must be blindingly obvious to anyone that Serena was the perfect candidate to take Finn and raise him. She had young children, Finn knew her well, it was a family environment, she was his mother's close friend.

Serena stared into middle distance. 'It's pretty crazy. I'm barely on top of my own two. And I want to go back to work soon. It's okay for now, but I never wanted a third child.'

'No, no, no, of course,' said Ana hastily. She didn't doubt for a moment that Serena would adopt Finn. It was what Priya would have wanted. Surely. Serena just needed time to get used to the idea.

Now at her desk, she rang the lawyer's number. A male voice answered, and she cleared her throat.

'Mr Moyal? Ana Haverfield, you rang me last week.'

A shift in his breath, a mutter to someone else, the sound of a door, or a drawer, closing.

'Ana, I'm very sorry about your friends' tragic accident.'

'Thank you.'

'You were obviously very close.'

Obviously?

'I lived with Priya at uni.' And we backpacked in India together, and I gave a speech at her wedding, and I attended the birth of her child; all the mementoes of a friendship, and yet it was the bits in between that were the real cement – the takeaways in front of the telly, the hours on the phone analysing our mothers, the mixed basketball competition that ended in near-violence every Sunday night.

'I rang you because I drew up Priya and Richard's will last year and they nominated you as Finn's preferred guardian, should anything happen to them.'

'What does that mean?' Paperwork, maybe. Signing bank statements.

'It means, in their case, that they wanted him to live with you and be raised by you, as if he was your own.'

'They *what*?' Her heart spiked with terror, until she realised the mistake. 'No, no, no, no, no.' She exhaled. 'You mean Serena. Serena McAllister.'

There was a pause. 'No, I don't.'

'Serena's the one with the kids. Married. Used to be a geologist?'

'Yes, and you're a journalist and you're unmarried and you work as a columnist for the *Morning Star* and you live in Fitzroy.'

'Oh.' She felt sweat on her top lip, watched her fingers shake.

'And they did nominate you to be Finn's guardian.'

'But they never told me.' The gift of trust, enormous, beyond flattering, was something she received in her heart. The reality of a whole, small child as her own responsibility, however, she felt horribly in her gut.

'They didn't? Well. I guess no one thinks they're going to die before their children.' He cleared his throat. 'I understand Finn is with your friend Serena now.'

'He's very happy there, he knows her well.' Her tone was plaintive. Thank God for Serena. She would see this was ridiculous.

'And might Serena want custody if you're ... unable?'

32

'I don't know. Maybe. I think we're all just taking it day by day at the moment.' Ana stared unseeingly up at the newsroom wall, up at the clock faces that showed the times in Paris, in Belgium, in Perth and Rome. Up at the figure of . . . her boss, Jason Lowenthal, leaning over her partition.

She jumped. He scribbled a note and slid it onto her desk.

'You know what I mean,' she said into the phone, distractedly. Lowenthal turned and left.

'Well, come and see me sometime in the next few days. Just call me first.' Moyal gave her an address of a laneway off Bourke Street, in the central business district. Where the serious legal players lived, she knew. Moyal and Maddison, not a firm she had heard of. But his name was in the title. He was a partner.

'Sure. Sure. I will.'

She sat back and stared at her computer. Had Priya been mad? Could she possibly fit a child into her life?

It wasn't that she had never wanted children, just that she had always wanted other things first. Once she had clawed her way into journalism she was desperate to get her head above the rank and file of cadets, and then once she'd got her first round – environment – she had been desperate to get a bigger round, so then she'd got health and broken the string of stories about hospital corruption that won her the Quill, and then she'd been desperate to get the London posting and once she got that she was keen to get back and make her name as a columnist – there was always something.

There had been boyfriends. Andy was the most serious. Lead singer in a local band, he had some chart success, with a top-20 hit in America. He and Ana were fascinated by each other's careers and spent long happy evenings planning fabulous futures. But then Acid Row flopped, and the relationship also started to sink. The band was dropped by its label, despite the front-page success of three years before. Andy couldn't get it together to organise another record deal and there were months of him sitting in pubs, ringing Ana and nagging her to leave work early.

Suddenly, like a threat, he proposed. Ana shrank from the desperation in the offer, romance replaced by a sense of sullen ultimatum. And she resented Andy's constant withdrawals from their joint account, to which he contributed so little. He wanted children, he said, but she didn't believe it. What he wanted, she believed, was to get her away from her job, make himself feel potent again. Within weeks, it was over.

Now thirty-eight and single, living in a city flat no bigger than Serena's suburban master bedroom, Ana sat at her computer and searched herself. Was she sure she didn't want a child, this child especially?

She wiped away tears. She missed Priya and Richard so much.

Still dazed, she looked down at Lowenthal's note.

'Come to my office.'

'Zac Banks will be away for a few months. He's been seconded to Sydney to help them start up a new section. You'll be minding his job,' said Lowenthal. His office was a vast, polished cube lined with framed front pages of the *Morning Star*. Ana recognised one of them as her own. She nodded. Just because she was the junior columnist didn't automatically mean she filled in for Zac. It was a good sign. Apparently she had been forgiven for her gaffe that morning.

'So that's three columns a week . . .' she said. She'd need to start brainstorming ideas.

'Five,' said Lowenthal. He folded his arms and stared at her. 'We'll see how you go for a spell doing every day.'

'You want me to do Zac's job *and* mine?' She was aghast. She'd be turning her brain inside out to come up with that many ideas.

Lowenthal shrugged. 'Well, only if you think you're up to it. If not, we can try some *new blood* in your position while you're doing Zac's —'

'No, no, that's fine,' she said hastily. 'I'll do both. It'll be great! Lots of fun.'

'Good stuff. And if you're any good at it, who knows?' Lowenthal rifled through some papers on his desk, already moving on. 'Zac might like his new job so much he stays. You could be our first female senior columnist, Ana. But we'll see how this month goes.' He looked directly at her. 'You know, we have big things in mind for you. Hang around long enough and you won't be disappointed.'

Ana glided out of his office, momentarily distracted from her grief and her shock. *My boss loves me. I have a future.* She rattled off a column about the outrageous shortage in childcare places and felt her ambition flicker back to life.

She spent the night watching car headlights slide across her bedroom window, and was wide awake when the first tram trundled by at 5.18 a.m. She got up, and made a list headed pros and cons, and then she got confused halfway through about whether cons were good or bad. She wrote: '*What Priya wanted*' in the same column as '*End of career. Single mother.*'

She stared at herself naked in the bathroom mirror, and something about her neat, trim body made her sad.

She drank her coffee on her first-floor balcony and watched the Brunswick Street flower shop below as workers ferried buckets of fresh blooms from the back of a truck. A clotheshorse laden with pantihose and bras took up half of her balcony and some folded chairs cluttered the rest. Her tiny flat had a dishwasher the size of a drawer, a stainless-steel stove top with two rings and an oven that was used to keep takeaway warm. Her table was big enough to accommodate a broadsheet newspaper, and while the bathroom didn't have a bath, it had a fully equipped laundry in one corner.

The flat was an efficient machine from which she emerged each day cleaned, fed and well dressed. It was no place to raise a child. And it was surely too much to ask that she uproot her whole life on Priya's whim.

No, Serena would fall in love with Finn. Ana just had to give it time. She herself would be present throughout Finn's life, dropping in on weekends, taking him on outings. She would be a loving aunt, an indulgent godmother. She would start a trust fund for him. She would help Serena choose schools and she would take him to help at missions for the homeless, that kind of thing. Be a big part of forming his character. She drifted into a happy daydream about Finn's wedding, his speech thanking her for a lifetime of inspiration. It would all be just fine.

5

Ana sat in Serena's kitchen and watched.

She drew her feet up onto her chair, as if to be clear of a briny tide. Angus leaned sideways in a high chair and drooled thoughtfully. Finn pushed a car around the floor, all the while clutching a balled-up silk pyjama top that had been Priya's. Cooper buzzed around Serena like a small cat baiting a big dog. He begged for an orange and his mother peeled one, split all the segments and cut them into halves.

He stared as the plate was placed before him, grave disappointment flooding his face.

'Not that.' He shook his head sadly. 'Want a samwich.'

Serena rolled her eyes and reached for the bread. Ana obligingly ate the orange, wanting to remove the offending thing from her friend's eyes. It was surprisingly delicious, cut up small. A sandwich was placed before Cooper, who dissolved into tears.

'Want an orange.'

Serena paused and brightened, turning to look for the plate of orange pieces. Ana felt mortified to have created more work.

'Sorry.'

She took on the task of dissecting the next orange. Cooper watched in absorbed silence until she finished it, and then he cried because he wanted Mummy to have done it, not Ana. Ana was *yukky*. She felt ridiculously hurt. Finn climbed on her lap and ate the orange, piece by piece, and Cooper melted to the floor in grief because Finn was eating *his* orange.

Serena took him to his room. She came back and slumped down in a chair. 'I just want to smack him sometimes.'

'Why don't you?' Ana lowered Finn to the floor. 'Or is it not the thing these days?'

'Dave's opposed to it. I guess I am too.'

Serena stirred some sort of stew. It smelled like something you might get in an orphanage, and Ana wondered if it was too late to suggest takeaway.

'When's Dave coming home?' Easy to be opposed to smacking when you were never home to spend any time with your kids.

'About ten. He's got a meeting.'

'He works late, doesn't he?'

'Tell me about it.'

Ana stood beside her at the stove and looked into the pot. It was worse than she had thought.

'Looks interesting.'

'Oh, it's terrible. Kai-si-ming. My mum always made it and we used to hate it. Her mum made it for her and she used to hate it too. It's just one of those things.'

'Character building.'

'The kids will eat it.'

'Can I buy us Japanese?'

Serena looked dolefully into the pot of mince and cabbage.

'Okay.'

They bathed the three kids, dried them and dressed them in nappies and pyjamas. They gave bottles, brushed teeth and read stories. The bedroom door was finally closed and Ana looked around the house. Drifts of wet towels piled up against the bathroom walls; toys crowded at the plughole of the bath. In the kitchen, cabbage scraps lay discarded under the table. Books, milky cups, trains and track pieces dotted the lounge room. Serena shuffled robot-like through rooms, throwing towels and clothes into a washing basket, stacking the dishwasher. Ana rang and ordered takeaway. She took the dirty dishes from the lounge room, swept every toy and book into a box, and matched *Playschool* CDs to their covers. She straightened cushions and swept the floor. By the time the delivery man knocked on the door with the box of food, they could see surfaces again.

Ana opened the plastic tray of food and clicked chopsticks over dainty morsels of raw fish and rice, bound with ribbons of seaweed and placed in meticulous patterns. She ached with fatigue.

'I can't believe you do this every night.'

'Only bath every second night.' Serena scooped up sashimi with her fingers and swallowed. 'It's a killer. I can see why some men prefer to hang out at work until it's over.'

'Do they?'

'Terrible, isn't it? Grounds for divorce.'

'But Dave?' She couldn't help asking.

Serena sipped her wine. 'He's not like that. He misses the kids. He just works too much.'

'Makes it hard on you.' Ana sensed the risk but said

it anyway. Serena's relationship with Dave dated way back; she had been the first to marry. These days however, it looked like something was wrong.

'Makes it really hard. Really hard.' Serena looked away. Ana was shocked to see her friend blinking back tears. She didn't move. Serena wiped her eyes and laughed a little, an apology. 'Self-pity. It's a curse.'

'You're entitled. Have you talked to him about it?'

'I've tried. He says it's short term. He keeps saying that. He says after this project he'll wind back. But he said that after the last project.' She laughed bitterly. 'I just don't see how he can, without leaving the company, or even changing professions.' She paused, her gaze landing on a wedding photograph on the wall. 'And the money's good.' An almost pleading tone in her voice. As if she were reasoning with herself.

'Is it?' Ana hadn't meant to sound so sceptical.

'It is. We're hoping to pay off the mortgage by the time Angus goes to school. Get an investment property.'

'Another one?' Serena had her own one-bedroom flat in Clifton Hill, which she'd bought before she met Dave.

'Property moguls, hey.'

'Well, that's great.'

'And I guess I feel that engineering is how I met Dave. Is it fair to ask him to leave it when it's what brought us together?'

'Well, you left geology. To look after the kids.'

Serena and Dave had met on a mineral sands project up near Horsham, a romance built in company-owned wheat belt farmhouses, and blindingly hot shipping containers, while geologists drilled and mapped and the engineers puzzled over how to make a difficult deposit feasible. Ultimately the mine failed, and Dave and Serena always joked that their marriage was the only good thing that came out of the six-million-dollar feasibility study. Although Ana hadn't heard that joke in a while, now she thought about it.

'Anyway. Enough about me. How are you feeling about Finn?'

Ana paused. She had only spoken to Elijah Moyal yesterday. 'I just can't believe Priya made me her child's guardian without telling me.'

'Looks like she did.'

Serena sounded rather brisk and relieved, Ana noted resentfully. She shook her head.

'You've seen my flat. You couldn't raise a child there. And my job. You've said it yourself, he'll need one-on-one care for a while. Not full-time childcare.'

Serena shrugged. 'You could move. Go part time at work.'

'Ugh,' said Ana. And kiss my career goodbye, she nearly said, until she remembered Serena had done just that. She had seen women go part time, watched good journalists get sidelined to writing obituaries, advertising features, anything that allowed them to race for the door at the end of the day while colleagues privately sneered at them and called them the Levis. Because they were out the door at 5.01. 'Maybe. But moving's expensive.' She didn't like to think about the substantial life insurance payout that came with Finn. Didn't want to think about any of it, but she looked at Serena and suddenly felt she had to; felt the first leanings of responsibility. 'I guess you want to know, don't you? What I'm doing. Of course you do.'

Serena shrugged. 'I love Finn, but I don't want to keep him forever.'

Ana stared ahead for a long time. Quitting her job, moving to the suburbs, changing nappies, just the thought of these things made her feel panicky and lonely. 'I don't know anything about having kids,' she said finally.

'No one does at the start.'

'I've got no parents to help me. No real family.' Her father didn't count, she had rarely seen him since he left her mother when Ana was sixteen and Nick eighteen. Too frightened to stay and face the spectre of Nick's illness.

'Do you think what happened with Nick put you off having kids?'

Ana considered it. 'I can't remember ever really wanting kids, not the way some women do.'

'It can be fun. They don't all get sick like Nick. Almost all of them grow up to be normal adults who you can do things with, you know, play tennis, have coffees. Grandkids.'

'I'd be a single mother.'

'It happens.'

Ana mused. 'Remember when Priya and Richard had been trying for years to have a baby and Priya was getting really sad about it? How she used to joke about just going out and bonking some guy, some one-night stand, just to see if she could get pregnant?'

A bitter joke it had been; more a muttered threat than an expression of humour. Ana sometimes wondered whether Priya would do it, how far she would go, but she didn't take her own ponderings on the subject too seriously. She was wary of her own judgement sometimes, knew it was skewed by years of writing news stories about the extremes of human cruelty.

Serena was silent.

'Remember?' Ana prodded. 'Priya used to joke that she might go out and pick up some guy . . .'

'Did she?'

'You were there!'

'I don't remember.' Serena twirled her wine glass, primly.

'Maybe she did go out and bonk some guy. Maybe Finn's dad was some sexy anaesthetist, or some throbbingly fertile male nurse.'

Serena poured herself another glass of wine. 'Have you thought about adopting Finn out?'

Ana blinked, vaguely offended. Had *she* thought about adopting Finn out? Suddenly it was all about *her*?

'No, no. I'll . . . I mean I guess . . . no, I'll take him. I will. If it's what Priya wanted.' Serena's whole body seemed to exhale as Ana spoke. 'I just need time. To absorb it. To restructure my life. Organise work, a place to live. I mean, even natural mothers get nine months to get used to the idea. Don't they?' She felt backed into a corner. What on earth was she saying?

'He can stay here for a few months,' said Serena, magnanimous in relief. 'Until June. Is that long enough for you to arrange things? A house, your job?'

'Yes!' Ana sat back on the couch, weak with gratitude. That would be long enough for Serena to fall in love with Finn, to change her mind. Or maybe in time, she herself would feel differently. The two women nodded at each other in a moment of communion, both reflecting on narrow escapes. 'Thank you so much.' Ana heard the emotion in her voice, recognised the words as an acceptance of responsibility. She paused. 'I feel guilty,' she said uncertainly.

'Ah. Welcome to motherhood.'

6

'I want to go back to work.'

Serena sat next to Dave, at the desk in his study. A paper called *Centrifugal fans, a viable filtration option* slid from the top of a pile on the desk and she caught it and threw it back. She knew more about centrifugal fans than she had ever wanted to, in fact, filtration systems in underground roadways was a subject she had been forced to passively inhale for the three years of Dave's master's thesis on the subject. Thank God he had finished. Whenever they drove past the filtration stacks by the side of the Domain tunnel, Dave's eyes flickered longingly towards them.

Dave stared at Serena as if trying to find her through fog.

'Okay.' More cautiously feeling his way than endorsing. 'The bookshop option?' They had talked about her working one night a week, in a local bookshop. Not geology, but at least part time.

'No. I want to go back to MRA.'

'Okay.' He nodded, let go of the computer mouse and turned towards her, like a manager preparing to handle a difficult employee. 'Are they offering part-time work now, Serena?'

'Don't Serena me.'

'Pardon?' He blinked rapidly, the word misused as a protest, a play for the role of victim.

'You heard me. I mean that patronising tone of voice.'

'Oh, fuck.' The round neck of his woollen jumper framed light brown hairs on milky skin. His broad shoulders hunched over like he wanted to be elsewhere. She felt sick with love and loneliness.

'They might be able to give me part-time work. I spoke to Michael English, remember him? He's running it past Sydney.'

He stared at her.

'Oh. Okay.' He rolled his chair back from the desk and gazed at his feet. 'Well, I'm surprised. I just didn't realise . . . and what about the kids?'

'They're on the waiting list. For Primrose Street.' And four other childcare centres in the area, she might have added. Centres that told her she could wait as long as two years for a place.

Dave smiled, like the sun cautiously emerging. He held out a hand.

'Hey, you've really thought this out, haven't you? That's great. You know, I don't think childcare's that bad. Cooper will like it.'

She accepted his hand, seeking a moment of physical comfort between the blows. Trust Dave not to have read the papers, not to know that no one these days just whisked their kids into childcare on a moment's whim. She rubbed his fingers.

'It will probably take a long time to get a place, Dave.' As in, Cooper might be in uni first.

'We can cope with that. And Finn will move on to Ana's soon, won't he?'

She felt like a crocodile toying with a newborn babe.

Tired of playing already. 'I mean a really long time. Like a year, even two. In the meantime, what would you think about going part time?'

He withdrew his hand and stared at her in alarm and then weariness, a soldier tricked back onto old territory. 'Hodsons don't do part time, Serena. They just don't. They're old school.'

'Well, make them.' She hated herself, knew she was a thorn piercing the skin of his lovely, worky world, but if she didn't, she would have to leave him and then his world would be truly stuffed. Or would it? She wondered.

He looked away. 'Maybe *you* could go back to full-time work. And I could stay home with the kids.' His voice flat, his eyes dead. A false parry, although a risky one. He was gambling that she couldn't leave her children five days a week, that she wouldn't sacrifice that many of their precious childhood days, not even to their father.

She felt the chains of that truth tighten around her. 'Look at us. We used to work side by side, we used to respect each other's careers. Geologist and engineer, we were so proud of ourselves, we were never going to end up like our parents. Before we know it I'll be ironing underpants and you'll be telling Cooper to join the army.'

He smiled wanly. 'I thought you wanted to be home for the kids.'

'I did. But not forever. And I don't mind being home for a reasonable working day with the kids, but I've been hijacked. You're never here. I'm getting up with them, I'm putting them to bed, I'm just a support system for them and you, and no one's supporting *me*.'

'But does that mean you want to go back to work?'

'I'd like to spend time somewhere where what I do is appreciated.'

'I appreciate you.' His face lit up, having sighted The Solution. 'I *really* appreciate —'

'Stop it. Please. You're telling me to go work in a bookshop while you become engineering master of the universe.'

'I don't know what you want me to say, Sreny.' He scratched the side of his face. 'I'm doing this for all of us.' He had a rash on his jaw, eczema. She touched his cheek gently, desperate to defuse the bitterness, even while she added to it. He turned in relief, and seized her hand.

'I want you to work less,' she said. 'That's what I want, for you as well as me. Look at you, you look terrible.'

His eyes clouded. She knew him so well.

'What?' she demanded. Her eyes slid over his shoulder to the desk. All the thesis material had been stacked and put to one side. 'Why are you reading about the Gilbert Freeway extension? I thought you weren't going to be working on that.'

He winced. 'They've asked if I'm interested in, er, taking over the running of it.'

Serena's mouth fell open. She was horrified and impressed. It was an enormous honour for Dave to be asked to run such a huge project. It would ruin her life.

'What happened to Frank Overton?'

'He had a heart attack three days ago.' He looked at her nervously. 'He was . . . stressed.'

'Well, obviously he was *stressed*.' She was stressed just thinking about the Gilbert Freeway extension and what it would mean for her. 'Can't you say no?'

'They ask you, but you don't actually have a choice.' He stared at the papers on his desk. 'And really, I can't believe they've asked me. The Gilbert Freeway . . .'

She knew what he meant. It would open doors. It would ratchet his career up to a new level. If he survived it. If any of them survived it.

While she got to pick sandwich crusts up off the floor and blow noses.

'It should be just for a year, Sreny. How about I do it, and then we see what comes of it? It might mean I can quit and go out as a consultant. Work less, earn more.'

She looked at her watch, sick of the whole thing. There was a time when news this big about one of their careers would have sent them straight out for champagne, had them talking far into the night about the intricacies of the project, about their plans for the future. These days she could see that success came to those who couldn't say no, those without kids, those with the most self-sacrificing partners.

'We could hire a nanny. Think about it, I'll do whatever you want.'

Except give up your career, she thought wryly. But could she ask him to give up this, now? She wondered: if she had been with Poss when he discovered the Aurora deposit, if she had been a part of that momentous thing,

and Dave had then asked her to quit for the family –
would she have?

The nausea returned. She swallowed back the saliva,
considered running to the toilet. It passed.

'Are you okay?'

She stooped, avoiding his eyes, and picked up a stray
piece of Lego. He reached down to her. Had he noticed
anything? She hadn't even done a test yet. She didn't
even know, for sure, she tried to tell herself.

'Just getting my period.' Had Dave noticed her
swelling breasts, the darkened nipples, the flush on her
cheeks? She doubted it. But maybe she had underestimated him.

'You're just not yourself,' he said.

'What do you mean, not myself?'

'I mean, maybe this is about losing Priya and
Richard.'

She stared at him. She had underestimated him,
although not in the way she'd thought she might.

'Maybe I've learned something,' she whispered.

'What?' He sounded nervous.

She struggled with it. 'Not to invest so much in . . .'
She waved around her at their home, at all of it. A child
began to cry from the bedroom and they held their breath.
Finn had been waking at nights, crying for mummy, but
tonight he whimpered himself back to sleep.

Didn't Dave get it? Surely a soulmate would just get
it?

Dave moved on. 'I'll be getting a payrise. A big one.'

'Great. Maybe we can buy a daddy for Cooper and
Angus.'

He drew back to the shelter of his monitor and reached haughtily for his mouse. 'Serena, what it will buy is a way for me, for us, to get out of all this. Please don't be so hostile.'

She shrugged and put on her cardigan. 'Just don't have a heart attack.'

She wanted to say something like congratulations, wanted to burrow into the tiny nugget of euphoria she knew he was hiding beneath the stress and the overwork and the worry about her, but she couldn't.

'Where are you going?' He murmured, as if to tiptoe away from their conflict.

'Playgroup committee meeting – Mario's.' A local wine bar. 'The tribe leaders meet and discuss territorial issues. Share gossip, challenge each other over which group leaves playdough in the carpet. Possible cautious truce between alien forces to raise funds for a joint sandpit.' She wandered glumly to the front door and stared out into the dark.

'Oh dear. Serena?' He got up and followed her.

'Yes?' She turned back wearily and let herself be hugged. Crushed into Dave's jumper, she stared at the glass Buddha that her hippy mother-in-law had given them as a wedding present, and which lived on the hatstand.

'Thank you for this. You are a great mother to our kids and I appreciate it. And you'll get your turn. I promise.'

She nodded, her face against lambswool and the heat from his chest. Her turn had never seemed so far away.

She swung out into the night and began to walk the

few blocks to the wine bar. It was still warm and she stretched out her arms in the dark, like Cooper would have done. Even on her own, the children's little ghosts followed her, sticking fingers into the mouth of the Davis's funny-face letterbox, clamouring to press the button at the pedestrian crossing, crouching with bum cracks showing to pat the small white dog. Go, all of you, she muttered, banishing the ghosts home to bed. They drifted out of sight and she felt a moment's pang for them; their truthful eyes, their gravity.

Hidden in the dark, she took out Dave's news again and turned it over in her mind, allowed herself a moment of pride before the despair returned. He was so talented, so good with people, so respected in there. She pictured his colleagues stopping him to shake his hand, emails of congratulations, and felt bitter that she couldn't even do that. How could she, when she was the one who would put his children to bed alone every night as a result?

Was she jealous? She remembered again Poss's call from the satellite phone, she at home with Cooper, then a toddler. Poss, who had been her field trip partner, telling her the news that would weeks later hit the business pages: he had found a copper deposit, a huge one, on line now to become Australia's biggest copper mine. It was a find that would write him into the nation's history books, and *she was meant to be there*. She had come so close. Cheated by a toddler's bronchialitis. If Cooper hadn't inhaled that germ, if Dave could have stayed home to look after him, if she could have left him with a grandparent . . . she fished the latest postcard out of her handbag, this one from Chile. '*Still doing the international business lunch circuit, same questions every day, different faces, different food ... coming home next week.'* The envy rose in her throat like bile.

The night air was like warm satin on her legs and she could smell sausages on a barbecue, hear voices from the houses she passed, the echo of footsteps on a deck, the clink of glasses. The shopping strip glowed from around a corner, the hum of restaurant conversations grew louder. The footpaths would be lined with tables tonight. She would go back to work in June, she soothed herself, stroking the jealousy away. It would all work out. She touched her stomach. If this thing she suspected were true, then she would deal with it herself. She would simply make it not true. She was thirty-seven years old, it was her body, her husband didn't need to know. She wouldn't succumb to sentiment about the thing. Just another medical procedure, handled with dignity and discretion.

She entered the wine bar. She was suddenly desperate for company, and relieved to spot Cate and the women she knew, drinking wine and rushing through agenda items so they could get onto the serious business of the evening, which was bitching about their husbands. She could hear Mel as she approached, telling the story about her sister who had recently discovered her husband was having an affair with the nanny. '... and then Emmy said she was so pissed off about losing such a great nanny!' Screams of laughter.

They greeted her warmly and Cate ordered her a wine. Elaine was feeding Iggy, his face hidden beneath the lip of her raised T-shirt. Serena remembered the impossibility of feeding a newborn; coaxing the vast pillow of breast into a tiny mouth like a parrot's beak. The sensation of milk being sucked, the way it made a nerve in the side of her jaw twinge. They all gazed at the baby, lost in memory.

'Toy hygiene,' announced Felicity. 'Who wants to draw up a roster to White King the playgroup toys?'

The usual arguments ensued over the benefits of bacteria versus the need for cleanliness. Serena sat behind her wine glass and mentally drifted away. So Poss was coming home. This week, now, any day. It would be good to see him, to catch up. Dave liked Poss too.

'That's it, we're done. Anyone see that story about how you shouldn't drink water during pregnancy?' Felicity's bulge was just starting to show.

'That would be tap water. Terrible stuff.' Cate the nutritionist.

'Oh please.' Serena rolled her eyes automatically, but she was still thinking about Poss. And Priya. About that night they had slept together. She could keep other people's secrets, she had always been able to, but she didn't like the sensation of them under her skin. Particularly this one.

Cooper was nearly one. Serena had been offered a short-term contract by MRA, a two-week field trip to East Gippsland to search for tantalum, and she accepted. Dave was on study leave from work, and she had just weaned Coop. At the last minute she suggested to Priya that she come up for a weekend, she could hang out and relax in the hotel room during the day and share the interminable pub meals by night. Priya said she'd see how she went.

Early each morning Serena and Poss met at the drill site, in the middle of the Dogwood bush, poring over big silver trays of drill core like giant broken pencil leads, of quartz and feldspar. Serena labelled each with codes in black texta: A147dr and WBx56. The field hand grouched in late with an armful of sample bags prepared in front of last night's footy. The banjo frogs chirped thoughtfully, unseen beneath foliage illumi-nated with early morning sun. Hot coffee steamed from the thermos and they ate chunks of bread and butter brought from the pub. Poss, her old friend, her favour-ite colleague, was a comfortable work partner. Together they took careful notes on laptops, compiled small bags of rocks and watched the drill rig grind its way into the earth, stopping it every now and then to survey its path. And every night, Serena and Poss ate veal parmas and surf 'n' turfs at the local pub.

'I know you've got to eat lots of fish.' Felicity leaned forward, her hand wrapped around a wine glass of mineral water. The waiter laid a plate of chocolate cake before her and the women stared. 'I'm eating fish every day.'

'No way!' said Cate. 'Too much fish and you're ingesting high levels of mercury. Can lead to brain damage.'

'Shit. Why doesn't anyone tell you these things?' Felicity wailed.

Serena laughed, her thoughts still far away. Priya turned up unannounced at the pub one night, was wait-ing for them when they came in from the rig. A long, sleek, dark-skinned creature with dewy black eyes, who requested a Manhattan at the bar; who smiled at the bartender's confusion and the field hand's dropped jaw. Brown fingers with loose gold rings. A bunch of long, velvety sticks.

Priya and her desperate sadness over Richard, their inability to have a baby. Priya, fresh from a week of devastation, treating injured patients flown home from the Bali bombings. Priya and her plan. From the moment she arrived she was casting her eye around the bar. Out here she might as well be in another country, as far as Richard was concerned. There were no links back to her real life, only Serena, who could be trusted. And entrusted Serena was, in the first long night of lying in the double bed and mopping up Priya's tears; the tears of a woman about to ovulate. Yes it's a wild plan, okay it might work, no, I promise I'll never tell a soul. Serena was late to the rig the next morning, sleepy over her note-taking, slow to recognise that the rig had drilled deeper than planned and budgeted, a slip which cost a few hours work and some thousands of dollars.

That night at dinner, she watched Priya size up the talent. The local blokes were examined – Jake with his pants halfway down his bony arse; Piggy Watson, with a belly so big his shirt was nappy-pinned over it because the buttons had broken; Smeg the local bikie with a beard to his waist and leathers that smelt, if you ventured too close, as if he'd been wearing them with no jocks for the past year. Priya checked out the local blokes in six seconds, and dismissed them in the seventh.

And then Possum came in, fresh from the shower, his blond hair wet and cheeks glowing from a day outdoors, asking the bartender about her sick dog. Priya couldn't shake his hand quickly enough. Serena thought uncomfortably of Richard, sitting at home alone while his wife ovulated a few hundred kilometres away, and she went to bed early, leaving Poss and Priya chatting by the fire.

Poss was late to work the next day. Serena and Priya never spoke of that night.

'And did you know you've got to get out in the sun every day? They've linked lack of Vitamin D in pregnancy to increased risk of schizophrenia . . .' Cate accepted her plate of orange cake and waved away the waiter's offer of cream.

'Oh no! I've hardly been outside all week.'

'But be careful of skin cancer.'

Serena smirked. Cate was a pregnant woman's nightmare.

'I met this amazing woman the other day, a reiki healer.' Felicity rubbed her belly. 'She's going to give me reiki pain relief during the birth.'

'Fantastic!' Cate nodded enthusiastically. 'Will she come to the hospital with you?'

'She doesn't need to. She does it by ESP.'

'Excellent. What about nail polish? Do you know you shouldn't wear any during pregnancy, because . . . Serena, are you leaving already?'

'I am.' Serena had risen, suddenly restless. She laid a bank note on the table. 'See you guys on Wednesday.'

She walked along the pavement, weaving around chairs and tables, checking how much money she still had in her wallet as she went. It was enough. She went into the pharmacy, chose a pregnancy test and laid it on the counter, glancing furtively back at the door. The teenage girl barely glanced at the packet before she scanned it and put it in a bag.

'Is that all?'

'Thank you.'

Outside, the cool change was starting to sweep through, and thunder rumbled. Serena walked. She knew the drill. The first morning urine, sleepily holding a cup down through your legs, your heart in your throat. Trying to remember what you had planned for that day, while you waited to find out what you had on for the rest of your life. Did the manufacturers of pregnancy tests know that each little box would be carried away like a nuclear rod, glowing in the bottom of handbags, each one offering something that was more like a question than an answer? Serena got home, went to bed and spent an unsettled night. Finn woke twice, crying for mummy each time, and just before dawn Cooper's nappy leaked and she stripped the bed in the glow from the night light. She woke an hour later, shivering. The cool change had blown through the screens and the part-opened windows. The house seemed cleaner for it. She felt the pressure of her bladder and didn't need to remember her mission as she tiptoed barefoot down the gunbarrel hallway to the bathroom. It felt rather as though she hadn't stopped thinking about it all night.

7

'You girls these days have it all,' said Serena's mother, the next day. Iris was calling from the Women's Support Centre, where she spent most of her days writing outraged letters to politicians and trading books on feminism with other retiree activists.

Serena sighed into the phone. Sure, Mum, we have it all. Kids, careers, guilt, stress, a mortgage six hundred and fifty times bigger than you ever had.

'But what does that *mean*?' There was a band of pain across her chest, a hovering sensation around her arms, a longing in the pit of her stomach. The pregnancy test stick lay now in her wallet, tucked amongst the receipts and cards and old shopping lists. Two stripes, loud and clear. Another secret rattling around her hull.

'All those marvellous jobs. All that marvellous childcare. I've never understood, Serena, why you . . .'

Serena slumped onto the kitchen table as if someone had pulled her plug. Amazing how mere words could reduce the body's energy, suck it out and drain it away.

'. . . Mavis' daughter, Therese, she's still working as a lawyer, and the kids are in a lovely childcare centre. Mavis says it all runs like a dream and we had a big talk about how lucky you girls these days are . . .'

'Mmm.' Serena slumped further, felt herself melting

with inertia, unable to stop the inevitable next step in the conversation.

'And I said to her, I really don't know why Serena stopped work to stay home with the children. I hope she gets her career back one day.'

Serena pondered her next words, knew she would regret them. 'I have actually talked to MRA about going back to work, Mum.'

'Darling, that's lovely! When do you start?'

She was regretting it already. 'Well, it's not that easy. It takes time to get childcare.'

Iris was off again. 'Oh, I'm so pleased. I've always said, you don't want to throw your life away on your children when you don't have to . . .'

'Well, thanks, Mum. I'm glad you found me so worthwhile.'

'And all that work you did to get into geology . . .'

'I do actually like spending *some* time with my children. I don't think I want to go back to full-time work.'

Iris paused, a sigh blowing down the phone. 'What about part time?'

'Well, that's what I've asked for, but it's difficult. I don't know anyone who's done part-time geology.'

'Well, *be the first*.' Iris's tone was bracing, a cheery Brave Betty Solves the Mystery ring to it. Serena could just imagine her mother waving a bejewelled fist for emphasis, stamping a black lace-up boot, her purple white and green crinolines flicking up behind her. '*Be a pioneer*. Pave the way for other —'

'Jesus, Mum.' Serena threaded her fingers through the hair close to her scalp and pulled. Like it was all a matter of will, or something, like you could just stride into the foyer of MRA and set fire to your bra and they'd rush out and say, 'Yes, Serena, here's a part-time job based in Melbourne and limited to nine-to-five just for you. Oh and we'll throw in on-site childcare as well, and surgically excise the guilt . . . '

'I don't understand you, Serena.'

What was new? She considered confiding in her mother. At least there was no doubt her mother would support her if she decided to abort. God, would Iris support her. She would *carry* her to the clinic if she had to.

'Anyway, I don't have childcare yet.'

'That will happen.'

'Unless, of course, you're offering to mind the kids on a regular basis, Mum?'

'Oh, I'm too busy.' Iris had been dodging this question for three years. 'I've got my volunteer work with the Centre. Got to support the sisterhood!'

'Of course.'

'What about Dave? Don't the men sometimes stay home with the children these days?'

'I always said you were a woman ahead of your time, Mum. But no. Hardly ever. Try the next generation.'

Dave had looked after Cooper that one time; the Dogwood field trip. He said he would write his thesis in Cooper's nap times. But after a few days he enlisted the help of his mother. Joanne drove down from her commune on the north coast of New South Wales, only too happy to feed her grandson lentils and play him sitar CDs. Friends brought casserole dishes of lasagne and uncles and aunts emerged from the woodwork to Help

Poor Dave Get By. Where were all these people when Serena was spending all week, every week, with a small child, that's what she wanted to know.

But she had been as bad as anyone, she knew, ringing Dave and Jo on the satellite phone at all hours of the day to remind them not to give Cooper juice, to use molasses on his porridge, and to just let him watch *Playschool* on telly, nothing else. And maybe Dave could take him to playgroup to see his little friends?

'He's gone,' Dave had said.

'Where?'

'To playgroup. Jo took him.'

Serena was sick with jealousy. 'Oh. Did you send a snack? They all bring something to share . . .'

'Yes. I sent along the cake Dorothy up the road made me.'

'Dave, have you lifted a finger since I've gone?'

'What do you want me to tell you, Sreny? That I've baked bloody pumpkin scones and knitted him a jumper to wear? Haven't you got rocks to be finding?'

'I'm sorry. I'm sorry.' She knew she had to give up control, let it go. 'It's just I'm . . .'

'. . . his mother. I know.'

Dave sounded resigned, and for a moment they were in despairing, silent, agreement. *I'm his mother*. It's like confessing to a disability. *I'm his mother and it's just something I have to handle with as much dignity as I can muster.*

She got off the phone from Iris and sank onto the couch. Finn and Cooper watched *Playschool* and Angus sidled around the furniture, his latest trick. She had to think. Think. What was she going to do?

Did she really have the right to have an abortion without telling Dave? Yes. It was her body and he was never home to help with the children he did have. *But why not tell him all that*, her voice of reason argued? Maybe it would make him change.

Because she was afraid he would talk her out of it.

So, she didn't know her own mind well enough to trust herself? Maybe she had doubts about this. What if she had another baby, how bad could it be?

It might be a girl. A girl. She made herself picture one and prodded this mental image carefully. Lace-edged socks, ballet classes, a woman friend when she was older. But the hard work of a newborn, the toil of breastfeeding for another year, when she had barely finished with Angus. She wanted her body to have its boundaries back, firmly in place again for ever. And wasn't it crazy, when she was barely coping with two? Irresponsible, she thought, and the new moral high ground about the word gave her some comfort. No, the *responsible* thing to do was to abort. She just had to be sure, very sure, that she would never regret it.

And she did want to go back to work. She needed to get back into MRA while she could, before the inevitable change of management came and swept away the faces that had known her and respected her work enough to help her back in. Another child and she would have to put all that on hold again for a year and a half, maybe two.

Another child. Oh, there was the joy and the excitement of it, for sure. The sea smell of a brand new baby, like brine and oil and starfish and chalk. How they spent weeks examining their fist, turning it in wonder. The way their breathing slowed when you sang to them. A baby's laughter, proof surely that people were born to be happy. Another sibling for Cooper and Angus.

'Stop it.' She sat up from the couch and rubbed her face. Cooper looked at her.

'I'm not doing anything, Mummy.' His face in the blue glow of the telly.

'I know. It's okay.'

She had to relax, to think about this clearly. Was looking after Finn adding to her stress, colouring her decision in any way? What about the shock of Priya and Richard's death, which hung over her like a grey sadness throughout every day? Did anyone ever regret having a child, or did people just never admit it? She went to have a shower.

Serena stood ankle-deep in plastic toys and let the water warm her, running hot rivulets down her back, turning her shoulders from fused bone to flesh again. She considered picking up the toys but discarded the idea, as she did every day. What was the point? They would all be back there tonight. She did a sort of nut-bush step with her left foot to try and clear some space amidst the boats and sieves and empty shampoo bottles. It was akin to other profound questions such as, should we get out of our pyjamas today? Should we change a nappy when the baby doesn't seem to care it's wet? Should we sort the Lego from the wooden blocks, or put the books back on the shelf, when chaos would be resumed within hours? Terrible questions. She must be a terrible mother. She should not have another child.

Once dressed, she still felt the stiffness in her shoulders. She cleared a space on the lounge room floor and laid out her yoga mat, a rubber raft in a tide of puzzle pieces and Lego and small cars. She took out her yoga book. She turned off the television, put on a children's storybook CD and shuffled the Lego into a pile away from her mat.

'On the faraway island of Salama Sond
Yertle the Turtle was king of the pond . . .'

'Can we have Winnie the Pooh?' Cooper took out a Norah Jones CD and let the disc drop to the floor. Finn was on his knees before the telly, an undone growsuit flapping over his nappy like a tail as he tried to insert the remote control into the video player.

'No. Put that back.' Serena did a star jump and let her feet land far apart, her arms out. Angus, on his knees giving the edge of the rubber mat an investigative chew, gave a yelp of fright and fell back on his bottom.

'Me do yoda too.' Cooper crowded onto the mat and threw himself into a wobbly star jump. Serena slid forward into what her book told her was warrior pose, pointing forward like a javelin thrower, and she glanced down at Angus's brown hair. When had she last washed it? Was that a dreadlock?

'Breathe regularly, feel the blade of the right foot pulling against the reach of the left hand . . .' said her book.

'Don' push me,' grizzled Cooper.

'Darling, Mummy's doing something for herself. Listen to the tape.'

'"I'm ruler," said Yertle, "of all that I see. But I don't see enough, that's the trouble with me."'

'I doing suthing for myself too!' shouted Cooper. He wailed. Serena blew out, hard, and concentrated on her stretch. 'Breathe regularly and imagine a place where you feel at peace . . .' said the book. She stepped back, shut her eyes, and moved into the Holy Fig Tree pose. A place where she felt at peace . . .

'"Turtles! More turtles!" he bellowed and brayed. And the turtles way down in the pond were afraid.'

Serena felt a small metal object being placed against the palm of her hand, and tapped there insistently. She recognised it immediately. A Ferrari F50 Coupe.

'Do cars, Mum. Do cars.'

She wasn't doing cars. She had done cars back to front, rolled them up halls and down arm rests; had made tunnels for them out of milk cartons and big slides out of wrapping paper tubes. She had years ahead of her of doing cars. She was not doing cars today.

She went to the phone book and looked up the East-land Fertility Control Clinic. Found the phone and dialled, her fingers trembling slightly. After making this call she would think about the shopping. She would hang the washing out. Maybe even open the craft box and get Cooper and Finn doing some finger painting. Or fill the shell pool with water and let them have a splash. A woman answered and Serena took a deep breath and straightened her neck.

'I'd like to make an appointment please.'

8

Ana walked around the city block for the third time, looping up the laneway, back onto Bourke Street, around the corner and down the lane again. She was crunching column ideas even as she searched for Moyal and Maddison amongst the cafes and corporations. *Something on more women surfing, a sort of tribute to firefighters, a call for bush properties to clear more trees* . . . She could see the imposing offices of Harrisons, the city's biggest law firm, which the lift directory informed her took up six upper floors of the building. But she couldn't see Moyal and Maddison anywhere. *Why nuclear power was good, how fencers were reporting a trend for higher fences, loss of neighbourliness, a rebuttal of Germaine Greer's latest tirade* . . . She had to submit five column ideas by the end of the day and complete one for tomorrow and it was already late morning. She walked around the block once more, almost running. Her sleeveless navy shift was damp on her back. Finally she went and asked in a cafe.

'Red door, across the road.' The barista flicked up the handle of his coffee machine. Men and women in dark suits milled up and down the cafe steps, some carrying takeaway coffee cups and paper bags. How could they bear wearing suits in this heat? One man carried black robes over his arm. Young people pushed trolleys of fat books.

Outside, she found the red door and examined the tiny gold plate on the front. 'Moyal and Maddison, second floor', in copperplate so small she had to squint. Mr Moyal obviously wasn't seeking passing trade. In the shabby foyer, she pressed the button for the lift. It clanked down to her, a toilet-sized cage with every cable, spring and lever visible. The doors crashed open. Ana glanced at the steep stairwell and then at her watch and reluctantly got in the lift.

At the second floor the doors crashed open again. A dark-haired man in his forties was writing at a desk. He stabbed the pen into the paper as the lift doors slammed behind Ana, and looked up.

'Ana Haverfield?' He rose from his desk, a tall man with a solid build. 'I'm Elijah Moyal. Please have a seat.'

He had brown eyes and a big bushy beard. He wore a mauve shirt and a blue tie. His office had one small window, which was almost completely obscured by a sign mounted outside, but there was enough of a gap to let in a little sunlight and allow a view of Harrisons' mirror-windowed offices across the road. A steaming coffee plunger sat on a sideboard and a calendar from the year before hung on the wall. An open door revealed another office, apparently empty. A fan swung lazily overhead.

'So, you've inherited a child.' His beard moved, indicating a smile.

Ana had always disliked beards on men; they seemed unjust when women worried over a downy moustache or a centimetre of armpit hair. She sat in a chair with foam bursting from a hole in the cover.

'Well, yes.' Her heart sped up at the thought of it.

'Finn. Yes. I'm hoping we can work out a . . . solution.'

'A solution. Ah.' He sounded amused and sat back, studying her carefully. Ana resisted the urge to tug her dress further down her legs. 'A "solution" doesn't sound like you want to play mummies.'

Ana frowned at his flippant tone. She glanced around the room and noted the legal tomes on the shelves, a framed picture of a greyhound on the wall, and a small stack of TAB betting slips on Elijah's desk held down by a paperweight in the shape of a lobster. Where had Priya dug up this guy?

'My life's not really set up for a child,' she said coolly.

'I see. I wonder why Priya was so definite about you having him?' he said thoughtfully, staring at her hard as if searching for an answer.

Ana blinked, offended. 'Well, we were friends for over twenty years. She knew me well. I guess she just . . . knew that I care about Finn.'

'But she was wrong.' It was part question, part statement.

'Excuse *me*?' She glared at him. 'Of course I care about him.'

'I mean she was wrong about you wanting to adopt him.'

'Well I might . . . I may . . . that is, I'm thinking I'll probably take him on, adopt him I suppose, unless somebody else wants to . . .' She strove for a more confident note. 'Like Serena. Priya's other very close friend, who has children and is much better placed. There's a chance she might want to do it.'

'That's where Finn's staying now, isn't he?' Elijah

looked down at some notes on his desk and stroked his beard. Ana leaned forward a little, but couldn't see what he was looking at.

'It is.'

'How is he going?'

'It's hard to say. Sometimes he's just playing and he seems fine. Sometimes he gets his little bag and sits by the door as if he still thinks his mum and dad will come for him.'

'Poor little boy. How's Serena going?'

'Okay. She says she can care for him for the next few months while we all . . . work ourselves out.'

'*Meaning*?'

How rude was this man? He rolled a pen in one hand and his fingers were long, with tiny dark hairs on every segment.

'Meaning if I do take him,' she was starting to feel under siege now, 'I'll need time to organise a larger place to live, and get childcare and reduce my work hours.' Like hell, she would.

'Well, that's very good of Serena.' He opened a brown paper bag on his desk to reveal four strawberry dough-nuts, the pink icing peeling away with the paper. 'Can I tempt you?'

She shook her head. 'No thanks.' She had her regular morning snack of toasted almonds and sultanas in her bag. Elijah bit into the doughnut, his moustache brush-ing the pink icing. He turned and wiped his mouth with a hanky.

She could smell herself sweating and checked her watch again. She had to be back in the office and writing by twelve, or she would never make her deadline. *The disturbing rise of government spin doctors, maybe something soft on the ongoing trade in harp seals, quickly followed by something slagging off reality TV, or praising it, something anyway.* There was a picture on the wall of a flushed and elated man in a snowsuit, holding skis. Could it be the lawyer, twenty years younger? His face crowded grinning into the frame with two other men, one holding a trophy, another punching the air. A different photo showed Elijah accepting a scroll of paper from a greying man who appeared to be the former Liberal prime minister. No photographs of children.

'You seem a little unsure about the whole thing.' He spoke gently and leaned forward. There was a remnant of pink icing on his moustache. She willed him to lick it off.

'Have you ever been offered an eighteen-month-old child out of the blue?' she asked irritably. 'Ever thought about throwing in your career to become a single parent at a moment's notice?'

He raised his eyebrows, looking a little startled. Touched his moustache, and the icing disappeared. *Go Hard or Go Home*! read a placard pinned to the side of a filing cabinet, with a bottle of a well-known brand of whisky depicted on the side.

'No. I'm sorry, you're right. It must be very strange for you. To inherit a whole human being, so to speak.'

Ana sat back in her chair. 'So how did you come to draw up Priya and Richard's will?'

'Priya's mother was a client of Harrisons and I was a lawyer there.'

'And what happened?'

72

'I left. Started my own business.'

Ana nodded thoughtfully.

'Can I ask you something?' She'd had this particular thing on her mind now for a few days. Memories of Priya that kept surfacing, as if asking to be tidied up before they could be put away.

'Please.'

'What would happen, just say, in this situation, if – and I'm not saying this is the case – what would happen if the father in question, for example, Richard, what would happen if he wasn't actually the father?'

'Sorry?'

'Just say, the mother had actually gone out and had . . . er . . . had a one-night stand with someone. And conceived Finn. I mean, the child. So, that man was still alive and around somewhere.'

'Although the husband never knew.'

She nodded. 'The husband never knew. Theoretically. This is all theoretical.'

He raised his eyebrows. 'Theoretically. Well, if the biological father came along, in the absence of a Family Court order, that father would probably have the right to simply turn up and remove the child, say from school, and take it into his own custody.'

'Without breaking any laws?'

'If it's his sperm, it's his kid.' He stared at her unblinkingly.

Sperm. Ana, unbelievably, felt herself blush. 'Oh.' Was that a really good shirt or a really bad shirt that he was wearing? She smelled something, a cologne that was not unpleasant and strangely familiar. Her foot touched something and she jumped back, thinking it was his foot, before realising it was just a table leg. He continued.

'Of course the person he took the child from would run to the Family Court immediately, stopping only at their lawyer. They'd ask for a court order to give them custody. The court would probably say, if this bloke hasn't been in this kid's life for the last however many years, be buggered if we'll let him take him.' He narrowed his eyes as he spoke, as if imagining the fight over such a child, and relishing it. She sensed he would be tough in court.

'Oh well, just wondering.' Ana slipped into her coat, remembering her column deadline and panicking again. *Maybe something legal, I could ring Pete at the Law Institute and ask for some leads. Something on insider trading maybe . . .*

'Just making conversation, hey,' Elijah said dryly.

She shrugged and stood. 'Just throwing around, you know, scenarios.'

'I understand. Well, call me in a few days about Finn, won't you? And what you decide to do. I'm the executor of the will, you know.'

'Meaning?'

'Meaning I'd like to see Priya's wishes carried out. As best I can.'

She nodded. 'And Richard's,' she prompted him.

'Of course.'

They waited in polite silence while the clanking and grinding of the lift grew louder. To think Priya and Richard had been in this office, had talked together about

74

their own deaths, had probably discussed the merits of various people to act as Finn's guardian and decided on her. A reluctant decision, an enthusiastic one? *Serena would be great but she's busy with her own kids, I suppose Ana would do.* Or, *Ana's the one, she'd be a great mother.*

Elijah was preoccupied and curt when he saw her into the lift and she was relieved when the doors flung themselves shut. On the way down the lift crunched and lurched to a sudden stop at one point, flinging her against the wire frame, which grazed her elbow, bringing tears to her eyes. The lift spontaneously started up again and ejected her onto the ground floor, where she examined her arm indignantly. *I should sue*, she thought, and headed out into the sun.

9

Serena bathed the three children, dressed them in their pyjamas and put them to bed. Finn whimpered in his cot and pressed his chest against the rail. He had dropped his beloved Jarmy on the floor. When Serena gave him back the comforter Finn buried his face in the now greying silk, seeking the last remnants of his mother's smell.

Cooper hugged his own blanky and stared up from his pillow. 'Are you having a party, Mummy?'

'Just someone to dinner.' Serena stroked her son's head and wondered what detail had given it away. The extra time spent cooking dinner, the laying out of coffee and milk and cups for the end of the night? Her bribe of three extra stories if they all went to bed half an hour early? 'How did you know, Mr Clever?'

Cooper chortled.

'No, you Mr Chatterbox!' He wriggled and giggled, a sound like someone was squeezing it out of him.

'Seriously. How did you know?'

He grew still and stared at her and she had a sudden sense of the older boy he would become. Watchful, grave.

'You put paint on your mouth.'

She nodded. 'Mummy likes to dress up sometimes.' But Cooper was already bored, flicking through his Mr Forgetful book again, resisting her attempts to regale him with grown-up details. As he should. She kissed him once again, tucked in the other two and turned out the lights.

She had half an hour to set the table and put on the rice. Poss was coming to dinner, and she was bracing herself for his exotic stories of South America; wary of the jealousy and longing she knew they would arouse. Dave was due home any minute.

At seven-thirty she called Dave's office, silently praying he wouldn't pick up. He did.

'Hodsons.' He sounded impatient.

'Did you remember Poss Davies is coming for dinner?'

'Oh, shit. Sorry. I'll be a bit late.'

'How late?'

'I've just got to write this letter to these bastards who stuffed up their estimate of the Doveton up-ramp construction . . .' He launched into recriminations against some contractor.

'Dave!'

'And then I'll jump a taxi home. I'll be there about eight-thirty, nine at the latest, okay?'

She sighed. She couldn't face another fight. And it might be nice to get Poss to herself. But she thought of Cooper noticing her lipstick and she felt a little bitter.

'Well, that's fine, I'll have my candlelit dinner with the other man then. Poss knows how to give a girl a good time.'

She heard the smile in her husband's voice. 'He does. Is he bringing a friend?'

'Just himself.'

'Handsome chap like him, surprising he doesn't have a girlfriend.'

'I suppose. Not getting jealous, are we?'

'Of what?'

'That your wife is having dinner with another man? A handsome one?'

He laughed. 'I can't see Poss running off with a mother of two. Not when you think of some of the gorgeous young minxes he's worn on his arm.'

The comment hit her like a punch to the ribs. Her mouth dropped and she stared at the phone. Since when was *she* not a gorgeous young minx? Since when was she just a mother, wearing her two children like some form of purdah? Did Dave really think he was that safe, her own lack of appeal his guarantee of fidelity?

She ended the call frostily, Dave already realising his mistake and furiously backpedalling. '. . . *didn't mean you're not . . . to me you're more beautiful than any nineteen-year-old . . .*' Arsehole. She went into her bedroom to change, hoping to find something to make her feel young, sexy. But her great all-rounder, the black dress from Cue, wouldn't do up over her hips. The jeans she had bought just three months ago were uncomfortably tight – maybe she shouldn't have put them in the drier? She pulled out her green jersey skirt, a guaranteed fat-day improver, and was relieved when it slipped on easily. But then she saw herself in the mirror and gasped.

She looked pregnant. At nine weeks? It wasn't possible. She was a slim build, but she didn't usually show until the start of the second trimester. But there it was, her stomach starting to curve unmistakeably. Could she just be bloated? She put her hand to her stomach and quickly took it away again, disturbed to feel the telltale hardness.

Thank God she had the appointment with the clinic tomorrow. The sooner this was dealt with the better. She threw on a long, loose top over the skirt, not caring any more what she looked like, as long as she didn't look pregnant. Maybe it was better if Dave came home late tonight. She didn't know how much longer she could hide this.

When Poss arrived, his blond shag had been cut into something more corporate. He wore the brown dungarees and heavy leather boots that were MRA-issue to all field workers, although these days they were as clean as a Toorak tractor. He was still lean and lanky, and she remembered all the different diets he had tried in an attempt to bulk himself up. All the meals they had shared on their field trips, from cans of baked beans cooked in a Trannier, to fish and chips on the front seat of a company ute. He had cried on Serena's shoulder when Renae left him and moved to London, taking their young son Zeke. And he had kept an eye out for Serena whenever she went drink for drink with the field hands and ended up blind in some country pub, the locals eyeing her like she was a cold beer in the desert.

They abandoned her carefully laid table and went and ate on couches in the living room. He told her stories of South America, of attempts by MRA to put him up in two-star hotels even while they were introducing him at luncheons with government ministers as the man who found MRA's biggest copper resource. Serena winced.

After a couple of glasses of wine, she told him stories about mothers' group committees and playground politics, and briefly mentioned a close friend who had died tragically. He shook his head.

'You should bring Cooper and Angus up to my place for the day. We can round up the neighbour's cows, give them the full country thing.'

'You're back at the church?'

'It's looking great now. Even finished the cubby.' His eyes were distant. He had started renovation of his country church with Renae, when she was pregnant with Zeke.

'I've applied to go back to work. To MRA.'

'Fantastic!'

'Just part time of course.'

He grimaced. 'Part time? Do they do that?'

'Michael's talking to Sydney about it. He seems positive.'

'I'm having dinner with him tomorrow night. I'll ask him about it, if you like.'

'Oh.' She was a little startled to hear he now had friends in such high places. He smiled.

'You should have been with me when I found Aurora, you know.'

'Thanks. Like I would ever forget.' It still stung. For so long they had worked as a team; he a minerals geologist, she a coal geologist. He the one who believed in luck and instinct; she a stickler for the rigour of science. Together they had found a medium-sized mineral sands deposit, while drilling for brown coal. He had spotted the black grain in the sandy layers and she had urged him to get it analysed. They were both credited with this discovery, but it was small fry when compared with Aurora.

'Do you remember the trip we went on just before you found Aurora – Dogwood?' Serena's heart sped up as she asked the question. 'It was after I took maternity leave, started doing contract work.'

'We were looking for tantalum.' He smiled lazily. 'That was a good trip. The one your friend came on.'

She was suddenly tense with all the things unsaid. Had to stop his smile.

'That was Priya. The one who died. In a car crash. Three weeks ago.'

'That was *her*? But she was your best friend. That's terrible.'

She felt her eyes flooding and brushed the tears away irritably. 'Her and her husband,' she said.

'God.' Poss was hushed now, wary. Priya's husband.

'Did you know she was married?' Serena was suddenly tired of the thing unspoken between them.

'Yes.' Poss spoke carefully and waited for more. When none came he said cautiously, 'Am I in the bad books here?'

'Then you did sleep with her?'

'Didn't she tell you?' A childish note of disappointment in his voice.

'Sort of. Not really. But I always thought that's what happened.'

He nodded. 'It did.' He paused. 'She seemed keen,' he said in a small voice. Serena burst out laughing and he smiled in relief. She wiped her eyes, and dropped her bombshell.

'Her little boy is here at the moment. Asleep.'

'I didn't know she had a child.'

'He's eighteen months old.'

Poss nodded, still mentally back in the tiny part of Priya's life that he had starred in. 'Maybe they were having a bad patch at the time.' Not really interested in Priya's life outside that. Or the child.

'Maybe.' She waited for more, but he had missed it, gone on to talk about Renae, and how she was still denying him access to Zeke. For a damn good minerals geologist, who had made his name out of careful observation and finely honed instinct, he had just missed the find of his life.

The next morning, Serena's heart pounded as she approached the small group of protesters. There was a handful of middle-aged women, which was to be expected, but also a couple of grave-faced young men with spotted, sore-looking skin. '*Abortion is murder*', read one placard. From the car park the group had looked lethargic, faces wiped of passion, but as Serena wrapped her arms around Angus and walked towards them they proved surprisingly rigid.

'Excuse me,' she said to an older woman, ignoring a young man who was waving a wooden placard close to Angus's head. Her youngest sat hugged into her hip, his weight on her arm. He sucked his thumb.

The woman's jowls wobbled disapprovingly and her scalp was visible through styled hair.

'Did you know that at three months the foetus is the size of a persimmon?' she said.

'Yes.' Serena placed her hand around Angus's arm and folded him closer.

'Sister, your unborn child feels pain and joy already. She can hear music. She dances.'

'Oh no, you've got it all wrong.' Serena blinked kindly. 'I'm a consultant architect, I'm here about a renovation.' She turned to see the young man stroking Angus's downy cheek, running the back of his spidery, adult hand over her child's flesh.

'So beautiful,' he murmured. 'How can they do it to them?'

Serena leaned close to him and lifted his hand gently away from her child. She sank her short nails in above his fingers and felt the bones, like little chicken wings.

'*Don't touch him*,' she said, tossing his hand back at his belted jeans. She saw the violence flash into his eyes before he lowered them, and she moved towards the old women. They parted for her, grumbling incantations as she passed, and she marched down the path of the inner-city terrace house that was the Eastland Fertility Control Clinic. Her muscles were hot with adrenalin. She was sometimes shocked by her own rage. Confronting six-year-olds in the playground who'd pushed in front of Coop; breastfeeding with a snarl in front of blinking businessmen; kicking strange dogs that ventured too close to her babies, feeling like she could kick them to death.

A nurse watched through a security grill. She unlocked the door and ushered Serena in, shaking her head.

'Do you have an appointment?'

'Serena McAllister.'

'What a sweetie.' The nurse reached out one finger and tickled Angus's small hand. 'It's nice to see a little one here,' she whispered.

In the waiting room, Angus was the only child. There was a woman about the age of Serena's mother, and a girl in her teens. They sat apart. Both stared at Angus as he slid to the floor and crawled.

Probably not the greatest place to bring a baby. Cooper and Finn were with Cate, but Serena felt she needed Angus's unjudgemental company. She was only going to talk to a counsellor about her options, but still. Maybe deep down she wanted to offer proof. *See I've done my bit, I've had my babies. I'm a good mother.*

There were bright landscape paintings on the wall, and magazines: *House and Garden* and *Country Style* and *Gourmet Traveller*. Serena thought of her obstetrician's rooms; a place where women sat choked with swelling breasts and fat tummies and leafed one-handed through copies of *Melbourne's Child*; where past success stories, now aged two and four and six, fought over shape sorters.

She knew there were infertile women who ached for babies. Maybe they even watched this place where other women came to end pregnancies. No one did it easily. That was the truth. She had been here before. She did a mental calculation; eight years old, her first child would have been. Their first child, hers and Dave's. Imagine that. She wouldn't have got her degree, had a career. They would have lost those romantic, carefree years before children, just getting to know each other. She didn't regret it. Eight years and four and a half months, she calculated. Grade Two? Three? No, she didn't regret it. She just didn't like to think about the fluorescent rooms that she knew lay beyond the edge of this carpet. How many little ghosts haunted those rooms, with their ears out for music, dancing even, like the woman outside had said.

Not fair that some had too many babies in their life and others went without.

Like Priya. It took three years for her to conceive Finn, three years of wanting.

'Will you get tested?' Serena asked Priya in a whisper one night, when the boys had gone outside to check out Richard's new deck, and Ana sat by the phone dictating last-minute news copy.

'I've already been tested,' Priya said, pouring herself another mineral water.

Serena couldn't remember the last time she'd seen Priya drink alcohol. God, months and years of taking the folic acid, taking your temperature to track your ovulation, following a clean-living lifestyle, getting your damn period every month and starting over again. Serena couldn't imagine it. She got pregnant each time so quickly, it had made her head spin. She and Dave secretly joked they were the weeds of the human race; they would multiply unstoppably while rare flowers like Priya became extinct.

'And?'

'I'm normal.'

'Well, there you go. It'll happen.'

'That's me anyway. Not Rich.'

'Has he been tested?'

'He won't. Just refuses.'

'Yeah?'

'He says we should give it more time. Do it naturally.'

Serena thought of the question Ana used in interviews when she was stuck for something to say.

'How do you feel about that?' She had been a little embarrassed by how self-conscious it sounded, but Priya leaned forward and spoke with emphasis, through clenched teeth, as the men clattered back into the room.

'Pissed off.'

Her eyes looked like tunnels.

Serena removed Angus from the older woman's handbag and feigned the usual dismay at his behaviour.

'It's all right,' whispered the woman. 'I have grandchildren, I understand.'

She seized Serena's hand for a moment and let it go. Her gaze drifted to the teenage girl, who glared at them both and looked away, through the bars of the glass door. She folded thin arms over her flat stomach.

Serena remembered Dave's words of the night before. *I can't see Poss running off with a mother of two. Not when you think of some of the gorgeous young minxes . . .* It was true. It was true. She wasn't even appealing enough that her own husband wanted to come home and have dinner with her. She was just the mother of his children, and the minx in her had gone forever. Who was she kidding, daring to think she would ever get it back?

'Serena McAllister,' said a brisk nurse, eyeing a folder and looking up at her. 'Oh dear, are you all right?'

Serena was sobbing. She scooped up Angus and

wiped her eyes, but her chest heaved again, out of her control. 'I'm sorry.' She shook her head and wiped her nose. The older woman stood to put her arm around her. The nurse put down her folder and handed her tissues.

'I'm sorry. I think I'll have to come back another day.'

'It's okay,' said the nurse gently. 'People cry in here, often. It doesn't mean . . .' she trailed off. *It doesn't mean you don't want to go through with it.*

'I'll make another appointment.' Serena's chest heaved again. Her lungs felt as if she had swallowed a balloon. 'It's just the hormones. I'll ring back tomorrow.'

She fled outside and through the protesters. Angus bumped along on her hip and shrieked, pointing one fat finger at the world ahead.

10

'You remember I told you I was working with the government?' Lily asked. She fumbled at her own neck, trying to button the top of her cardigan closed. Ana gently batted her mother's hands away, and did it for her.

'Sort of,' she mumbled, momentarily stifled by the stench of cigarettes and some sort of nursing home-issue lavender soap. Lily must need help dressing every morning now. Ana glanced at her watch. She had thirty minutes allocated for this visit, which was, like yesterday's trip to Moyal and Maddison, in work hours. They were really the only hours she had, some weeks. Thirty minutes would appease her mother and tamp Ana's own guilt down to a manageable level. She got tired of hearing about the guilt of working mothers, paraded as if it were of a higher order than the garden-variety guilt everyone else felt. Aged care and childcare, there was little difference. They both left someone feeling sick at heart.

'At the time Gough Whitlam was sacked?' Lily patted her top button and peered at Ana.

'You did tell me about that,' Ana lied. Anything to avoid hearing it. Oh, she was bad, let the poor soul have her say. How many buttons had her mother done up for her, once upon a time? How many nappies changed and laces tied? The least Ana could do was listen.

Lily leaned close.

'Me and Gough were having a bit of . . .' she raised her eyebrows, and showed perfect teeth.

White whiskers grew thick on her chin now, like the underside of uprooted turf. Should Ana do something about them? She remembered the rituals of waxing that her mother once undertook regularly; the miniature saucepan with wax frozen mid-flow, taken out of the oval beauty case along with the little strips of cut cloth and heated on the stove. Ana had fossicked through the pink silk pockets of Lily's beauty case while her mother painted the steaming brown goop onto her own top lip. Lily had stared at herself in the mirror, frozen still, and then torn at the wax moustache as if launching an ambush.

Was that a daughter's job now?

Ana didn't have time. She had to get back to the office and come up with two column ideas before three. She had lied to Zac Banks, told him she was going to check out a lead at Victoria Police HQ, and he had asked her to return a book to a contact there, so now she would have to double park outside the bloody St Kilda Road offices on the way back. She had a letter in her bag from a politician threatening to sue because Ana had left her name off a list of up-and-coming female ministers. She was in desperate need of a haircut and she either had to do her washing, or buy new clothes. She should be a better friend, and wanted to offer a night's babysitting to Marnie, but if she did that she really should do the same for Serena. She had to meet a contact at four and transcribe two taped interviews. And the daily demand for column ideas was milking her brain.

The court case against the tobacco companies, the new panty liners for G-strings, the maternal monopolisation of guilt . . . She furtively scanned the nursing home's craft room where they were sitting; one woman reading a magazine, two more staring silently out at a garden. A young Asian nurse passing through. Nursing homes would be good. She just needed an angle.

'You know what I mean?' Lily's trembling hand reached for her daughter. Ana clasped her mother's hand with both of hers and stroked it. Still such a feminine hand. She could cry at how old it was now, how fragile the skin.

'About working with Gough?' she mustered.

'Yes.' Her mother peered.

'You enjoyed it?' She would be kinder.

'Oh yes. The nookies.'

'The what?'

'The nookies.'

'Sorry?'

'We had . . . relations.'

'Mum! Don't say that!'

Lily Haverfield gazed mysteriously past her daughter, out the window. 'It was lovely,' she murmured.

'Oh, God.'

It was getting too much. Her mother's 'memories' were growing madder with every visit. Last week it was her years as a Hollywood actress. The week before it was designing dresses for Queen Elizabeth on her 1956 visit to Australia. She had also told Ana in great detail about her adventures as a nurse in the war, single-handedly saving the life of General someone-or-other, who had of course proposed to her, but she had declined the handsome and wealthy war hero, breaking his heart, so that she could go home and get hitched to flaky Robert Haverfield, VPS1 clerical employee in the Federal Public Service, Air Force Logistics purchasing. Who would leave her years later when Nicholas had his breakdown.

'I'm thinking of adopting a child.' Ana spoke mildly. The conversation couldn't get much more bizarre than it was.

Her mother looked at her, suddenly alert.

'Oh, you don't want to go doing that.'

'Priya's child. You know my friend Priya, who died?' She had told her mother about the accident and her mother had been terribly sorry, had launched into a long discussion about fictional car accidents she herself had starred in until Ana fled, weeping.

Lily looked a little dreamy.

'Poor little coot.' Then she eyed Ana. 'But you never wanted children, did you, my love? Too much else to do.'

Something inside Ana screamed silently.

Ana's mother had cared for her son for fifteen years after his nervous breakdown. On the eve of his thirtieth birthday, he took a rope and a chair and put her into retirement. By then Lily was sixty-two, and she only had a few good years left before ailing health, both physical and mental, forced her into a nursing home. She had spent a quarter of her life taking her son in and out of hospitals, getting food into his mouth, listening to his terrors, washing his clothes, replacing his Medicare card every time he lost his wallet. No wonder she was dreaming about nursing generals, and designing dresses for a queen.

Having children was a lottery, Ana knew that well. All those breastfeeds and nappies and christening gowns, and you could end up clutching them round the waist and screaming for a knife to cut the rope. Sometimes she envied Serena her bland family history, her ignorance. It was all such a risk.

Don't have children, Ana remembered her mother whispering after Nick had tried, again, to kill himself. That was the time he drank toilet cleaner. Ana and Lily sat in the waiting room, outside intensive care, a long dark night of hard plastic chairs, chips from a dispenser, and hard plastic dreams that were a respite from the fluorescent lights.

'Don't have children,' Lily breathed. As if she were trying to brainwash Ana in her sleep. But Ana had heard it all before.

'Are you going in?' she asked briskly, nodding at the swinging door of the ICU.

Her mother buried her tears in her hands.

'My life is ruined.'

Wet, wet, wet, in those years, salty tears and long moist sobs all over the place. Ana went into intensive care, pulled up the chair beside Nick. A nurse flicked back a curtain.

'Your mother's having a sleep, is she?' she said.

Ana looked at the floor scattered with used tissues, and back at the nurse.

'Yes.'

She held Nick's hand gingerly, careful not to disturb

the drip. His bed was a palette of white: the snow of his sheets, the faded-page hue of a loose-woven blanket, the deep milk of his face, stark against black eyelashes, eyebrows and stubble, and the rose-white of his lips.

She could remember being little and thinking all families had one boy and one girl, and all parents were named Lily and Robert, and anything different was just wrong. She remembered running around the circular pool in the back yard with Nick to make a whirlpool, all the dry leaves and dead bugs flying past in the wake. Later, drying in the hot sun, they massaged the soles of each other's feet, adding codes to each different touch – one for a stroke, two for a brisk pat, three for pinching. She remembered Nick paying her a dollar to clean his golf clubs and the long hours of dispiriting work with a toothbrush, jiggling away at all those tiny divets and trenches. She remembered him in his early teens, tall and sinewy, filling a bucket of water and swinging it, up and over, without spilling a drop. Coaxing her, begging her to try it as well, and then she, smaller, had spilled it all over her head, and he wept with laughter. Her own sense of sopping outrage, her secret delight at how he lay on the ground and clutched his sides and ached with silent laughter, almost like he was sobbing. She liked to make him laugh.

'Don't have children,' her mother had muttered on that occasion too, as she stripped the soaking clothes off her and hurled them in a wash basket.

'Do you wish you hadn't had me?'

'Of course I don't wish that,' her mother said crossly. 'What sort of mother do you think I am?'

'Do you wish you hadn't had Nick?'

'What a question. I'm glad *I* had children. I'm just saying *you* don't have to.'

Ana thought hard about all this. She didn't really get it.

At twenty, Ana had a boyfriend and she got pregnant. She told her mother.

'How could you do this to me?' Lily wailed, as she reached for the phone and booked Ana into an abortion clinic.

'Are you sure?' asked Ana. Meaning, was she herself sure? She was so fuzzy-headed and nauseous, she could barely think.

Lily stared at her, then pushed her into a chair, made her a cup of tea and sat opposite.

'Ana, you don't want to have children. You're not cut out to be a mother. I just don't think you'd be very good at it.'

'No?' Ana wished she knew someone, anyone, who had a baby, so she could make such an assessment for herself. She wished she could stop throwing up long enough to think about it.

'And there's your family's genes to think about.'

Ana knew what her mother meant by the family's genes. There was Nick, bidding for auctions with car engines. Her mother's own brother, Ana's Uncle Doug, wrongly believed he was the Channel Nine newsreader.

'And anyway, you don't want to get bogged down with children.'

Her mother often said things like this. Don't get bogged down with a boyfriend, or don't get bogged down with that friend whose mother had died, who cried in her room and played guitar all the time. Don't get bogged down with a mortgage, or with living in one city, or owning a dog. Ana pictured herself doing an eternal high step, keeping clear of boggy territory.

'And think of your talents. A lot's been invested in you. Things are expected of you.'

This was the only argument that made Ana lift her eyes from the grain of her mother's kitchen table. She had skipped a grade, won an undergraduate scholarship. She had expectations of herself. To be everything her mother wasn't, for a start.

And now, years later, Lily could muse that Ana had never wanted children. 'Too much else to do.' Was that a note of *criticism* in her voice? Would she dare?

Lily came with her daughter as far as a coffee shop two blocks away, and said she would wait there. It went without saying that Lily would not enter a place like the Eastland Fertility Control Clinic herself.

Just as she didn't want to go back into intensive care again, to sit by Nick. It was killing her, she told Ana. So Ana sat beside her brother all night. She was there in the morning when he opened his eyes and found life still gnawing on his bones.

'It didn't work.' His hair so black against the pillow it looked like it could have left a stain. 'Why does it never work?'

'It's just that we won't let you go.' She stroked his hand, then patted it, then pinched it. 'Number four? Number five?' she asked him, trying to jog his memory back to a good time. She could be dry, hard, lean as beef jerky, because their mother was out in the waiting room crying enough tears for all of them. Enough tears to get herself well and truly bogged.

11

At the swimming pool, Serena put Angus into the creche and took Finn and Cooper to the indoor pool. The air was soupy, stinging with steam and chlorine, and it was still early enough that parts of the water were like mirrored glass. In the big pool, a senior aerobics class waved foam dumbbells and flapped upper arms in time to 'Big Spender'.

The boys held onto the edge of the toddler pool and stared across at the oldies, fascinated by the wrinkly faces, the eyes with all their history in creases like footprints. A few wore clear shower caps over their hair, elastic frills framing their soft faces like petals. One was a bit younger, still a grey-hair but around Iris's age, smiling a little embarrassedly as if to say, 'I'm not old really, I'm just here for fun,' looking as though she might later tell her friends the whole story of the class, as a big joke against herself.

'And over to the right, that's it,' called the instructor, insultingly young and gorgeous.

In the toddler pool, a baby swimming class was fenced off behind a big plastic necklace. Mothers with first babies, all of them, Serena would lay money on it. They stood around a foot-shaped foam raft and their babies took turns crawling across the foam to the instructor, and back again to Mum, always a quicker, more successful trip on the way back because they were heading for Mum's beaming face. How on earth this was meant to prepare babies to swim was beyond anyone to see; it was really just something for new mums with not enough else to do.

She knew the classes well, and she leant back on her arms in the shallow water and smiled. Next they would do the hokey-pokey; there, off they went. *You put your right hand in* – long pause while the startled babies had their arms arranged for them – *you put your right hand out* – repeat above. Invaluable contributions to water safety.

Oh, the things you did with a first baby, convinced they were bored and understimulated, when in actual fact it was you, the mother, who was going out of your mind. The babies would have been happy or sad or grumpy regardless of whether they were crawling over a big wet foot, or home playing with the car keys.

Serena and Cate had taken the boys to music classes a few times, a community centre session run by two stern and wholesome looking women who went around singing an unnerving 'Hello' song to each child individually as they arrived. The mothers were expected to smile approvingly – Serena knew this because she anxiously observed Other Mother behaviour – and wave madly at the instructor, wave hard and wide like you were drowning and signalling for help, even though Mrs Music was only a hand's length from your face, all in the hope that your brilliant child would mimic you and catch the Hello bug.

Neither Cooper or Matty caught such a bug from the

class, nor any sort of musical tendencies at all, although they liked their turn at banging the tambourines. Their favourite thing was to chase each other madly around the room, while the other mothers and babies sat in pairs in a big circle and chanted obediently. Serena and Cate were left cross-legged and facing each other.

'Pat-a-cake, pat-a-cake, baker's man,
Bake me a cake as fast as you can . . .'

Two thirty-eight-year-old professionals clapping each other's hands smartly, staying in time with the teacher, and trying to ignore their children running riot.

Cate had leaned forward and muttered to Serena, clapping all the while, 'I'm *so* glad I did that Masters in Public Health.'

Finn let go of the side of the pool and wobbled. Serena caught him under the arms and walked him back to the shallows, where he sat down in an inch of water, cushioned by his swimming nappy. Cooper smacked his hands on the water's surface, his little buttocks clenching under lycra bathers. An old woman reached out one jewelled hand to pat his precious head as she paddled past and Cooper screeched and splashed back to Serena.

'Mummy!'

'It's okay.'

She watched her son watch the world around him. The elderly woman retreated, and he turned his attention to the baby class. She knew Cooper's three-year-old craziness would one day pass, and leave him with this reserve that she glimpsed occasionally, this private inner world. And then she would be jealous, would want to drag him back to her. She could hear herself already, as she had been with almost every male she had ever known. *Tell me how you feel. More. Talk to me.* One day she would yearn for these exhausting times, when his every emotion was laid bare and she sometimes had to lie down and cover her head from the beautiful bushfire that was her three-year-old son.

'I love you, Coop.' She hugged him and he watched over her shoulder and pushed against her with one hand to be free. She released him and he splashed away after someone else's ball.

She crouched in the water, watching her two charges. Self-conscious about her already-showing pregnancy; that someone she knew would spot her. Just a fat day, she could always say. She would ring the clinic as soon as they returned home, would make another appointment. What had happened in there this morning? What had possessed her to flee the waiting room like a frightened teen? Did she have doubts about this? None that time wouldn't deal with, she told herself grimly. If she had this, this thing – she wouldn't let herself call it a baby – she would be almost forty before she returned to work, and even then she would be coming home to three small children. Three lots of vaccinations, three lots of little friends, yet another round of kindy waiting lists. Three adolescents.

Three little people who loved her best.

Stop it.

She sighed and waded after Finn, walking doubled-over to keep one hand on him, the chlorine steam making her light-headed. Down the track she might feel differently, but it was just too soon now after Angus. Not even a year since her youngest was born, since the weird magic of birth. One week late, he had been. Seven days in that timeless state of overdue, when you were regarded cautiously by all. *Not on my new carpet*, her mother had said, only half-joking. All the details of birth; how her favourite Stevie Nicks song had come on the delivery room radio, how Dave had tried the gas and said it did nothing, how the hot towels worked best when placed on the bottom of her back rather than the middle. The midwife had placed the towel on her coccyx and she had almost shrieked with relief, but then the next hot compress was too high, just missed that perfect spot, and so it went on, with Serena locked inside herself, unable to find the words to tell anyone, *Down a bit! Further!* Like one of those dreams where you couldn't scream to save yourself. All those details you thought you would have time, one day, to relive, to savour, and yet you forgot how birth was like a starting gun; it started you running and running for months, years, and by the time you slowed down and regained some perspective on your life, you had forgotten whole chunks of it.

'Finny. Careful.'

He turned his liquid brown eyes on her and toddled away, his back arched, his limbs still soft with baby fat. Children's skin was so perfect, it was like someone had drawn a fine outline around them. In the few weeks since Finn had been orphaned, he had learned to spoon-feed himself. He was fighting back harder when Cooper took a toy. He rarely let go of Jarmy and when he was tired, he would cry when Serena moved out of sight. The words he'd had before the accident – book, moon, dog, blanky, bye – had been wiped back to baby gabble. Serena felt the loss of Priya in her solar plexus, and wondered where Finn felt it most. Probably in every surface he touched, every sound that he heard. Every moment that Mummy and Daddy still didn't come.

In the change rooms, Serena commandeered the big disabled shower cubicle and let the boys take turns squirting each other with the shower-hose. She shampooed two heads of hair and rinsed them off. Always hard to dry small, wriggly bodies, you just had to flap enough towels around and hope they made contact. Cooper and Finn made a game out of slapping the walls of the cubicle and listening to themselves howl in the high-ceilinged change room, and Serena sorted small singlets, T-shirts, long pants, nappies. Outside she could hear the senior cits class coming in; low meandering conversations, as if they weren't sure the others were listening. '. . . it's a nice cheap price, that . . .' and '. . . Doris's knee's a bit bung this week . . .'

Cooper pushed open the change room door and stopped in shock. The opening revealed an enormous, naked bottom – elderly, tissuey, hairy at its lower extremities – meaty and magnificent. Right at his eye level. Cooper's hands flew to his mouth and his eyes boggled at Serena's over the top.

She gently shut and locked the door and crouched to the two boys. Cooper screeched, and he gave Serena the giggles, and Finn started to chuckle just watching them, and as the tide of old age washed up outside their door, Serena laughed silently until the corners of her eyes were wet.

12

From: Ana Haverfield

To: Marnie Atkinson

> How's the milk flowing? I liked your story yesterday on mothers' groups getting thrown out of cafes, and the one the other day on the Russian woman who went to prison to escape from her children. And the one on rising rates of caesars. Where do you find this stuff?

From: Marnie Atkinson

To: Ana Haverfield

> I usually find it on my desk. Other people hear stuff and pass it on to me. My byline should be: Marnie Atkinson, Bad News About Mums Reporter.
>
> Milk situation is DISASTROUS. Only getting 70 mL an express, when Lucy needs 200 mL a feed. Am getting RSI in my right hand from working breast pump handle. Should get an electric pump but they scare me. Might malfunction and chew up my nipple. Lucy's creche is ringing, saying I'm not leaving enough milk and they'll have to start using formula. Bitches. I hate them.

From: Ana Haverfield

To: Marnie Atkinson

> Is formula so bad?

I'm not going to be one of those mothers who dumps their baby in creche and just takes the easy way out with formula!!!!

Ana understood. Everyone needed to feel there was someone making more of a mess of things than them, especially mothers. She stood and tried to catch her friend's eye across the office. Since returning from maternity leave Marnie had taken to eating her lunch either at her keyboard or, she told Ana, over her breast pump. If Ana ever ran into her downstairs, she was always in a hurry, usually coming from the chemist with sorbolene or cortisone cream or breast pads, clutching her coat closed over her chest and frowning at the ground as if trying to remember something. Who she used to be, maybe.

'Come out for lunch,' Ana pleaded at Marnie's desk. 'We haven't done anything to celebrate you coming back to work. You are allowed to take a lunch break, you know.'

'Okay, okay. I'll finish this story, pump some milk and I'll see you at Bonnies.'

They ordered salads, garlic bread, one glass of white and one of mineral water. It was a warm day, and elm branches stretched around them on the restaurant's first-floor balcony, leaves starting to turn gold at the edges.

Ana thought her friend looked ten years older. She seemed to have stopped blowdrying her hair and taken to letting it dry in stiff strands, scarecrow-style. The creases around her eyes looked thirsty, as if baby Lucy and the breast pump had sucked out the last drop of moisture.

'How's childcare?'

Marnie shook her head. 'Exhausting.'

'I'm sure Lucy's fine.'

'I mean it's exhausting for *me*. By the time I drag some clothes on, dress Lucy, change her nappy again, take her to creche, settle her in, get the expressed milk in the fridge, talk to the carers, get back out to the car, drive to the station, get the train in here, I'm absolutely shagged. I feel like I've done a day's work before I turn on the computer.'

'What are the carers like?'

'Two of them are lovely, one's a dragon. I walked in the other day and she had some ghastly story tape playing, a sort of New York badass version of The Three Little Pigs and I swear, I heard gunfire in the background of it. I was horrified. I wanted to say something but I didn't dare. Dragon woman terrifies me. I tell her Lucy doesn't like to be wrapped, I come back and she's bound up like a mummy and the old cow reckons she's had two three-hour naps like that. She knows everything.' Marnie took some straws of sugar from the bowl on the table and fidgeted with them.

'Two three-hour naps? What are you paying them for?'

'Well, they're not likely to do it for nothing, are they? Anyway, dragon woman keeps calling Lucy *Laura*.' A paper straw exploded in her fingers, scattering sugar across the table.

'No Christmas present for *her*.' Ana swept the sugar

off the table. Marnie put her hands in her lap and held them.

'And everyone I meet at work, every single person says, "'Oh hi, welcome back and Who's Looking After The Baby?" and I say, "She's in childcare", and the *tragic* expressions on some people's faces. *It goes so quick*, they say.' Marnie leaned close to Ana. 'I had three months at home with Lucy and I love her to bits but I'm here to tell you, it actually doesn't go so quick, not when you're in the middle of it. There were days where I felt like there must've been some nuclear event that had slowed down the clocks and wiped out the nights and three weeks had gone by, only I was ringing Kurt every hour and he was saying, "Yes, Marnie, it really is still Tuesday, yes, still Tuesday the 23rd".' She drank some mineral water and sat back as the salads were placed before them. 'Anyway. Enough about me. How's things with you?'

'Same. Work's full on. My mum's getting lost in her memories. I spend my time with her feeling either profoundly guilty or wildly irritated.'

'How's poor little Finn?'

'He's with Serena still. A bit fretful sometimes, by the sound of it. But she's so good with children.' *And I'm so bad*. Ana ground pepper over her salad and sent up another silent prayer. 'I think he'd be much better off staying with her family than coming to me.'

'You're probably still in shock. It's all so . . .' Marnie shrugged. 'God. That poor little boy.'

Ana shook her head, a mouthful of food suddenly like straw in her mouth. Finn's loss, her loss, was like a toxic tide that overwhelmed her sometimes.

Marnie pressed on. 'Don't you want to have children? I know women your age who would see this as a gift from the gods, who would cut off a limb to . . .'

'I know. I know. I *might* want children one day. But I feel like this . . .' She grimaced into her salad. Such a selfish thing to feel.

'What?'

'It sounds awful, but I feel like this isn't the way I wanted it. It sort of excludes me from the dream ever happening.'

'What dream?'

Ana glanced around and lowered her voice. They were only a stone's throw from the office. You never knew who might be listening. 'You know, fall in love, live happily ever after . . .'

'Oh, *that* dream.' Marnie smiled grimly. 'Look, if you meet a guy and he's put off because you've got a child, then he's not worth it anyway. Think of it as a filtering device.'

'I feel pressured to do it. Like everyone expects me to take Finn, like everyone would think better of me. People *love* mothers.'

'I hadn't noticed,' said Marnie.

'Zac told me the other day that someone did a study and found the word "mother" was the most popular word in the English language.' She snorted. She had asked him why he was telling her that and he looked hurt and replied, 'Just thought you might be interested.' Arsehole.

'He wants you off his tail.'

'Exactly. And I don't know if I *want* a child. I can't

imagine being so . . . so needed. I mean listen to your-self, you don't exactly make it sound easy.'

Marnie frowned. 'I know. You hear the worst of it. I'm sorry. I don't mean to put you off. There are great bits. I mean, you love them so much. Really you do. More than words can describe. You know why I don't like coming out for lunch any more?'

'Oh, it's too expensive, I know, and you can't get a really good Caesar salad any more, it's all this Nicoise crap . . .'

'No, no, it's because all these mums come here with babies in prams . . .' Marnie waved down at the prom-enade below, where what looked like a mothers'-group outing had emerged from under an awning '. . . and I just cannot bear to see them, it makes me miss Lucy so much, it fills me with *panic*. I think what am I *doing* swanning around here while my baby's being cared for by strangers?'

Ana nodded slowly. She sensed this was going to be a very quick lunch.

'Not you, Ana! I mean it's great to catch up with you, it's just I feel guilty, like if I'm away from her I should be working and not doing *anything* else. And I have to leave work by five-thirty at the latest, to get to creche before it closes and they leave all the leftover babies with the cleaner or something, so I need to show the editors I'm working hard during the day. Especially now I'm only working four days a week. Shit, you know I just remembered I have to go to the chemist and get Eucy Bear and saline and cotton balls . . .'

Marnie started shovelling her salad into her mouth

furiously, bending low near the plate, even as she rose to her feet. Ana exchanged glances with an older woman at the next table. 'And I have to make some phone calls and express milk again at three, so would you mind, Ana, if I headed back?'

'I don't mind, but we've only been here twenty minutes. You are entitled to a lunch break.'

'We are. We are, aren't we?' Marnie looked struck by the idea. 'That's why work is so fabulous. Mothers at home don't get lunch breaks. Or sick leave.'

'You're not doing a very good job of selling this gig.'

'Next time. Next time I'll tell you only the good bits. Is ten dollars enough?' Marnie stood and finished her water. Her salad was half-eaten.

'It's plenty.'

The next Saturday, Ana headed out to Serena's, having offered to take Finn to the zoo. It was a month since his parents' death and Serena needed a break. Ana was met at the door by a pile of brightly coloured backpacks adorned with various banana folk and train faces.

Both Cooper and Finn peered out at her; little tin-men in stiff raincoats. A definite going-out look about both of them. She felt suddenly anxious.

'Hello, you two! Cooper, where are *you* off to?' Surely not, please God no. She was nervous enough about taking one. Then remembered she only had one bolt for a child's car seat in the car, so she couldn't take two anyway. Coop must be going to kindy. She hugged him, affection renewed in her flood of relief.

'Would you mind taking Cooper too?' Serena drifted

into the hall, holding Angus on her hip while she put a hat on him. Cooper gazed up at Ana, eyes wide with hope, body frozen with suspense.

Ana hedged. 'Doesn't he need a car seat?'

'We can swap cars.' Serena handed her some keys and Ana stared at them in dismay.

'Are you sure? I mean . . . it's nice that you trust me but . . .' But what if I lose them?

'I trust you completely.'

'Well, of course then, that's great!'

Cooper shrieked with joy and Ana regrouped. It was hard not to feel flattered, anyway. There weren't many people who greeted the prospect of a morning with her by jumping on the spot with excitement. No one at work, that was for sure.

Twenty minutes later, she pulled away from the curb, reflecting that getting two baby goats arranged into car seats would probably have been easier than inserting these two. Her back ached with the effort. Finn had sobbed on being parted from Serena, and Ana had hopefully suggested postponing the trip but Serena just kissed Finn and walked quickly back into the house. Serena's car was, predictably, a mobile garbage dump, but it did at least have a CD player. The CDs were apparently stored loose on the floor, where they slid around with a bag of shell grit, a fire engine, a couple of foam cups bearing dried coffee rings, two small jumpers and a clear-lidded lunchbox which held emergency supplies of crusty orange peel. At the lights, Ana examined the musical choices: *Wiggly Safari, Yule Be Wiggling,* and *It's a Wiggly Wiggly World*. She groaned. *A Wiggly Wiggly World*? What was that, a Best Of or something?

She was regaled by the sense that real life was happening elsewhere.

'Ana?'

She glanced in the rear vision mirror. Cooper smiled at her deliciously, with that toddler skin that looked like it had been buttered on thick. Eyes enormous and shining. How did we lose all that gorgeousness, all those generous layers of gloss? Her own skin in the mirror looked leathery by comparison; cross and withered.

'Ana, what your name?'

'Ana.' She should try to fit in a regular weekly yoga class, she was thinking, only why did they make them so long? An hour and a half? She was fuming with impatience by the end of them.

Cooper pressed on.

'What your name, Finn?'

Finn's tears had subsided into hiccupping, and he gazed dreamily at the passing cars.

'What your *name*?'

Silence. Finn's dignity under pressure was impressive, Ana noted. That's how she should handle the next bout of bullying in the conference room, just stare coolly out the window and . . .

'What your *name*, Finn?' Cooper again.

She couldn't resist. 'His name's Finn.'

'No, *Finn*! Finn say. *Finn-what-your-name*?'

'Just trying to help.'

'What your name, Finn?'

There was a sharp scuffle in the back seat and a cry of protest. Ana changed lanes and frantically tried to remember which road led to the zoo.

Finn wailed.

'Cooper, you didn't hit Finn, did you?' Ana was filled with dark rage at the very thought. She could see in the rear-vision mirror that Finn's face had turned down in comic book outrage. That face so like Priya's, that motherless little face, grizzled in grief. And she had taken the wrong bloody lane.

'No.'

'Because if you do it again I'll . . .' She would what? Smack him? Stop the car and put him out on the side of the road, with his address written on his forehead? '. . . I'll be very sad.'

Sad? *Sad*? She blushed. Oh, well now, that was *really* showing him who's boss. Appeal to his obviously highly developed sense of compassion. She darted across two lanes of traffic and waited in a break in the median strip, her heartbeat rising as she saw the traffic bearing down on the tail of her car. They were all about to be smashed to smithereens. This car was so ridiculously big. She did a U-turn, whisking the car out of oncoming traffic just in time, and was rewarded by a sign that said, '*Melbourne Zoo This Way*'.

'Finn, what your name?' A pleading little voice from Cooper's corner.

Finn whimpered, but revealed nothing.

'*He doesn't want to tell you his name.*'

You know, this wasn't so different from being in an editorial meeting after all.

At the zoo car park, she took Finn out first, buttoned up his red coat and stood him on the pavement.

'Wait here, Finny.'

She went back to extract Cooper. Cooper insisted on holding a truck in each hand, which meant the harness straps had to be eased over not only his arms, but also various scoops and backhoe devices, at one stage becoming entangled in the string of a crane. Ana accomplished all this while bent at an unhealthy angle inside the car door, banging her head twice, both times when she tried to get a glimpse of the pavement to check on Finn, who, thankfully, seemed momentarily frozen by his new freedom. Through the horror of Cooper's car seat extraction, Ana was sustained by a smug and breathless delight that Finn was standing still and waiting for her, something Serena had sworn toddlers never did. Ana mentally practised telling Serena about it in a casual, expert sort of a way. 'I just said, *Finn, wait here*, I said it loudly and firmly, and I reckon that was the secret, *he knew I meant it*.' Cooper was finally lifted free of his bonds: if Ana had had the energy she would have raised him to the sky and shouted in triumph, but all she could do was push him towards the pavement and slump on the car, resolving to call a chiropractor that afternoon, and noting in disbelief that the impossible-to-let-go-of construction machinery had now been discarded on the ground in Cooper's joy at being at the zoo.

At this point Ana realised she could not see Finn. She dashed onto the footpath, hoping each step would reveal him behind a tree, just out of her previous line of vision. It didn't. He wasn't there. She looked frantically up and down the footpath, not even daring to look out into the car park. Finally, beyond a group of elderly people and a couple of mothers with prams, she glimpsed a little red coat toddling along jerkily, before it disappeared into a crowd again.

'Cooper, *please, please* stay here.'

She dropped her handbag and ran, hoping as she did that no one would steal her bag, or her friend's firstborn for that matter, then found a moment between pounding steps to berate herself for her distorted sense of priorities, before she glimpsed Finn again, getting close to the big road upon which a convoy of meat trucks was just now thundering along. The two women ahead with prams paused and looked back to where she was bolting, crazy and red faced through stumbling old people who were probably suffering cardiac arrests in her wake. One of the women left her pram and ran to Finn. She scooped him up under the arms and chatted to him conspiratorially, smiling as Ana pounded up. Her hands trembled. He had been so close to the road.

'Thank you so much.' Ana was almost in tears as she took Finn onto her hip. 'He just ran . . . I didn't know they could run so fast . . .'

The women nodded kindly, probably wondering how anyone could not know toddlers ran away. Probably wondering whether Finn should be reported as a suspected kidnapping victim. Then Ana realised they were looking over her shoulder at Cooper, alone way down the footpath.

She ran back, Finn jolting against her hip.

Cooper, however, had obediently stayed put. He was crouched over her handbag.

'Good boy, Cooper. Next time I get *you* out of the car first.' She reached behind and rubbed her back. She had definitely pulled a muscle.

'I don' run way.' He held up a small bottle, and the powerful smell of Estee Lauder Beautiful, mixed with the three-week-old remnants of an apricot and almond bar, met her nostrils.

'Perfume,' said Ana. One hundred and forty dollars a bottle perfume. Her back pain branched out into a headache.

'All gone.' Cooper smiled at her cheerily. Ana reached in and patted the wet but exquisitely scented innards of her bag.

'It has indeed.' There did seem to be a small pool in the bottom corner, but she would bet it was now rich in ingredients that the good people of Lauder had not intended for the scent Beautiful, including the yellow crumbs of a vitamin B tablet, and some stray sesame seeds.

Inside the zoo, they saw vervet monkeys, waterbuck and cheetah. The Asian elephants, Mek Kapah and Bong Su, were having sex in front of the tourists.

'They're making love,' a woman near Ana told her children. Ana blushed and hurried the boys away.

Inside the butterfly enclosure Finn grabbed a no-doubt priceless tropical specimen, which had to be quickly pried from his small hand so it could limp to safety or quiet death behind a monsteria plant, and they all emerged gasping from the humid enclosure. Ana was striding along when she realised Finn wasn't with her. She turned back and there he was, standing a few paces back, his face pressed against the butterfly enclosure.

'Finny!' She ran back to him. He murmured something. 'What, darling? Say that again?'

'Buf-fly.' It was a whole new word, emerging from the wasteland of baby gabble like a green shoot after a bushfire. Ana had the eerie feeling that people other than herself should be alerted. He was so real, so there, when Priya, day after day, continued to not be there. Ana crushed him to her and he flailed to escape as she wept into his dark hair. He even smelled like Priya.

When she looked up through her tears, Cooper stood watching her with calm interest.

'Finn's a bit sad,' Ana said, wiping her nose.

'Poor Finn.' Cooper crouched slightly, hands on his corduroyed thighs, eyebrows raised, mimicking an adult's patronising stance. 'Okay, Finny?'

Ana stretched out one arm to pull Cooper in behind Finn, to hold them both close. She watched the butterflies over the tops of their heads, and saw how they blurred away with her tears.

13

Think of Vanuatu, Serena was telling herself. As she lay on the operating table with her legs spread.

It was their last overseas holiday before children. Not that they had known that then. They had a cabin on a lagoon. They walked through cabbage tree palms at twilight, reaching ahead of themselves in case they blundered into the unspeakable giant spiderwebs, so strong they made a twanging noise when they snapped. Serena squealed, even Dave shrieked like a girl whenever they flapped their hands into one of these webs. They stamped and brushed down their clothes. Dave peered mischievously behind her ear. 'Don't move. I see something.' They ran back to the hut, from which they could hear the waves crashing on the sand. More kava, more mad giggling.

She always liked to think it was on one of those nights, with the warm salt winds blowing through the open louvres and the Do Not Disturb sign on the door, that Cooper was conceived.

'Does that hurt?' said the nurse.

'No.'

Back to Vanuatu. They took a canoe from the resort one day and . . .

But that *was* starting to hurt. What was this woman doing?

'This is just the prelim check-up, isn't it?' she asked.

'Oh yes! Don't worry, you'll be knocked out for the real thing,' the woman said. 'You're booked in for Thursday morning, aren't you?'

'Tomorrow,' said Serena.

'Tomorrow! I can't believe it! The weeks go so fast,' the nurse marvelled, her Ansell-sheathed hand apparently up Serena to her wrist.

Serena gritted her teeth and shut her eyes.

They took a canoe from the Blue Island Resort and paddled it feebly, city types that they were, zig-zagging and splashing their way upstream a little until the resort was out of sight. To their right was dense forest, impossible to see through. To the left was a palm plantation, deserted, Narnian with its meticulous rows of trunks. As they jerked along, they could see down one avenue of palms after another, each row running out of sight.

They pulled in at a tiny bay. There was a shed, a windowbox of flowers, a wheelbarrow filled with coconut soap. No one to be seen.

Dave wandered off on a diagonal line through the palms.

Serena climbed an old tree, a craggy remnant of pre-palm vegetation, that looked out over their canoe. She laid her belly along a branch and hung down her arms and legs.

Dave came back and stood below her. She watched him through the leaves as he looked around, first towards the river then back to the hut. If she had been holding a palm frond she could have stroked his head with the tip of it.

After a minute he called her. 'Sreny! Sreny!'

Nothing. Just the lifeless rattle of the palms. It was getting dark.

Serena didn't want to answer. She felt she would never be so beautifully alone again in all her life. So whole.

The nurse withdrew her hand and helped her sit up on the narrow bed. Then she showed her into another room, which had a television screen mounted on the roof.

Serena reached around to hold the back of her hospital gown closed. 'You're giving me an ultrasound?'

'We need to date the pregnancy,' said the nurse. 'You seem quite big for ten weeks. And if it's too big, we may need to use a different procedure.' She helped Serena lay down on her back and gently parted her knees then she reached up and turned the screen away.

'Don't you let people see the ultrasound?' She felt the need to nail every delicacy in this place; to be sure she wasn't deluding herself for a moment about what she was doing. That was the only way she could live with it.

'If they want to. But we don't encourage it.' The nurse watched the screen as she held the probe. Serena knew from previous pregnancies what she would be looking at; an indecipherable swirl of black and grey in the shape of a fan, with one kernel, one nut, with the incredible potential to become a child. A heartbeat that flickered like a disco light.

'Why not?'

The nurse was calm. 'Because people without a

medical background can read the wrong things into an ultrasound. The uterine sac can look like a head with eyes and a mouth. People can think they see their baby's face.'

'And what, they change their minds?'

'Not usually. But it can give them nightmares.' The nurse frowned and stared at the screen. What could she see?

'I've had two children. I'm pretty familiar with ultrasounds.' Serena braced herself against the uncomfortable probe. 'I guess most people who come here haven't had children.'

The nurse seemed distracted when she answered. 'You're wrong, actually. Many of them already have children. So, did you want to see the ultrasound?'

'No.'

The nurse withdrew the probe, left the room and returned with a doctor. They stared at the screen and murmured. The doctor nodded and left and the nurse reached back between Serena's legs. 'We're just preparing the cervix now . . .'

It seemed to go on forever. Finally the nurse withdrew her hand and sat back with a smile, peeling off her gloves. She reached out and helped Serena to sit up.

'Is there a history of multiple births in your family?'

'No!' Serena's breathing was shallow and the room suddenly felt too small. *Multiple births?*

'Because the scan is showing two heartbeats.'

'Two?' Serena spluttered. 'But what does that mean?'

The nurse looked at her kindly.

'It means it's twins.'

Serena stared. '*What*?'

'How do you feel about that?' This nurse should be reported. Why was she telling her these things?

'What . . . I don't know. Are you sure?'

'Yes. That's why I got the doctor in, to double check before I told you.'

'But why tell me? What does it matter if I'm going to . . .' She couldn't finish. It was impossible. No one in her family had twins. How could her body have done this to her?

'We always tell people if it's a multiple pregnancy. They need to know. Sometimes people get a bit funny when they hear it's two.'

Serena wiped away tears. This nurse was definitely a plant, linked to the angry women standing out the front. Accepting two pays, taking secret orders. 'What do you mean, people get funny about it?' There was something so conspiratorial about the idea of twins, as if they had made their plans regardless of her.

The nurse smiled mildly and blinked, holding up a calming hand.

'It changes things for some people.'

'I'm not having twins.' Serena pulled on her under-pants. 'I've seen women with twins. Breastfeeding two, chasing two toddlers around supermarkets. And I've already got two. *And* I'm minding a third.'

The nurse nodded briskly. 'Well, it sounds like you've made up your —'

'How does it change things for some people? Knowing that it's twins.'

The nurse shrugged. 'It doesn't matter how other people feel. What matters is how you —'

'How would it *change* anything . . .' But she already knew. Because there was a witness. Because every human is more real when they have a mate and twins came equipped. Because she was outnumbered.

The nurse shrugged. 'It's a bit special, or people sometimes see it like that.'

Special? Special? Serena felt the word slice under her heart. They shouldn't be allowed to say these things! 'But that doesn't make sense! Twins is twice as bad! If you didn't want one, why would you suddenly want two?' Another nurse entered the room silently, exchanging a wordless glance with the first.

'Would you like to see the counsellor?'

'No!'

'You need to see them once before the procedure, anyway.' The second nurse murmured and the first one corrected herself. 'Actually the counsellor is busy at present. But when are you booked in for the procedure?'

'Tomorrow.' Serena zipped up her skirt.

'Well, you'll need to come to a counselling session first. Do you think you're going to go through with it?'

'Yes!' She buttoned up her shirt and did up her shoelaces, wrenching them so tight her feet hurt. 'I'll be here. I will *so* be here.' She hated them all.

'Tissue?' The nurse held out a box.

Serena took a wad and wiped her face. The nurse moved to touch her shoulder, her face sympathetic, but

Serena glared her off. She gathered up her bag. 'Well. I'll see you tomorrow!'

'Tomorrow it is.'

'I'll be here.'

'Good-oh.'

Serena slung her bag over her shoulder. 'It just gave me a shock. I'm fine.'

'Of course you are.'

'It doesn't really make any difference to me if it's two. It's funny isn't it, that some people get funny about it?' She felt fine, now. Just a little dizzy.

'It is funny.'

'Maybe it's because there's two of them in there and . . . maybe they already know each other . . .' *Stop. Don't think about it.*

'Sorry, Serena. My next appointment's waiting.'

'Sorry. Well, I'll see you tomorrow.' *Stop saying that. You sound irrational.*

'Okay. And, Serena?'

'Yes?'

'Take the rest of those tissues.'

That night, she put the kids to bed and waited up for Dave. It was ten o'clock before she was woken, in front of the television, by the sound of his keys at the door.

'Hey.' He dropped a briefcase and took off his jacket. She rubbed her eyes and reached for the remote, turning the telly off.

She held out her hand and he took it silently. He sank onto the couch beside her, letting his head fall back on the cushions and closing his eyes as if he were sliding underwater. She watched the profile of his face, the straight lines of his nose and his forehead and his jaw, and the inward undulation of his cheek.

It was time to tell her husband the truth. *Pregnant . . . already dealing with it . . . just thought you should know . . . a simple medical procedure . . .*

He opened his eyes and frowned.

'Hey, Serena. Could you not . . .' She gritted her teeth. They had way too many of these conversations, the ones that began *could you not . . .* As if they were trying to sand off each other's edges, get rid of each other piece by piece.

'Could you not put the garbage bin right up against the front of the house like that?'

Serena released his hand.

He rubbed the heel of his hand against his eye. 'It's just, you've pushed the down-pipe out of kilter and it's not lined up anymore with the grille that leads to the drain.'

'Okay. Where do you want me to put it?'

'Maybe under the eaves.'

'Well, where are the billycart and the trikes meant to go? And the firewood?'

'Maybe we could put the bin around the other side of the house . . .'

'*We*? You can, I'm not hauling the Sulo over bloody hill and dale every week.'

'I'll do it. I do the bins.' He sounded hurt. 'How are the kids?'

'Okay. Sad they missed out on Daddy saying goodnight to them.'

'But I rang. Why didn't Cooper want to talk to me on the phone?'

'He was busy right at that minute. He was executing a particularly tricky manoeuvre with Thomas, Percy and Harold, all passing through a cardboard box tunnel we'd made.'

'Oh. Well, that explains it then.' He snorted huffily.

'I can't *make* them talk to you. Cooper doesn't want a phone daddy. And a phone daddy is useless to Angus, seeing as he can't talk. You might as well leave him a video of yourself. These hours are crazy.'

'I'm doing this for all of us, you know. It's not like I'm working my arse off fourteen hours a day for my own pleasure. We'll all benefit from the money.'

'We don't need more money. We need *you*.'

'Okay, okay. And look, when I'm on the phone with Cooper, could you not . . .'

She rolled her eyes and knotted her arms across her chest so tightly she could feel her swollen breasts being crushed. Could you not exist, Serena? Could you not have a single bloody need of your own?

'Could you not prompt him to answer me, could you just let him speak? It's just that if he wants to sit on the phone and *not* talk, if he wants to just listen to me talk, then that's okay. But if you're telling him what to say to answer me, and I'm talking in his other ear, then it's completely confusing for him.'

'Well, could you try getting home by seven so you could say goodnight to him in person? Could you not walk in at ten and start telling me off about rubbish bins? Could you not leave me to run the house for fifteen hours straight and then come home and start issuing orders?'

'Serena, I'm sorry, but the downpipe thing is really important. It's causing a puddle to develop around the side of the house, which could eventually rot the foundations.'

She stood, knotting her dressing gown tightly around herself, tears in her eyes.

'You have no idea what's important, Dave. Maybe there are things happening around here that are even more important than rotting foundations.'

'Are there? Well, tell me. Fucking hell, the foundation thing should be a communication exchange of twenty seconds, it shouldn't exclude you telling me about more important things. Are the kids well? Is everything okay?'

She stared at him. It was now half past ten. If she let herself say what she really felt, they would be up half the night. And then, after they finally got to bed, at least one of the three kids would wake, with a cough or a nightmare or some inevitable thing, and then they would all be up at six tomorrow anyway, and she would feel like death. The scratchy eyes, the feverishness, the hunger cravings of the sleep-deprived. More than war, or even peace, she wanted sleep.

She shook her head and turned to leave.

'Everything's just fine, Dave. Call me sometime, I'll tell you all about it.'

14

'I'll have the lamb salad, thanks.' Ana smiled at the waitress.

'Make that two.' Elijah handed back the menus. No thank you, Ana noted disapprovingly. No please. Barely a smile. And yet the young perky waitress beamed at him.

'Two lamb shanks,' she said brightly, scribbling on her notepad. The obligatory strip of bare, tanned stomach, revealed between a too-short shirt and an incidental black apron. But Elijah didn't look even momentarily at the bare young flesh. Arrogant? Unobservant? Gay?

She suddenly heard what the waitress had said.

'Lamb *salad*,' she corrected. 'Thank you.'

'Oh, sorry. It's my first day.' The girl beamed again, this time a little conspiratorially, at Elijah. Ana watched the girl saunter off. Was Elijah attractive? Did she find him attractive?

Did he find *her* attractive?

He had rung her that morning at work and asked her to lunch, to talk about aspects of the will. That was what he said, anyway. So far there had just been polite small talk about weather and work lunch habits (he never brought sandwiches from home, she did intermittently; he occasionally forgot to eat anything for lunch, hell would freeze over before she ever forgot to eat, that sort of thing). She had been relieved to meet him in a restaurant rather than his uncomfortable office. Maybe the beard been trimmed, or maybe it was the white shirt, but he seemed a little more lawyer, a little less dungeons and dragons. Although she could still imagine him running a Jethro Tull fan club, or being the sort of *Lord of the Rings* freak who had read *The Silmarillion* as well.

Not that she was the sort to stereotype. It was just that, after breaking up with Andy, she looked back at their early days and realised it had all been there to see, in their first meeting. Andy's insecurity, his neediness, his tendency to moodiness and a sort of feminine, hysterical bossiness, which she loathed. And she had noted it all very rationally, and then quickly put it aside so that she could fall in love with him, the way people did when it was their time. This was Ana's theory, that when it was Your Time, you just met someone right enough and decided which bits of them you would need to ignore. And later those parts resurfaced and then you had to deal with them, make a call on whether you could live with them or not. And having worked this out, she had resolved to be far more wary with every man she came across.

'So, Priya's will.' She folded her arms, elbows on the table. 'No surprises? She hasn't bequeathed me any more unexpected gifts, has she?' Trying to lighten the sick misery that arose whenever she thought about Priya and Richard.

'I was just thinking about the scenario you raised last time we met.' He raised his eyebrows. 'The what-if-Finn-had-another-father scenario.'

'Oh. That.' She felt faintly disappointed. 'What about it?'

'Do you know anything more?'

'It really was hypothetical.'

He smiled, as if reading something flirtatious into her reticence. 'Oh, come *on*.'

'No, really.' She find herself almost simpering, enjoying an unusually coy moment for her.

'Ana, this is important.'

She blinked at his change in tone. 'Oh. Okay. Well, it was just a thought I had. They were having trouble conceiving a child and it went on for a couple of years. And then Priya got really sad and she used to joke privately to me and Serena, that she could always go out and, you know, have a one-night stand and get knocked up that way.'

'I see.' Elijah put his long fingers together and stared down at them. He was, for a long moment, mentally absent from Ana, and she felt herself pleasantly liberated to examine him. The smell of his aftershave snagged at her; she knew it well from somewhere. How did they make these smells for men, she wondered, these trust-me, fuck-me smells?

The waitress appeared with two steaming plates and laid them on the table, sneaking another smile at Elijah. Ana felt irritable and old. She really should shop for new clothes that weekend. Then she looked at her plate.

'These aren't our meals.' She gestured at the chunky dish before them, fatty lamb shanks in vegetables and chickpeas, with cous cous and probably a lazy four thousand extra kilojoules on the side. 'We ordered the salad, thanks.'

'Oh my God, you did too.' The girl looked distraught, and glanced back towards the kitchen as if a wild animal was about to burst through the doors and bite her. 'Oh, shit.'

'It doesn't matter. It looks much better than salad. Don't think twice about it.' Elijah shrugged and earned a grateful smile from the waitress. Her slim body almost doubled over in thanks. He gestured magnanimously, indicating she could go.

Ana bristled.

'No, sorry, I would still like the salad.'

Elijah glanced at her with what could have been distaste but said nothing. She decided she didn't care what he thought anyway, if he was the sort of man to speak on her behalf without even asking how she felt. This was a man who confessed to forgetting to eat. No wonder he didn't care what he was brought. She, however, was a woman who liked to eat, and liked to get what she wanted.

Elijah spoke again to the waitress.

'I'm hungry, I can eat two of these, so just leave it. But we'll order a lamb salad for the lady.' He nodded at Ana as the waitress departed. 'It's my shout anyway.'

'Now you make me feel bad.' Ana spoke a little resentfully.

'I'm sorry, I don't mean to. But it's her first day. She'll get into trouble if she has to admit she made a mistake like that.'

'I have to go soon.' Ana looked at her watch. What was his point, rescuing some strange girl waitress he didn't even know? She felt herself on shaky ground and didn't like it. Had she been rude to the girl? Had he felt forced to compensate for her? He looked like a caveman, sitting with his beard in front of two steaming plates of lamb shanks. Was he just a bit of a goose?

'Oh.' Elijah also looked at his watch. 'You have something to do . . . ?'

'I have to write a column before four, and I have to present ideas for three others before five.'

'Of course. The *Morning Star.*' His expression was blank as he perused his two meals, but she detected a faint note of amusement. She said nothing. She was used to people like him looking down on the tabloid *Morning Star.* They were the sort of people who read the *Financial Daily* or the *Observer* magazine, people who rolled their eyes over the dreadfulness of the vast mass of middle Australia.

'I'm sure you don't read it.' She looked at her watch again. She really wasn't going to be able to wait for them to prepare a whole new meal.

'You're wrong. I do.'

'Do you?'

'I like horses. The racing section's good.'

'Oh.' He really wasn't her type, after all.

'You disapprove of gambling?'

'No, no.' She shook her head. 'I write about it sometimes . . . well I've written a few things about its . . . effect on families . . . I mean I know people can't help it.' She blundered on, trying desperately not to offend him. 'I know it's addictive, like smoking or something . . .'

He laughed openly at her. 'You write for a mass-circulation newspaper and you think everyone having a bit of a flutter is a problem gambler?'

She glared. 'No. Not at all. I just didn't think lawyers hung around the TAB in their lunch breaks.'

He studied her with a curiosity that made her blush. 'Well, you're not like what I thought tabloid journalists would be like either.' His voice was quiet. 'And to be honest, when I was preparing myself to ring you and tell you about the will, I thought I would be making this person, you that is, pretty happy.'

'Why?'

'Well, you know. Unmarried 38-year-old woman, childless, bereaved best friend . . .'

'You thought I'd be jumping at the chance to have a child.'

'Of course, if you're already in a relationship I can understand . . .'

'No. I'm single.'

'Tell me about your family.' He tilted his head to one side.

'Middle class, Dad left Mum, brother had mental illness and killed himself, Mum in nursing home.' Her lamb salad landed before her and she stabbed it with a fork.

He nodded, still scrutinising her face.

'Is that maybe why a childless 38-year-old woman isn't jumping at the chance to adopt a young child?'

'What! Enough of the barren spinster stuff already. I'm not on a walking frame yet. I've said I may want him.'

'Ah but you don't, really.' He leaned closer to her. 'Ana, I'll tell you something. I don't think I want children.'

'Really.' She sipped her wine. 'Well, let's hope no one ever dumps one in your lap.'

'I can see how much hard work they are and it's not for me. I'm only telling you this because I can understand totally if you feel like that. In fact you'd be the most rational woman I ever met. But ask Serena to take the little boy, if that's how you do feel.'

She stared at him. She wished she could. Bloody Priya and her mad wishes.

'I'm scared of having a child. I might stuff him up. And my career's . . . important to me.'

'I see.' He seemed almost amused by her again.

Ana put down her fork. 'You seem to know everything about me. What about you, are you married?'

'Single.'

Ana sat back. Was he flirting? Was she interested? He seemed a little solid, a little conservative for her. Something church-going about him.

'I bet you're from the country. I can always tell,' she said.

'Bingo. Family from Swan Hill. I spend a lot of time on the Calder Highway.' He beamed. She smirked. Country boys were like something from the fifties. Their world view was one shaped by a lifetime of general-store trust and kindness, which was why they usually married country girls. And they said things like bingo. And they ate whatever was served up to them, even if it was the wrong thing.

'Ah.'

'How can you tell?'

'Country boys are . . . sweet.'

He snorted.

'So you think I'm a sweet country boy with a gambling problem. Who's a pushover for a pretty waitress.'

They laughed. Ana glanced at her watch again, and reluctantly picked up her handbag.

'I must get going. But tell me, did you know Priya very well?'

'I knew her a little.'

She nodded, her eyelashes suddenly heavy with tears. She rose, and took out her wallet.

'Leave it. It's on me.' He waved at her. 'Go on, go. Call me sometime.'

She thanked him and left, deadline panic rising with every step she took back to the office. She had remembered a recent survey on how little the public trusted lawyers, and she was going to dig it out, hook it in with the most recent case of slack sentencing in the courts, and shape a column out of it. All by four.

But she had enjoyed talking to Elijah. And the lamb salad had been delicious.

Back at the office she went through her mail. A PR company had sent her a CD with an enticing pink cover note that asked her to, 'slip this into your CD-ROM and learn more about the magic of Magdalan cosmetics'. CD-ROM? Were they joking? People always assumed journalists would have state-of-the-art communications equipment, such as a CD-ROM player. Or maybe she did have one? Ana frowned at the box under her monitor and poked the CD nervously at a promising looking slit, but it was just the join between two parts of the plastic cover.

Lowenthal poked his head over her partition and she jumped, hoping he hadn't seen her complete lack of IT savvy.

'Got some very interesting news for you, young lady.'

'Really?'

'I just had lunch with the chiefs of Parker Publishing. Your name was raised.'

Parker was an international book publisher, owned by the same group as the company that ran the *Morning Star*. She felt her breath quicken.

'My name?'

'Mmm-hmm. They're looking for a young female to do a book for their summer year-after-next collection.' Lowenthal often referred to women as females, much as a zoologist might have referred to a subsection of species. 'Either reprint a series of columns or take one good argument and expand it into a sort of thesis-stroke-definition of contemporary life, all smart and intelligent but conveyed in a very quick, *Morning Star*-ish sort of way.'

Ana couldn't speak. A book?

'You know the sort of thing. Something that half the people agree with, half are offended by, something that hits talkback radio with a bang and gets lots of free publicity. Something people can read in two days on the beach but talk about over dinner parties for a month and feel like they're hip and up with things.'

A book, was all Ana could think. A book. Strangely the first person she wanted to tell was her mother, and for a moment she felt sad that she'd be lucky now to catch her in a lucid moment. Her mother would be telling her she had won the 1956 Olympic 400m for Australia, and Ana would tell her she was writing a book, and neither would believe the other, if they even listened long enough to hear it.

'But maybe they want someone else to do it.'

'No, they like you. They like your stuff. This move of Zac's has been good for you, a lot more exposure. But there's a catch. They want to be able to say you're our senior columnist.'

Well. That was the end of that, surely. Zac Banks was stuck there like wet cement.

'Don't think like that,' he said firmly, seeing her face. 'There's a chance that's just what you could be in a few months. If Zac decides to stay in Sydney, you're in. And I'll be giving him every encouragement.'

15

Twins. Serena woke at seven on the morning of the abortion, to find Dave standing over the bed, fully dressed in a suit and holding his youngest. He lifted the blankets and tucked sleepy Angus in beside her with a bottle.

'Coop and Finn are watching cartoons. I have to get going. Early meeting.' His expression soft as he watched her struggle to wake. She saw a steaming cup of tea on the bedside table, an epaulet of regurgitated porridge on the shoulder of his suit coat, and realised he had made an effort to let her sleep in. In the comforting morning tangle of warm bedclothes, with Angus' chubby baby toes pressing into her bare thighs, she took one of her husband's hands and felt momentarily at peace. Their weapons of war simply laid aside. Could it be this easy?

Twins. An abortion. Today.

She sat up. 'Dave, I really must tell you something.'

He looked in anguish towards the door. 'Sweetie, I have to go. It's a breakfast meeting at the Hyatt with the upramp designers and we have had nothing but problems with these pretentious bastards. I told them we had to meet at seven-thirty and get this resolved by nine, so that I can go into the nine-thirty meeting with the financiers and tell them exactly what the cost will be, and that's in preparation to meet the Roads Minister at ten-thirty at Parliament House, so he can hold a press conference this afternoon on the total cost of the project . . . my morning is just hell. I've hardly slept all night worrying about it.' He picked up his briefcase and looked back at her apologetically, poised for flight at the bedroom door.

'This is important, Dave.'

He looked at his watch.

'Can you call me at work? Or tell me tonight?' His body now half out of the door, just his head leaning back, hoping for a word of release.

She considered him. Some things you didn't say on the phone. Some things, it was never the right time to say them. She opened her mouth, words hovering around the tip of her tongue, *Sure, we'll talk later*, as if she were leaving it up to her lips to make a decision about whether to tell or not.

'I'm pregnant.'

His astonished face reappeared wholly in the door. He put his briefcase down. A mixture of wonder and puzzlement and delight.

'Sweetie!' He came and sat on the bed beside her, took her hand, turned it over. 'Are you sure?'

'Yes. And it's twins.'

The emotion on his face turned to shock.

'*Twins* . . . Shit. How long have you known this?'

'And I'm having an abortion. Today.'

He sat very still and regarded her. Turned quite purposefully toward the bedroom clock and checked it. Turned back to her, his expression chilly.

'Say that again.'

She told him again. She felt ill with morning sickness

and fear. She recognised the look on her husband's face: cold fury. He might have been sick with guilt, he might have been shocked at the news, or her resolve, or recognised her decision as one that reflected on his absence as a parent. He might have felt all these things, but unfortunately he had moved straight to anger. Crisis containment. Project management skills. *The rights of the father*, one of Dave's favourite soapbox subjects. Suddenly she wanted him to go away, go to work.

'You'll be late.' She glanced at the clock again. He didn't take his eyes off her.

'How pregnant are you?'

'Ten weeks.'

'And let me get this straight, you have an appointment for an abortion today?'

She felt ill. 'I've been trying to tell you for a few days but you're always so busy . . .'

'And what, you thought you'd secretly abort our child, our children . . . are you mad?'

'Well, what am I meant to do, discuss this with you by email?'

'These are my children!'

'Well it's my body! And are you planning to quit work for the next five years to look after them? Or even be home enough to know who they are? It sure doesn't look like it!'

'And you choose this moment to tell me, as I'm walking out the door to one of the most stressful mornings of my life. Doesn't that strike you as a bit manipulative?'

'Dave, every fucking morning is the most stressful of your life.'

'I can't believe you didn't tell me this!'

'What do you think I just *did*?' She heard the anger in her voice, but it wasn't genuine. She was more scared than angry, and already bitterly regretted telling him at all. And she was sympathetic, despite herself. Watching him, intrigued and puzzled by the glimpse of joy she had seen cross his face when she said the word 'pregnant'. Saddened by it.

His mobile phone started ringing and he checked the screen and turned it off. She could see sweat glistening on his cheekbones, could smell it on him.

'Dave, I'm sorry. It was bad timing. I didn't plan it. I nearly didn't tell you at all. I shouldn't have.'

He slumped, and suddenly looked so young, like a boy dressed up as a man. His freshly shaven face crumpled, his mouth trembled and his hand flew to his eyes, the way it always did when he cried. As if to push the tears back in. Serena couldn't bear it.

'I'm so sorry.'

'Can you cancel it?' A sob lurching up in his voice. Men always cried so badly, like it was something to fight.

She touched his cheek, helpless. 'I don't *want* more children.'

'Just cancel the ... thing, the appointment, today. We'll talk about it tonight.'

She grimaced. 'I've made my decision.'

'Well, I *haven't*. I need time to think about this.' He shook his head. 'Don't do something I might never be able to forgive you for. I'm the father, I have a right to be part of this decision. I mean, maybe I'll come to the same decision as you . . .' He looked doubtful. 'But whatever happens, I need to be part of that decision.'

She sighed. 'Okay. I'll postpone. But you must make time tonight to talk about this. Or I will go ahead and do it without your input. Do you understand? I mean that.'

'Tonight. I promise.' He stood again, reached for his briefcase. Rubbed his temples. Put it down again and kissed her. She rested her hand on the back of his slim neck, the curves of it so like those of his sons, like the children she had already borne him. Could an abortion bring two people back together, the way a baby could?

After he left, she reached for the phone. If she was going to resist the pull of the clinic she would need to arrange something for the day, something far from the city. She listened to the dial tone. A sleepy voice picked up.

'Poss? It's Serena. Are you home today?'

There was a rustle. She pictured him sitting up. Did he have someone with him? Did he think she was mad to call him at such an hour? But it was geologist, labourer hours; once upon a time they had been out in the field by now, oiling parts and positioning a laptop on their knees to get it out of the sunlight.

'I'm meant to be preparing for this talk I'm giving at Weipa but it's boring me stupid. Are you going to come and visit me? With the kids?' She listened for any note of dismay, but there was none. He sounded hopeful.

'Is that okay?' She stood up and peeked through the window. Sunny, clear blue sky.

'It would be fantastic.'

She packed a bag, turned off the telly and changed the boys out of their pyjamas. She studied Finn as she tugged elastic-waisted jeans over his nappy. There was a rosy blush in his brown cheeks and his black curls shone. That jawline, was that Possum's? The shape of the eyebrows?

'What doing, Mum?' Cooper held open his own jeans to examine the cartoon character on the front of his undies.

'We're going on an adventure, Coop. To the country. To see some cows.'

His eyes widened.

'A farm?'

'Sort of.'

'And Angus and Finn?'

'They're coming too.'

Behind the wheel, leaving the city behind them, Serena relaxed. The land on either side of the road expanded into paddocks; occasional mobs of cattle, the odd blue gum plantation. She had always loved long drives, and the meditative state they brought on. It was one of the many things she missed about the field trips, the chance to watch the kilometres flash past, the momentum. The thinking time. *Dave crying.* There was a time when she would have cut off her hand to stem his rare tears. Today she had watched with a worried but distant sympathy. She loved him, yes, but was that still enough? Married love wasn't maternal love: it wasn't unconditional. And he had breached so many of the conditions. Every night that he left her to put the kids to bed without Daddy, to eat her dinner alone, she felt another chip in that protective wall around all their lives; that wall she thought would last forever.

Could she leave him, she wondered, as she pulled over and called the clinic to postpone? How would her life be: single with two small children?

She drove on. She might meet someone else. People did. Maybe she would never find anyone as wonderful as Dave. Maybe the romance of true love only came once. But she would settle for someone who wanted to eat dinner with her. And breakfast. Someone who liked to mow a lawn and potter around with tools; someone who had an opinion about what sort of schools the boys should go to. Someone who could get home in time to put the children to bed, to hold hands with her on the couch and watch bad television.

Mount Misstep was an old mining town, where the tide of gold money had long since flowed out and left one main street with shops housed in heritage buildings, used by local dairy families and tourists. Serena asked at the pub for directions to Possum's place. He lived in what had once been Mount Misstep's Church of the Holy Madonna, now decommissioned, a small building with lancet windows and doors. Inside, light spilled across floorboards and through dust motes.

Seats had been built under the three high windows along the western wall with a small step ladder set in under each one. Shallow shelves stretched over all the lower walls; like looking at the ribs inside a great whale, Serena thought. She stepped closer and saw that rock samples were placed at even spaces all along the shelves.

Chalcocite from Dogwood. Purple and green stichtyte, from Western Tasmania.

'Is the malachyte from South America?'

'The Atacama Desert, up in the Andes.' Poss wore old khaki MRA pants and a flannelette shirt. A framed photograph of Zeke sat between some rock samples. 'Let's make coffee and get the kids set up and I'll show you the photos of the trip. You guys, come here.'

He led them all out the back to a cubby with a slide. Poss had made it himself when Renae was still living with him, even as their relationship fell apart. Zeke had barely had time to play in the cubby before he was taken to London to live with his mother and her new boyfriend.

'I cleaned out the cobwebs this morning.' Poss helped Finn follow Cooper up the ladder and the boys were soon squealing as they did circuits of the ladder and the slide. An old claw-foot bath, painted with a bright mural, was mounted on a slab of Castlemaine slate in a stand of black bamboo at the side of the garden; a hose from the outdoor laundry indicating Poss might still favour hot moonlight baths. Serena settled down with Angus on the grass at her feet to look through Possum's photo albums.

She smiled as he turned the pages. Picture after picture of drill rig, bare rock, blokes in overalls – he could have been anywhere in the world. But then there was the colour and flash of La Escondida, Chiquicamata, home to some of the world's richest copper veins. Serena almost salivated with desire. She asked questions and he told stories and the boys came and collected cake to take back to the cubby and she relaxed amid the sunshine and coffee steam and let images of foreign places and dusty drill sites roll past.

An easy silence fell and they watched Finn and Cooper, now intent on making a bed in the cubby with cushions and blankets dragged from inside.

'So this is Priya's child?' Poss nodded at Finn. 'What's going to happen to him?'

'Shhh.' She lowered her voice. 'She left him to Ana, remember her? But Ana's a full-time journalist and she's never had a child. I said I'd take care of him for a few months while she got herself set up.'

'Would you like to keep him?' Poss whispered.

'If Priya wanted Finn to go to Ana, then that's where he should go. And I've already got two. That's enough.'

Poss sat back and watched Finn, and Serena in turn watched her friend's thoughtful face. Should she say something? Might he just get it?

He turned back and smiled.

'More coffee before we go out and look for some cows?'

'Sounds great.'

I made a promise, she reminded herself as she watched him carry the cups inside. A promise to keep a secret forever.

If someone died, did that absolve you of your promises to them? Was it in fact time to break this particular promise?

Tell me, Priya, what I should do.

Later that day, she strapped the kids back into the car and climbed out to say her goodbyes. The boys had met cows, sheep, a rooster and a small frog, which was in a jar on her front seat. They had all taken turns sitting on a real, working tractor, and Possum's neighbour Norm had even started the engine so they could feel it rumble beneath them. They had run and crawled and climbed until they were exhausted. Finn had said a new word: 'cow'. Angus was already asleep, a bottle upturned in his hand, its teat dripping milk. Cooper had an old, dried, cow's skull in the back of the car and he kept turning to look at it. Possum had brought it out of his shed to show the boys and had ended up giving it to them to take home.

'Oh, you shouldn't have.' Serena stared in horror. 'You might need it.'

Poss shrugged with mock forbearance. 'I can bear the sacrifice. I want Cooper and Finn to have it.'

Cooper glared. 'It's mine, Mum.'

She glanced at Finn and Cooper through the rear-vision mirror as she drove off down the drive. The boys twisted back in their car seats to wave at Possum. By the time they reached bitumen and passed through the small village of Mount Misstep, all three were sound asleep.

Halfway home Finn woke, screaming. The car swung slightly and Serena gripped the steering wheel hard.

'It's okay, Finn. It's okay. Sreny's here. Just a bad dream.'

'No! No!' Finn howled, twisting around in his seat to see the cow's skull. He screamed anew. It was white with age and bits of it were ragged with the gnawing

teeth of time. She was not surprised it had given someone a nightmare.

'Mumma! Mumma!' He was becoming hysterical.
She flicked on the indicator and pulled off the highway.
Swung out, opened the boot, and started pulling on the
horns.

'Nooooooo!' Cooper howled in fury. 'Mine! Mine!'

But Finn's cries were the ones that wrenched Serena's heart.

She jumped back as the cow's head finally slid out
and landed on the verge, and then she slammed the boot
shut.

They pulled back onto the highway and left the
skull behind. Cooper sobbed. Finn whimpered. Angus
turned his head away from them both and settled back
to sleep.

Serena glanced at Finn in the rear vision mirror as
she drove. His eyelids drooped and she willed them
down further, further. Sleep, little boy. He nuzzled his
precious Jarmy as he hiccupped. The scrap of silk was
filthy now and any smell of Priya must be long gone, but
Finn held it constantly. His cry had frightened Serena;
it was a few days now since he had called for his mother
and she had wondered whether he would again. Sometimes Serena felt like shouting for Priya herself.

What if Finn had a living father? What if he was a
good man, a kind man?

Later, she stopped to get petrol, and peered
through the shop window at the car. No movement
within. She took out her mobile phone and called
Priya's lawyer.

'What if I told you I thought Richard wasn't Finn's father?' she said.

There was silence at the other end. To one side she had rolling hills as far as she could see; to the other was the highway, the dull whine of trucks passing.

'That would be interesting,' Elijah Moyal said at last.

'Because it's possible he wasn't.'

'What's your theory?' He sounded cautious.

Serena leaned one elbow on a tattered phone book. 'Priya and Richard had been trying for three years to have a baby. She had tests and she was fine, but he wouldn't even talk about it. I think she had sex with another man just to conceive a child.'

She heard the lawyer inhale, but he didn't speak.

'Did you hear me?'

'I did. Sorry.' He cleared his throat. 'So how certain are you?'

'I'm sure of it. At least that she had sex with someone else around the time Finn was conceived. And that she was trying to conceive.'

'Really?'

'She slept with a former colleague of mine, a geologist. A man I've just been to visit, up in Mount Misstep.'

There was a long silence. Serena sighed. She had obviously caught him at a bad moment. Maybe he was eating lunch or something. 'Look, I just thought you should know. Seeing as you're overseeing who Finn goes to. Just in case it matters. I don't know, maybe it's irrelevant. But please don't let what I've told you go any —'

'A *geologist*?'

He couldn't have sounded more appalled if Serena had revealed that Priya had slept with a farm animal. Serena felt indignant, and cut the call short. She didn't feel Elijah Moyal had understood a word she'd said.

16

Ana tugged at the legs of her one-piece bathers and put her goggles back up on her bathing cap. She had just done her twentieth lap of the indoor pool, and she held onto the edge and let her body go limp in the soupy water. Around her was the rhythmic splashing of other lap swimmers. In the next lane was the long, solidly built man in green baggy shorts she had noticed before. He stopped for a rest too.

She watched the lights of the trams passing outside. This was a city pool, used by workers, open late and early. She had slept with a yoga instructor, Nathanial, who worked here, and her impulse to swim tonight was flavoured by a nostalgic hope that she might see him again. But his name was no longer beside any of the yoga classes on the timetable, and she slipped into the water feeling a little deflated. At work earlier that day she had indulged in a brief fantasy of some poolside chat with Nathanial in his bathers (not Speedos, but a close-fitting, short-legged sort of trunks affair, Ana mused, as with some other section of her brain she wrote a column on industrial action by construction workers), and then the fantasy morphed to some seedy city alleyway where they were tearing at each other's clothes as they pushed aside garbage bins and the cooler temperatures of recent days somehow became conducive to sex up against the wall or on bluestone pavers. Ana thought about all this while she typed languorously.

'When electing their new secretary this year members of the CFMEU must think carefully about the security of their jobs and the stability of the city. The future of $6.4 billion in building contracts could be affected by this election . . .'

But how had they got to the alleyway? Ana often got distracted by such detail in her sexual fantasies. She liked to build them carefully so they could stand a bit of use and re-use. Maybe they had gone for a hot chocolate in the pool cafe, and one thing led to another . . .

'. . . Organiser Butch Freely must be sent a strong message by members that they don't appreciate the direction he's taken them on this year, and that they want a leader whose aim is industrial peace, not continual strife . . .'

Who was she kidding? When had a hot drink in the chlorinated air of a pool canteen ever led to wanton sex outside in an alleyway? Ana hastily moved herself and Nathanial to an atmospheric bar, and then had to puzzle over how they got there.

But here she was in real life, at the pool, and there was no sign of him. She watched as the tall man in the next aisle powered off again in a splashing of muscular legs.

She was crouched in the shallow end, thinking about Nathanial, when she realised Green Shorts was swimming back into harbour. He grabbed the edge, raised his goggles and shook his dark head, splashing Ana.

'Sorry, did I splash you?'

'Er . . . no.' She wiped her eyes and had a pleasant thrill to find herself arm's length from a good-looking and nearly naked man.

'How are you, anyway?' He wiped his own eyes. There was no one immediately near them. The friendly type.

'Good, thanks.' She kept her tone cool, but spoke again to keep him standing there. 'Just having a rest.' She blushed and muttered. 'Well I guess that's obvious, I've been blocking up the end of this lane for the past fifteen minutes.'

He stretched out long legs under the water. 'Oh I don't come here to swim, I just come to dog paddle around the edges and then have a coffee and feel virtuous afterwards.' Friendly *and* self-effacing. And hanging around as if he were interested. Ana found she was grinning stupidly towards the far end of the pool.

'What's the coffee like in the canteen?'

'It's actually really good, Ana. Can I buy you one?' He sounded amused. She turned and stared at him. Someone she had written a story about? Someone from her old school?

The lawyer. She sank as low in the water as she could without submerging her mouth. 'What happened to your beard?'

'I shaved it off.' He laughed. 'You didn't recognise me, did you?'

'Of course! Of course!' What would he think she was, some desperate woman going around trying to pick up strangers in public pools. 'I mean, I *knew* I knew you from somewhere.'

'I'd understand if you didn't. My nan didn't recognise me when I went and saw her yesterday. Although she doesn't recognise me a lot of the time anyway.' He laughed again. He looked ten years younger. His eyes were clearer, his mouth like something she needed to taste. 'So do you still want a coffee or have I scared you off?'

'Yes! I mean, I wanted a coffee anyway . . .' She followed him out of the pool, blinking away the image of his long, brown body as the water fountained off it. Her upper half was suddenly freezing. He looked back and she saw him glance down at her bathers, in the direction of her nipples, which she knew would be screwed tight as her jawline.

'I thought men only grew beards when they were losing their hair. Or if they had acne scars.'

He rubbed his cheek thoughtfully. 'I went camping last year and I wanted to grow one.'

'Oh.'

'But it gets in your food. It's hot and it's itchy. And I didn't get any women trying to pick me up at the pool when I had a beard.' His eyes twinkled at her and he pulled out a chair for her in the pool canteen.

'Excuse *me*. I was *not* trying to pick you up.' She sat, now demurely wrapped in a beach towel from her armpits down. Maybe she should say she couldn't stay for a coffee, retire with some dignity.

'No? I was *hoping* you were.' He smiled down at her, all jawline and brown eyes and beads of water still on his broad brown shoulders. She opened her mouth and closed it again. She felt delicious, as if she had just won some unexpected prize. *I was hoping you were.* Did that mean . . . ? Was he trying to say . . . ? She felt suddenly awash in uncertain and pleasant possibilities.

Elijah ordered two pink iced donuts.

'Two?' She stirred her black decaf.

'They're my weakness.' He cut one into small pieces and pushed the plate towards her. 'I used to do triathlons with my friends but I couldn't get serious about giving up cakes.'

Elijah gave himself a cursory pat down with the towel and Ana tried not to watch as he stepped into a thick, navy blue tracksuit. She grieved for the covering of his long brown limbs. The tracksuit made him look sort of Sheraton health club, nurtured and luxurious. A long way from the shabby chic of Nathanial's yoga classes. She remembered the picture of Elijah with the conservative Prime Minister; one that she, an ardent left-wing voter, would blush to hang behind her desk. Then the fresh memory of near-naked Elijah almost made her blush anew. She watched his mouth move with the fascination of a scientist, and the way he stirred his coffee. What had he said?

'You do triathlons?'

'I used to. Now I just train with friends sometimes. So, how's Finn?'

She told him the story of taking Finn and Cooper to the zoo. 'What with the spilt perfume and the emergency visit to the chiropractor after, I reckon that was the most expensive trip to the zoo ever.'

He sat back and laughed, a hearty belly laugh that she wanted to hear again. 'Hey, I had a chat to Serena the other day.'

'Oh?' Ana felt a little miffed. Serena hadn't mentioned talking to Elijah. 'What about?'

'About Finn. Sounds like he's doing pretty well, considering.' He watched her carefully and she straightened her back, and touched her fingertips to her throat. 'She was talking about a friend of hers, a geologist, a former colleague, I think. I can't remember his name.'

'Oh?'

'I think she thought I knew him from somewhere, and I didn't think I did. But now I think about it, I might have been at uni with him. But I can't remember his name . . .' He trailed off and stared at her. 'Do you know who she might mean?'

Ana thought about it, as eager as a first-grader to come up with the right answer. 'She did have a partner when she worked at MRA, a guy she always went out in the field with. They found some sort of deposit together, and then he went on and found —'

'That sounds like him. What's his name again?'

'Possum Davies.' Ana had met Poss a few times, had thought he was pretty cute too, but unfortunately he was married with a pregnant wife at the time.

'Possum Davies. Possum Davies. And where does he live?' Elijah seemed intrigued. Ana, however, wanted to get back to the deliciously dangerous topic of herself and Elijah.

'I have no idea.'

'It doesn't matter.' Elijah shrugged. 'How did you and Serena and Priya come to be friends, anyway?'

Ana smiled. She was very fond of these particular memories. 'We met at uni. Priya and Serena took a science subject together, biology I think, and I was studying journalism, and editing the student newspaper, and they

155

came in together and volunteered to work on it. The three of us sort of . . . clicked. Then we shared a house in St Kilda, and after that in Windsor. It just went on from there.' And would have gone on forever, right to the old folks' home, if Priya hadn't been killed. Now there was just the two of them, and Ana had a sense these days that she didn't know quite what to do with Serena. As if the friendship was like a three-wheeler bike that, with one wheel fallen off, didn't automatically convert to a bicycle, but rather fell to the ground. The loss of their third wheel was so destabilising that sometimes Ana found she almost resented Serena.

Elijah regarded her kindly. Priya's death stood so clearly between them, they could almost see it. 'It must be hard for you.'

Ana nodded and silently declined the unspoken invitation to unload on him. While most of life's troubles could be thrashed out for the better with a good long chat, she had had enough experience with grief to know that, for her, grief was better left alone.

'But worse for Finn.'

'Uh-huh.' He looked at her. 'So, when are you seeing him next?'

'Well, I'm meant to be taking him to the beach this weekend. Serena's family have a holiday house at Sorrento and she said no one's using it at the moment, so I could have it.'

He raised his eyebrows. 'A whole weekend. Very impressive.'

'Actually, I'm terrified.'

'Hang on. Let me check something.' Elijah took a

diary out of his bag and flicked through it. 'I thought so. I'm seeing a client in Portsea on Saturday. Could I drop by the house on the way home? Maybe I could take you guys to the beach. I'm good at building sandcastles.'

Ana finished her coffee and licked her lips. How absolutely delightful. Her workplace fantasy was sort of materialising, although in a far more decorous way than the violent lust of her dreams, and with a different man. In fact, it was coming together in a vastly improved form. Sex on cold bluestones, really, she was losing her class. Sex in friend's holiday house was a much nicer fantasy.

'That would be lovely.'

'Yes, it would be.'

They beamed at each other, buoyed by an exquisite sense of the synchronicity of the universe.

17

'I do not like green eggs and ham!
I do not like them, Sam-I-am . . .'
Serena closed the book and let the boys' breathing surround her. Cooper, his lashes long, his cheeks rosy and slack. Angus, like someone had dropped him face down from the ceiling. Finn on his side, as if he had fallen asleep in the midst of an Olympian sprint, eyelids blank like someone had wiped his face with a sponge. All exhausted after their long day in the country.

She made herself pause a minute, and touched each one gently on the head. Just a few moments with sleeping children could smooth over some of the ragged hours of before.

Although a glass of wine in front of the television could go even further.

She watched the news like someone else might have watched a fire in the hearth. It flickered and snapped while she sipped her drink and tried to find herself again. A politician and a circle of journalists did their familiar two-step on the screen, a pale and ill-looking young man hovering somewhere behind the politician.

She sat forward. Shit. That was Dave. The State Minister for Transport, Will Sanders, was speaking. She seized the remote control.

'. . . almost certain that a twenty-million dollar blowout

on the Gilbert Freeway extension won't result in increased tolls . . . problems with upramp design, I've been informed by our construction engineers . . .'

Dave strayed into the camera shot again. Serena stared at him, tonight's face of Hodson's Engineering. She wondered what was happening behind that tight, white face. Had he been able to find a moment in the day to think about the reality of twin babies, of a family of four, or of the sadness of an abortion? Had he had a moment to think about his existing children? Who was that serious, grey-faced man who looked like he was about to have a heart attack? Was *that* the man she had married?

Soon after, the phone rang, waking her from a doze on the couch.

'I'm just leaving now,' Dave whispered. She could hear deep, cross voices in the background. 'I'll be home in thirty minutes. And we can talk then.'

'Dave, I saw you on the news. You look terrible.'

'I'm fine. I'm just . . . check it with Anderson, will you, and get back to me tomorrow . . . sorry. Just leaving now. Hang on a minute. Tell Sanders' man we can't do it before tomorrow afternoon . . . sorry, Serena. This is a fiasco.' He sounded desperate.

Serena sighed, resigned. 'I'm going to have an early night. Why don't we talk about things in the morning?'

'That would be better for me.' He sounded relieved. 'How about I pick up croissants on the way home and we'll get up early and put the kids in front of a video and have a proper talk before I leave for work?'

'Six a.m.?' The kids were all up by then anyway.
'We'll do it.'

Serena hung up and shook her head. It had come to this. She was scheduling a dawn meeting with her husband to discuss whether or not to abort a pregnancy. And right at this minute, she didn't even care. She stripped down to her singlet and undies, and went to bed.

She woke a little later in the dark, Dave's sleeping bulk beside her. 12:45, the clock said. She could hear a child crying and she went down the hall to check, rubbing sleep out of her eyes. It was Cooper.

'Mummy, my bed's wet.'

His night nappy had leaked. She turned the lamp on and stripped her son and then the bed. Cooper curled up foetus-like on the carpet as she did, his vertebrae protruding like knuckles from the fist of his bare back. She rubbed him down with sorbolene to ease his itchy skin, dressed him in dry pyjamas and tucked him into clean sheets. Back in her own bed, Dave turned over and murmured at her, and she fell asleep.

A hacking cough from the children's room penetrated her dreams. Finn. She opened her eyes. 2:20. Dave turned over. More coughing.

'I'll go.' He got up, and she felt the bed shake in the darkness, exhaled and stretched her limbs across the luxury of the empty bed. Heard him open the kitchen cupboard where the cough medicine was kept, and movement in the children's room. He returned and she tidied herself back to her side and they went back to sleep.

Another cry. 3:40. Angus this time. Serena got up

and, desperate now, gave him some milk in a bottle. Anything to get some sleep.

More crying. 4:20. Dave started to stir but she sat up, in martyr mode now. 'I'll get it.' Angus had vomited. She changed his pyjamas, washed his face, combed milky vomit out of his hair as best she could. Shampoo would have to wait for morning. She added his soiled sheets to the pile of dirty laundry in the corner.

'Mummy, is it morning time?' Cooper, ever the opportunist.

'No. Back to sleep.'

She woke again at 4:50. Something was beeping.

'Is that the smoke alarm?' she whispered in the darkness.

Dave sighed and got up. Smoke alarms were his territory. He returned. 'Where's your mobile? I think the battery's going flat.'

She rose and together they searched for a few minutes until they found the phone and went back to bed, wordlessly.

At five-thirty she was still awake, fretting about getting back to sleep. At eight, Dave woke her and she groaned. She stared at him resentfully, hating him for tearing off her beautiful shroud of sleep.

He pointed at the clock. 'I couldn't wake you. You needed to sleep. But I have to go to work.' He stared at her desperately. 'I'll call you later and we'll talk about it?'

'Okay.' This is getting ridiculous.

Sleep deprivation always made her hungry. She ate fried eggs, baked beans and toast, and drank a strong coffee while the children watched a video. She threw a load of sheets in the washing machine, lined up yesterday's dishes in the dishwasher, and took meat from the freezer.

Friday was a kindy day for Cooper. He had begun one weekly two-hour session of three-year-old kindy, and so far, it seemed to take three hours of effort to get him there. She stared at the kindy note from last week. *Please bring a picture of your child's family, and their favourite book and an object that represents something from their favourite book. And some fruit to share. And some autumn leaves to represent the change of seasons.* God, were they serious? She sagged with the weight of kindy optimism, and then chided herself as she dragged out the photo albums. She should be glad Cooper was getting this lovely whatever-it-was, this rocking-horse innocence, this relic from the age of wet nurses and steam trains. She should appreciate it. And while she remembered, she had to do something, anything, to mark Angus's first birthday tomorrow. And she put her hand on her growing belly, and knew she had to do something about that too.

And if Dave couldn't find time to talk about it, then he didn't have time to be more of a father than he already was. She rang the clinic and was told the two-day procedure would have to begin again. She had to see a counsellor and have her cervix prepared on the first day, with the termination on the second.

'The counsellor has just one appointment left for Monday,' the receptionist said.

'I'll take it.' Serena spread peanut butter on a slice of bread, gave it to Finn and took the phone from its wedge between her head and her shoulder. 'Hang on, I'll just find a pen.'

'But I can't give it to you.' The receptionist spoke smoothly. 'The counsellor books her own appointments. She'll be in at one.'

'Can you ask her to call me?'

'Yes, but she's seeing people so it might be tonight . . .'

'But the appointment might go . . .'

'Best you ring at one then. But ring on the dot.'

Serena hung up and wrote on the back of her hand, a habit that dated back to high school, *ring cr at one*. She loaded up the boys and took Cooper and his various offerings to kindy. At the kindergarten she propped Angus on her hip and held Finn back, like a rearing horse, from the sparkly glue sticks, while she made broken conversation with two other mothers. They were going to the same fairy party the next morning and they exchanged hasty reports on birthday presents and tin-foil wands. Finally she reloaded the two younger boys and drove off, singing a throaty version of 'I Am Woman' at the closed car windows and reaching around at the lights to tickle Finn's knees in her giddy relief to be away from the gentle newness of kindy.

It happened at the lights.

A little boy, not much older than Cooper, was standing with his father, waiting to cross. The father held a new baby in one arm, and a bag of nappies in the other, and the little tableau had already caught Serena's eye. What made her look again was that the boy stood unanchored beside his father. The father, obviously too weighed down with shopping to hold the boy's hand, was barking something at him, probably to stay close, don't run. The little boy was obedient, and he didn't run. He walked just two small steps, and that was all it took to place him in the path of the motorcyclist.

It happened so quickly. The little boy was lying on the crossing and the noise of the cyclist went from a roar to silence as he threw down the machine and ran back to the crossing, struggling with his helmet. Serena turned off the key in the ignition, swung out of the car and checked behind her. The woman behind lifted her hand. No one was going anywhere right now.

There was a crowd around the boy. Not dead, unconscious, came the word back. The man's baby was screaming so fiercely, it hurt Serena's throat to hear it.

'Does anybody know first aid?' someone shouted.

No, thought Serena, as a doctor was brought to the boy's side. But I know babies. She touched the distraught father and lifted the little girl out of his arms. She tipped the hot wet face toward her shoulder and stroked the tiny back with her whole hand, feeling the lumpy pink knit of a home-made cardy. The baby's head was still so small that it flopped forward, a velvety melon under Serena's palm. She positioned herself at a point where the two boys in the car could see her, and where the father could see his baby when he rose from the boy's side. An ambulance siren sounded from far away, and Serena checked her watch.

When she finally got home at one-thirty, having handed the baby over to an hysterical mother, she rang the clinic.

164

The last counselling appointment was taken. There wasn't another until next Friday, a week away.

It might as well have been a year. She couldn't, any longer, hold herself apart from the pregnancy, couldn't harbour these invaders for another week without giving in to the reality of them. She just couldn't.

She wouldn't have the abortion. It wasn't going to happen, and she was stunned at her own relief, and her dismal terror. Four children! A mother of four! Where had this treacherous joy emerged from, she wondered? How had she hidden from it for so long?

She sat on the floor and wept. Angus held the side of a chair and shuffled along it. Finn dumped a truck in her lap and Angus flung one arm out to the centre of the room, let go of the chair and took his first step.

She watched him in wonder.

She remembered Cooper's first steps. Dave had been there to see them. They were making breakfast during a weekend at Sorrento, when Cooper stood, stared at his feet questioningly, and moved one, then the other. Serena inhaled sharply. Dave shouted. They were both more slain by this moment than anything since the birth. Such a sign of time's relentless march. Serena had suddenly felt very old, as if Cooper had just taken the car keys from her and slouched out to the Subaru with a six-pack in his hand. Dave danced, jumped, regressed to the exuberant idiot she had fallen in love with and married. He put on a Billy Bragg song, the one they had been playing for weeks as they watched all the nearly-first-steps, 'Waiting For The Great Leap Forwards'. Cooper fell back on his bottom and watched them, astounded.

Dave dragged Serena off the couch to dance, shouting the song, *'One leap forward and two leaps back . . .'* but Serena was limp in his arms, weeping. Her baby would grow up and leave her, she knew it now, and she looked at Dave anew, critically, wondering if he could ever be enough for her again after their children were gone. She remembered when Cooper was born that she had pondered, who will I love more, Dave or the baby? Oh, she blushed to remember it. It was so long since she had asked herself such a stupid question, not now the children had moved their belongings into her heart and colonised it.

Cooper, delighted, had risen and taken another step and his parents stood side by side and clapped him fiercely, one laughing, one crying, and the music blared, too loud, too loud, the seagulls would be rising in alarm from the ti-trees outside.

'Here comes the future and you can't run from it . . .'

18

Ana woke at dawn to a grizzling Finn, and the sound of seagulls in the ti-tree outside. Finn whimpered between the mismatched sheets, paisley above, spotted below, and she stroked his black curls. His toes pressed into her thighs. He smelt of urine.

'Mumma,' he wailed, looking around him.

She reached down and patted his nappy nervously. Squashy. Sunlight peeked around the edges of a torn blind. Were they waves she could hear, or distant traffic?

'We're on holidays, Finny,' she told him. 'Beach!' She put one hand on his tiny chest and shook it gently in a wave of nervous joy.

His breathing slowed almost to a halt.

'Beach?' he said.

'Beach! Beach everywhere!'

Hmm. He responded to her ridiculous excitement, like an animal catching a scent, and smiled. He giggled. She chased him out of bed and into the lounge room.

The Sorrento beach house had worn carpet, a rose couch from the fifties and a modular lounge from the eighties. A poster of sea birds and a cane blind that sagged in the middle. A dining table with magazines dated two years earlier. A women's group newsletter on a coffee table with the headline 'Now *She's* Bringing Home the Bacon!'

'I'll just have a quick shower, Finny.' She brought him her car keys to play with and hastily stripped off. She had the shampoo through her hair when she stuck her head out of the bathroom to check on him.

He had wandered behind a three-legged stool on which a television was perched. Cherubic in his growsuit with the built-in feet, he was reaching into a tangle of black cords, tugging curiously. The small monitor had inched backwards on the stool. As Ana wiped the soap from her eyes and took in the scene, the TV began to teeter. About to fall on the black curly head of the baby below.

She ran from the bathroom, grabbed the TV and pushed it back just in time, leaving wet footprints behind her on the carpet. Held Finn and squeezed him until he squealed. She could hardly bear to look at the soft black curls flopping all over his vulnerable head.

'I'm so sorry, so sorry,' she told him. She had nearly killed him.

'Na-na.' This was his word for food.

'You want to eat?'

He started to cry.

At eight a.m. she rang Marnie.

'Did I wake you?'

Marnie moaned. 'As if. You would've had to ring me four hours ago to wake me.'

'Oh, I know. We were up at six.' Ana heard a bragging note in her own voice and checked herself. 'Listen to me. One night with a child and I'm feeling sorry for myself.'

'Tell me about it. I fed three times last night and then Lucy threw it all up.'

'Hey, I couldn't get the portacot thingy up.'

'So where did he sleep?'

'In bed with me. He woke twice and I gave him a drink of milk each time. Does that sound okay?' Finn had coughed intermittently through the cool latter half of the night, and Ana hadn't slept for more than a few minutes at a time, nervous she would roll on him, listening for changes in his breathing like a robber with his ear pressed to a door.

'I guess so. No, Kurt, use up the smaller nappies first . . . the ones over there . . .'

'I'm just wondering, is there anything I should be doing with him?'

'What do you mean?'

'I don't know . . . what do you do with them all day long?'

'You stop them killing themselves, from what I know about toddlers. Maybe you should call Serena if you're worried.'

'Hmmm.' Ana had secretly resolved not to call Serena all weekend.

'Hey, Lucy's got her first tooth, did I tell you? How early is that?'

Bloody mothers. Couldn't stop talking about their own problems. Ana hung up and went back to her charge.

She felt part of some new club, having charge of a small child. Before heading down the beach she had stopped at her local 7-11, where a man in his twenties slumped on the counter reading the paper.

'Ana.'

'Randall. Just minding a friend's child here.' She felt rather marvellous, telling this to Randall the acting student. Sort of competent and on the run; newspaper columnist one day, babysitting friend the next. She quite liked the feel of that nappied bottom on her hip; like having a little buddy. A pet, even. She carried Finn up and down the aisles until he got too heavy and then she put him down. Within five minutes he knocked over a sunglasses stand, and Ana found herself playing the breathless, disconcerted mother. *Oh dear, there he goes again. Poor me.* She threw a packet of best-quality Swedish muesli on the counter, along with some nappies.

'Taking him down the beach tonight,' she beamed. 'Ah, you'll be out raging again, but I'll be in bed by eight-thirty.'

'You're not feeding him that stuff, are you?'

'It's all organic. See, extra omega threes . . .'

'It's got whole nuts in it.'

'Yeah. Protein.'

'They're not meant to have nuts until they're five.'

'Says who? Some fascist doctors' lobby, anti-health food group?'

'They can choke on them. Get him some Weet-Bix.'

'Oh.'

'And these nappies look too small for him. Try those ones.'

'How do you know this stuff?'

'Because of my Sebastion. See?' He took out his wallet and showed her a photograph.

At the beach, Finn chased the seagulls and dug a hole. He splashed through the sea puddles and ripped his sunhat off, again and again. Ana bought an ice-cream from the kiosk and Finn curled into her shade and she fed him pieces of chocolate coating. Then he put his head in her lap.

'Ni-ni.'

He fell asleep in the car and Ana put a blanket over him. She tiptoed away and into the house. She could try again with the portacot. Or she could have a shower and rinse her hair properly. Or she could have a go at starting the gas heater, which had refused to work the night before. Or she could sit and read the paper, which she had bought at the beach. And then there was Elijah, who had said he would drop in some time that day. Her heart was thumping and she was sweating. She rang Marnie.

'I think I'm scared of children.'

'Really?'

'My hands are shaking. I'm exhausted. I feel like I've been holding my breath all morning in case he cries.'

'They all cry. Don't let it worry you.'

'I know. It's just . . .' *It's just, I can't give him back to Priya.* 'I mean, he's an orphan. What if he's suffering some sort of . . .'

'I know. Grief. And how well does he know you?'

Ana mused. 'Pretty well.'

'You'll be fine. Just be nice to him.'

'But what is being nice to a toddler? I want him to like me but all I seem to do is say don't touch this, don't do that . . .'

'Find him something to play with. Get him some saucepans to bang, they like doing that, don't they? Or get some plastic bowls and let him stack them.'

'Yeah?'

'And then let him get on with it and you relax. Take some downtime. You're getting too wound up about it. He'll sense it.'

Later, Ana and Finn sat out on the wooden deck and played with shells. Across a sea of ti-tree tops to either side of them, other holiday houses peeped up to get their share of the view. A weak sunlight fell over their hands; Ana's fingers long and criss-crossed with tiny lines, Finn's short and fat. There was still no sign of Elijah. Ana had carried her mobile phone out to the deck in case he called.

'Sell,' said Finn.

'Shell,' agreed Ana.

He carefully put the shells, one by one, into the bowl.

Ana rang her mother, her chest full with her big news.

'Guess what? I'm spending the weekend with Finn. The little boy.'

Her mother was predictably confused and had to have it all explained to her again. Then she said, 'I had a little boy once.'

'Yes, yes, yes,' said Ana impatiently. 'But I think he *likes* me, Mum.'

'That's nice.'

'He's *happy*.' Where did this ridiculous sense of defiance come from? Who, at the age of thirty-eight, was still trying to rebel against their mother's expectations?

'That's nice, dear. Could you pick me up some cigarettes on your way over?'

'I'm not . . . Do you remember telling me I'd be a terrible mother?'

'Mary gave me her *New Idea* today.'

'Because, I think maybe you were wrong.'

Her mother started to cry. 'I didn't even know you were married.'

'I'm not! This isn't my child, he belongs to a friend . . . remember Priya?'

When she hung up, she checked her messages in case Elijah had rung, but there was nothing.

She even managed to open the newspaper. Zac Banks had a column in the *Star*, Tax Reforms Just Tax Reworn, and she bristled at the sight of it. Back off, you bastard. The opinion pages are mine, for now anyway.

She read his piece and smirked. Too highbrow, not reader friendly. Conceptualise? Who would use a word like that in a tabloid paper. Her piece on malicious parking ticket inspectors was better. But he did make some good points in his piece and the financial-page readers would applaud it, she worried.

'More?' said Finn, pushing a shell into her hand.

'More,' she said absently, dropping it into the bucket and reading on.

Finn whacked her paper so hard that the page tore.

She looked up and laughed. A warm breeze was blowing the clouds across the sea, cleaning up the sky. Finn threw some shells off the deck in a punching gesture. She copied him and together they threw them all.

She rang home to check her messages there and found four from Elijah. He had lost her mobile number. She quickly rang him.

'Where are you?'

'Halfway back to Melbourne.'

'Do you want to come back?' Casual, her heart in her mouth. She gave him the address.

'I'm just doing a U-turn now. I'll pick up fish and chips for dinner.'

'Oh! Okay! Well, see you soon!'

She put down the phone and did a mad jogging tattoo which made the deck rattle. 'He's coming, Finn! He's coming!'

She moved Finn inside and raced into the bathroom to put on some make-up. Checked the double bed was remade. Finn would have to sleep somewhere else tonight.

When Elijah arrived he was wearing black jeans and a jumper, the collar of a white business shirt making his clean-shaven face look ruddy. He carried a briefcase and a laptop, which he didn't want to leave in the car, and a white paper swaddle that steamed with the scent of fish and chips. He smiled at her and she grinned back giddily. Then he looked around and frowned.

'It's a bit cold in here.'

'I couldn't get the heater working.' Ana said. Finn coughed, hard, and she watched Elijah turn his gaze on him. Her heart fell.

'He's got a cough.' Elijah crouched in front of the little boy, who twisted away from him, towards Ana.

'Well . . .' She heard her own indignant tone. 'What is this, a spot check or something?' She tried to laugh.

He smiled mildly. 'Sorry. How was last night, you get some sleep?'

'Ah, yeah.' She lied. 'Although, if you could have a

go at putting up the portacot for me, that would help for tonight.'

'Where did Finn sleep last night?'

'In bed with me.' Finn coughed again and she stared at him. *Please stop.*

'He's got cough medicine?'

'No.' It hadn't even occurred to her to try some medicine. She sat on the couch and folded her arms. 'I didn't think of it.' Her voice was small. This was obviously nothing but a work trip for Elijah. He was the executor of Priya's will. He had a professional interest in Finn's welfare. It seemed incredible to Ana now that she had, so hopefully, made the double bed.

'You look tired.' Elijah frowned at her. She knew her hair was still dull with un-rinsed shampoo, and her eyes were puffy from lack of sleep, despite the make-up. 'Do you want to go and have a shower and I'll watch Finn?'

She emerged from the bathroom later in a cloud of scented steam, to see Finn emptying a basket of toys she hadn't seen before. The open-plan kitchen and family room was tidy and the fish and chips were spread out on the table. The heater cast a radiant warmth and Elijah was opening a bottle of red wine.

'You got the heater working.' She hated him. She wanted him to leave, and she wanted him to stay the night, if nothing else so that she wasn't alone with Finn any more, now she knew she was no good at it.

'You just needed to turn on the gas bottle outside.'

'Oh. Where did the toys come from?' She picked at a chip.

'I found them in the cupboards. And I hope you don't

mind, but I looked through Finn's bag and found this.' He held up some cough medicine. 'Serena must have packed it. Can we give him some?'

Ana stared at him. She felt utterly hopeless. Clearly, Priya had made a terrible mistake. Even a childless lawyer with no desire for children had more of a clue than she did.

She put down her head and wept, turning sharply away from Elijah. She was exhausted, but she had felt strangely earthed for the past two days. For the first time, she had let herself imagine keeping Finn. Without thinking about how she would manage it, without worrying about the childcare or her job, or doing any realistic calculations, she had just considered having that little person to dress and giggle with and protect. And . . . serve, was the word that came into her head. How stupid. But that was it, as if maybe she could shuck off the burden of thinking about herself, and think about someone else.

She felt his arm on her shoulder.

'I'm sorry,' he said. 'You've done amazingly well. He seems really happy.'

She couldn't speak. He turned her around.

'Why don't you go and have a sleep? You're exhausted,' he said. 'I'll have a go at the portacot. Although if it wouldn't work for you, it probably won't for me.'

The last thing she heard from her bed as she drifted off to sleep was Elijah murmuring to Finn, and the sound of the portacot being snapped into place. She wondered again if she could hear waves, and then she didn't open her eyes until morning.

19

Serena opened her eyes and found herself alone in the bed. Her body felt strangely limp, her mind slow and stupid. The clock said 9:30. She could hear Dave and Cooper talking in the kitchen. Heard the kettle boil and click off. She sat up and shook her head, drugged by a surfeit of sleep. When had she last slept in this late? Why hadn't Dave gone to work, as he had done on Saturdays for the past few months?

She put her hand to her belly and stood, holding the curve in her palm. My children. It was a relief to have made a decision, to let go of the panic of the past few weeks. Now the pregnancy unspooled ahead of her, all its stages predictable.

She still hadn't talked to Dave. She had gone to bed early the night before, just after putting the children to bed, and she couldn't remember getting up all night. Impossible that all three could have slept through; Dave must have got up to them. She heard the far off whine of a motor mower; the sound of a weekend. She padded up the hall to the kitchen, where Dave was reading a broadsheet newspaper, Cooper at his elbow. Angus looked up at his mother and fell hard on his nappied bottom with a crow of delight, clutching a handful of wrapping paper. Serena scooped him up and he shrieked with laughter. His hair, never yet cut, hung in wispy flaps over his ears.

'Happy birthday, my darling.'

'Mumma!' He smacked her happily.

'You're not working today, Dave?'

'Not on my boy's birthday. Do we have a present for him?'

Serena brought out the present and Cooper tore off the wrapping for his brother. A picture book.

'How long's Ana got Finn for?'

'Just the weekend.'

'Do you want a coffee?'

She glanced at the clock. 'No time. We've got Mia's birthday party at ten.'

He sagged. 'Do we have to . . .'

'Yay!' shouted Cooper. 'Can I take my lightsaber?'

'Okay,' said his father, folding his newspaper. 'Okay.'

At the party, children tripped on netting skirts and trailed oversize wings. A grown-up fairy called Fairy Beatrice, who it was murmured charged fifty dollars an hour, wore a pink net skirt over her jeans. Fairy Beatrice gathered all the children into one room where they shouted and waved tin-foil wands, and the adults poured out on the back deck and scrutinised the plates of fairy bread, lolly-face biscuits and butterfly cakes for anything edible. They murmured, horrified, about the accident at the local shops the day before; the little boy in hospital, serious but stable was the word. He would be okay. Serena felt her body tremble with gratitude to hear it; the child's reprieve somehow linked to her own. She took Dave's arm and they wound their way through a cluster of rose bushes and sat on the edge of a sandpit amidst the low buzz of cicadas and occasional laughter from the deck.

She took both his hands and stroked his long fingers.

'Dave, I've changed my mind. I do want to have these babies,' she said. Up at the house, knee-high fairies streamed out the back door. Fairy Beatrice trudged behind them and stabbed her wand downwards to look at her watch.

Dave's eyes were achingly wide, his whole face was falling into the slack openness of joyful shock. She watched it remotely, as if her husband was an actor in a film. She felt irritated by his joy. He wasn't remembering night after night of pacing with crying babies; he wasn't remembering endless breastfeeds and long lonely days without the importance of work, without the camaraderie of colleagues. She wasn't sure what he was remembering, as his face lit up with almost cartoon-like emotion. She wished *she* could remember it, whatever it was.

'I still want to go back to work,' she said. She wanted to nip that smile right back. 'One day.'

He moved his head slightly, as if an insect had touched him, but his expression didn't waver. 'Serena, I'm so happy. So . . . grateful you listened to me.'

'I'm not having them because you wanted them,' she snapped. 'I'm having them because . . . because they're here.'

'Darling.' He was beaming, already casting his eyes hopefully up at the crowd, their friends and neighbours. 'Can we tell people?'

She let him lift her to her feet. Let him lead her back up the garden, his face alight with his news, his victory. *Man make two babies! Spread his super-seed!* She knew many of the women, keener-eyed than Dave, would have already noted her stomach, but they would feign delighted surprise, would disguise their sympathetic dismay, or envy, at the news of twins. More champagne would be bought from the local bottle shop and Fairy Beatrice might hang around for a drink, and amidst the handshakes and congratulations there would be at least one moment of champagne-swallowing silence, like a crystal of precious tantalite in the core after days of labelling grey granite. A whole few seconds in the party chatter when no one spoke, all of them coasting on the gentle breezes of private thought, intimate memories of their own babies' beginnings. Two whole new lives in the world. The tremulousness, the godliness of it. Two new lives.

'Oh, no.'

Iris spoke as though she had just sighted an incoming cyclone while standing on a rocky outcrop in the middle of the ocean. She rose to her feet in Serena's kitchen like a footy fan objecting to an umpire's decision. In short, she was less than pleased to hear that her quota of grandchildren was about to be doubled.

'Yes. Well. No use moaning about it.' Serena slung the wet teabags into the sink and held an open biscuit jar down low for Cooper. She had resolved on no false joy about this pregnancy, but she'd still had to brace herself to tell her mother.

'Oh, my darling. What were you thinking?'

'Well, obviously I wasn't thinking at all,' Serena smirked.

'Oh, sweetheart. Your career.'

'I might still get back to it one day.' She wasn't going to write off her life yet.

'Are you disappointed?'

Honesty, Serena reminded herself carefully. 'Well, I am a little . . .'

'Oh, you must be devastated.'

'Not *devastated* exactly . . .' Ah, here it was already, the rose-tinting, the great maternal mask. Why couldn't she tell her mother just how bad it was, how she had come so close to snuffing out those two little lives? But here she was, already their mother, pushing her cubs behind her and fending off the vultures.

Iris sniffed. 'Well, it must be Dave's turn to stay home and look after them. You've done your time.'

Serena was surprised by the grit in her mother's voice, touched by it. Relented a little.

'I can hardly get him to come home by bathtime, Mum. I don't know about my chances of getting him to stop work.'

Her mother looked like a four-year-old who's just been told there's no Santa Claus. 'But . . . he's such a lovely boy. He'd do anything for you.'

'Anything but stay home and spend time with us.'

'Well, what about all that marvellous childcare that's out there?'

Serena sighed. She was never going to convince her mother that her choices were still so limited. Yes, she could get a nanny for the four children, but they would be virtually orphaned with their father at Hodsons and Serena at MRA.

And if a nanny was what it took, then Serena would consider leaving Dave and raising the children alone. It would be a colossal amount of hard work, but at least if she went to bed alone, night after night, it would be by her own choice. She would be finished with the daily indignity of pleading with a man to spend time with her.

Jo, Dave's mother, rang to say congratulations.

'And is my son doing the right thing?'

'Which is?' Serena often had a little trouble keeping up with Jo, but she liked her mother-in-law, and wished she saw more of her.

'Treating you like a goddess.'

Serena snorted and then felt a little disloyal. She answered carefully.

'He made me a cup of tea the other morning. Before he left for work.'

'Oh *dear*.' Jo's voice was heavy with dismay. 'Is he still working all hours with that job of his?'

'He works hard.'

'He doesn't work as hard as you, my love.'

Serena felt tears start to flood, and tilted the phone away from her face so Jo would hear nothing. There was a long silence, as if Jo was listening for something beyond sound. Serena recovered.

'Going to come and see your grandkids soon?' she asked brightly. Jo usually made the trip down twice a year, and stayed about a week. Her presence was like lubrication on the screeching, squealing, malfunctioning machine that was Serena's home.

'I'll come when you need me,' Jo pronounced.

Serena ached with need. Her need was so infinite, it was almost pointless to express it. She thought of Jo's visits, the house fragrant with vegetarian curries, story-reading marathons with Cooper, the rainbow-coloured sling she carried her grandsons around in when they were little. But with desire choking her up, strangling her vocal chords, she said something that came out sounding brittle and cool. Jo got off the phone to go and check her mud bricks, and Serena felt so terrifyingly alone she went and held Cooper's hand while he watched telly.

She told Ana on the phone.

'Oh.' Ana sounded alarmed. 'How long have you known?'

'A couple of months.'

'You're very secretive.' A note of reproach.

'Well, it's what people do. They wait until they're sure.'

'I just . . . I guess that's why you were so definite about not taking Finn for good.'

'Well, yes.' A convenient story now. 'I certainly won't be able to keep Finn.' Serena sensed this was a revelation to Ana, that she was hearing her say this for the first time. 'What, you thought I'd come around?' Good old Serena, her life's over, she might as well take another child. Well, this would well and truly drive the point home.

'No, no. How is he?' Ana had dropped Finn back earlier that evening, after their weekend at the beach, the little boy carried in asleep in his pjs, in the arms of Elijah. Serena had done a double-take to see the lawyer

183

with her friend. Ana was sun-pink across the bridge of her nose and had seemed smiley and familiar with him. She had bustled Serena out of the way to make sure Finn had Jarmy with him in the cot, and Serena stood well back, amused to see how a hint of maternity translated to her friend. Bossy and anxious, that was the sort of mother Ana would be, she secretly predicted, but it would be better for Finn than insanely busy and hopelessly distracted, which was the sort of mother Serena would soon become to any child in her care.

'He's good. And that was very *pastoral* of Elijah, to come and visit you both at Sorrento, wasn't it?' She smirked.

'He's a dedicated lawyer.'

'So when did this begin?'

'I don't know that anything *has* begun.'

'That's a terrible double bed, that one at Sorrento.'

Ana sighed. 'Well, we're not at that stage, and I was so terrified to be sleeping with Finn the first night that it could've been a slab of concrete for all the sleep I got. The next night I was so exhausted I just sort of hoicked my hip across the ridge down the middle, and I barely even noticed it.'

'I believe I was conceived in that bed.'

'Yuk!'

'Thank you.'

'I can't believe you're going to be a mother of four.'

'Neither can I.'

'Are you happy?'

'Do you want the horrible truth, or a nice lie?'

'You need to ask?'

'I'm horrified. My life is over.'

'No it's not. Wait a couple of years and you'll be one of those supermums, school lunches all lined up on the bench by six a.m., briefcase packed the night before. How's Dave, is he rapt?'

'Yes. I don't know why. It will probably be the straw that breaks us.'

Ana hesitated and Serena waited in resignation. She had done it now. Sure enough, Ana waded in, all concern.

'I can't imagine you guys ever . . .'

'No.' Meaning no she couldn't imagine it either, and no, don't put it into words, and just an all-round no. No. A word which Ana, being a journalist, took as an invitation to continue. Like a hysterical child told to stop giggling.

'Would you ever leave him?'

Serena considered a flip 'no comment', but suddenly felt too sad.

'Maybe,' she said tremulously, and knew that just saying it made it all the more possible. It left her feeling limp, but she knew it was important. She would need everyone in her team on her side if she left Dave; would need all the help she could get. And if she had to sacrifice marital privacy to make the move, well, that was just the way it was. Every journey had its price.

She expected Cate to be the easiest, like telling herself. A relief. She sat at her friend's kitchen table before a bowl of biscuits, which Cate was chattering on about. No sugar, extra fibre, incredible GI rating. Serena raised her eyebrows and tilted her head to feign interest, waiting for Cate to draw breath.

'I'm pregnant with twins.' It was a blurt and she added apologetically, 'They're nice biscuits.'

Cate screamed, pushed her chair back from the table. 'Really?'

Serena nodded sheepishly.

'Congratulations.' Cate became deadly serious and reached over to shake her hand. 'That's wonderful news.'

Serena gave her a look. 'Cate, this is me you're talking to here. You can cut the bullshit.'

'Whatever you think now, you won't regret it. An abundance of children.'

'I haven't been taking folic acid. I've been drinking alcohol, I've done all the wrong things.'

'They'll be fine.' Cate poured the tea. 'Hey, I've got news too.'

Serena's mouth fell open, her heart leapt. Cate was going to tell her she was pregnant. They would go through it together, they would be able to support each other, the way they had with the first babies. Serena sat forward, her hope before her, like hands waiting to catch falling fruit.

'I've got a job.'

Serena almost groaned. She stopped herself in time. 'That's fantastic news,' she said. She could feel her features contorting in disappointment. One look at Cate's sympathetic face was enough to assure her she wasn't hiding anything. 'I'm sorry.' Oh God, now she had tears in her eyes. 'Sorry. Pregnancy hormones. Makes you very emotional.'

'It's only three days a week, Serena. We'll still see each other lots. And I've made sure I'm not working on playgroup day.'

'No, really, Cate. I'm crying for joy. For you.'

'It's okay. I know how I'd feel if I were you.' Cate pulled her chair next to Serena and put her arm around her. 'But it's only three days. Maybe four, sometimes.'

'I know. I know. It's just, I feel very alone with this pregnancy. I'm a bit freaked out about it.' She wiped her eyes. 'So what's the job?' She swallowed. Cate would start three days, then four, then she'd end up full time, and Serena would be alone in babyland.

Cate shrugged awkwardly. 'Sports nutritionist for the Australian Ballet. I'll be one of a team of about five.'

'But that's fantastic. And Matty?'

'He's got a place in Arnott Street.'

'That's great.'

Cate smiled, looking slightly guilty. 'I know. We need the money desperately. That's the really good thing. Are you okay now?'

'Fine. Fine. Really, I'm just crying left, right and centre at the moment. It's nothing to do with you. I'm very happy about your job.' She briskly collected drink cups and sultana boxes. Cate watched her.

'And it's fantastic news about the babies, Serena.'

'Yeah.' Serena gave up. She put her head on the table and wept.

20

Ana smiled at the Macquarie dictionary above her desk. She stroked her computer mouse dreamily. She licked the froth off her coffee, and reflected it had never tasted so good. She picked up her phone and played her messages. She heard Elijah's voice and leaned forward on her desk, the abundance of the universe raining down on her shoulders as his words rolled over her.

'I just wanted to say thank you for a very enjoyable day yesterday,' his recorded voice said. Ana hugged herself and dropped her chin to her chest to hide her lunatic grin from her colleagues. 'I was thinking about it this morning on the way to work, because there were some seagulls on St Kilda beach that needed a good chase.' She laughed out loud. On the way home from Sorrento they had stopped at a beachfront cafe and had coffee while Finn chased the flocks of seagulls, squealing and flapping his arms. Suddenly Elijah took off his shoes and socks and ran after Finn, squawking and jumping around until Finn was hysterical with giggles.

'But I think I left my address book in your car, and I was wondering if you found it? I'm a bit lost without it. And if you've got it, maybe I could buy you some more fish and chips for dinner tonight, and we could go sit on the pier in St Kilda?' His voice faltered on a high note of nervous hope that Ana recognised, wanted to rush to reassure. 'Anyway, give me a call.' He hesitated, said 'Ah . . .' as if he had thought of something else, or was simply reluctant to go, and then he hung up.

Ana felt her body flush, as if the sun had just come out above her desk. Already so happy, and there would be more! More! But she would have been devastated, gutted, if there hadn't been more. That was love, wasn't it? You got a taste of paradise and from then on anything less was worse than nightmarish. Humans were like that, she reflected, they climbed onto the higher rung and immediately kicked out the one they'd just left.

She scrawled 'seagulls' and 'fish and chips' and 'Elijah'. Three times she wrote his name. So Biblical. She did a quick internet search, feeling newly possessive of every shining letter. Elijah. *Jehovah is my God.*

And realised she had not heard a word of the eight messages that followed Elijah's, although she had obediently pressed delete at the end of them. She had to ring IT and get help to retrieve them.

Elijah's address book. She did indeed have it. She reached down in her bag and took it out. A small, black leather Filofax. She had been reading it on the train, and had only got up to N. Elijah's writing was jagged but straight: dramatic capitals, evenly spaced. She kept reading, feeling less shame about it at work than she had on the train, where she had hidden the book inside a newspaper in case she happened to be spotted by someone he knew. In here though, all gloves were off. I'm a journalist, she told herself, flicking the pages to O. Trained observer. Naturally curious. Paid to pry.

Under 'S', she was a little surprised to find her friend's name. Priya Sreepada. Well, Priya *had* been a client. But there was her mobile number, and her hospital pager number, written in her own handwriting, a lighter touch than Elijah's. Numbers Ana had in her own address book.

She frowned. Elijah must be very diligent.

She closed the book, and tapped shut its little clasp. Stroked the front of it. After lying down for a nap on Saturday evening at the Sorrento beach house, she woke in the morning with a jolt of alarm. She had slept right through. She found Finn in the next room, tangled in blankets on the floor of the portacot, like a toy put in its box. Elijah emerged yawning from the third bedroom, unshaven in a rumpled T-shirt and jeans, and together they cooked up a feast of eggs, bacon, toast and mushrooms. Finn pattered around in his footed suit and Ana read him a story, and Elijah found him some clean clothes. It was a balmy autumn day with some of summer's last kiss in it and they had gone to the surf beach. Elijah chased Finn on the sand, and Ana marched, a little self conscious in her bathers, down to the water, so keen to have her body shielded again that she strode in without hesitation, and hyperventilated with the cold. The waves dumped and churned and spat her back out on the sand, her heart thumping, her nipples aching, and she shivered her way to the public toilet block for a hot shower.

And when she met them again at the car park, Finn said 'Ana!' and struggled out of Elijah's arms to get to her. She gathered up his warm little body on her hip and he poked her in the eye.

'Oh, he's been going on endlessly, Ana, Ana, Ana,' complained Elijah cheerily.

They dropped Finn off at Serena's together, and then Ana drove herself home. Her own flat was cold and stale, empty and fussing at her in its solitude. It seemed like a long time since she'd left.

She made some hot chocolate, took the remote control to bed, and missed Elijah and Finn. Missed herself as part of them. Three unrelated people who had felt, for a moment in time, like a proper family.

And Finn. Those fat legs, that ready smile. Finn, who knew her. Who liked her.

Was that the true secret of a child's power, when they were so glad to see you, with a joy that was unfeigned? That they cried when you left? That they were small and new and beautiful? Or was it the intimacy of your own, shared, routine? The cups in the bath and the elephant pyjamas and the song where the crocodile goes snap and putting a nappy on teddy too, all the little things that become your special things to do between you.

Like lovers.

Ana lay in her big bed, with the tram lights passing overhead, amongst the images of a boy and a man. Long, heavily muscled legs that had existed for years before she saw them. The flawless curve of a toddler's cheek. Man shoulders; broad enough to sprout wings. Small, archless feet in the shellgrit.

But it was baby flesh she dreamed of when she fell asleep. A little boy with overalls criss-crossing his shoulder blades, black curls flecked with sand, toes in the foam of an ocean's salty fingers.

191

Zac was in news conference, shouting by the window with Pete Pryor. They boomed over each other about the weekend's footy. Zac called to her.

'Nice work with the column, Ana.'

'Thank you, Zac. What brings you here?' She smiled at him so warmly he looked alarmed. He wasn't that bad, she reflected. In fact, they were all very nice.

'Oh you know. Checking the bases.' Code for seeing his wife and kids. He hesitated between two chairs and, as if encouraged by her newfound friendliness, took the one beside her. 'And a meeting later today. Back to Sydney tonight.'

She nodded to indicate she was interested, although she wasn't, and she smiled out the window at the view of the bay. Thought about Finn's little hand, how she had held it yesterday and turned it over so she could see the palm. He had let her, his breath stilled, and she felt how at any second he might pull it away, but also how hungry he was for attention, for a kind face turned full on him like the sun.

'Round and round the garden, like a teddy bear . . .'

Funny how humans are born with a crease on their palms, a long wrinkle that looks like something an eighty-year-old might have earned.

Lowenthal shut the door and slid into his chair.

'Okay, people, I want your best stuff . . .'

Elijah picked up Ana after work, and she took him to Westgate, to the *Morning Star*'s printing press. Something so old-fashioned about newspapers, that at the end of it it was still the cat's cradle of paper woven through reels and handles and barrels, flashing past at high speed with headlines and pictures and advertisements and the grey blur of the classifieds. She watched him watch it, get hypnotised by the machines. She felt proud. This is my world. It's not just suits in a room, it's not just he-said-she-said, it's machines that need oil, and reels of white newsprint that could crush your foot. Men in overalls and beanies.

He wanted to see the newsroom. She took him back to the office. A few cadets wandered around, night editors sipped on cans of beer and a full bank of sub-editors hammered away at keyboards, glancing up at clocks.

'What time is it finished?' Elijah asked.

'Midnight it's off the presses and in the delivery vans.' Out at Westgate the white vans would start queuing soon, snaking out of the presses and into the street. Gunning their engines, ready as soon as the bundles hit the van floors to swing into the night and start driving; start the race to bring the news to the state's wheatbelt in the west, the cattle country in the east, the riverbank towns in the north.

Later, on St Kilda pier, Elijah spread open white paper and the steam from the fish and chips rose. She watched his hand hovering over the food. Long brown fingers, crisp blue cuffs and the glint of cufflinks under his jacket. He had been in court that day. He sat cross-legged on the weathered wood of the pier with no regard for what must be an expensive suit. They ate chips companionably, while the sea lapped at the pier's footings and, far away on the beach esplanade, cars moved without a sound. They saw one couple kissing on the way up the pier, and another kissing couple moved ahead, in Ana's vision. She didn't mention it.

A heavily pregnant woman walked slowly by. She breathed deeply and clutched her stomach, staring out to sea. 'I think we should get to the hospital,' the man with her said, frowning towards the shore, the car park, jingling keys in his pocket. His voice as taut as the rattling cables on the anchored yachts. 'Deborah, it's time we went.' The woman grimaced, and turned her bulk away from the darkening horizon, but reluctantly, casting a glance back over her shoulder, as if leaving in the middle of a loved film. He moved to support her and their figures became a silhouette, smaller step by step, as they moved back towards the beach, towards a delivery room and the first day of the rest of their lives. Piers were a halfway point, neither land nor water, that attracted people in certain situations. Times when nowhere on dry land felt like the right place to be.

Ana and Elijah ate the last of the chips. Elijah folded up the white paper, wrapping the scraps like a present, squeezing it small. Then there was just a diamond space between their crossed legs, their knees almost touching, the invisible sea splashing below. It was cold, but Ana didn't want to leave. She wiped one salty, oily hand with the other. 'I need a tissue,' she said.

Elijah took her hand gently in his. He lifted it to his eyes as though mesmerised by it, and he kissed the tip of one finger, and then another. His eyes met hers and they were suddenly grave, touched with fear and hope. She leaned into him, wanting to kiss the fear from his eyes.

A sea breeze blew them apart and Elijah seized her

shoulders, rested his forehead against hers.

'Can we go for a coffee at your place?'

Ana shivered violently, almost hiccupping with cold. Her flat was still strewn with half-packed bags from the weekend; takeaway containers from the night before, hastily washed underwear. There was hardly any coffee and no fresh milk, and she knew none of these things mattered. She was glad they would be on her territory for their first time. Knew without question that that's what it would be. So many first times to come. She nodded and they grinned at each other, elated, in delirious, unspoken agreement.

A freezing wind blew up and they spontaneously stood, held hands and ran down the pier. The beams rattled as their feet pounded over them, and they swerved around the pregnant couple, onto the silent concrete and towards Elijah's car.

21

Serena slid the top down over her belly, hitched up her pants and stared at herself. At three months pregnant, she was showing more than she had with either of her two earlier babies. She stroked the lycra over her belly and studied her face. An expression of alarm and wonder. A twin pregnancy. She would be a whale.

'How do the babies get out?' Cooper asked, his little face at the bottom corner of the mirror, where an artist might have signed a painting.

'They come one at a time.' Serena spoke gravely, purposely misunderstanding him.

'They take turns?' He left her mirror face and turned his big eyes up to hers.

'They do.' She placed her hands either side of her belly and turned side-on to examine herself.

'But *how* do they get out?'

Serena sighed. It didn't bear thinking about, really. 'Mummy has a door,' she said briskly. 'Is that the postman? Can Cooper get the letters?'

Finn was spending the day with Ana, and Serena parked her own two in front of the telly and opened the letter. It was the rates notice for her flat in Clifton Hill, currently tenanted by a university student named Shamala and, Serena suspected, at least three of Shamala's uni mates. Serena had bought the flat in her mid-twenties, using a small inheritance as a deposit, and laziness stopped her selling it in the following years. By then, it had doubled in value and when she married, it became part of Dave's master plan for their financial future, one which involved paying off the mortgage on their home in the next five years and buying more investment properties. Serena looked at the rates notice, and discovered a figure in the top right corner which made her mouth fall open. Could that really be the current council valuation on her property? It was now more than five times the price she had bought it for twelve years ago.

'Is it the last day?' It was Cooper. He was asking her every few minutes, these past few weeks, after overhearing someone mentioning the last day of summer. She had noticed children got these things like verbal tics. 'Is it the last day?' he persisted.

'Not today,' Serena said, with a calm confidence she hoped would quell the subject. She rustled through the mailbox debris that lay on the kitchen table for the real-estate brochure she had seen. Let Us Value Your Home.

Imagine. The council valuations were always conservative. Her humble little flat was probably worth even more than this figure. What would an agent say? Should she get a market valuation?

Her flat. In *her* name. Bought, well partly anyway, with her money. An intriguing thought. Mad money, her mother had once called that sort of thing. Although in her mother's day, mad money was a few fivers in a biscuit jar, so she could storm off and buy herself a dress when she and Dad had a fight. It wasn't a piece of prime real estate, partially paid off by her husband, that a woman would consider selling to fund the desertion of same husband.

Desertion? Did you call it that when you were planning on taking custody of two, soon to be four kids? Some would call it liberation, not desertion. But she knew it would be desertion in every sense of the word for Dave. In some ways, it would kill him.

Ah, but would it make him work less? That was another question altogether.

In the last few days, as news of the pregnancy filtered through their family and friends, Dave only seemed to work harder, to come home later. He had arrived home near midnight for the past four nights. The Gilbert Freeway extension had become a political football, with Hodsons under pressure from the government to make impossible budget cuts. Two more times, Dave appeared in a press conference on the evening news, lurking nervously in the background. Serena, newly armed with the energy of the second trimester, had bought a small chest freezer and set about cooking enough meals to see them through the first three months of the twins' lives: twelve weeks, eighty-four nights. Thin them out with a few takeaways and the inevitable gifts of meals from friends and it could last four months. She stopped complaining to Dave, stopped begging him to come home for dinner, and wondered if he even noticed that she had given up. On Saturday mornings, Ana picked up Finn to take him for the weekend's househunting, sometimes with Elijah in tow, and then Serena packed the other two in the car – Dave was working weekends – and trawled the markets for the freshest meat and vegetables, going home again to fill the kitchen with steam and smells. Every time she made a new deposit in her food bank, she closed the freezer door with a sense of satisfaction.

She discovered frugality, penny pinching. She bought more things from the market, fewer from the supermarket. Each week she calculated what she had saved on this item or that. Then she took out the difference and stuffed the cash in her underwear drawer. Mad money. She watched it grow, like the mad meals in the freezer. She wasn't sure why she was doing it. Dave would give her more money any time she asked for it. But she wanted to take it from the fat, from the excess of their lives, as she learned to live differently. She was practising to be poor, to survive on less. Her options swirled endlessly in the back of her mind and she made herself wait for them to line up into an answer. She knew from geology that the best solutions didn't come from being forced. They came from sitting with the problem for a while, giving it time to grow, ripen and fall off the branch.

Could she seriously leave Dave? Four children under four, on her own, with no back-up. *So what's new?* Weekend trips to the park, where other kids had dads and hers didn't. *Again, what's new?* Children asking: Where's my daddy? *You can have holidays with Daddy every second weekend. Bring it on.* Abandoning the dream of a happy family. *Might find it with someone else. Could get my self-respect back.*

But, no Dave. Family holidays without Daddy. Newborns without Dave around, walking the floors at night with the little bundle on his shoulder, his nocturnally erect penis flapping like an unnoticed flag down below. The taste of his kisses, his polite contempt for fools, the spartan elegance of his mind. His kindnesses. The hot biscuit smell of the crook of his neck.

Damn. Serena threw the rates notice aside.

Cooper wandered into the kitchen and picked up an apple.

'Is it the last day?'

'Not yet, Coop.'

Don't think about it. The answer will come.

Later that morning she was doing laps of her kitchen – from Angus's highchair to spoon in some food, to the big table where Cooper was drawing, to admire, to the stove to stir a monster pot of minestrone, four empty freezer packs waiting to be filled – when the phone rang. It was Poss, back from another speaking tour, this time in Europe.

'I heard your big news. Michael told me.'

'Ah.' She smiled to hear his voice.

'Twins. You'll be busy.' He hesitated. 'Michael was disappointed. He'd lined up the work for you.'

'He took it well.' She had been embarrassed, calling her old boss and announcing she was pregnant again, after begging him for part-time work.

'Are you tired? Sick?'

'I'm feeling better. Second trimester, you know. It's the good one.'

'I wanted to ask you a favour. I've written a paper on some local geology, the Tasman fold belt, for publication. Would you read it for me?'

Serena waited for the envy to pass. The Tasman fold belt had been her specialty. Oh, get over it. 'Sure. Why don't you come for dinner tonight?'

'Fantastic. And might I catch Dave this time?'

'No. He doesn't get home before eleven these days.' She heard her own robotic tone, knew it revealed more than her words.

'Yeah? That's crap. How about I pick up some take-away?'

Serena glanced over at her minestrone, scenting her kitchen with rosemary and tomato and the promise of a warm house on winter nights.

'You do that.'

By lunchtime, she was sleepy. Ready for her daily battle over nap time. It was not unusual for Angus and Finn to sleep for two hours after lunch. It was just that Cooper, at three, was growing out of his daily nap. But still, she hungered for it. A whole two hours, once a day, to herself. Every day, she tried again.

'Where's Giraffe?' snapped Cooper, surly as an old man. Serena scurried out to the cubby and came back triumphant. Giraffe was accepted suspiciously by Cooper, halfway out of bed. Angus had a bottle and was snuggling down in his tiny, painted pine jail, watching Cooper with great interest. When Finn was there, the two littlies were almost winking at each other in expect-ant delight. *Argh, the big fella, gotta keep your eye on him! He'll give the warden a run for her money.*

Cooper dropped Giraffe on the pillow, no longer interested in him. 'Where's Monkey?'

A short tour of the house located Monkey embedded

in some playdough under the kitchen table. Serena scurried back.

'Hmm. Where's Froggy?'

Not behind the telly. Not under the big bed. Not in the book box, or even out in the car. Froggy, it seemed, was gone. Serena caught sight of her strained expression in the bedroom mirror as she waddled past, and raised her hands at her own image. What was she doing? Her own mother had probably sent her to bed with an oily rag for a comforter, and slapped her with it if she complained; and here she was touching her forelock and all but backing out of the bedroom to embark on his lordship's next mission for exotic animal recovery.

She was the mother. The Mother! She strode back down the hall purposefully, empty-handed.

'Where's Froggy?' shouted Cooper.

'That's enough about bloody Froggy! Go to sleep!' She glared at him and slammed the door.

There was a moment of stunned silence from within and then the howl arose.

'*You make me sad!*'

It was something he pulled out of his armoury a bit lately, and she didn't know where he had learned it. She winced and rubbed her forehead. Only three years old, and he already knew how to stick a jagged knife into her heart and twist it.

'You sound tired, my love.'

'You know how it is, Jo. Small kids.'

'Up here the little ones run wild through the commune and the parents barely see them all day. The older ones care for the younger ones, make sure they don't go under the waterfall or get lost in the bunya trees.'

Serena was barely able to disguise her scorn. 'Well, I think three is a little young to take responsibility for a one-year-old sibling.'

Joanne laughed gaily. 'Oh, goodness yes, of course it is. Much too young. Hold on a sec.' There was a long pause during which Serena could hear her mother-in-law apparently accepting a gift of honey from a friend passing in the street. Serena rolled her eyes and resisted her own slightly ashamed impulse to turn down Bob the Builder. Jo returned. 'But really, Serena. I've been having dreams about you. And I can hear it in your voice. There's a sadness about you.'

Serena swallowed. 'It's just a lot of work,' she said finally, in a small voice. 'I don't want to . . . I mean Dave's a fantastic dad, but his job seems to take so much time . . .'

'Of course. It's ridiculous. You put out all this mothering energy and you need someone to bring it back to you.'

Serena felt her face flush.

'Where's Iris?' Jo asked. 'She isn't around to help?'

'She does a lot of charity work . . .'

'Well. Serena, there's always help in the universe when you need it. You just have to believe it. Believe the universe will bring you everything you need, it's just a matter of recognising it when it arrives. There is mothering energy everywhere.'

Serena exhaled, and laughed helplessly. 'Jo, I'm sorry, but . . .'

'. . . but you've never heard so much hippy shit in all your city-dwelling days.'

'Well . . .'

'Okay, to put it simply, in a way a modern girl understands, you need to learn to ask for help.'

'Sorry?'

'You heard.'

'Are you offering to come down?'

'No.'

There was a long pause. Serena had a sense she was being asked to decode some foreign language.

'Okay. I need help.' What was Jo going to do, anyway. Light a candle for her?

'Well. Just give me a day to pack the Bedford and I'll get driving.'

Serena smirked as she got off the phone, but her heart felt lighter as she tried to get the place in some kind of order for Poss.

Poss squatted by the bath, his sleeve rolled up, bubbles up to his elbows. He swatted Angus with a flannel and tried to answer Cooper.

'The last day of what?'

'Just the last day. *You* know!'

'Is it the last day of bubbles?'

Cooper's eyes widened. 'No, silly!'

'Is it the last day of shampoo?'

Cooper hiccupped with laughter. Possum lowered his voice to a whisper. 'Is it the last day of . . .' he looked around him with mock fear '. . . the undies?'

Cooper threw his soapy hands over his mouth and

turned his rapt gaze quickly on his mother. 'Undies?' He chortled.

Serena rolled her eyes affectionately at her friend. 'Uncle Possum's a very silly man.'

Later, the children in bed, Serena and Poss ate food from plastic boxes and drank wine.

Serena sat with her knees apart to make room for her belly. She was wearing black pants and a pale-blue maternity top that gathered under her breasts and fell loosely over her stomach. She had pinned her blonde hair high at the back of her head and darkened her eyelashes with mascara. Something about Poss, the contact with the long-lost world of work, made her want to look nice. As if she were coping.

'Do you miss Zeke?'

Poss paused, chopsticks halfway to his mouth, then he lowered the food back to the container. 'I'm considering taking Renae to court. To force her to move back to Australia.'

'Really.'

'She had no right to move Zeke to England without consulting me.'

'I take it that's a yes.'

'Sorry?'

Serena smiled. 'I asked you if you missed Zeke.'

Poss laughed, a little bitterly. 'You ask me a question about how I feel and I answer with details of the war.'

'Well, that's men and women for you.'

Poss was already nodding in agreement and they both laughed, remembering old conversations along these lines. That was the thing about spending two-week stints together on drill rig sites; you sometimes ended up discussing things in greater detail with your field partner than you did with your spouse.

Poss shrugged and spread his hands open. 'I miss Zeke desperately. Every minute of every day. I get butterflies every time I see a little boy. Or a family. Is that enough for you?'

'Sorry.'

'It's okay. It's good to talk to someone about it. I don't really talk about this to anyone, except my family court adviser.'

'You don't have a lawyer?'

'Not yet.'

'Might need one.'

'That reminds me, there's been some lawyer snooping around Mount Misstep, asking the locals for my address.'

'Renae?'

'Has to be, doesn't it?' Poss reached for his briefcase and took out an envelope. 'Anyway, this is the Tasman fold belt paper I wanted you to read. Can I leave it with you?'

She took it and regarded him. 'Can I ask you something? You're not asking me to read this just to make me feel good are you?'

Poss stared at her for a long moment as if she were deranged. 'No,' he said finally. 'Now, can I make the coffee?'

She skimmed through the paper, slyly watching him move around her kitchen, and she thought about her life. It was a whirlwind of domesticity, life on a tiny scale – the kindy mums' chatter about renovations, and the price of nappies and who was pregnant and who was trying and somebody's kid's hearing problems and another kid's learning difficulties, and the rising dissent because the Barb the local kindy teacher hadn't taught the alphabet song – and yet when it was her kids, when it was Cooper with bronchialitis or Angus who was bitten at playgroup, then she was hurling herself in that maelstrom, and no one could suggest to her that maybe it all mattered less than she thought. Her life was so intense, so inescapable, it needed a counterbalance. A secret life. Some cold, hard, very ancient rocks.

There was a time when she managed rigs that could sink diamond drill bits six hundred metres below the earth's surface, while at the top she fussed over precise angles and shouted at drillers to pump more water. At Dogwood, she and Poss heated meat pies on the rig's noisy manifold, smirking a little to be domesticating this big giant. They calculated it took seventy metres of drilling to heat two pies. She discussed drilling with mining legend Noel Peterson once, after she had won the Young Geologist Encouragement Award, at a ceremony where there was another award named after him. You always drill more than one hole, he told her. Move along fifty metres and do it all again. You could be just metres away from something good. She had remembered that when looking for tantalite in Mitta Mitta, zinc in Zeehan, nickel in Waratah.

Almost every deposit he'd discovered, he said, he'd been looking for something else entirely. In Hamersley he'd been drilling for copper for weeks, and had grown tired and frustrated and homesick. But when the light plane lifted him out of there to take him home, he looked out the window at the red rock below and thought, iron. Made the plane land again. It took him just a few more days to nail what was now one of the world's biggest iron ore resources. So, of course, look for what the company tells you to, because they're paying you. But remember you're an explorer, and every field trip is new territory. You can find whatever you want to. It might not even be a bloody rock.

It might be a child. A friend, a lover, an escape route.

Poss left at ten o'clock and she had a feeling he didn't want to cross paths with Dave. At the door he turned and kissed her in a friendly way on the cheek and she felt the warmth of his skin, the smell of him in the gap between his collar and his neck. Her hand rested lightly on his sleeve, and she felt the curve of muscle underneath. He looked at her with an expression she couldn't read.

'Are you okay?'

'I'm fine.'

He paused. 'Because someone as fabulous as you deserves to be happy, Serena.'

He looked at her with a mix of concern and a defiant embarrassment. She stared at him in surprise and waited for him to walk away. He didn't. She struggled for words, felt herself blush.

'Well, Poss, that's very . . . flattering of you.' A jokey tone, trying to regain the solid ground of their years of friendship.

'I mean it, Serena. I hope Dave knows how lucky he is.' She slid her hand on her belly, to stop her clapping it over her mouth. Slivers of desire shot through her, so strong she feared he might feel them off her skin. She felt how close he was standing to her. Just a handspan of air and some marriage vows separating them, their breaths coming quickly. Then Poss noticed her hand on her belly, and he looked down at it.

He reached out, touched her stomach gently.

'Twins. It's so . . . amazing.'

'Yes.' Don't stop, she thought, willing his hand to stay in contact with hers.

She raised her fingers and lowered them again, on top of his. Skin to skin. Don't go, she said with her flesh. Stay with me.

But the contact broke the spell. He snatched his hand away, as if to look at his watch.

'God, will you look at the time? I'd better get going, got an early one tomorrow.' Red spots on his cheeks, his brown eyes horrified. 'Thanks for dinner, Serena. Lovely. Sorry to rush off . . .' He plunged his fists into the pockets of his suit coat and scuttled off into the darkness, towards his car.

Serena shut the door and rested her forehead on it. The kicking in her belly was going wild, as if the babies were reading the messages of adrenalin and hormones flooding her body. She shook her head and frowned at Jo's glass buddha. *What the hell was that about?*

'You expect too much from life,' said Serena's mother, the next morning on the phone. 'You always did. To be happy every moment. It's just not realistic.' She paused. 'It's probably my fault. Something in the way I brought you up. Maybe I spoiled you.'

Serena paused. She had had the same thought about

Cooper. That maybe he should suffer a little more, to prepare him for real life. Three disappointments a day, that sort of thing. Although he was quite capable of manufacturing his own disappointments, at the rate of three every five minutes, some days. He couldn't play with the kitchen knife, he wasn't allowed to open his birthday present three weeks early, he couldn't paint on the walls, that sort of stuff.

'Oh, I think I'm all right,' she told her mother. And she was, despite a restless night replaying those last few minutes with Poss over and over, trying to work out what they meant. She had woken at three to find her husband's sleeping body next to her in the bed, and she had thrown her arm around him, pulled him back towards her, and felt him wake in surprise, turn to her. They had made love without speaking, just an exchange of murmurs and touch, and fallen asleep entwined, his body pressed against her back, his hand over her belly. She was all right, she reflected, possibly even more than all right.

'Yes,' said her mother thoughtfully. Then she made a small noise in her throat, like a door slamming shut. 'Oh, of course. I'm just thinking aloud. You're wonderful, darling. Kids and house and David working such long hours . . . and you had that wonderful career . . . which you could maybe go back to one day.'

Serena sighed. Now she was getting a headache.

'Bye, Mum.'

Later that morning she picked up the phone and rang the number on the real-estate flier.

'I'd like a professional valuation on my flat,' she said. 'How soon could you get it to me?'

22

'*I feel like someone is pouring liquid sunshine over my bones.*'

Ana stared at her computer screen and hastily deleted that sentence. It was not a very good start to an op-ed on nuclear power. But being in love was simply not much of an aid to being any sort of journalist at all.

Two months since she had first kissed Eli, taken him home to her flat, and it was like someone had taken her heart off a dusty shelf and blown light into it. Creamy, lubricating, was how she would describe new love. People looked different, as if she could see into their minds. She found herself seeking out complex things to look at, like the fingers of bare autumn trees, to relieve the pain of joy, because the hard angles of city buildings only made it worse. She yearned for some sort of ritual to pin it in time, this grinding back into motion of her long unused heart muscles.

She saw him every few nights, and on the weekends. In between she scuttled back to her work or her flat like a magpie returning to its nest with its latest shiny trinket, turning over and examining whatever new thing she had learned about him. He has three sisters! He doesn't believe in God! He went to private school! He hates synthetics!

On bad days she worried it was too good, that it was

going to end, and her joy began to tip over to panic. Sometimes it was as if the sun were shining too hard, and she had to close her eyes, shut out the light. *I'm showing him too much. He'll get to know me too well, and he won't like me.* Or maybe there was something wrong with *him*, to be in love with her; something she would soon discover. He emailed her: *I adore you,* and she worried. Maybe he was just saying it to be nice. To be kind. Out of pity. But then she would see him and it was like falling through the universe again, to see the joy he took in *her*. To have another night in his bed where they fell asleep at dawn, sated, and she would wake later with his juices still between her legs, like a plant that's been deliciously watered.

She went into conference and forced herself to locate the dry, dead, minuscule part of her brain that she now realised she used for work. It was an act, but a comforting one. One she was well rewarded for.

Lowenthal was away today, and Morrie Lumiere was standing in. A new associate editor had been appointed from the ranks; David Williams, formerly courts, environment, federal politics and show biz, with a stint in LA under his belt. Younger than her, a new generation, a golden-haired boy touted as a future editor-in-chief, she noted with a pang of nervousness. Each editor gave their rundown, but Ana found it hard to concentrate. She shuffled her papers and a listing of that weekend's house inspections and auctions slid out. Eaglemont, Alphington, Northcote, Thornbury, Brunswick. Three bedroom, renovator's delight, low-maintenance courtyard, each one full of possibility until she saw it or went to the auction. She wondered whether Eli would do the rounds with her this Saturday, as he had done the past few; holding the Melways, carrying Finn and distracting him, stopping in parks for takeaway picnics while Finn played on slides and swings. The three of them looking for all the world like a family.

No, she wouldn't let Elijah come this week. She loved playing families with him, but she didn't want to scare him off. He had, after all, said that he didn't want children.

Had news conference really once sent her into a state of nervous anxiety? These days it seemed she could barely stay awake.

'Ana?' said Lumiere, slapping down his pen and staring at her. She jumped. She had put on yesterday's shirt when she dressed at Elijah's that morning, and had resolved to keep her jacket on to cover the creases and ink marks. Now she was hot, and sweating. She went to unbutton the jacket, remembered the shirt and hastily did it up again. She ran her hand behind her neck, under her hair, and it was moist. She couldn't think.

'Uh . . . nightclubs,' she said. 'The Carnvier report, about how drugs are being openly sold in clubs. I went to three nightclubs the other week . . .'

'Go, girl,' murmured Pete Pryor.

'. . . and was *instantly* offered drugs in each one.' She stared around solemnly. The fact that it had taken careful observation in each club, and a few murmured queries in one, to spot the dealer, was not worth mentioning.

'Nice . . .'

Lumiere frowned at his list. 'Good, but not this

week. We've got Professor Rubenstein doing a piece on drugs.'

'Oh.' Ana hastily scanned her list. 'Okay, okay. Assumed joint custody for separating parents. Been proposed, I think should be accepted . . .'

'It's a mistake,' said Pete Pryor, folding his arms. 'Kids will always choose their mother first.'

'Yeah, if women badmouth the fathers all the time!' bristled Morrie Lumiere. Must be having a bad time with his ex-wife.

'Mate, you talk to any single young bloke,' said Pryor, nodding generously, like Moses on the Mount, delivering the final wisdom on a subject. 'They don't want to have kids. If it weren't for women, the human race wouldn't continue.'

'Mate, that's true,' said golden boy Dave Williams, spreading his ringless hands on the table. Everyone looked at him. 'It's really hard to find a woman over thirty who doesn't want marriage and kids before you've even bought her a second drink.' His first contribution as associate editor. The older blokes laughed uproariously. Ana, feeling slighted, grew stony.

'Nice trying, I bet,' said Pryor, with a leer. 'Heh, heh, heh.'

'Thanks for your contributions.' Ana rolled her eyes sarcastically. 'Actually, I know quite a few single women who don't want marriage or children.'

'Batting for the other side,' murmured Zac.

'Can I have their numbers?' Williams smiled smugly as the men around him roared laughing. 'But seriously, Ana, women won't go for the joint custody thing. Women are naturally conservative.'

She gave him her most incredulous, you-are-an-idiot look. He wasn't the editor yet. 'Really,' she said flatly.

'It's true. There is no breed more conservative than the young mother.' Pryor sounded like he was mounting his soapbox. 'Suddenly awash with the vulnerability of her charges and her enormous responsibility, she would see paedophiles executed and the price of nappies a matter of national debate.'

'That's crap.'

'No, it's the truth. I've seen women who previously devoted their spare time working to abolish refugee camps, these women, they have children and suddenly they're directing their radical energies into campaigning for all shops to install pram ramps at the doors, and for school canteens to sell gluten-free sausage rolls. The young mother is the cornerstone of social parochialism.'

'Rightio.' Ana stared out the window, bored with defending her gender.

'Are we all done?' Lumiere looked around.

Ana remembered something. 'Actually, I had an idea for something that might be good for the paper. Why don't we give over a page to the police to publicise their unsolved crimes, see if the public can help?'

Lumiere looked doubtful and glanced at his watch. Ana regretted raising it in front of him, when all he wanted was to get away to his lunch. She should have saved it for Lowenthal. But she'd started now, so she pressed on.

'Citizens' Arrest, we could call it.' She had the idea while talking to Eli about some of the police prosecutors he worked with. 'They get to make public requests for information and we get to expand our police contacts and publish more juicy details of crimes.'

'Interesting. But probably something for advertising to look at. The police should pay for stuff like that.' Lumiere was already at the door, the others leaving around him.

'And we'd get to look public-spirited to the community,' Ana pressed, following him out.

He smiled. 'Nice try, Ana, but I don't think it's us.'

She shrugged it off. Better to have a few crap ideas than none at all.

Now she had more important things to think about, like finding a house to buy, and visiting her mother.

She went to visit Lily that Saturday, and with her heart in her mouth, she took Elijah and Finn. It wasn't planned. But Eli had stayed over Friday night, and pleaded to spend the day with them.

She hedged. 'I'm worried you'll get bored with all this househunting. Shouldn't we be doing something romantic, instead of poking through other people's homes?' She pulled her dressing-gown around her waist and held the paper cup of coffee he had brought her, with all the Saturday papers.

'This is romantic.'

'And I promised to go see my mother this morning, and bring her some things that she needs. I can't inflict that on you.'

'Why not?' He crossed his arms, and looked hurt. 'Are you that worried about me meeting your mother?'

'Mr Moyal, you sound a bit sensitive on this subject.' She examined his face curiously. 'Would you *like* to meet my mother?'

He pouted, trying to make a joke of it. 'Oh, you know, I don't care. It's just I sometimes think, maybe Ana's ashamed of me, that she doesn't ever. . . .'

Ana leaned over and kissed him. She loved his moments of insecurity, never felt he was more hers than when he revealed them, and showed her she wasn't the only one to worry this was all too perfect. 'Give me five minutes to shower. We'll pick up Finn and head straight out there. Just promise me one thing?'

'What?'

'Don't tell me I'm anything like her.'

At the hostel, Lily looked Elijah up and down. In a business shirt and jeans, he held Finn on his hip. He smiled and held out a hand to her but she looked at it incredulously.

'Your what?'

'My boyfriend, Mum.' Ana blushed to use such a word, but knew she had to keep things simple.

'And what's his child's name?'

Lily looked paler than usual, thinner. Ana resolved to ask the nurses whether they'd thoroughly checked her recently.

'It's actually not his child, Mum, he's Priya's. Remember I told you . . .'

'Ah.' Lily nodded thoughtfully, looking from the man to the boy. 'Did you know I had a boy once?'

Elijah nodded, his face sobering. 'Ana's told me all about Nick. It's very —'

'Ana never wanted to be a mother. She wanted more.' Lily spoke gravely.

Ana had a mad urge to stamp her foot, to point at the man and the boy. She took Finn from Eli and put him in her mother's lap, not caring whether the robust toddler was too heavy for her mother's thin legs. Hoping he hurt.

'But this is Finn, Mum. I'm going to be his . . . mother.' She felt dizzy with daring and fear at all this labelling. *Boyfriend. Mother.*

And Elijah. Who had said early on that he didn't want children. If she took on Finn, would she scare Elijah off? Just one day at a time, she resolved. Because being Ana, she had to dream big. Her dream of family now was the whole thing at once; the boy *and* the man.

Lily stared at her and then smiled off into the distance.

'I hope you don't regret it . . .' she whispered.

'*Mum!*'

'So, do you feel sure now about taking Finn?' Elijah poured her a glass of red and sank his teeth into a piece of pizza. It was Sunday night and they were in Carlton, ensconced in a booth with plastic garlic pinned overhead and pictures of Ferraris taped to the brown brick walls.

'It still scares me. Having a child. It always has. I'm too selfish.' Ana drank some wine. 'How will I do things like this? Just spontaneously whip out for dinner with an attractive man?'

She smiled flirtatiously but Elijah only raised his eyebrows in the smallest acknowledgment. He was watching her, listening. She stared. 'Sometimes I still have moments when I wonder if you're just spending time with me on behalf of your client, to investigate whether I'm fit mother material.'

He looked hurt. 'Of course not. I'm here because I want to be with you.'

'Because if you were, I could save you the time and tell you right now I'm not. Fit mother material, that is.' She finished the glass and he topped it up. She could feel the wine going straight to her head.

'Who is fit mother material? Maybe you're being too hard on yourself.'

Ana shook her head and thought about it. Serena was a fit mother, although she didn't seem very happy lately. But that was it, *could* you make the right sacrifices and stay happy? She thought of Marnie.

'My friend at work has just come back from maternity leave and she's so stressed it's hard to have a conversation with her.' Ana twisted a paper serviette around her greasy fingers. 'She spends half her working day pumping breast milk and the other half writing mummy stories and ringing the childcare centre to see if her baby's all right.'

Elijah nodded and wiped his mouth, leaving her the last piece of pizza. 'I know. My sisters went through all that with work. But it's only that hard when they're babies. It gets better. And then the last kid starts school, and their mums are sitting around weeping because they wish they'd had a third. Or a fourth.' He shook his head.

She liked it that he had sisters.

'Maybe I won't have the patience a biological mother would have.'

'I didn't notice my sisters growing superhuman patience.'

'I read this story today about this woman who tried to kill her four children, and it said she had been abandoned by her own mother when she was eight years old. And you read that and instantly you know: it's history repeating itself, it's the scars of childhood. Imagine being a mother and causing that much damage.'

He stared at her. 'What? That woman overdosed on Prozac. It wasn't necessarily —'

'It's *always* the mother's fault, though, that's what scares me to death. That woman whose baby starved to death because she fed it rice milk; everyone said how stupid she was, but I was just thinking well, yep, that could be me.'

'You read too many newspapers.'

'When I was doing court reporting, defence lawyers always brought up their clients' terrible childhoods, the shocking parenting they received, and the judge *always* took it into consideration.' She pointed her finger, now a little drunk and convinced this last point proved her case. 'See?'

Elijah leaned over the table and wrapped his hands over her finger. 'Well, people like that should be reassuring. There'll always be someone who's a worse parent than you.'

Ana watched her hand being held, and felt her body melt as he stroked her fingers.

'Serena's a good friend, isn't she? She'd give you advice.'

'She would.' Ana nodded and looked away, distracted from her lust. She was ashamed of how much Serena had offered, how good Serena had been. 'But Serena scares me too. I'll never be as good a mother as her. Finn will have to go to childcare, for starters.'

'Plenty of kids do.'

She sighed. 'Serena . . .' She swilled her wine around her glass.

'Parenting's not a competition sport.'

'And the whole single parent thing . . .' She finished another glass and watched gloomily as Elijah filled it. What had happened to their moment of closeness a minute ago; and why couldn't he stop grilling her about this whole uncomfortable thing with Finn?

'Don't give me that. I know how much money Finn comes with. You'll be able to buy whatever house you choose, with cash.'

'It's not that. It's the responsibility of it. The never having someone to take it in turns with.' Okay, she was fishing. She finally couldn't bear it any more. 'You said you didn't want kids,' she said in a small voice. 'Are you going to hang around if I adopt Finn?'

He put his hands over hers again and drew her close. He slipped one hand behind the nape of her neck and tugged gently at her hair, his eyes large and wandering over hers as if he were about to take a bite out of her. She laced one hand through his fingers and he pulled at her hand until she came and sat on the bench seat beside him. They kissed and she felt his hand behind her head, the other around her back and she was almost dizzy with lust for this man. She could smell pizza and red wine and a tinge of chlorine still in his hair from his swim that morning, and the sweet musky smell of his chest, rising from his collar . . .

'My place?' he murmured.

She frowned. 'You didn't answer my question.'

He stared at her, and held her delicate jaw with his two hands. 'Ana, have you been worried about this?'

'Yes.'

'Well, listen. Don't. I don't care if you have a child. I actually quite like Finn. You won't get rid of me that easily. Now, can we please go back to my place?'

She smiled, swallowed back a throatful of emotion and stopped herself throwing her arms around his neck. That might really scare him off.

'Sounds good.'

23

Ana woke. 3:12, said the digital clock. She was in Elijah's bed, and damp between her legs. It was eerily quiet – that brief window when public transport stopped running, and traffic on St Kilda's streets slowed. There was the odd, far-off shout, muffled by Elijah's hydronic heating. His flat was art-deco, renovated with modern fittings. The bedroom was spartan; a headless queen-size bed, a few weights stacked in a corner, and a bedside table piled with books and legal briefs. On her side, there was nothing but a stretch of carpeted floor and an elaborate leaded window framed in dark wood.

Elijah's long body was still spooned behind, his arm thrown across her, over the cover, the way they had fallen asleep. She remembered their lovemaking, and blinked in the darkness, twisting a corner of the pillow between her fingers. It was always so good. She smiled and felt her face flush, felt the desire rise in her again like a tide. She turned to him and breathed in his scent, felt the body warmth of him. *Hers*. And if she took Finn, he wouldn't be scared off. He had said so. She took out her dream of a little family and turned it over tenderly, privately.

But she couldn't get comfortable. Although they always fell asleep naked after making love, she still wasn't used to it, didn't like the tendrils of air that crept in around her shoulders. She wriggled the doona up higher and Elijah breathed peacefully on. She closed her eyes and tried to relax. But still, the wetness between her legs. It was cold. She eased herself out of bed, and crept out to the bathroom.

Ugh. She faced her squinting face in the mirror, her naked self, fluorescent lights bright off white tiles. Blood was fanning down the soft insides of her thighs. Damn. Her period. She should have brought something. Tidemarks where it had flowed and dried. As she stared down in despair, a red drop fell on the white tiles between her feet. She pulled down handfuls of toilet paper and wet it under the tap. Wiped herself and scrubbed the tender skin of her thighs, the tissue shredding between her fingers. She used a face washer to clean herself. She needed a tampon, or something to staunch the flow. Even if she just used folded toilet paper, she would need her underpants, which were tangled somewhere in Elijah's snowy doona. Maybe not so snowy now.

She looked around her at Elijah's bathroom. A shower, the erotic potential of which they had already explored twice in the past weeks. A modern, low toilet. A mirrored wall cabinet, holding shaving foam, a few out-of-date packets of medicines, a bottle of aftershave. Nothing that would help her. She closed it. Below her, another red drop fell. What a mess. Her period, when it came, usually did with a vengeance. She kept looking. A sink cabinet, with a cup holding two toothbrushes, the pink one a present to her from Elijah, on the condition she didn't remove it from his place. She smiled as her eye fell on it, hugged the memory of that gift to herself. *He wants me in his life*.

She squatted, and opened the cupboard doors below the sink, hoping to at least find a new roll of toilet paper. There was one shelf, with a pile of discarded razors, some folded towels, hair gels, sunscreens. There had to be *something*. Maybe she should cut up a towel, and buy him one later to replace it? She got on her knees on the cold tiles to squint in at the bottom shelf, and then she saw it.

A blue toilet bag with pink piping around the edges. Stained with toothpaste in one corner, lipstick in another. A woman's toilet bag.

Ana, shaking violently, pulled out the bag and stood up. She turned and locked the bathroom door, suddenly horribly aware she was prying. She stared down at the bag.

She'd seen it before. It was Priya's.

But it couldn't be. What would Priya's toilet bag be doing here, in Elijah's bathroom? Ana unzipped it and folded the lid back.

A toothbrush, the head jammed in a plastic cover. Hotel soap from the Sofitel, unopened. The same Cedel normal-to-oily shampoo that Priya always used. A hair-clip made of black shell, passed on to Priya from her mother. One jade earring, from a pair bought to match the green dress Priya wore to Angus's christening. Priya's lipstick, Clarins Plum Passion, the only shade she ever wore. She had the same lipstick in her car, in her bag, in her office at work. A tiny vial of parsley tablets for fresh breath, with Hindi lettering on the side. A thermometer. Two tampons.

Ana couldn't seem to think, or to move her legs. She was aware, as if from a long way off, that she was cold. But her mind was completely still, as if waiting for an answer. *This must be here because* . . . Still no answer. She could hear her own fast breathing, and she felt sick. *This must be here because* . . . there was no answer. Not one that didn't involve a secret of which she was not a part. Finally another drop of blood fell to the floor, and Ana reluctantly took out a tampon. Grabbed a towel and wiped herself, and then the floor, clean.

She went back to the bedroom and switched on the bedside lamp. Elijah didn't stir when she dropped the toilet bag on the bed, and she used the time to fossick for her underwear in the doona, slip on her jeans. He began to blink awake, smiling, and sat up to look at the clock. He frowned at the time and stared at her.

'What are you doing?'

She nodded down at the toilet bag and sat on the edge of the bed to pull up her boots.

'What's that?' she said. She was trying to look calm as she zipped up the boots but her fingers were shaking so much they couldn't get a grip. Her arms were milked of their strength. She wasn't even sure why she was getting dressed, except that she needed another layer on her. Like armour. She could always take it off. After Elijah explained to her what this was doing here. There would be a reason, a reasonable reason.

He stared at the toilet bag, his face scrunched and blinking, but she saw the caution slip over his eyes like a curtain.

'It's a . . . er . . . ladies vanity case,' he said. He was sitting up now, pulling the sheets tight around his waist. He watched her. He didn't look puzzled any more. He looked like a man who was waiting. Waiting and worried.

'It's Priya's,' said Ana. Her heart was hammering. 'I'm sorry to wake you but I found this in your bathroom, and I know it. It's Priya's.

'Is it?' he said cautiously. Fell back into a watchful silence.

'What's it doing here?'

'Actually I think it's my sister's. She stayed the other week and . . .' Half-hearted. Trailing out even before he'd finished, at the sight of her face.

'It's Priya's.' She tipped the contents out on the mattress. 'I know this stuff. All of it. I've borrowed this hairclip before. I've *worn* it.' He stared at the small pile as if it were a dead animal. Ana dropped the bag. She had a horrible sense that she had fallen asleep with a friend, a lover, and woken up with a stranger.

'Did you go through my cupboards?' His eyes were cool.

She stared at him, her heart falling at the words. The rejection she had been fearing every week of the past two months. She scrambled to defend herself.

'I got my period. I needed something.'

'You could have woken me . . .' He pressed his lips closed. He looked suddenly fed up, as if she were a nuisance. Tears filled her eyes, but she looked again at Priya's bag and had to know.

'Elijah, I'm sorry if I've intruded, but this is freaking me out. Please, just explain it to me. What is it doing here?'

He stared at her with a sullen expression she had never seen before. She asked again, her voice thin now, petulant, pathetic in her fear.

'What's it *doing* here?'

He slapped back the sheet, stood up and wrapped a towelling robe around his naked body, tying the sash with vicious jabs of his elbows. He folded his arms. 'Why should I have to explain something you found while snooping through my cupboards at three o'clock in the morning?'

Ana gasped. *Snooping?* Her world was tilting. Elijah hated her, her relationship was ending and there had been a deception, something unspeakable, incomprehensible.

'Because it belonged to my best friend! Because she's dead!'

'And if she had a secret she really wanted you to know, don't you think she'd have told you herself?' His voice was low, exasperated.

Ana stared. 'What are you saying?'

He rocked back on his heels, now fully awake, watching her warily. They were both breathing too fast, pale and wide-eyed. Her heart was pounding, and she glanced towards the door. How well did she know this man after all?

He reached towards her and she shrieked and jumped back. 'Don't touch me!'

He whipped back, shocked, then sunk his head into his hands. 'Shit,' he muttered. 'Ana, please calm down.'

With tears sliding down her face, she moved towards him. 'Could you *please* tell me what it's doing here?' She wiped her eyes.

He rubbed his forehead and glanced at her again.

'I don't want to tell you, Ana. I made a promise and it doesn't make any difference now that she's dead.'

A promise? She? Ana almost doubled over at the intimacy of it. She stood, shaking her head.

'Are you saying something happened between you and Priya?'

He shook his head, his face becoming stony.

'I can't talk about it. I'm sorry.'

'And you didn't think to mention it before now?'

He pressed his lips together, shook his head. She picked up her bag, her coat. Stared at him.

'You'd better . . .'

'I made a promise —'

'Fuck you and your promises Elijah! You can either tell me what happened right now, and why you concealed this from me, or I'm walking out that door and that's it.'

'But, Ana, it doesn't matter to you and me . . .'

'Obviously it does matter, or you'd tell me. I'm getting out of here.' She was filled with fury at not one, but two of the people she loved most. She felt as angry as if she had found Priya alive and in her lover's bed; as lonely and excluded. And something in her felt justified. *I always knew there must be something wrong with him, that he was too good to be true. I knew I shouldn't open my heart so far, so fast.* Why hadn't she listened to her instincts?

Ana snatched up the last of her things. She picked up Priya's toilet bag and considered taking it. Why not? Priya was more hers than Elijah's, surely? But after a moment she threw the bag back on the bed, and slammed her way out of the apartment. Maybe nothing was what it seemed, after all.

24

'Are you serious?'

Serena stared at the phone in shock. The figure the real-estate agent had quoted was one that, in her mind, should be attached to a designer four-bedroom home with wall sockets for vacuum cleaning, not her tiny inner-city flat.

The agent assured her that the flat's period features, such as the pressed metal ceilings, were a selling point. Serena declined to tell him that the last time she had tried to paint those ceilings, her brush had gone right through the rust in so many places she had been forced to stop. If a dustball was dislodged within the roof cavity, it could probably collapse an entire room.

'And the outdoor toilet?' she inquired cautiously, stroking her belly.

'I wouldn't call it that. It's attached to the house.'

'Sorry? Did you call it a house?'

'Well, maybe we'll call it a unit. But it's virtually on its own piece of land. It just shares one party wall with the neighbouring place.'

She paused. 'I'd like to believe you. I just find it hard to believe this is a realistic price.'

'I can show you ten similar properties that have been sold at higher prices. Self-contained unit, period character, onsite parking . . .'

'Onsite *what*?'

'Just get rid of that flowerbed out the front and you could park a small car. Doesn't matter if it sticks out on the pavement a bit. It's the location that matters, anyway. Butterworth Street is considered a very desirable area these days. Now, Serena, would you like to put this property on the market? I'd be very keen to sell it for you.'

Serena bit her bottom lip and blinked hard at the phone.

'Let me think about it.'

Cooper dragged Serena's backpack, the one she used to carry the nappies and spare clothes and apples and drink bottles, all the way down the hall to the kitchen. He dropped it at her feet and stared at her pleadingly.

'We go to Matty's house?'

Serena sighed. 'No. Matty's in childcare today. But we might go to someone else's house.'

Cooper crumpled. 'I want Matty!'

Serena privately agreed. She wanted Matty too, or she wanted Cate. But Cate had started her job with the Australian Ballet and Matty was in childcare. And Serena felt like she had never needed Cate more.

She forced her voice to sound cheerful. 'Never mind, Coop. We'll find other people to play with.'

She loaded up the pusher and they walked four blocks to visit Mel. On the way they passed three other pushers, all propelled by elderly women. It was the grandma invasion of the northern suburbs. As house prices rose, women were more likely to go straight back to work after their babies were born, and the local childcare centres were full to overflowing. So the grandmas were left behind with the littlies to explore the remnant parklands, and the gentrifying coffee shops. Each of the passing elderly women smiled, the affection of the older woman for the young pregnant mother, and Serena returned the smile hesitantly. She rather resented the grandma invasion. Could she befriend a grandma? Sit in her lounge and drink tea while the kids played? Did she want to be reminded by someone older and wiser that these were the best days of her life? No, she wanted a friend who sometimes hated her husband, someone who was still trying to get rid of the pregnancy fat, who pined for the perfect black boot, who had got up to children six times the night before. She wanted Cate.

'*Broomm, broomm,*' said Finn. He held a small steamroller and twisted in the toddler seat, where he was perched above Angus.

'Lovely,' said Serena absently. 'Come *on*, Coop.' She tugged her son's hand and he reluctantly rose from the snail he was examining.

She manoeuvred the pusher around a corner and past another old lady. The worst thing about the grandma invasion was how badly she wanted one. A grandma, that is. A real one. Not one who was too busy making sandwiches for the feminist movement. Not one up north on a commune. A nice, solid grandma who lived a short drive away – not too close, but close enough – and whose heart did a little jump for joy every time her daughter or daughter-in-law rang and asked her to babysit. She didn't have to knit or anything like that. She just had to be around.

However, she reminded herself, she did have one delightful, if largely absent grandma in her life. Jo might only come to stay for one week a year, but it was always fantastic. And Jo, or Jo-jo as Coop called her, was on her way at this very minute, driving south in her Bedford van. Serena couldn't wait. She passed another grandma with a pram, and this time she beamed at her.

At Mel's, the children were ushered out the back to the paved courtyard. Stone statues struck poses along the fences and a figurine of a woman lifting a jug stood in the middle and doubled as a water feature. The woman's stone arm was raised so the water pouring from the tilted jug fell from a point above her scarf-wrapped head, on her right. To her left, a life-size ceramic child gripped an armful of her mother's peasant skirt and pressed a cherubic cheek against the fabric.

In one fenced-off corner of the paving there was a plastic shell of sand with three buckets and three spades, still so new they had price tags.

Mel, bone-slim in black hipsters and a clingy blue top, crouched down to the children. 'That's Edward's little play area,' she announced enthusiastically. Cooper stared at her with distrust. 'Would you boys like to have a play? I've put enough toys there so there'll be no fighting. Red for Edward, green for Cooper, blue for Finn.'

'Eddie likes red,' said Cooper gravely.

'It's *Edward*, sweetie.'

'Mummy, there's water coming out of the lady's head.' Cooper shrieked and ran towards the water feature. But Mel moved her lithe body to intercept him, quick and low like a goalie trying to block a ball.

'It's nice, isn't it? But just for looking! You boys stay in the lovely sandpit.'

Serena and Angus followed Mel through her immaculate open-plan living and kitchen area, and watched while she made tea and took poppyseed cake out of a container. Then Mel took Serena upstairs to her study, where she had flow charts for her new business, Slingshot!, manufacturing a complicated-looking baby sling.

'I've got four retail outlets for it now, including David Jones.' Mel picked up a spidery tangle of what looked like occy straps. 'You put it on like this.'

Serena submitted to having the thing strapped around her and privately reflected she had always been too fond of her personal space to use a baby sling. Everytime she was lashed to one of her babies, heart to heart, face to face, she felt a mad urge to slap herself free.

'Just turn around.' Mel was on her knees now, frowning up at Serena. 'It looks a bit . . .'

Serena turned and found herself looking out of a window, down at the three boys below. They had made a quick bid for freedom, having trampled the small fence and taken possession of the wider courtyard. Now a slow and steady transportation was underway, with sand being carried and dumped in the shallow pool at the bottom of the water feature.

'Oh dear,' she murmured.

Mel bounded down the stairs and reappeared under the window. 'Oh no, no, no!' she cried, rushing to re-erect the fence. 'Naughty, naughty boys.'

On the way home, Serena stopped and bought them all ice-creams.

'Naughty, naughty boy,' Cooper told Finn.

Serena crouched and looked them each in the eye.

'None of you are naughty. You are all my very, very good boys.'

'I'm naughty,' said Cooper. 'Eddie's mummy said so.'

'Well, it only counts if your own mummy says so,' said Serena. 'And I say you're good. So you are.'

Finn watched her with his big dark eyes, and then his ice-cream dripped on his hand and he sobbed inconsolably.

'Mawlting!'

Sharon brought her children over for a play the next day. Dhakota and Shakylah arrived with matching yellow streams under their noses, and Dhakota had a guttural cough. Shakylah's earrings were gone, the holes now oozing pus. Sharon drifted around the house while Serena made coffee and Dhakota and Cooper got into a screaming argument over a fire engine.

'Sharon, I think Dhakota's bitten Cooper.' Serena tried to say it calmly, in a measured tone. Tried not to shriek, *My child is not a bone for yours to chew on!* The small red circle of teeth marks already turning blue on the delicate skin of her son's neck. Cooper sobbed in raw misery, his face buried in Serena's lap. Finn hugged his beloved Jarmy and stared fearfully at the visitors. Dhakota raised and lowered the fire engine's ladder, his head on one side.

'Oh God, I don't know what to do with him,' Sharon said. 'Dhakota, you're very bad, honey. You're a bad boy. Give Cooper the fire engine or Cooper's mummy will get cross with you.' Dhakota ignored her and she wandered disconsolately over to the newspaper, sitting unopened on the couch. 'Do you get the newspaper delivered? That is fantastic. I wish I could do that . . .'

After Sharon and her clan had left, Serena held the teatowel-wrapped icepack on Cooper's neck and wondered. What was it about her mothers' group? As a group, they were an endearing collection of strengths and eccentricities. Individually, they were just . . . strange.

Was she any better? Sitting at home with her reluctant pregnancy, brooding over whether or not to leave her husband? She stared at a scrap of paper and wrote down some figures. That much for the sale of the flat. That much on weekly rent of another house in the area. That much for food, that much for petrol and clothes and kindy fees and chemist things and stuff. That much for a nest egg, until lawyers worked out how to divide up the house and the car and the mortgage and all the things that were a life. That much for some home help, to get her through the worst times. Why not? It would be her money, her life, her decisions. No more waiting for Dave. She felt the lethargy of a thousand lonely nights slip from her shoulders at the thought of it. Her gaze fell on a photo of Priya and Richard, a wedding picture, and she felt a flutter of panic at how brief life was, how many precious days she had already spent.

She took another piece of paper and headed it, *Things to Do While Jo Here. Go swimming. Night out with Ana. Buy new clothes, lipstick, earrings. See P.*

P for Poss.

She would ring him when he got back from his trip

to south-east Asia, some time this week. She would ask him out for dinner, away from the family chaos of the house. She would take out her new feelings for him, carefully, gently, so as not to scare them away. And she would examine them.

Someone as fabulous as you deserves to be happy . . . I hope Dave knows how lucky he is . . . She hugged the memory of those words to her. How long had Poss felt this way about her? How had she never noticed?

She looked out the window and saw a Bedford van, with a spiral rainbow snake painted on the side, parking in the street. She ran into the lounge room and turned off the telly.

'Jo-jo's here!'

'You're not really having an ultrasound, are you?' Jo wore a purple cheesecloth skirt and a long crocheted top with batwing sleeves. Waves of grey hair framed her brown eyes and she sat on the floor, Angus on her lap, and watched Cooper draw. 'I read somewhere it's so loud, it makes the babies silently scream.'

'Well, as long as it's silent.' Serena sat cross-legged against the wall and rested her coffee cup on her stomach. She tried for something less flippant, and a little more explanatory. After all, this woman was about to give her her first day off in two months. 'It's to check for abnormalities.'

Since Jo had arrived, Serena had had a scented bath, washed her hair and put on the dress her mother-in-law had bought for her. It was a cobalt blue, in fabric that stretched over her bump, with small white flowers at the wrist and the hem. She could always cut off that lacy bit at the neck after Jo left. Jo unpacked her bounty of dream catchers and scarabs and ribbon twirlers from her local market for the children, as well as a pair of drawstring pants printed with Chinese symbols that Dave wouldn't wear in a million years. Corn and tofu curry bubbled on the stove for dinner and Jo drank dandelion coffee with soy milk.

'Ah yes. Abnormalities. So. How are you, my girl?' Jo watched Serena closely.

Serena drew a rainbow with Cooper's crayons and thought of all the answers she could give.

'Tired,' she said, finally.

'Is Dave working too hard?'

'Yes,' Serena said cautiously. 'Long hours.' She was secretly looking forward to Jo seeing it for herself, wondered whether his mother's presence might make Dave spend a bit more time at home.

Jo nodded, as if she expected as much. 'His father did too,' she said, with resignation. 'A workaholic. That's why I left him. Best thing I ever did. Now, are you going to this ultrasound or not?'

'Will you be okay here with the kids?' Serena was dizzy with the prospect of freedom, the question a mere courtesy flung over her shoulder as she mentally headed out the door.

'I'll be fine. Go have a massage, there's some good reiki healers here in Melbourne. Get your chakras aligned. Take your time.'

Serena watched the screen above her and waited while the nurse pushed the sonar over her greased stomach.

She had mounted the stairs to this twenty-week ultrasound with growing nervousness, almost relieved to see that Dave, as expected, had not made it. Was it abnormalities that she feared? Down syndrome, cystic fibrosis, a lifetime of dependency?

Or was it the girl thing?

When she had her first baby, she hadn't cared what sex it was. Then with Angus, a girl might have been nice but she had been just as keen for another boy, so they could play together. But with the prospect of two more children, she suddenly, despite her best intentions, cared. With four boys, would she feel like an outsider? A reluctant pusher of cars, a flier of superheroes, who would never get to revisit her own childhood? When she was old, would any of them know to paint her nails or bring her women's magazines?

'There's one; its kidney, fingers, toes, brain and a *penis*. It's a boy!' The nurse slipped the sonar around the jelly. 'We'll find the other one now.'

Serena waited, turning over the words. A boy. A boy.

'And here's number two, see the fingers quite clearly there, and look at those two spots, they're the ovaries, and there's the kidney and the brain . . .'

'Hang on. My ovaries?'

'No. This is a girl. You have one boy and one girl in here. How does that sound?'

When Serena stopped crying, she dressed and went into a nearby cafe for a piece of cake and a juice. A boy and a girl, she whispered silently. A boy and a girl. A girl and a boy. They would know each other in there, long before she knew them.

She checked her mobile. One message from an hour earlier. 'Serena, it's Dave here. God I'm so sorry, but I'm just getting dragged into a last-minute meeting, is there any chance you could reschedule the ultrasound? I really don't want to miss it . . . give me a call.'

Serena stared at the phone for a few minutes, then she dialled the real-estate agent.

'It's Serena McAllister here . . .'

'Yes, I've thought about it, and I've decided to go ahead with the sale of that Clifton Hill flat . . . Butterworth Street . . .'

'That's great. As soon as you can.'

25

Ana woke again, this time in her own bed. She sat up and pushed away the doona. It was late. Nine-fifteen. The *Morning Star* office had been ticking over for hours without her. Her head ached and her heart felt bruised, and it was a few seconds before she remembered why.

She saw her jeans on the floor, the blood-stained underpants. Elijah. She had slammed out of there in the middle of the night and caught a taxi home. Was it a home? Sometimes it felt like nothing more than a hole in the wall, a shelf on which to park herself when she wasn't working. She crossed to the bedroom window and peered out, wrapping the matchstick blind over her semi-nudity. Half a dozen people dressed in black stood at the tramstop, holding briefcases. Two of them still with wet hair. She had to be at work in time for news conference, and she had to have an idea for a column or three. It never ended.

She dressed, gathered up the papers and took them on the tram, trying to hang onto the strap and read at the same time. She scanned every article for something, anything from which she could squeeze some outrage. Anger was easy, anger was the short cut for days like this. Anyone could write an angry column, there was an endless supply of things in the world to be indignant about. You could even make it seem slightly original if you paired your anger with an unlikely cause, such as, for example, this story on one council's plan to bring in a curfew on cats. All cats indoors by seven o'clock or shot on sight. It was an article to have a laugh over but maybe she could throw her lot in with the cats, defend their natural right to yowl around in the dark and destroy wildlife. The tram stopped, and she rested her head on her arm, fully extended to hold onto the strap. Around her, passengers swayed and the iron of the tram clanked and dragged.

She sighed, sick to her stomach about the night before. She felt newly and definitely single, cold winds circling her. She thought about the scene she had caused, Elijah blinking helplessly in the light, this man she'd had sex with just hours earlier, tender, fantastic, sexy sex, and then there she was like some harpie grilling him about something in his private cupboard. A nicer girl would have simply kept a polite silence about it, or waited until breakfast to raise the question, instead of ripping into his sleep like she had. Did she really have to *resolve* everything, *get it all out in the open*? Could she not find a little dignified reserve from somewhere, a little aloofness maybe?

I don't care, she told herself. Creepy, secretive lawyer type. She wiped away tears and ducked her head to peer under somebody's arm, to see where she was. Parliament House. A few minutes to go. Time to think up at least one idea.

'Nice of you to come, Ana.' Lowenthal glanced at her coldly as she crept into conference and took the last seat.

'Sorry,' she winced. They continued talking, apparently about some brilliant idea that poster boy Dave Williams had conjured up, for a page called Crime Watch. Police furnished the paper with juicy detail of unsolved crimes and the *Star* published it on a set page as a community service, therefore making themselves look like a good citizen at the same time as they got exclusive and hopefully lurid crime detail.

Ana's face dropped as the concept grew more and more familiar. 'What a great idea,' she hissed to Pete Pryor as the meeting broke up. 'Why didn't I think of it myself?'

'Citizen's Arrest, I seem to remember yours was called.'

'What's the difference? He's stolen my idea, and renamed it.'

'Marketing is everything these days, my love.'

'Don't you think that's outrageous?' They were the last two in the conference room.

'No. I think it's newspapers. And why were you late to conference? Out romping with the new boyfriend again?'

She felt her eyes fill with tears. 'I think we've broken up.' She heard the sob in her voice, and pressed her hands to her face in horror. 'Oh God. I'm sorry.' Was she, Ana Haverfield, grown-up career woman, really crying like a teenage girl? Pete closed the door and guided her into a chair.

'Don't be sorry, Ana. Human beings do this all the time. You'll get the hang of it.'

Oh, God. Awash with loneliness, she remembered

Finn, and thought, wouldn't it be awful if he ever felt like this? Awful at two, awful at five, awful at thirty-eight. Maybe she should go and get him right now, take him to the park. Or she could take him to see her mother again. Maybe if Ana joined up all the lonely people she knew, they could – what? Make a family? Make a newspaper? She knew there was a better life outside these walls, but it seemed so distant, she wasn't sure she'd survive the trip there.

'Did I ever tell you I was a surf lifesaver?' Lily asked.

Ana had dropped in from work, with some primal urge to throw herself in her mother's arms.

'No,' she said, sadly. 'Mum, I broke up with my boyfriend. Remember Elijah?'

'Yes, dear. Anyway, I tried to save Harold Holt from drowning,' her mother whispered, cognisant enough to conceal her revelation from Doris Kneebone, who was knitting on the next couch. 'He put his arms around my neck and I tried to swim for shore with him.'

'Mum . . .' Ana kneaded her own forehead. 'Did you hear me? I really feel . . . pretty sad about this.'

'He had big shoulders,' said her mother, her head cocked as if she were listening to something far away. 'I held his back against my breasts and he laughed, because the fish were tickling his legs.'

'Right.'

'He said it felt like they were kissing him, so gently.' Her mother held up her fingers like a beak and made kissing motions.

Ana could feel herself starving for oxygen.

'But he was too heavy for me.' Lily suddenly had pools of tears in her eyes and she glanced furtively at Doris Kneebone, quickly wiping her own face.

'One pearl, one plain, one pearl, two plain ...' whispered Doris, eyes fixed on her steel needles.

'I couldn't hold him. He slipped through my hands like ...' She held out her arms helplessly. The same arms that had held Nick's waist, that had pushed against gravity and the tyranny of the rope around the neck, too late, too late.

She covered her face and sobbed. Doris Kneebone knitted on. Lily suddenly lifted her head.

'So you won't be a mother then, will you?'

'What do you mean?'

'If you've broken up with that man and his son, you won't have to be a mother. To that boy.'

Ana considered her for a minute.

'You know, Mum, I will still be a mother. I will.'

Driving back to the office, Ana considered her family. Once, it was something an observer might have envied, but that was so long ago. Once, it was Nick's job to shine all the shoes on Sunday nights, and Ana's job to feed the guinea pigs. Lily had cooked hot dinners and Ana's dad came home to eat them and he could always make Lily laugh.

Then one day Nick, a tall fifteen, went to the auction of the Andersons' home across the road. Standing alone in a suit, he bid, again and again, until he won the house, and was escorted inside by the agent to meet the beaming owners. Their jaws dropped when they recognised their neighbour's child.

'I'd like to pay you in car engines,' he announced. 'I have access to many.'

Then the bad years began, and soon after that Ana and Nick's dad went to find Some Sort Of A Life with another woman he knew through work.

From then on, her mother was always crying. It was the soundtrack of their lives. Ana would come in from school, make herself a sandwich and go to her room. Nick would be in his room, watching TV in a medicated haze. Lily would sob quietly at the kitchen table.

'Ana, can we talk?'

It was Elijah. The blood rushed to her head so she could barely think. 'Okay.'

'I mean can we get together? Maybe tonight?'

She paused. 'Are you going to tell me what happened with you and Priya?'

She heard him sigh. She could picture him, sitting in his small office with the gable windows and the sticker that said *Go Hard or Go Home!* on the side of the filing cabinet.

'I can tell you that it doesn't matter, that it makes no difference to us, that it was a long time ago.'

'Exactly when did it happen, this thing you won't tell me about, that doesn't matter?'

He hesitated, and in that pause she heard the weight of his own fears. 'I can't remember.'

'A bit less than three years ago?' She sketched some figures on her notepad. 'October, maybe?'

'I don't —'

'She was happily married, you know.' Ana suddenly

hated him, wanted to hurt. 'There was only one reason she would have cheated on Richard. And you know what that reason was, don't you?'

He was silent.

'She used you. You thought she was a married woman driven mad by lust for you, didn't you, but she just wanted one thing from you.'

He sounded indignant. 'Look that's really none of your . . . That's a completely unacceptable thing to insinuate.'

'What, that she wasn't driven mad by lust for you?'

'You know what I mean.'

'So you did have sex with her?'

'Look, I really don't think I have to discuss that with you.'

'Don't you? Well, it's your choice.'

'What's that meant to mean?'

'It only means that it's up to you. But I can't love someone who's concealing something so important from me . . .'

'Ana! What are you saying?'

'How would I know what else you might be concealing from me?'

'Ana, please. I can't bear this.'

'Well, tell me then. I mean, obviously you did sleep with her.'

'I'm not discussing it! And if you can't treat me like an adult, well maybe you're right.'

'About what?' Her heart suddenly thumping.

'You're the one making ultimatums.'

'What are you saying, you want to break up?'

'Well, what choice are you giving me?'

'Okay. Okay. If that's the way you feel about it . . .'

There was a long pause, her disbelief growing to fill it. He would say something to stop this happening. He would. He would.

Elijah sighed. 'Okay, Ana. My partner will handle Finn's inheritance from here. He'll call you in the next day or so.' He paused as if waiting for her to say something, to drag them back from the brink. But she couldn't speak, and he continued. 'Good luck.'

And he hung up.

26

Ana moved through the next week in a daze. That was it for her. There would never be anyone else like Elijah. She would grow old, and remember him as the best man she had ever met. She would always be single.

On Friday morning, Marnie rang and invited her to come to her mothers' group. It was a plea from the heart.

'I need you. And you need to take a day off work. Give yourself time to absorb this?'

'I'm too sad.'

'Please? These people scare me.'

Ana raised her elbow onto the mattress, her curiosity piqued. 'Scare you? Marnie, I remember when Jeff Kennett told you to fuck off and you still kept asking him that question, in fact *AM* replayed you asking it six times. You cannot be scared of a bunch of lactating mothers.'

'I know. But I am,' Marnie said, sadly. 'I just feel like I'm doing everything wrong when I'm there.'

'So why do you go?'

'Because I learn things from them. I'm hoping I'll learn how to do it all better.'

Ana rolled her body out of bed. She felt lethargic with misery, but once she started moving, she found all her limbs still working as normal. It almost surprised her. She arranged to collect Finn and to meet Marnie at her local community centre.

Fridays were Marnie's day off, and she spent the mornings with this mothers' group, where, as far as Ana could see, she was made to feel guilty for being a working mother. It didn't seem like much of a way to spend your one weekday at home with the baby, and she made a mental note to say so to Marnie, later.

In the community centre, the babies were placed on mats in a circle and the mothers sat behind them. Finn played with some blocks and the women threw out their hands when he strayed too close to their mats. They ate Tim Tams and compared sleep routines with the precision of scientists.

'Tully's waking every two hours to feed.'

'Oh my God. I don't know how you got yourself here. Lachlan's waking just twice a night now.' A weary looking blonde, who might have been, and could still be, attractive, if she could be bothered, or maybe if she could get enough sleep.

'But when do you put him down? What do you count as twice a night?' A very fat woman with greying hair scraped back in a ponytail. Her daughter was in the latest pink designer gear, while the mother wore a shapeless tracksuit, as if she had funnelled all her sartorial energy into her offspring at birth.

'Down at eleven. Feed at two, feed at five, sleeps 'til eight.' The blonde spoke proudly.

'You go to sleep at eleven?' Grey Hair was aghast. Ana wondered at her age, she looked well into her forties.

'Well, no, I go to sleep at nine-thirty. Mike stays up with him.'

'Well that's three times a night then. Isn't it. Really.' Grey Hair made a broad appeal for consensus. The blonde one turned away irritably and busied herself with her nappy bag.

'Mia's waking four times a night.' A friendly looking Italian woman. Grey Hair piped up again, the police-woman of the truth.

'Really? But what do you call four times a night?'

'Ten, twelve, four and six.'

'Six isn't night.'

'Jesus, it is for me. She'll go back to sleep then until eight.'

'Are you feeding both breasts?' Marnie spoke, sounding nervous. They all stared at her in surprise.

'No.' The Italian woman sounded thoughtful. 'I get too tired. And she falls asleep after one.'

Marnie was speaking so quietly Ana could hardly hear her. Her feisty friend was drowning in this place.

'Well maybe if you wake her up and feed both breasts she'll fill up better and sleep longer.'

The women all stared at her, as if waiting for some-one else to address the puzzling issue of which language she was speaking.

'Well, that makes sense.' Ana nodded encouragingly at them. Like she knew anything about breastfeeding. But somebody, please, speak to her friend Marnie, who looked like she was going to burst into tears.

'Are you still expressing milk at work?' Grey Hair

directed the question at Marnie. The room fell utterly silent. Even the babies seemed to hold their breath, waiting for the answer.

'Yes. She's fully breastfed still. We'll start solids this week.' Marnie stroked Lucy's head, her hair still just fuzz on her peachy skull.

'She gets five feeds a day?'

'Sometimes six.'

There was silence and the Italian woman spoke sympathetically. 'Did you have to go back for financial reasons?' She was almost nodding, as if prompting Marnie.

'No. I love my job.'

All seemed to release their breaths simultaneously. Two women exchanged quick glances. The room was silent, but screamed with things unsaid.

'I think they're just in awe of you,' Ana said later. 'Really, they're so impressed they don't know how to handle you.'

'Do you think?' Marnie's face lit up.

'What does it matter what they think?'

'It doesn't, it's just . . .' her voice trailed off.

'Why don't you find another mothers' group. There must be other ones in your area.'

'Where would you find them?'

'You're a journalist. That's what you do, you find things. Do you have the internet here?'

'Yes.'

'Get on and look up mums' groups in your area. Ring around from work and find one with working mothers, people who are on your wavelength. Or start one.'

'I will, Ana. I will. Just as soon as I get through this pile of washing, make dinner, feed Lucy and express some milk.'

'Excellent. And this cutlery needs a good polish too.'

'You really have no idea, do you?'

'You're right. What would I know, I can't even seem to keep a boyfriend longer than two months these days. Hey, Marnie, I was joking.'

'I know you were. But you still have no idea.'

'That's crap. I have an imagination. I know what it is to feel tired, and depended on, and done over at work, and disapproved of by women my own age. I can put that all together and have a rough guess at what you're feeling.'

'It's the guilt. The love, the responsibility . . .'

'You must come and meet my mother some day . . .'

'And I want these women to *like* me . . .'

'*That* feeling I know. That one is not unique to new mothers, and really, can't you find a nicer group of women to want to like you? I mean, give yourself half a chance here. Go and choose your own mums' group. Do interviews. You deserve something friendlier than this. More supportive.'

'*Choose* a mums' group?' Marnie feigned shock. 'That's just not how it works, Ana. That's like saying go choose a family. You get *put* in a mums' group by the maternal health nurse, and then you have to cut it. To shop around for one, it'd be like cheating.'

Ana spent her day off wandering restlessly around Melbourne, unable to settle to anything. She went to the organic fruit and vegetable shop over the road from Elijah's apartment block, and sauntered around a trolley of biodynamic bananas. She frowned at some Daylesford apples and ran a fingertip over some mandarins; pores open, jackets loose.

Why had she said those things to him? *Priya used you . . .*

There was no one, no one in the world she ached so much to talk to right now. She took a Nashi fruit from its paper cradle and rolled it between her two palms. She had a terrible feeling that it was a moment, a fork in the road to which she would never return. She looked over at his apartment, his window. She saw nothing but a curtain.

'Please don't handle the fruit.'

'Sorry.'

'Unless you plan to buy something.'

She stood at the door of the shop, East Timorese coffee on one side, a stack of Barwon Heads strawberries in-process-of-organic-accreditation on the other, and touched her fingers to her lip.

Elijah came out. She quickly stepped behind the strawberries. He was with a girl, a young woman, dark haired, attractive, familiar looking. She had a baby on her hip, and Ana recognised her, with relief, from the photos in Elijah's flat: one of his sisters. The youngest. He stretched one arm behind her as they crossed the road, shepherding her, because it was his road and his traffic and he was a worrier. She could see that now. For all his bravado, he worried that people would get hurt. She wondered where that came from. Now she would never know.

And he was beautiful, she could see that too. It was in his eyes, his mouth, his patient face, the mature restraint of him.

She drove to Serena's and chased Finn and Cooper out into weak winter sunlight to play hide and seek. She found herself in the cubby, knees pulled up to her chest, sitting beside a plastic train with no wheels, and a pile of rocks. Each was cut smooth on one side, ragged as a shadow on the other. Tiny black lettering marked each rock; X105 Mitta; RF200 Dogwood. She turned them over, stroked the smooth sides. Felt a fondness for Serena's neat handwriting. Wondered whether twenty years ago a woman like Serena would ever have felt compelled to have a career; something to leave behind for children.

For herself, journalism had given her life direction, after the losses of her adolescence. Jason Lowenthal offered her a job while she was in the top ranks of her university course and she accepted. In the newsroom she rediscovered the routine and order of her childhood. She worked with people from happy families and wrote about other people's disasters. She learned to drive by getting in *Morning Star* cars and travelling out to murder scenes, car crashes, court dramas and later, political stoushes. She learned that everyone has their personal tragedy in life and if they haven't had it yet, well, it's still coming.

'Ready or not, here I come.'

She climbed down the ladder and cast a glance around the garden. Cooper and Finn's arms and legs stuck out from behind a tree and there were giggles. She veered off in another direction and wondered aloud.

'Where could those boys possibly be . . .'

After several games, Ana retired to sit cross-legged on Serena's couch, sipping a mug of hot chocolate. Cooper fossicked through the pocket of Ana's jacket, keeping one eye on his mother. Finn drove a train down her thigh.

Serena stared at Ana.

'*Priya*'s toilet bag? In his bathroom cupboard?'

Ana nodded. Serena shook her head.

'But why?'

'Well, it seems fairly obvious why. Something happened between them.' She raised her eyebrows suggestively at her friend. 'But he won't tell me. It's all, you know, can't reveal a friend's secret, blah blah blah.'

Serena looked shocked. 'When do you think this happened?'

Ana looked meaningfully at Finn, who was pushing a train around a wooden track. 'Who knows?'

Serena shook her head. 'I can't believe it. She didn't say a word.'

'Well, I don't know for sure. I'm only guessing.'

Serena nodded, lost in thought. Ana watched her.

'Do you think Priya would have set out to . . . I mean, you know how they were having trouble conceiving . . .'

'I don't know.' Serena pulled her into the kitchen, away from Finn and Cooper. She put the kettle on to boil, her back to Ana.

Ana held a rattle and turned it over. 'Lately I've been thinking about all the things I didn't like about Priya. Do you think that's bad?'

Serena examined a teabag and spoke slowly. 'I guess

256

when people die, you make them out to be perfect for a while. But that can't last.'

Ana stared out the back window at the garden, drifts of dry leaves up against fences and trees. The branches were bare against the sky, and without their protection, the suburban homes behind were stark and intrusive. The chickens were nowhere to be seen, probably huddled inside their hutch against the wintery weather.

'Priya wasn't perfect,' she said, with tears in her eyes. 'She had secrets she didn't tell us.'

Serena folded her arms, her eyes vacant. 'It seems so,' she said at last. 'It seems so.'

'She was so regal, like she thought she was some queen.' Ana was sobbing now. Serena hastily closed the door between the kitchen and the lounge room where the boys played. Ana rubbed her eyes. 'We shared everything with her, and she, she was holding out on us.'

'She was just a private person.'

'She was inconsiderate of other people. She only ever thought of herself! How could she have cheated on Richard? How could she have left me her son in her will and not bothered to tell me? Not even prepared me for that possibility?' Ana wept hopelessly into her hands. Had she ever liked Priya? Right at this moment, only four months after the car accident that killed her, Ana couldn't think of one good thing about the woman she had called a friend for so long.

Serena put her arm around her. 'Ana, if what you think happened really did happen, then it was a long time before you even knew Elijah. Priya didn't sleep with your boyfriend. She slept with someone who would become your boyfriend. And if he wants to keep a promise not to discuss that, I think he sounds very honourable.'

Ana stared at her through her tears. Very honourable? Had she broken up with a man who was not only good-looking, kind and funny, but very honourable?

Oh God.

The boys clattered into the kitchen as Ana was wiping her face. Finn crouched over Ana's handbag, dressed in only a woollen jumper, and extracted her mobile phone. His bare bottom cheeks were the colour of milky coffee, his thighs still pudgy, and he pressed the phone's buttons with furious concentration, narrowing his eyes at the tinny beep each button made.

'Ana's a bit sad,' Serena whispered to Cooper.

He held up his digger and leaned on Ana's legs.

'I give her my digger.'

Ana burst into fresh tears and cradled the digger to her heart. Cooper looked anxious and Finn stood and stared at her.

'My turn now,' Cooper said gravely. Ana gave back the digger and mopped her face again.

Cooper rested his chin on Ana's leg.

'We're havin' a barby,' he said.

'A barby? In your backyard? How lovely.' She blew her nose distractedly and smiled at Finn. His face broke into a shy grin and he lifted the edge of his jumper, revealing his round belly. Ana wanted to gather him on her lap and squeeze him.

'No, a barby. We're havin' a barby. In Mummy's tummy.' Cooper patted his own. 'Two barbies.'

'Of course. You are, aren't you?'

Ana looked down into Finn's waiting brown eyes and felt her blood quicken.

27

'You've just missed Ana,' Serena told Elijah, bringing coffees out to her deck and pulling a chair into the weak winter sun. 'Did you check there's nothing wet on that seat? I'd hate it to wreck your suit.' She and Angus had just been startled from a rare hour alone by the lawyer's knock on the door.

'Ana?' Elijah paused with a spoon of sugar hovering above his coffee. 'Was she here?'

'She's taken Finn to see Priya's mothers' group. They've rung me a few times and I haven't had time, and she had today off, so she said she'd take him.'

'And your older boy?' He looked around.

'My mother-in-law's staying with us. She's taken Cooper out, to a drumming workshop.'

'Ah.'

He stirred his coffee and stared into it. He smiled. 'Ana at mothers' group,' he murmured. 'Now there's a thought.'

'Mmm,' said Serena, preoccupied by her old maternity pants, which kept sliding down under her belly to reveal her flesh. Well, it wasn't like he'd called to warn her he was coming. She tugged her top down. What on earth was he doing here?

Elijah sipped and leaned back in his chair, smiling. 'She'll have interrogated them all in the first hour, and informed each of them of their problems and various faults, and then she'll move on to advising them how to raise their children.'

Serena laughed. He obviously knew Ana well.

He reached into his coat pocket and put a brightly wrapped package onto the table. 'I brought a little present for Finn.'

'That's nice of you.' She waited.

'I was thinking about what you said that last time you called me? About how maybe Richard wasn't Finn's father?'

'Yes.' She bit her lip as she remembered. It seemed Priya had been unfaithful with not just one man, but two. But when? Serena thought about that weekend at Dogwood, nine months before Finn was born. Could Priya have been sleeping with Elijah as well, at about the same time? Fed up with Richard's refusal to be tested, could she have finally decided to take matters into her own hands with not just one but two men? Or three, or more even?

'I was wondering, did Richard know Priya was being unfaithful to him?'

Serena looked out at her chickens. Angus tottered across the grass and fell on his padded bottom. She shifted her weight in the chair to get comfortable.

'No,' she said, and hastily corrected herself. 'I don't think so.'

He nodded thoughtfully, and she went inside and brought out some biscuits. Angus tottered around them.

'The three of you were good friends at uni, weren't you?' He took a biscuit.

'We were.'

He smiled at her, watching her with a curiosity that made her blush. She stood, one hand on her round belly to hold her misbehaving pants in check. 'Angus! Not for eating!' Her son took the end of a garden hose out of his mouth and regarded her sorrowfully. Elijah smiled and the brown skin around his eyes wrinkled. He was good looking, intelligent, kind . . . how could Ana have let him go?

'You've got a lot on your plate. You must be getting keen for Ana to take Finn.'

Serena nodded, sitting down. 'She's been househunting pretty hard.'

He nodded. 'She has.'

'I'm sorry it didn't work out with you two.' Might as well wade in boldly. But his face closed down, and she regretted her words.

He nodded curtly. 'I just wanted to let you know that my partner will handle everything with Finn from here on.' He handed her a business card. 'He's very good. It's just that it's no longer appropriate that I . . . what with Ana . . .' He trailed off awkwardly.

'That's a shame. I think Finn had grown to like you.'

He nodded, expressionless now, and rose to his feet. Again, she wished she hadn't spoken, and she struggled to get out of the chair to show him out.

He grasped her hand and helped her up. On her feet, she found he was still holding her hand, regarding her with curious admiration.

'It's a wonderful thing you've given Finn,' he said.

'To open your heart and care for another child at such a time. Priya could not have wished for better friends.'

Serena's eyes filled with tears, as if they had been waiting there all along.

All too soon, it was Jo's last day. Tomorrow, she would load up the Bedford, fill the tank with petrol and start the long drive north. Her visit had been a nugget of blessed reprieve for Serena. Jo rose every day at dawn with the children, and silently observed as her son threw down a coffee and whirled out of the house. She pulled the plug on the television and brought a crate of craft materials out of the belly of the Bedford. She sent Cooper and Finn outside to collect leaves and sticks and treasures, and then sat with them at the kitchen table sticking them onto sheets of brown paper, Angus crushing leaves in his fat little hands. She got Finn finger painting, and Cooper threading spaghetti necklaces. Mid-morning, she loaded up the pram and walked them to the park, where she sat on the bench and drank nettle tea from a thermos and read her *Unicorn* magazine, in between pushing swings and catching children at the bottom of slides. During this time, Serena sat in the echoes of her empty home and waited for the racket of her mind to quieten. At first the silence was faintly alarming, but after a few days of such breaks, she befriended the quiet. She could sit and feel her babies kick inside her, a sensation she was usually too busy to even notice. Her tense limbs unwound, and she drifted to sleep on the couch, in the winter sun through the window, or on her bed, the smell of Dave still in it like some ghost creature.

Sometimes she felt she had already left Dave, as if in spending so much time thinking about it, planning the possibility of it, she had somehow erased him from her life. He came home at nine o'clock, ten, eleven, and she found her anger had gone. Maybe watching Jo's growing disgust at her son's absence relieved her own need to be angry. Or maybe, she had simply given up.

'They grow up so fast,' Jo whispered, backing out of the children's bedroom one night. 'It seems every day I've been here Angus has learned something new.'

'Mmm,' said Serena. She studied the TV guide and considered plugging the set back in. Her mother-in-law sat on the couch beside her and folded her arms. Her long grey hair was loose on her shoulders and a chain with a silver fairy pendent sat on the leathery skin of her cleavage. She leaned down to catch Serena's eye.

'Before you know it they'll be at school.'

Serena closed her magazine. 'So people say.'

'Well, it's true. They're like this for such a short time. Make the most of it.'

Serena nodded and stroked the remote control thoughtfully. *Make the most of it.* She didn't know how she could make any more of it without giving up eating, or showering, or breathing. All the videos she had taken of her babies, hardly any of them replayed, because there was simply never time amid the deluge of the real thing. *Make the most it.* Make less of it, now there was a goal to strive for.

But now, after two weeks of Jo, Serena's cheeks were flushed the pale pink of the well rested. She had the ragged ends of her blonde hair trimmed, the natural highlights of summer already making way for a more honeyed winter growth. She bought new maternity clothes to get her through the last three months of the pregnancy – sleek jeans with cunning tricks at the belly, stretchy tops that flapped around her thighs and showed off her slim arms, muscled from picking up toddlers. Her blue eyes were dewy and deep with the polish of pregnancy; her skin shone. Her breasts were swollen, her round belly was so huge it made her legs look thin. She was a picture of health and life, and both men and women turned in the street to watch her pass. She basked in this pregnant glow. It was like being nineteen again, although with the assurance to stand the stares, and the wisdom, now, to know it would fade all too quickly.

It was in this state that she rang Poss and asked him out to dinner. She felt guilty about asking Jo to babysit on her last night, but Dave promised to come home early and spend some time with his mother. Serena doubted he would, but that was their problem now. She lied, said she was going out with a girlfriend from school. Jo bathed the children and packed them off to bed with her usual efficiency. She watched the care Serena took with her make-up, and said nothing about her new clothes.

When Serena entered the restaurant, people turned automatically, paused in their conversations. Then, most turned back to their companions, having silently registered her heavy state of pregnancy – only six months, but she looked about eight. She sat at Poss's table and he stared at her.

'You look . . . incredible.'

'Thanks. How was your trip?'

He nodded. 'I gave the paper on the Tasman fold

belt. Thanks for helping with that.' He kept glancing away from her, into the crowds around them.

She felt dreamy, floating in other people's consciousness, drifting on the furious life within her. She recognised Poss's nervousness, the memory of the awkward moment at her front door still between them. She asked him more about his trip, the paper he had given, and he relaxed a little, although still staring at some point over her left shoulder most of the time. They ate their entrees and finally she couldn't stand it any longer.

'Can we talk?'

He paled, his face shutting down. 'We are talking, aren't we?' A sort of flippant irritability.

She leaned forward as best she could, her legs splayed under the table to stop from squashing her belly and lungs.

'Last time I saw you, I felt like something had changed between us.' She wasn't nervous, felt every word she spoke was inevitable. Watched the guarded look in his brown eyes with patience; she had known him in every mood, every season of emotion, too many to be intimidated by him. He was a good man, an attractive man, more unpredictable than Dave, edgier, less solid. But just as kind. He had been there in the wings all those years, and suddenly she could see he had been there for a reason. Some ember between them had been blown on, had flared up like the future.

He said nothing, just watched her warily. She wasn't afraid.

'We've been friends for a long time, Poss.'

'We have.' Quick to agree with that one.

'Are we . . . am I . . .' She hesitated now, unsure for the first time.

He said carefully, 'We've been friends for a very long time, Serena.'

'I think a lot of you.'

'I think a lot of you too, Serena. You're a very special person.' Again, the watching, the waiting.

She quailed, lost her nerve completely. 'Well, that's good, isn't it?'

He smiled, a grin that touched his eyes for the first time that night, as if he were amused, relieved.

'You're funny tonight.'

She shook her head. 'Things are falling to shit with Dave.'

He nodded. 'That's a shame. He's a good man.'

She felt rebuked. 'Maybe. We're growing apart.'

'Serena, I can't believe you're saying this.'

'He's obsessed with work. I never see him.'

'He cares a lot about you.'

She stared at him, puzzled. 'I think I'm going to leave him.'

He raised his eyebrows, dropped his eyes to her belly. 'Hell of a time.'

She blinked. 'I've got money. I don't need to stay in a bad marriage just for the children.' Had she got this wrong? Was he scared of what she represented, a woman with children?

She suddenly didn't want to be there any more, had to blink hard. 'Actually, I don't feel so well.' She pushed her chair back and clutched her napkin, dropped it on the table. 'I might head home.'

'I'll take you.'

He walked her into the foyer. Outside it was raining and they hesitated in the doorway, Poss's arm under hers, lightly touching. He opened an umbrella over them both and they stepped out and hesitated again, together.

'What are we doing?' he murmured into her hair and she started to laugh helplessly, tears still in her eyes. He pulled her outside, into the dark, and still under the umbrella she turned up her face and kissed him.

He smelled of grass and bush and of all her favourite memories of field trips. He felt like coming home, more than Dave had ever done. He held her like she was the most precious of things, kissed her with one hand behind the crook of her neck, cradling her jaw, his fingers in her hair. She felt dizzy with joy, with possibility, and when he pulled away, she saw his eyes were shiny with tears.

'You are beautiful,' he whispered. 'You are the most beautiful pregnant woman I think I've ever seen.'

She stared at him, breathed him in. 'Take me home,' she whispered back. 'Where are you staying?'

He stared at her for a long moment, agonised longing in his eyes. Then he shook his head, stepped back. It had stopped raining and he shook his umbrella, closed it. 'I can't do this.'

'What?'

'I can't do this to Dave. I couldn't put another man through what Renae put me through.'

Serena stared at him in disbelief.

'You should try to work things out with Dave. You

have two kids, soon to be four. He doesn't deserve to have them taken away from him.'

Serena curled her lip. 'What would you know? Don't tell *me* what *he* deserves . . .'

He stared at her, winced. 'I'm sorry.'

She couldn't believe it. He had literally pushed her away. She felt huge, fat, ridiculous.

'Oh.' She sounded mildly indignant, when what she really felt was fury.

'You are beautiful, Serena. A gorgeous woman, and if it wasn't —'

'Oh, please.' She wrapped her jacket more tightly around herself and stared away from him, towards the taxi rank. All she wanted now was to get away from his embarrassing apologies. She waved furiously at a taxi. Poss huddled into his coat as the taxi wheeled slowly around and headed toward them. He was at her shoulder again as the car slowed.

'Can you tell me something before you go?'

'What?'

'Do you really think I'm Finn's father?'

She turned and stared at him, aghast. 'How did you . . . I mean, what makes you think . . .'

'You've dropped enough hints.'

'I have *not*. What a crazy idea.' She yanked open the back door of the taxi and threw in her bag. Turned to glare at him one last time. He stared at her.

'Please don't be angry with me. You're one of my best friends, my favourite person, a gorgeous woman. But I just couldn't do this to Dave . . .'

She shook her head, mortified, and lowered herself

into the taxi. 'Northcote,' she told the driver. She looked at Poss one last time through the window, but the raindrops blurred his image, and he retreated to the warmth of the doorway as the taxi pulled away.

28

Ana pressed save and looked up from her keyboard like a diver surfacing. Out through the eleventh-floor windows, ship lights twinkled on the mass of black that was Port Phillip Bay. Sub-editors arrived and slung bags under desks, trailing the aura of work-free days with pre-schoolers and golf clubs and all the other pleasant compensations of shift work. Ana checked her personal file with satisfaction: the rough drafts of three columns sat like cash in a wallet. Rainy-day pieces. Good to have something in case you got sick. At least breaking up with Elijah had helped her get ahead with work. Maybe this was her fate – single career woman for the rest of her life. She hoped the *Star* would have something for her to do when she was sixty-five and still rattling around these halls. Dusting the library window sills, or dementia correspondent, or something.

It was two months since her last curt conversation with Elijah, and winter had truly set in. The deepest point of a Melbourne winter always felt like it would last forever: rain-whipped train platforms, the unsociable rush from office to home and back again, the bitter snow clouds hailed as gifts by those heading for the ski fields. There were fewer houses on the market and Ana met the same people again and again at inspections, obediently leaving shoes in a wet pile at doorways, shimmying in socked feet down the ubiquitous baltic floorboards, or drifting back to cars in despair after auctions. Her rivals were mostly couples, and she tried not to stare longingly at their whispered conferences, held in lean-to extensions or while staring at asbestos garages. She made her own notes, pressed agents for reasonable estimates of prices, and drew circles on folded pieces of news print, which littered the otherwise empty passenger seat of her car. She picked up Finn every weekend, and avoided the cafes where she and Elijah had once stopped for morning teas. She bid at auctions, at first tentatively, but quickly getting the hang of it. While her confidence rose, her hopes sank with each auction lost, each record reached and broken. It was the worst of times to buy property. Her latest dream home was a double-fronted Californian bungalow in Northcote, its gracious front porch hidden under sheets of ugly masonite, like a gift wrapped in newspaper. Painted a monstrous shade of green, the house had brown striped carpet on the floors, a kitchen where every cupboard door stuck, and smelled of dogs. But there was an elegant old elm tree in the front. A back yard so big and bare, tumbleweed fluttered over it. A gate in the back fence leading out to parklands; banksias, wattles, eucalypt. Best of all, it was a fifteen-minute walk to Serena's house.

Every day she thought of calling Elijah, and sometimes she even got as far as dialling his number, but she would be shaking violently by the time she pressed the last button and she always hung up. Early afternoons, late nights, she yearned for him the most. On bad days, she would give herself small treats for every hour she endured without dialling. A five-minute break to read the paper. An extra coffee. A piece of chocolate. Her treats were like Hansel and Gretel's white stones, leading her through the forest of her winter days one by one. Hour by hour.

She had taken Finn again to visit her mother. Ana had woken at dawn one Sunday morning in a cold sweat, having dreamt she found Finn cold, blue, dead in the little bed beside her own. Waking, she hurled herself at the lamp in a sightless terror, almost knocking it off the bedside table. The room jumped out at her in a golden pool, and Finn, in a real-life bed beside her own, turned his head restlessly, as if to comfort her. Ana watched him breathe and wondered if she could stand this.

Later, she asked Lily, 'How do you stop worrying all the time, that something bad will happen to them?'

She didn't really expect an answer. But her mother, this time, took Finn onto her lap and studied him carefully. Her breath seemed short, almost panting, and the doctor said she had been complaining of headaches. Finn reached out for Lily's shiny glasses and she gently checked his hand, and stroked his cheek with the back of a finger wizened by nicotine.

'You leave them in God's hands,' she said thoughtfully.

Ana switched off her computer and headed for the lift, exchanging monosyllables with Zac as they passed. He had been filling in for the past few weeks while Lowenthal visited sister papers in New York. Zac believed in an unnerving permeability between people's roles, and had a habit of springing a week in news on a sports reporter, or throwing a real-estate cadet into court reporting for a month. He had already made Ana do a few stints on news, a temporary demotion she had objected to on principle. Secretly, she hadn't much minded doing the news days; like most journalists she had a short attention span and was pleasantly distracted by the variety.

She was walking to the underground car park when her phone rang. It was Zac.

'Could you come back in and write an obit for Dizzy Harris? We're in the shit here, three reporters off sick and this arsehole has to crash his plane and die. Can you come?'

'Dizzy Harris?' Ana lost her breath. He was an Australian rock star gone global; his was the music of her teens. She had grown up with his face on her bedroom door.

When she got back upstairs, Zac gestured to the clock.

'Twenty minutes 'til second edition deadline. It'll run front page, not the splash but a runner. Library's been asked to do a search.'

Ana got onto the wires and checked the story – just two grabs so far.

Australian rock star Dizzy Harris believed dead in French hospital, AFP reporting. MORE

And then:

Australian musician Dizzy Harris confirmed dead in French hospital, after his light aircraft plummeted into the Mediterranean just off the coast of France. MORE

A third popped up while she was watching.

Swiss starlet Anya Horovitcz has also been confirmed dead. The pilot of the aircraft remains in a serious condition. MORE

Ana looked back at the first take. The wire service had a policy of marking urgent stories with a star, or two or even three stars. Dizzy Harris's death was rated only one star, probably by some aging editor who didn't even know who Dizzy Harris was. Ana rang the library.

'Cuttings for Dizzy Harris?'

'We'll bring them up in ten minutes.' Thank God, it was Brian Mitford, who had a brain and understood the meaning of the word deadline.

'Could you make it ten seconds? We go to press in eighteen minutes.'

'We're going as fast as we can.'

She hung up and started writing from memory. She soon discovered that there wasn't much there. She could name two of Dizzy's big hits – unbelievably, the rest had vanished from her memory. But there had been dozens. And hadn't he been in a couple of films, later in his life, when he was a little more drug wasted?

She could remember the last three celebrity girl-friends, she had at least kept up with that much of her trashy magazine reading. She jotted down their names and did a spell check on the internet. She fretted.

'How's it going?' The chief sub-editor leaned over her partition but backed away quickly at her glowering face. 'Sorry. Deadline's in —'

'I *know*!'

Be calm. Children. He had children, didn't he? And

parents. God, he had parents living in Melbourne, Ana realised, tense with adrenalin. Journalists the world over would be writing the same story, but she had Dizzy Harris's parents living just down the Eastern Freeway. She seized the phone book, panic rising as she glanced at the clock. This could be a giant waste of five minutes.

Harris. There were five pages of them. She despaired, then remembered Stephen Monkford, from high school. He had been an obsessed fan. He would know where Dizzy had grown up. And these days Stephen Monkford was a spokesman for the ACTU. Someone would have a mobile number for him.

She rang the industrial relations reporter. 'Jamie, hi, it's Ana. Have you got Stephen Monkford's mobile?'

'ACTU Monkford?'

'That's the one.'

'Is this an IR story? Should I come in?' Bristle, bristle.

'Not an IR story, but I can't explain. Bit under the pump.'

He suspiciously read off the number and Ana hung up, then rang it. Brian appeared at her desk with a stack of cuttings. Jesus, she only needed a tenth of that. A trickle of sweat ran down between her breasts. Ten minutes to go.

Breathe.

'Steve! Ana Haverfield here, from St Mary's. I hope I didn't wake you.'

'Ana! This is a surprise.'

She paused. To break the news of Dizzy Harris's death like this might render Stephen senseless with grief. He would hear soon enough and she would ring him back tomorrow.

She asked him where Harris's parents had lived, saying there was a rumour he had had a child with a supermodel whose name Ana hastily dragged out of her mind. She added she was right on deadline.

'Sure.' He mused thoughtfully. 'They lived in the next street from my cousins. My cousins lived in Primrose Street, Balwyn – the Harris's were in the next street, some name like a flower or a vegetable. I think it started with T.'

She thanked him quickly, hung up, grabbed a Melways and found Primrose Street. The next street along was Tulip. Zac appeared.

'What are you doing? We just need a wrap of his life, don't make phone calls. Start typing.'

He was right. She didn't have time for this. She nodded and threw the Melways aside. Forget it. All she needed was the basics. Who, what, where, when and why. It was a cut and paste job. Songs, girlfriends, drug problems, when he topped the US charts, brief mention of where he was born, and string it all together in a few short paragraphs that mixed the stately tone of a funeral procession with the rush of greedy, lewd detail. She shuffled back and forth through stories. Down in pictorial she knew they would be madly trawling through file photographs of Harris in his prime, then in his later decline, with this girlfriend, with that one. She typed hard, like she always did under pressure. As if pounding the keys instead of tapping them would somehow help.

'Leave her,' barked Zac. She looked up and he was

277

standing in front of her desk, sending a photographer away. 'No. No. Ask someone else.'

She felt a moment of deep gratitude and went back to hammering her keyboard until she wrote the last paragraph. ENDS.

She read back. It was all there. How he'd died, who he was, the crucial opening three pars heavy with emotion. It read easily, smoothly; not at all as if the author had written it with her heart smashing and her shirt soaked in sweat and the stale taste of panic in her mouth.

She still had three minutes. She checked the wires again. A new catch said Harris had been flying his own plane. Sources said he had been drinking alcohol and had consumed a considerable quantity of cocaine. Huge. She felt another rush of adrenalin, copied the new take and fed it into the second paragraph.

Zac swung around.

'Done?'

'Almost.' Fuck it, she had ninety seconds and she was going to do it. She dragged the phone book towards her, newspaper cuttings scattering on her lap and the floor. She found the number. Dialled and glanced at her watch. Almost eleven-thirty.

'No!' snapped Zac. 'Just send it.'

She ignored him. Her skin crawled.

Would they know? It must be on the radio by now.

'Hello?' A woman's voice. Elderly, well spoken, sleepy.

'Mrs Harris?' She sounded tight and breathless to herself. Zac froze and stared at her. 'Mrs Harris, it's Ana Haverfield from the *Morning Star* newspaper here. I'm terribly sorry to bother you but I'm calling in relation to your son Dizzy.'

'What? Please don't bother us at home. All queries should go to his agent in London.'

Ana paused. It was the right number. And the woman didn't know. But then, in that moment of silence, with an entire newsroom waiting at the other end of the line, Mrs Harris realised. Mothers of rock stars must dream these nightmares long before they happen.

'What?' she cried. 'Tell me!' Ana hesitated. The second hand ticked toward the deadline and she no longer cared. Zac raised a hand at the subs.

'He died in a plane crash tonight. I'm so sorry, Mrs Harris.'

There would be no rushing this call. She simply couldn't. She pressed the button and watched her existing story disappear, en route now to the subs' desk. She nodded at Zac and picked up a pen.

'My baby,' cried Mrs Harris. 'My baby.'

Even drug-addled rock stars were somebody's baby.

Ana quietly typed out three heart-rending quotes in the first sixty seconds of listening to Mrs Harris. She sent them through and waved at Zac, who might still have time to feed them into the story before it flashed through to the waiting printers at Westgate. Whether the quotes had missed the deadline or not, she no longer cared. At least there was a story. Ana turned on her telephone tape recorder and let the waves of Mrs Harris's grief wash over her. She went through the wires again, explaining what had happened and when, over and over. She waited for Mrs Harris to remember she was talking to a journalist, a stranger, because she knew that would come next. And it did.

'Well, thank you. I'm sorry. I must go.' Mrs Harris was suddenly aloof, although still crying. A new note of reserve. A sleepy, masculine voice spoke in the background; the next in line to have his world shattered. The family would shut down after this, she knew; they would issue a measured four-paragraph press release expressing their grief, and that would be the end of their public emotion, no matter how many of the world's newspapers came knocking. Mrs Harris might regret having spoken to Ana, but Ana didn't think she should. It was just the grief of a mother, after all.

'I'm so, so sorry, Mrs Harris.' Ana had tears in her eyes, and her clothes were drenched. 'I loved his music so much when I was a teenager. He brought a lot of joy.'

'Thank you, dear. Thank you.'

Ana tidied up her desk, cold in her damp shirt, feeling small in her skin, as if she had just given a few litres of blood. It would be ecstasy to stand under a warm shower, to soap away the grime and emotion and pressure, to fold herself up in a dressing gown and sit neatly, calmly, beside her wall heater and turn the pages of a book. She switched off her computer, stacked up the phone books and wound the microphone cord around her tape recorder before locking it in a drawer. It was this, this exact moment, that got her addicted to newspapers. Not the rush and the bustle, and the self-importance of the day, but this. The moment when it stopped.

She could even drive out to Westgate at midnight and pick up a paper so fresh from the presses the pages would stain her fingers and the inky smell of paint thinner would fill her nostrils, but she was well past that now. She had done it as a cadet, when she couldn't sleep with the vain hunger to see her name in print, and the terror that she had got something wrong. But that was a long time ago. These days there was just this thrumming peace, a peace that descended between finishing a story, and seeing it in print. The knowledge that her work was done, that other hands were batting it closer to the finish line.

She thought of herself and Nick as children, making whirlpools in the pool. Giant strides around the rubber edges, chasing each other's thin shoulders, swinging arms, until the moment when Nick yelled *Go*! and they both sank into the spinning current, bobbing in a circle, with the eucalyptus leaves and the sticks. The wonder of centrifugal force, and a free ride. The wonder of a tide.

She bent down to gather the scattered cuttings and when she stood, Zac was there.

'Can I buy you a drink?'

He didn't smile as he spoke. He was unshaven, grey-skinned, and there were dark trenches under his eyes. He had lost a button on his shirt. You really got to see your colleagues at their worst in this job, Ana reflected.

She looked down at her own damp shirt. Her hair would be flat and dreadlocky and her face would be pale. Her mascara had probably smudged. But who cared what Zac thought.

'Sure.' The hot shower could come later, and would

be all the better with a glass of wine in her belly. And some food. She was starving.

Down at Bonnie's, waiters were wiping down tables and stacking chairs, but the *Morning Star* provided plenty of custom and *Star* journalists were never knocked back. The manager showed Ana and Zac to a booth and took orders.

'A red wine please.'

'A double whisky and a beer, thanks.' Zac threw a hundred dollar note on the table. 'And a hamburger. You ordering food?' He looked at Ana.

'A Caesar salad.'

Zac smirked. 'I remember when a journo would have blushed to his toes to order a Caesar salad.'

Ana gritted her teeth. One drink, one quick meal with Zac, and she would make a run for it. She had heard Zac's views on the decline of journalists before, and the last thing she felt like doing was sitting there watching him get drunk and obnoxious.

'*His* being the operative word,' she said. 'What you really mean is you remember the good old days when all journos were men.'

He leaned back and folded his arms, regarding her with a wry smile. 'Well. Whatever. Thanks for coming back in tonight, Ana. My only other option was a boy cadet who hadn't started shaving yet. And he'd never heard of Dizzy Harris. So this one's on me.'

'Oh. Okay.' She almost blushed. Well, she could do civilised too. 'So, how's the family? Coping with seeing less of Dad?'

'Seems like it.' He threw back his double whisky and

glared at the empty glass. 'Francine's sleeping with some arsehole delegate from the textiles union and the kids both hate me. I'm living out of home at the moment.'

Ana barely blinked. 'Deary me.'

Zac shrugged. 'It was always coming. I've been away too much, with work. The kids hardly know me, and Francine and I have lost whatever connection we had.'

Zac had been foreign correspondent during the Bosnian war; he'd had overseas postings in three countries, as well as a stint as finance editor. If there was one thing Ana did envy about Zac, it was his heavyweight experience. She got him talking about his time in New York, and quickly finished her salad.

'Well, I'd better head off.' She rose as her fork clattered into the empty bowl. Outside it was raining heavily, windy and wild, and she felt a reluctant pang of guilt about abandoning a colleague. 'Can I give you a lift somewhere?'

'You could drop me home.'

In the car park, her car threatened not to start and she clenched her jaw. Was this night never going to end?

'Stop turning the engine over, you'll flood it.'

She rolled her eyes at him and turned the key again, and the car revved in the cavernous space. 'Thank Christ,' she muttered.

Zac was renting a flat in North Melbourne. As Ana pulled up out the front, her windscreen wipers working overtime against the rain, there was a crack from across the road. In the glow from streetlights, they saw a massive branch separate from a tree and fall to the ground, the storm and traffic muffling any sound. Then the engine cut out and it was as if the volume of the rain had been turned up. Again and again Ana tried to start the car.

'Shit.' She hit the steering wheel with both hands.

'I'm sorry, but I'm hopeless with cars.'

She nodded. She expected as much. None of the practical, mechanically minded men she had known had been journalists. He reached for the door handle.

'Do you want to come upstairs and call the RACV?'

The flat was like student digs with some extra money thrown in: a bedspread thrown over a couch, a new Sony television, a cardboard box with Sony printed on the side upturned to use as a coffee table. The place smelled faintly of alcohol and smoke, although she could see a packet of Nicorettes on the table. There was a pile of *Morning Star* cuttings; recent opinion pages, she could see, some of them bearing her pieces. She had an eerie sense of life through Zac's eyes – cranky young women nipping at his heels; wife sleeping with another man; a routine of words and alcohol and cigarettes and cricket and takeaway food, and the daily appearance of the newspaper as reliable as a heartbeat. Needing the sight of his byline as fiercely as a junkie needed their next fix. Zac did have a network of powerful mates throughout the company that would keep him slowly climbing up the ladder, but she could see he clung to the paper in the same uneasy way she did; hoping it would keep giving him an emotional home, fearful it would betray him.

He rang the RACV for her, and came back with bad news.

'Two hours, they said. This weather, everyone's breaking down.'

284

She nodded. Her head hurt. 'Well. Better get me a drink then.'

He poured her some Baileys and himself some Scotch, and then, as if hoping to cheer her up, said, 'I know some good news about you. Something good that's coming your way.'

She raised her eyebrows. Had he heard about the book? He did, after all, play golf with Lowenthal. 'Can you tell me?'

'Well. I shouldn't.'

'Well, don't then.' She crossed her legs and he looked disappointed.

It occurred to Ana on her second glass of Baileys that Zac found her attractive, which shouldn't really have given her as much triumphant glee as it did. She was, after all, probably fifteen to twenty years younger than him; she was slim and healthy, in close-fitting business pants and a pink business shirt open to a hint of cleavage. There would be something wrong if an old sleaze like Zac Banks *didn't* find her good-looking. But there was something strangely intoxicating about knowing a rival was sexually attracted to her. Sort of like being fifteen and discovering your ability to saunter into a room and make your male schoolteacher blush. They were playing Scrabble by now and she felt Zac watching her as she mused over her letters, studying her face as if trying to read something. She felt herself drunkenly exaggerating her facial expressions for his entertainment: here's Ana puzzled, here's Ana anxious, ah, here she is triumphant as she lays down her tiles.

'Luting is not a word,' he protested.

'It is,' she said, as solemnly as she could manage. She drank another Baileys, and reflected that maybe the night could be salvaged. 'It's a component in food, a sort of hermalcuous protein.'

'A hermalcuous protein?' He stared at her in a sort of admiring disgust and she blinked back at him. He took out a dictionary. 'If that's a word, I'll scull my next drink.'

'If it's a word, you can tell me the good thing that's in store for me at work.'

He sat beside her and perused the dictionary. 'I don't believe it. It's another word for *lute*.'

'There you go. The benefits of a university education. And healthy food such as Caesar salad. Stimulates the brain.'

'You smartarse. It wasn't a hermalcuous protein though. Well, I'll tell you your good news.' He was so close on the couch now she could smell him, an encompassing blend of cigarettes and alcohol and male sweat. It was a smell that reminded her of teenage parties, when boys smoked and drank and had pissing competitions. The bottom button of her own shirt had come open and pulled awry as she turned to face him, and she saw him glance down at her milky patch of belly skin, and the three or four fine, dark hairs marking out a path towards the button of her pants.

Thunder shook the windows and the rain pounded down harder. Zac cast her a smug look.

'There's been mention of you helping me. With a book.'

'What? I thought we were writing it together. I'm not bloody *helping* you.'

'You know about it? Lowenthal said not to say anything.'

She was outraged. 'He never mentioned *you*.'

Zac was uncharacteristically mild. 'Well, I'm okay with it if you are. Writing it together. What shall we do it on? They want some columny thing. Let's brainstorm it now.' He took the paper and pen from the abandoned game.

Ana shook her head in disgust. Well, they had to pass the time somehow. 'Something pop culturish. What about the way communication has become briefer in everyday speaking life, because of text messages and emails? How that sort of stuff's affecting our speech?' She was having trouble putting her own speech together. He nodded and wrote.

'Or, or . . .' She gazed at him. 'How clothes get sexier as society drinks and smokes less. We give up bits of one vice and we take on more of others.'

He looked doubtful. 'I don't know. I was actually thinking we could do something on how the unions are destroying the Labor party . . .'

'Oh my God.' She slid off the couch and collapsed on the floor, her face a picture of agonised boredom. 'Don't do it to me. I couldn't bear it.'

He smirked. 'Get up, you bloody drama queen. What about the growth of the nanny state, more laws to protect us, less violent crime and accidents, but people more fearful . . .'

She grimaced, climbing back on the couch. Zac's world was such a colourless, gritty place to be, she almost felt sorry for him. 'Can't we do something we can have some fun with? What about, how two-dollar shops are taking over from op shops?'

'Says who?'

'Or, Girlfriends: are women these days closer to their friends than their husbands?'

'Ugh. What about Melbourne and Sydney, what people talk about in each city? Top ten topics of . . .'

She mused. 'Not bad. Not bad. I know! I know!' She let her voice fall to a hush, her eyes wide. '*What we email about* – research the top ten topics of emails and analyse what they say about modern preoccupations. That's bound to bring up sex, money, clothes, careers, something to attract everyone.'

She waited breathlessly for his reaction. If they went with one of her ideas it would be at least equally her project.

'Not bad.'

Two hours and a bottle of Baileys later, he had told her about his disintegrating marriage. She had told him about the lawyer she had loved and lost, and about her dead brother, and about inheriting a child.

'Are you going to take him?'

She nodded. 'I'm scared though. I know how things can go wrong with kids. Look at my brother, a lifetime of care.'

'But look at you. How proud your mother must be.'

'I feel guilty. I should visit her more.'

'We all carry the burden of our parents' love. It's hardly ever fully reciprocated.'

She thought about Finn, as she tucked her bare toes under the couch cushions and hugged her knees.

Watched Zac put two steaming coffees on the cardboard box table. She could smell tobacco and wood grain and coffee beans.

'What if something goes wrong? What if he starts petrol sniffing, or turns to crime? What if he gets sick, like my brother?'

'What's that quote? "Having a child means forever to have your heart go walking outside your body."'

'So true.'

Later still, after another chaotic game of Scrabble, the storm still wrapped around the window like padding, she beamed at him drunkenly and punched him on the shoulder. He rubbed it.

'If you keep hitting me I'll file a harassment suit.' He spoke with a stern coyness that made her roar laughing, another button on her shirt popping open. Somehow her legs had stretched out across his and her feet were bare.

'Oops.' She fumbled one-handedly at her button. He put down his drink.

'I think you're very drunk, Ms Haverfield, if you can't do up the buttons of your blouse.'

She lay back and watched him help her, until she realised that instead of doing her buttons up, he had undone another one. He looked down at her playfully.

'Uh-oh. *I* can't remember how to do it either.'

She was thinking of how he had said blouse, instead of shirt. What a lovely old word that was.

He studied her expression and went thoughtfully back to the next button.

'Oops. Look. This one's come undone too.' His voice was a thick murmur, and her shirt fell open to reveal her bra. She watched him gaze at her, watched his eyes travel down her bare belly, and his fingers open the waistband of her pants, and start to slowly, slowly unzip them. This is *Zac Banks*, she told herself incredulously. This is *really* happening. This is *terrible*. *Terrible*.

And if he was going to be that slow about getting her pants off, she would just have to help him.

It was four a.m. before her mobile rang, waking her out of a deep sleep. She opened her eyes to a searing headache and the stench of stale alcohol. She was naked, with a naked man lying beside her.

The past twelve hours came flooding back and she lay still and let them pound like waves on her temples. Had she really . . . ? And then did that honestly . . . ? And was this man next to her Zac Banks?

It was. She edged away from him, horrified. He snored and she got up and went out into the living room, a mess of Scrabble pieces and bottles and glasses and scraps of paper with writing on them and her clothes. Oh Jesus. She was muck, she was gutter life. Her head had a life of its own, a painful one. She found her phone and answered it.

'RACV. We're downstairs now with your car.'

She hastily dressed, grabbed her bag and closed the door quietly, praying that Zac wouldn't wake up. Had they used something? A condom? Please, please.

Outside, the storm had gone and the night had dropped to perfect stillness. A branch had fallen on a van up the road and hazard lights flashed up ahead. A young man waited at her car.

'Sorry it's taken a while. It's been a wild night.'

'No worries.'

She wrapped her coat more tightly around her while the mechanic worked, and she stared up at the dark shadows of old elm trees. Through the branches, the clouds had cleared and she could see stars, like tiny Christmas lights. She wondered how the green house in Northcote was travelling in the storm, and she knew that more than anything in the world, she wanted to go home.

29

In August, when Serena was seven months pregnant, Dave finally took a whole weekend off. He announced this like he was the Prime Minister about to tour a remote electorate, and Serena had to stop herself snarling. Then she thought fuck it, and she snarled.

'Even divorced dads see their kids every second weekend.' Listen to her. A chainsaw whinge that Cooper would have been proud of. 'I wouldn't get so excited about it.'

'Well, I am excited about it,' Dave said cheerfully, handing Cooper some toast and jam.

'The kids have chopped fruit on cereal in the morning,' she said. She had already turned the video off after Dave put it on, and dressed the children after he said why not leave them in their pyjamas, arguing that they looked like tracksuits anyway. It left her gobsmacked how she worked so hard all week and then he got home and took every shortcut in the book.

'Well, Saturdays are special. Saturdays are jam day.' Cooper opened his mouth full of half-processed toast and jam, and nodded at his dad in conspiratorial agreement. They leered joyously, and high-fived each other. Dave started reading a picture book.

'. . . and Scruffy took Wendy's phone and buried it . . .'

'It's *Scrufty*, not Scruffy.'

'Shush, Mum.' Cooper glared.

She couldn't help it. It drove her mad that he worked such long hours, yet now he was home everything he did seemed an affront. She watched him load the dishwasher half-full, close the door and turn it on.

'You've left all the dishes out.' She waved at the sink, full of dirty crockery.

He blinked. 'That stuff never gets clean in the dishwasher. I'll do it by hand.'

'Well, *I* put it in the dishwasher. What are you saying, I've been doing it wrong?'

'No, I'm just saying those deep bowls don't get clean in the dishwasher.'

'So, what, I should be washing half the fucking dishes by hand? As if I haven't got enough to do.'

'Get off my back, Serena. You can do what you like, this is the way I'm doing them.'

'There's no need to speak like that.'

'You're the one swearing in front of the kids.'

'Oh sorry, Saint fucking David,' she hissed.

'I'm going to open the fridge door now, and I'm going to use my right hand to reach for the bacon, and I'm going to do it like so.' He demonstrated. 'Is that to your liking or are you going to have a go at me about that too?'

She snarled but retreated, a hungry animal temporarily scared off its prey. She would be back.

She had survived two months of winter since her embarrassing night with Poss. Two months during which Poss called intermittently, between overseas trips, timidly asking her out for a coffee, a dinner, a repeat visit to his place with the kids. She had been cool; they were always busy. Two months where it seemed every time she caught up with Cate, Matty was bearing some new illness from childcare, which then swept through Serena's small tribe like a grassfire. Colds, which made Angus cry almost all night, unable to understand why he couldn't breathe properly. Gastro, with its frightening vomits, leaving children pale and thinner. Cooper's eczema always flared after an illness, and there were nights of him scratching himself and wailing. Days when one child was infectious and they stayed inside, away from winter mists that melted into rain. Telly became like a drug, something she doled out in limited quantities, for herself as much as the boys. An hour in the morning, an hour in the afternoon. The boys whined for more, and a part of her whined for it too. But Jo had left behind games, new books, ideas, and something more. A model for mothering, a role Serena tried on for size. Days when she would try to be Jo for a few hours and get the boys building elaborate cubbies out of folding tables and blankets, zoos out of blocks and an array of toy animals.

One hellish, day, when she thought they would all claw each other's eyes out with boredom, she turned the heater in the bathroom on full, stripped the two older boys, put them in the empty bath and squirted Dave's can of shaving cream over the floor of the tub. The boys played uproariously for an hour in the foam and Serena felt the stirring of something long forgotten. Optimism. Joy. *I could do this*, she thought. *I could be a mother of four.*

She had kept Finn safe and loved through his own terrible winter, all the while urging Ana to spend time with him, to form a bond. Ana and Finn had a relationship now, and as soon as Ana found a house they could begin the process of moving him into her care, his second big upheaval of the year. Finn still clung to his relic of Priya's pyjamas, but he was picking up new words every week. He had bonded closely with Cooper and followed him everywhere. He still needed cuddles more often than her own children, but she thought of the lawyer's words, and knew she had done the right thing by Finn. She might stuff up everything else this year, but at least she could hold onto that.

Dave went to the shop and came back with half a dozen stackable coloured crates for the kids' room. He filled one with wooden blocks, another with animals from various sets, another with Lego, one with cars, one with train set pieces. She stared at the room in silent amazement. You could see the floor. Cooper lay on the carpet and rolled and Finn jumped on him.

'Well, that'll last five minutes,' she predicted sourly, and skulked back to the living room. She was awful, she was terrible, and he was really trying. *Trying to show off*, said the evil voice. *Trying to make you feel like you're hopeless at it.*

The agent had rung the day before. He had a serious buyer for the Clifton Hill flat. Serena felt nervous about selling it behind Dave's back, but she was still determined. She had been rocked by Poss's rejection, newly aware that when she left Dave, she could be single for a long time. Maybe forever. A woman with four children was a lot for any man to take on. But she decided she didn't care. She was sick of having things happen *to* her, wanted to be the one to make them happen. She remembered the adventurous spirit that had led her to geology, mourned it like a dead friend. She needed her native recklessness, her once anarchic impulses, to steer her out of this time. But still, hesitant, she had put a ridiculous price on the flat. A good twenty per cent higher than the price the agent had quoted, and his price was crazy, a figure pitched at winning her business. He had objected, but she had been firm. Let the fates of the property market decide. If anyone wanted to bite at that price, she would sell, leave her husband and set up her life anew.

'Well, I must admit I'm surprised about this, but you have a potential buyer,' said the agent. 'A woman who is desperate to buy in the area. She's offered just ten thousand below your asking price.'

'Really?' Serena's heart lurched in her chest. She almost had to lean backwards these days to give her lungs room to move, as the babies pressed against her diaphragm.

'And we both know your price was very high. This sale would set a new record for the area. What do you say?'

'Let me think about it for a few days.'

'What's to think about? You won't get better than this.'

'Just give me a few days.'

The figure ticked across her brain, like a subtitle at the bottom of a screen. She wondered why this woman was so desperate to buy.

'I boop you!' Back in the bedroom, Dave lay curled on the floor, three children jumping on him. 'I boop you!' cried Cooper, echoed by Finn. 'Boop you.' Dave laughed helplessly, raising his hands in self-defence.

'Don't hit your father.' Serena spoke irritably, folding clothes. Cooper looked at her indignantly.

'Not hitting. *Booping*.'

'Don't teach them to hit, Dave.'

'Booping's not hitting.' More hilarity.

She scowled and went out to the laundry.

Dave followed her. 'Why don't you take a day to yourself? Go have a facial or something.'

She sorted washing, whites in the basket, coloureds into the machine.

'Why? Do you want to get rid of me?'

'I do. You're cramping our style.'

'Thanks a lot.'

'I just want you to relax. Look at you. You're huge. Take this chance, have some time to yourself.'

'Fine. I'll go shopping.' She grumped out, slamming the door behind her.

She ran into Cate at the butcher and dragged her off for a coffee.

'I feel betrayed. Cooper just wants Daddy. He doesn't want me.'

'Matty's the same.'

'I'm just not *fun* with them. Like a dad.'

'They're boys. Maybe it's because we're just not into cars and stuff.'

'But will they know I love them as much as Dave? It seems so unfair. I give up so much more, and yet their best childhood memories will be riding on Daddy's shoulders, or play-fighting on the floor with him. Not me hanging out the washing, or me not-having a career. Or me making them eat their vegies.'

'Serena, you just need a rest. Fun is an optional extra, fun is what they get from a parent who's had enough time to themselves.'

She waddled towards home, breathless and warm despite the cold day, the only person on the street not wearing a coat. There were things that she loved about being a mother. Watching children eat a meal with vegetables; their solemn faces as you unfurled a bandaid on a finger. The first time they said please to a grandparent. The way they called Mummy when they woke, or when they fell. Watching them dance to a song she'd loved for years, since way before they were conceived. Their pudding bottoms. The way children learned, starting by making things too complicated. Saying engine-gine-gine, scrawling dozens of mad circles to represent one, as if they were hopeful of finding a life as complex and energetic as they were.

When she arrived home Dave had drawn up elaborate plans for a two-storeyed cubby house and dug stump holes. He had laid out timber and was starting up the chainsaw. She shrieked.

'No! No!'

'What?'

'You can't use power tools around small children.'

'Why not?' He looked genuinely baffled, the chainsaw swinging from his hand. Finn solemnly inspected the sharp point of an electric drill.

'Because it's dangerous. And don't think you're going to spend the whole weekend building a cubby while I look after the kids.'

'Okay, okay. That's it.' He threw down the drill. 'We're going away. We're getting away from this house before we kill each other.'

Dave made her sit on a couch with a herbal tea while he packed a case for them, and another for the children, and a third for Finn, who was to spend the weekend with Ana. Twice she started pulling herself out of the cushions to remind him of something, and both times she gave up and sank back again. *Let him do it*. She read the paper. She could hear crashing and laughter, Angus wailing and Cooper running. She breathed out, and Dave finally came in.

'Okay. We're done. Can you think of anything I might have missed?'

'Baby Panadol? Finn's Jarmy? Drink bottles, woolly hats, sleepy suit for Angus? Portacot, toothbrushes, eczema cream, waterproof bed liner, gum boots? Teething gel for Angus . . .'

Dave looked bewildered. 'I might have missed one or two of those.' He walked out.

Serena smiled and went back to the paper.

They drove out to the Mornington Peninsula, dropping Finn at Ana's flat en route, to visit Romeo and Katrina, who had done the seachange thing ten years before and bought twelve hectares of paradise. Romeo grew llamas, and painted, and Katrina raised three children, and they shared boundaries to the east with a national park, and to the north with cliffs that overlooked the bays of Cape Schank. It was clear land, grassed, but the land was just an accessory to the sky, really, the sky that arched over them, putting on an everchanging theatre of waxing and waning moons and scudding cloud sunrises licked with rose.

Katrina, an old school friend of Serena's, had quit her job after the first child and Romeo had inherited money and invested in the llamas, working just a few hours every day before returning to the house to whisk his two-, four- and six-year-old away for a play. They had an in-ground trampoline and if you jumped high enough you could see the breaking waves, as if you were a seagull. They had two guest bedrooms with ensuites and were always telling their friends in the city to come and stay.

Serena watched Katrina as she read a story to the five children, night falling in magnificent drama through the panorama windows before them. Katrina had been a wild girl in school: the first to smoke, the one who disappeared for two hours with a boy when you played Spin the Bottle. That girl's a worry, Serena's mother had muttered. But not any more. These days Katrina was the very picture of a woman fulfilled by family. She breastfed her first two children until they were two, and would probably do so with her third.

'Do you miss your job?'

'Not for a second.'

Katrina gazed at Serena, waiting to hear more. She was a listener, Katrina, and her long silences often extracted bubbling confessions. Serena felt them rising within her and pushed them down. How could Katrina understand how she felt?

Katrina blinked and went back to the picture book.

The children went out and said goodnight to the llamas, and collected lemons from under the trees. There was a last pyjama jump on the trampoline, and then they all ran inside to sit on the rug by the fire, where the labrador slept, snoring faintly. Every second picture was a framed fingerpainting, toys and books poured from every crevice. Serena wandered around studying photographs, turning over placemats, pretending to pack up Lego. She even peered into the fridge, the freezer. She found a stack of frozen pizzas in the freezer, and stared at them curiously.

But it still wasn't what she was looking for.

There was a double swag and a bed for the children to sleep in, but they all fought for the swag. In the end they crammed in together and shrieked for joy for the next two hours in the darkness. Finally the lights were turned on and children were redistributed by parents through beds and rooms.

'Do *you* miss your job?' Katrina had this quality of watchfulness, and could pick up a conversation hours after it began. She wrapped a home-knitted shawl around her shoulders (the wool spun and dyed from the llamas), and curled around a glass of red wine. She had surprised Serena, after the children went to bed, by going out in the dark and jumping alone on the trampoline, a shadowy figure under the rising moon, a memory of the hungry girl she had been before motherhood came and filled her up.

'I do miss my job.' Serena sipped her wine. 'I really miss it.' It felt treacherous to admit such a thing, in a place where happiness was an art form and children the centre of the world.

Katrina nodded thoughtfully.

'You had a good job. I was bored with my job anyway.' She had been a medical receptionist. 'But yours, it must have been hard to leave it. Getting out to the bush on your own. Reading all that history in the rocks.'

She unwound herself and brought out some cake. When she came back she sat next to Serena. 'I don't want to go back to work,' she said. 'But I have days here where I think I'll go crazy. Completely insane. The older two are in creche one day a week, and Emmet will go in as soon as he gets a place. I'll just read books and go for walks on the beach. I don't know how you get by without at least a day to yourself.'

Serena nodded. She savoured the words, replayed them in her mind. She curled her feet into the borders of her armchair and felt like she might break.

Dave and Romeo were off in Romeo's studio, looking at his paintings. Serena knew that Dave, with not an artistic bone in his body, would be studying the paintings with his head on one side, as if politely puzzled by their very existence. He would be more interested in the economics and logistics of raising the llamas. She heard her husband's voice, his footsteps coming down the hall and when he came back in the room, his eyes sought hers.

They slept there that night, Dave and Serena, in a four-poster bed, and they made love. In previous pregnancies they had made love constantly, both of them aroused, as now, by her changing body. Her breasts were full, the nipples were dark, she had a sort of pelt over her, she knew. The obscene mystery of pregnancy always seemed to heighten her libido. It was the strange rudeness of carrying a baby, and having a man's penis inside her. Like, how much more of the world could she take in? Anyone else want to hop on board? As if this small army of people, babies, her husband, were creeping closer to her own life flame, burning just under her clavicle, as if they couldn't resist it.

She woke in the morning before Dave and she watched him breathe. With her hands on her bare belly, she could feel the dawn chorus of tiny legs and arms within, pressing on ribs, reaching for room. Dave. Just when she had given up on him, sealed up her defences, here he was, stealing back into her heart. The wretched truth of it was she loved him. She didn't want to be without him. But she wanted it to be like this, all the time. And it wouldn't be. But here she was, once again, hoping. She groaned and burrowed her face into the crook of Dave's arm, felt herself falling back into his orbit with reluctance and relief. She would not accept the offer on the flat. The buyer, that faceless woman, would have to take her desperation elsewhere, into someone else's life. Sea breezes blew the ti-trees outside and Serena could hear the waves, or the rain, she wasn't sure which.

As they waved goodbye later that morning, Cooper cried.

'I want to live there. I don't want to go home.'

The car crunched over gravel; bags of lemons on the back seat and an oil painting of Romeo's in the boot.

'Wouldn't you miss Mummy and Daddy?' Needy mummy, thought Serena. Always fishing for more.

Cooper considered it carefully.

'Mummy can come too.'

'And Daddy?' Dave, petulant.

Cooper paused, watching the clouds above the sea. 'Daddy go to work.'

It was surprising, Serena reflected, as the car bumped up off the gravel and onto the bitumen, how little pleasure she derived from the hurt that flashed across Dave's face.

30

Ana sped through her office on Monday morning like an Olympic walker. If it was possible to become invisible through sheer force of will, she would have done it. At her desk, she locked eyes with her computer screen and held the contact as fiercely as an operating surgeon. She read through the newswire without absorbing a word.

Zac, still acting editor, was also a vision of industry. However, with four reporters off sick, his busyness was possibly genuine. He called Ana over, and she picked up a notebook and pen and slunk across. Was that cadet smirking at her? Were the subs talking amongst themselves and looking her way? Oh God, why on earth had she done it?

She was horribly conscious of her body, her slim-cut pinstripe pants today feeling like they offered little more coverage than a pair of lycra stockings. She had worn a vile, baggy shirt that hid the shape of her upper body, but she was worried that when she leaned forward it revealed her bra. She stood as straight as a soldier to stop this happening.

Zac looked exasperated. 'Can you come here? I'm not going to bite you.'

Ana reluctantly closed the gap, and crouched at his desk. Zac took a phone call, sweat breaking out on his face, and she relaxed a little. She was not his biggest problem right now.

He hung up. 'We're short-staffed, we need you to do courts today.' There was a popular entrepreneur on charges of insider trading in the County Court, and the parents of a child with cerebral palsy in the Supreme Court, suing the state. And if she could stick her head into the ongoing trial of six men charged over a local nightclub murder, and pick up the transcripts of a magistrate's court case for the police reporters . . .

'Shit, anything else? How am I meant to do all that?' Ana could feel her heart rate speeding up already. 'Isn't there a spare cadet?'

'No. And check these court lists before you go. There's a bunch of North Melbourne footballers due up on D and D any day now, we don't want to miss them.'

'Oh, come on! I shouldn't have to —'

'It's a newspaper, Ana, no room for princesses.'

Looked like everything was right back to normal.

He had rung her on the weekend, a message on her machine that she heard when she returned from Saturday's househunting, Finn in tow. An awkward few words that said everything she didn't want to hear.

'Ana. Zac. Hope you got home all right. Just wondering if you'd like to go out for a coffee this arvo. Here's my number.'

Coffee? Follow up? This could be worse than she thought, and she was already sick with fear about it. Had they used something? That was all she needed at this point in her life, to be pregnant to Zac Banks. Oh, dizzying, mortifying thought. Something in the message made her replay it again; a note in his voice that rang an even greater alarm bell than possible pregnancy. A note of hope. A hint of . . . optimism.

Oh dear.

She rang him back. No use tiptoeing around this one. She could only hope he wouldn't tell the whole office.

'Did we do something really stupid last night?'

He paused. 'I had a good time.'

Her body surprised her, feeling slightly sensual, as though non-thinking parts of her recognised the sound of his voice.

'Did we use anything?'

'You don't remember?'

She did. Details that made her blush to her toes.

'Not much.'

'That's a shame. Because you had a great time too, as far as I can remember.'

'Right.'

He laughed. 'Could I . . . take you out somewhere nice for dinner tonight? We could talk about the book? And anything else, of course.'

She blinked and grimaced at the phone. Could she, should she slide easily into another night with Zac? It was comfort. Company.

'I don't think so.'

'I really like you, Ana. I mean, I *really* do. I have for a long time. We're . . . sort of alike, you know.'

She was appalled, and deeply touched.

'I don't think it would work, Zac.'

'How can you know that? Just take it day by day, you might be surprised. Give me a chance. Let me take you out somewhere special.'

'I can't. I've got Finn for the night.' But she knew she had to shut this door properly, not leave it ajar. 'And I really don't want to, Zac. I'm sorry. But last night was a . . .' She hesitated to call it a mistake. '. . . a one-off.' He was right, they were alike. Too alike. It was Elijah she really wanted; someone who was a better person than her in some ways, worse in other ways. Someone she would never completely understand, who took her to a different part of herself. 'There's someone else I like. Love. Still.'

'The lawyer? But you're not *with* him.'

She sighed. He made a sound, a low grumble of resignation.

'Okay, I get it. Well, we did use something, Ana, so don't worry.'

'Great.' Thank God for that.

'At least you can't say let's still be friends, because we've never been friends, have we?' He laughed bitterly.

'No. But maybe we could start being friends? It would make life a lot easier.'

He sighed heavily. 'Sure. Sure.'

'And, Zac? I did have a good night. But can we keep this to ourselves?'

'Off the record.'

She travelled to the courts with a photographer called Nick Hodge, a surly bastard who drove with one hand holding a mobile phone to his ear, and the other hand flitting between gear stick and steering wheel. There were unspoken rules at the *Star*: the photographers always drove, they drove like maniacs, and journalists who dared complain about the likelihood of their own death by car crash would be treated like the weakest of kittens. Ana said nothing, but resolved, as always, to lodge a complaint with HR on her return, an intention she never carried out. Once at the courts, she checked out the media scrum at the door and noted the opposition.

A closed hearing on the entrepreneur. She ticked that off with relief; Hodge could camp here for the day to catch the parties leaving, and she could pluck the comments off the wire service if she missed them. She sat in on the nightclub murder trial, which seemed on the verge of hearing some salacious evidence to do with a broken bottle, a gun and the nightclub owner's girlfriend's husband, just as soon as the lawyers could agree on the legal definition of a term used three days before. Two hours later she gave up on that and dashed over to the Supreme Court cerebral palsy hearing, where the weeping parents, the charged atmosphere and the smug looks of her rival from the opposition newspaper made her heart sink. The horse had bolted on this one. She would have to try for the transcript later. Which reminded her, she had to pick up a transcript for the police reporters.

'All rise.'

Lunch. She spent the hour chasing barristers, pleading with them for details and being treated like some form of parasitic insect life. Back in the case of the entrepreneur, now regrettably open to the media, she struggled with the finer nuances of corporate fraud, completely at a loss.

Nicking out to check on the nightclub hearing again, she noticed a group of people wearing the scarves and beanies of the North Melbourne football club, straining to see through the doors of the Magistrate's Court.

Shit. She'd forgotten to check the court lists. The drunk and disorderlies of the footy team must be up today. She almost wept. She ran inside the court's cavernous front foyer, bag flying off her shoulder, ring-binder notepad fluttering from her hand, vile shirt flapping around her like a spinster's nightie, and suddenly found herself face-to-face with Elijah.

He looked impeccable. Charcoal suit, white shirt, navy tie. Hair cut even shorter, skin a little shadowed around the clear brown eyes. Same strong jaw, a gold watch she hadn't seen, which glinted as he touched his tie. He had just turned away from a group of men and begun walking, but he paused in front of her. His face was blank and closed, and still so dear.

'Hello, Ana.'

For a horrendous second she couldn't remember his name. She had thought of him every hour of every day for the past two months, had replayed his every word. She had fantasised about a chance meeting like this, and now she couldn't remember his name.

'Hi.' He was gorgeous, perfect, whatever his bloody name was, and she was a ragged mess. She was about to miss a front-page story and she no longer cared. 'Sorry.' She gestured down at herself crazily. 'Bit flustered.'

'Can I help you?'

Could you take me in your arms? Kiss me? Take me out for dinner, take me home to your bed?

'You wouldn't have a court list, would you?'

'Certainly.' He produced a clean sheaf of paper. 'Are you after the footballers? They're in court six.'

'Oh. Lovely.' She hugged the court list to her chest.

'You can keep that.'

'Thanks.'

He looked a little amused. 'Bye, Ana.'

She nodded, her heart breaking all over again. 'Bye.'

She wandered without direction for twenty minutes, uncaring where she was, until Nick Hodge found her, his eyes bulging out of his head. 'The Kangaroos! The Kangaroos!' he shrieked.

It was a second before she realised what he was talking about. 'Court six,' she shouted, and they ran.

At the end of the day, Ana had a notebook with shorthand from four different court cases. The pages were dog-eared, her shorthand barely legible. She stared at one page for ten minutes, trying to work out whether it was from the entrepreneur or the nightclub murder. She had ducked away at one point and taped the ABC news from a small transistor she carried, and she thought from that she could cobble together the entrepreneur's story. The newswire reporter had been in the nightclub hearing and Ana had miraculously caught the footballers' case at the right time. The cerebral palsy was a lost cause, and the opposition would run it big because they knew they had it to themselves. Win some, lose some. All in all, she had done pretty well.

'You missed the cerebral palsy case?' Zac stared at her in bitter disappointment.

'I've got three stories here, one of them a possible

front page. Who cares about the bloody cerebral palsy case?'

'That's the big one for us! You should have let the nightclub one go if you couldn't stay on top of them all. We didn't really need that.'

'Well, why ask me to do it then? Sorry, I'm not bloody psychic!'

She rattled off the North Melbourne story and sent it, before she checked her phone messages. She was typing while she listened, and she only half clocked the first message from her mother's nursing hostel to call her at one p.m. The next one, at two p.m., said her mother had had a stroke. Ana drew a deep breath, held the telephone receiver with both hands and braced herself like a truck driver staring at an oncoming tree. A few messages later, after a couple of calls from a contact about a possible union story, there was another message from the hostel, this one a deep-voiced male, who identified himself as the managing director. His voice sent a chill scudding across her skin. Official. Slow. Formal.

Please ring.

After she made the call she sat at her desk for a full twenty minutes without moving. Her notebook, loaded with two more stories, sat bristling at her elbow. Finally she got up and forced her legs to walk over to Zac. He took one look at her and rose to his feet as she spoke.

'My mother died today.'

A massive ischaemic stroke, the doctor told Ana. They stood outside the hospital wing of the hostel. Her mother had been seen falling from a garden chair, her thin body landing silently in a newly mulched bed. She had been holding the *Morning Star*, which she read every morning, and the paper had clapped closed as she fell, conveniently providing a clean landing place for her face. She had drifted in and out of consciousness for a time. A few hours later there was a haemorrhagic consequence, the doctor said, and Lily passed away.

'A 72-year-old woman, still smoking – she always had a high chance of this,' he said apologetically.

A nurse led Ana to her mother's room and sat her gently in the only armchair. Ana sank into the loose cushions where her mother had sat, the hollows and depressions from her mother's body welcoming her. She watched the steam rise from a cup of tea. A nurse crouched in front of her and touched Ana's arm.

'The girls in palliative are just preparing your mother's body,' she said. 'I thought you might like to wait here, and when they're ready, I'll come back for you?'

'Okay.'

Ana heard the word come out from her own mouth. There. She could still speak. Grief moved its heavy machinery into her heart, and she felt the steamroller begin its inevitable crushing, the pneumatic drill to hammer holes. She was shocked at it. She could hardly breathe.

The nurse left, closing the door behind her. The room was small; space for a single bed, an armchair, and a television, with the DVD player Ana had bought last Christmas. There was an ensuite the size of a cupboard. Floor-to-ceiling curtains, closed. A bedside table with a photo of Ana and Nick on a seaside holiday when they were five and seven. Nick holding Ana's hand, she remembered, to make her stand still. There was a pile of newspaper clippings, already creamy with age; columns of Ana's from earlier that year. A shelf on the wall held an open packet of her mother's Twinings Irish Breakfast tea, a few packets of matches and an ashtray. The smells of lavender talcum powder, Johnson's baby shampoo, stale cigarette ash – as if her mother were standing just out of sight.

But the smells would fade and go, just like everything Lily knew about Ana. Lost. Things Ana didn't even know herself, had not had time to ask. *Did I cry a lot as a baby? How did Nanna meet Grampa? What was your first memory?* Ana's own first memory was of her mother, sitting at the kitchen table, carefully cutting up a bandage with nail scissors. She was telling Ana she was very brave, as blood flowed from Ana's tiny knee. Ana touched her knee now, and through the fabric of her trousers there was still a scar from that day. Dashing greedily for ice-cream, concrete steps rising traitorously, something along those lines. She remembered Lily dancing with Robert in the lounge room, Lily on a chair lift, wearing a furry hat and waving at them as she dangled skis and sailed up and away over snow.

She desperately wanted another chance to care for her mother, to spend more time with her, to come running when Lily called for her only remaining child in the world. She wished she'd been kinder, wished she'd understood Lily better, but she had been so busy *not* being her mother that it never felt safe to stand in her shoes, even for a moment. And what had she been frightened of? That, like her mother, love would be taken away from her? Here she was, flitting through other people's lives, watching and writing and angling for a better run. Was she ever going to take the risk of loving, of letting herself be loved, of losing and hurting and starting again?

She wept, with Priya and Richard, Lily and Elijah crowding around her, the losses so raw they could all have happened that day. Her world felt so empty. There were not enough people left. And the remaining few were so fragile, so very mortal. Elijah – how had she let him go? Why had she been so high-handed with someone who cared for her? She should have forgiven him anything, anything at all.

She sobbed silently, gulping for air. What was it her mother had said the last time Ana visited, when Ana asked how you stopped worrying about someone you loved? *You leave them in God's hands.*

Ana, an atheist, sat in her mother's room and struggled with the slippery words, as if they held a secret she had yet to unfold.

31

'Four hundred and ninety thousand, we have four ninety over here in the red, four ninety and we are on the market, ladies and gentlemen, this fine property will be sold today . . .'

The auctioneer, well-shaven neck rolling out of his collar, beamed at his assistant. The crowd turned like the audience at a tennis match to watch the family – mother, father and two young children. A small group who looked like neighbours whispered greedily, wide-eyed at the price. The young man blinked away his fear and firmed up his face.

'Four ninety-one.'

The crowd turned back to the opponents: two young women, one heavily pregnant, with a pram and two toddlers at their feet; the children cowed into silence by the sheer number of watching faces. The neighbours looked a bit worried. Two women with children – how were they going to explain *that* to the kids?

'Four ninety-two.'

Ana was dizzyingly over her own limit. But since her mother's death, all limits were off. She would bid all weekend if that was what it took to get the key to this ugly green house with its back gate onto magical parkland. She would bid Finn's whole inheritance. She had passed what she could pay with the small capital she had in her own flat and an acceptable mortgage. She was bidding into Finn's money now and she glared at her rivals. They were costing her boy cash.

'Four ninety-three.' The man spoke quickly, glanced at Ana and squared himself, feet apart. His wife stood at his shoulder, and stared out defiantly at no one in particular.

Ana drew a deep breath and took hold of her future with both hands.

'Five hundred.'

She picked up Finn and held him on her hip, his small sturdy boots hanging idle at her side. She squeezed him tight in this moment of hushed, whispering silence, as she watched and waited for the last walls to fall before them. The young couple's shoulders sank. Their faces turned towards each other like a book closing. The neighbours rotated as one to examine Ana. She gazed at the auctioneer and he nodded, and raised a rolled piece of paper.

'Going once, going twice . . .'

In the second that the auctioneer hit his own palm, Serena and Ana crushed Finn between them as they hugged.

In the freefalling days after Lily's death, life felt to Ana like something which could end at any moment. Every face she looked into was marked with its inevitable death; every beautiful tree or poignant music was something the dead were missing. Life was just one loss, one parting after another.

Death was forever, but Elijah, he was still a phone call away. God, if she could have one more chance to ring Priya, all the terror in the world wouldn't stop her. What would she say?

Finn has a new word — bert-day. *I've bought him a floor mat with roads marked on it to push cars around on, and a red dump truck with eyes, called Muck. He's been practising blowing out candles. It takes twenty minutes to walk to the corner with him, because he stops to examine snails and bits of rubbish. He can do all the actions to Miss Polly Had A Dolly. He thinks me doing the hula hoop is hilarious for some reason, and laughs until his eyes fill. He's looking more like you. He still cries Mumma when he falls, or when Cooper won't share, but I'm not sure he knows any more what it means . . .*

She dialled Eli's work number and wondered how many thousand times she had done this in the past two months. This time she held the phone tight through the dial tone, and his answering machine message, and she took a deep breath.

'You don't have to call me back. I just wanted to say that I behaved badly back in . . . on that night . . . and I'm sorry. I had no right . . . well anyway, I'm sorry.'

He rang her at home the next day.

'Apologies accepted.' He sounded quiet, reserved. 'What brought this on?'

She rolled in the cadences of his rich voice, and despaired. She had resolved to leave the message and hope for nothing, and here she was, hoping for everything.

'I just got thinking. You were right to keep . . . your secret. I mean, I didn't have a right to demand you tell me.'

'Oh.'

'And I shouldn't have implied that Priya was just . . . you know.'

'Using me for my sperm.'

Ugh. 'Did I say that?'

'You meant it.'

'I'm sorry.'

'Well. It's okay.' His voice was calm, nothing like her own strangled tones. 'So how have you been, Ana? Still househunting?'

'I bought a house yesterday, at auction. In Northcote.'

'Sensational! Renovator's delight or something different?'

'Renovator's delight. Huge dustbowl of a backyard, close to Serena's.'

'That'll be handy. How's your mum?'

Ana steadied herself. 'She died.'

'I'm so sorry. When did that happen?'

'Oh, a little while ago.' She was reluctant to admit how recently, didn't want him to think she had run back to him in the throes of grief. 'Well, I'm glad you're okay about . . . it.'

'I was pretty cut up, actually.'

'Yeah?'

'Yeah.'

'Could we maybe – see each other sometime?' she said. Her traitorous voice had dropped to a whisper.

He drew a deep and ragged breath. 'I don't know, Ana. Maybe not.'

'Oh.' She fell back into the boiling pit of grief within, where all her losses lived. Life was just misery. Why had she ever thought otherwise?

'We could try being friends. I don't think I could bear to . . . I don't know. But I appreciate the apology. And I'm very sorry to hear about your mother.'

'Okay.' Friends. She spiralled deeper. What would being friends entail? Meeting his girlfriends? Being on his group email list for jokes? He had seen through her, realised her flaws. She never really deserved him. She scrambled to say something, anything to retrieve her dignity. 'Thanks for that court list the other day. That really saved me.'

'You looked pretty stressed.'

'It was a mad day.' Was this how to be friends? Was she doing okay at it? Maybe if there was enough of it, lots and lots of just being friends, it might fill a tiny portion of her howling heart.

But he was already making wrap-up noises.

'Anyway. Nice to talk to you. Give me a call if you're doing courts again and maybe we can grab a sandwich.'

'Yeah. Yeah, sure.'

She went to Serena's for lunch. It was Finn's second birthday, and she and Serena had resolved to keep it small. Dave was at work, and it was just Ana, Serena and the children. Ana was meant to have made a cake. She stopped at a bakery and bought the only remotely suitable thing they had – a pink fairy cake. She sat it carefully on the seat beside her. Tried not to glance at it, tried not to think about her mother, and Priya, and Richard, and Elijah, and hoped it was safe to drive through all these tears.

'. . . happy birthday, dear Finny . . .
Happy birthday to you.'

Serena sliced up the cake and handed it out. Cooper picked off the musk lollies and disembowelled it for the icing. Finn watched Cooper and copied him. Ana trembled, accepted the steadying glance Serena sent her way. She knew Serena felt strongly about Finn not being swamped with other people's grief, and she was right. It was almost six months to the day that Priya and Richard had died.

'What a year,' Ana murmured.

Serena reached out and squeezed Ana's hand. 'So, did you get a quick settlement on the house?'

'A week. I've got the money and the house is empty.'

'Wow.'

'I know. I'll have to use most of Finn's money as a bridge, but when the flat sells, hopefully within a few months, I'll return it.'

'You don't have to explain anything to me. He's your baby now.'

'Are you sure another week is okay?'

'It's fine. You can't possibly arrange a funeral and move house with a two-year-old in tow. Serena touched her belly. 'As long as these guys don't come early.'

'Thanks, Serena.'

Ana picked up the Saturday *Morning Star* from Serena's recycling basket. It seemed like weeks, not just days, since her shift covering the courts. A late-breaking story on a state politician caught speeding had bumped Ana's footballers back to page eighteen, where the now seven-paragraph piece was dwarfed by an ad for a treatment for erectile dysfunction. Thanks, Zac. She tossed the paper back on the pile. For the sake of seven paragraphs on page eighteen, she had missed out on saying goodbye to her mother. So many wrong choices. *If only I'd checked my messages in the lunch break. If I had carried a tampon that night, and never found Priya's toilet bag. If I had bought the first house I looked at four months ago. If I'd been kinder to Nick. If I had walked away from that abortion all those years before, ignored my mother. If only I had spoken to Mum one more time.* Then again, it was Lily who had always told Ana not to get bogged down in other people's lives.

Ana looked over and met Finn's eyes. Get bogged down, she would tell her son. *My son.* Get bogged down and dirty, in other people's lives. Have a child's imprudent courage, and show me how it's meant to be done.

Finn rose from the floor, still holding his cake, and regarded her. In that moment there was something very regal about him, very Priya, as he licked icing from his fingers. She crouched and held the little body, pressed the soft curve of his cheek against her own.

His breath was quick and soft as moth wings on her neck; sugar sweet.

'I'll come back for you,' she told him.

He stared at her with his dark eyes, appraisingly.

'Back,' he agreed.

32

A cry broke through the house, through the night, and into Serena's dreams. Finn. Once again, she had the agonising cramps in her left leg and ankle, foot pointing down in a ballerina's arc. She bent her leg to break the cramp, and lifted her head to look at the red figures of the clock, all she could see in the dark.

3:15. She tried to remember what they had said the last time she had been woken. 2:10? 1:20?

The nest of her blankets shifted as Dave turned over, his back to her like a wall. He had a presentation to give to the minister in the morning. His shoes were polished, his shirt was ironed, his briefcase was filled with documents filed in careful order. His perfect stillness and shallow breathing told her he was awake. She listened to her own breath, the panting of late pregnancy. The two of them breathed at each other in an unspoken exchange. There were some true economies achievable in marriage, and communication was one of them. Since visiting Katrina and Romeo, things had been a little better. Dave had been home the last few nights before bedtime, had talked about taking time off when the babies came, and cutting down his hours. Serena's bitterness was diffused by the dreamy mental retreat of the heavily pregnant, the instinct to leave the daily problems to others more able. Now, she guided her belly back onto the supportive pillow that was buried in the blankets, and felt the bed move as Dave hastily sat up to pre-empt her. She heard him stumble his way to the door.

'Make sure he's got his blanky,' she called after him. 'He's had cough medicine already.'

She lay, eyes open, and heard the crying grow louder as the children's door was opened. Finn's tone grew plaintive, disappointed at the sight of the man he hardly knew. 'Seny,' she heard him cry. 'Mumma.'

It seemed to go on for ages, until she couldn't stand it any longer. She could have dealt with it in a minute, she knew, but Dave was going to dither around for half an hour, getting everything wrong and making sure everyone was well and truly awake. She growled, and flipped the blankets back viciously. Inside her a baby kicked a foot against her bladder, and she put her hands to her stomach. It was swollen hard and round as a full-term pregnancy, although she still had four weeks to go.

In the bedroom, Dave held Finn and patted his back, while the little boy roared. Cooper sat up in a puddle of blankets and grizzled as the hall light splashed across him. Serena got Finn a drink of water and held the cup to his lips. Her husband looked at her.

'Why can't you let me do it?'

'You're taking too long. I don't feel like lying there for an hour hearing Finn cry, that's all.'

'Well, what should I be doing? Tell me.'

'Don't get him up, for a start. Just tuck him back into bed. But it's too late now, he's awake.'

'Well, fine. No point both of us being up.'

He thrust Finn into his cot and stalked back to the bedroom.

Serena tucked Finn back under the blankets and stroked him until his crying turned to a whimper. Maybe a bad dream? She didn't like to think of the dreams Finn might have, but at least he had the even breathing of her own children near him, to bring him back. And there was always a shadowy Priya, standing silent behind Finn's bed, watching expressionlessly as Serena checked his forehead, gave him a drink of water.

Serena leaned over him.

Just a few more days, Priya. Help me get over the line here.

But at the head of Finn's bed there was nothing, just a dark patch where the nappy holder hung on the wall.

Serena went out to the kitchen and made herself a cup of hot chocolate. She sat on a child's chair and refolded clothes into a bag. Finn's clothes, small singlets, T-shirts, pants, in preparation for handing him over to Ana. She squeezed in a teddy and looked at the back door. It showed a dim reflection of herself; a very pregnant woman with pyjama bottoms pulled up over her bump, sheepskin boots and messed blonde hair. A woman packing a little boy's bag, for the second biggest move of his short life.

She reached up and turned out the light and her reflection disappeared. Her own moonlit garden was laid out before her. She felt through the coat rack, found her old MRA-issue bluey and put it on. She went outside, into the chill night, brushing her hand over the lemon balm bushes, ripping off handfuls of leaves. She dragged a deckchair down over the chickweed, past the mint and the pear tree, to the little shanty chicken house. She would sit under the moon.

Within the chookhouse there was an occasional murmur. They had heard her outside, were shuffling nervously, maybe wondering if she was a fox, if chickens could wonder. She had known nothing about chickens when they first came to her, had looked up everything in books. When the shells had grown thin, breaking messily when she touched them, she learned to put shellgrit in the chooks' feed, and toss them the shells when they had oysters. She gave them two laying boxes but they only ever used the left one. Some days she had opened the laying-box door to find two chickens crammed in one side, while the third stood outside hopping from leg to leg in her impatience to get in, ignoring the other empty box. She clipped their wings once, timidly, leaving soft shavings like dust stuck to the scissor blades, to stop them jumping over their fence. Then after they had escaped and eaten their way through her lettuces, silverbeet, french sorrel, she clipped them again, angrily this time, crunching through the white stalks of their feathers. She thought of the wonder of their bodies producing one egg a day, a thing bigger than their own heads.

She knew how they would be now, inside on their perches, clustered side by side. She opened the laying-box door, hoping to peek through to the perches, but she was met by a wall of feathers. Blackie was still in the laying box, had been for a few days now, she realised. She was broody, sitting on eggs that hadn't been fertilised, eggs that would never hatch and now could not be eaten. In the moonlight she saw Blackie's eye, fierce and threatening. She closed the door.

The next afternoon, coming back in from kindy and shopping, Serena saw the answering machine blinking. She parked the kids in front of *Playschool*, made a cup of tea and played the messages.

One from Possum, ringing to say hi in the nervous, pleading tone he used now, since that uncomfortable night. One from the real-estate agent, asking her to call. The last was from a woman from Melbourne Uni.

'I've got a message for David McAllister, just in relation to his query about PhD studies . . . we're very happy to meet with him to talk about that further, please just give us another call during business hours.'

A PhD? Dave?

Serena jolted her tea, sloshing it over her hand. She swore and ran to the sink to run her hand under the cold tap. How could he be even *thinking* of doing a PhD? He'd only just finished the Masters. When did he think he was going to get the time? It was impossible, with just weeks until the babies were due. She suddenly felt as alone and betrayed as if her husband had died.

She went back to the phone and rang him, hitting the numbers so hard she had to redial twice. Finally she got his assistant, Mary.

'Hi, Serena. He's just in a meeting with the board about the Bell Circle Road project.'

Serena bit back an urge to scream. First she'd heard of this.

'Is he? I didn't know he was involved with that.'

'It's exciting, isn't it? It was mentioned in the business section of the paper this morning. A huge affair. He's really kicking goals, your Dave, you must be very proud.'

Serena laughed dangerously. 'Oh, we're all very proud of him here. And doing his PhD too.' Might as well see if Mary was up to speed on that too.

'Ooh, is that what he's been arranging so secretly? I don't see how he'll have time really with the Bell Circle Road project . . . twice the size of the Gilbert Freeway extension. But he's the man of the moment now, especially since the company won that design award for the Gilbert.'

'Ah.' Her husband had obviously given up on telling her anything to do with his working life. 'Well, he *will* be busy, won't he?' She could barely keep her tone civil. Another huge job, months more of Dave never being home, with two new babies. Her mind was spinning. How could she have been stupid enough to think he would change? She had to get out of this house straight away. She would take the kids and move in with her mother, she would . . .

'Well, he'll be busy, but he always manages to keep a balance, doesn't he?' Mary was cautious, sensing the hostility. 'He's known for that around here. The way at least once a week, he insists on leaving the office before eight o'clock. Very modern young man.'

Serena almost sneered as she hung up. She stared at the phone for a moment and then she rang the real-estate agent. He was jubilant.

'That woman has raised her offer. I must say, I thought you were crazy to knock her back but —'

'Sell it. She can have it.'

'Don't you want to hear what she offered? Another five thousand dollars. That's a record price for the area, for that type of property . . .'

'Good. It's hers.'

She put the kids to bed, and waited up for Dave. He came in just after nine, and leaned down to kiss her on the head. She turned off the telly, as he took off his coat and flopped on the couch opposite.

'Serena, could you not park the car half on the curb? It throws the wheels out of alignment.'

She stared at him.

'Sorry,' he said hastily. 'How was your day?'

'Cooper cut his hand on a nail in the cubby.' She smoothed her top down over the globe of her stomach. 'I've been asking you for weeks to climb up there and check it out for jagged bits.'

'I did. I went in there three weeks ago. I banged down some nails and sanded some wood back. It should be fine.'

'Well, it obviously wasn't!' she snapped. 'He's cut himself. It was quite serious.'

'Okay, okay!' He glared at her, and then turned away, shaking his head. 'Fuck. Is *everything* my fault?'

She muttered, holding back tears. She had loved Dave, loved him so much, but he had ruined everything. There was no trust left now, nothing. She watched as he turned on the kettle and started to fold clothes in the washing basket. He was such a perfectionist. He smoothed down the tiny singlets before he folded them, frowned as he sought matching socks – as if *she* would have the luxury of doing anything perfectly ever again. She felt a pain in her back, and shifted her position.

'Oh God, don't bother,' she burst out irritably. 'You're mixing up all their clothes.' Didn't he know by now whose small socks were whose?

He threw some baby socks back in the basket. 'What's wrong with *you*?'

'What's . . . I'm like this, and you still think this is a fit time to come home.'

'I can't even have a conversation with you any more. I'm so sick of this.'

'I'm sick of it too. Sick of you.'

His eyes widened and she manoeuvred herself out of the couch.

'You know, the only difference between me and my mother is I gave up a better career,' she snarled. Her tummy was tight and the babies kicked mercilessly. 'Mary told me you've taken on Bell Circle Road, so that's more time without you around. And you've applied for *a fucking PhD*. The nerve of you.'

He reached out and gripped her shoulder hard.

'You're getting hysterical.'

'Don't manhandle me!' She grabbed a coat and car keys.

'Manhandle? I was trying to hug you.'

'You *pushed* me.'

'How *dare* you imply . . .' He clenched his fists, his face white and as he turned away he bumped against the hatstand, knocking off the glass Buddha that his mother had given them. It broke into three pieces, one rolling into a corner. All Serena could think about was getting away from him, getting her unborn babies out the door. He followed her into the cold night air, light spilling out after them and he shouted. 'Where are you going? You're in no state to . . .'

She turned and hissed into his face. 'This marriage is over. It's over.'

She got into the car and quickly locked the door, suddenly fearful Dave would reach in and stop her, his strength against her cumbersome helplessness. But he spun around, stalked back inside and slammed the door. She wrenched the key around in the ignition, pressed down on the accelerator. The car lurched away from the kerb and she hurled it around corners, headed for the old Tullamarine Freeway. The soullessness of concrete overpasses and dark empty lanes, the indicator clicking close like a heartbeat. She had always loved the long, long drives of the field trip days, becoming a mindless part of a machine, pressing it onwards. She put her foot down hard and shot out into the world like water released from a dam. Finally, finally, she could run.

33

Ana sat surrounded by cardboard boxes. She had spent the day packing her books, and her bathroom, and tomorrow she would do the kitchen. Over against the wall were two cardboard boxes of a different vintage, loaded with pieces of her mother's life. Her mother's TV and DVD player sat beside Ana's own, cords and plugs trailing. A man would come in the morning and collect a load, to be sold at a charity shop. Ana felt guilty about handing over Lily's things with so little ceremony. But what choice did she have? She already had a list of forty-eight things to do, carefully written on butcher's paper and stuck on her wall. She had to carve a path through the stuff of three lives – her own, Finn's, Lily's – so that she and Finn could start again.

She wanted to be in the green house by this weekend, just five days away. She had to pack up her own things and have them ready to go by Saturday. Her real-estate agent was adamant she had to leave at least one piece of furniture in each room, so it didn't look too abandoned to potential buyers, and Ana had to choose which of her paltry stock of furniture she could afford to leave behind for a few weeks. As it was, the green house was so much bigger than her flat that she and Finn would be rattling around almost empty rooms. She wanted to have the house professionally cleaned before she went in, and there was a dangerous branch that had to be lopped off the elm tree. Serena pointed out that the branch had been there this long, it could last a few more weeks. But Ana was preparing for motherhood with a grim intensity. Nothing that could possibly hurt her child would stay. My child. She whispered the words in wonder, and wished she could believe them. She had bought a pile of books on child care and development, and they sat on the table like homework. Thankfully Serena would be only fifteen minutes away, on call if she needed help. Although Serena would soon have more than enough on her plate.

Ana had taken Finn to Lily's funeral, braving Serena's disapproval. It was the first time Ana had openly disagreed with Serena about a child-raising issue, but as Serena herself had reminded her, Ana was Finn's mother now. And Ana felt strongly about this. Lily might not feel like Finn's grandmother now, but in time, in retrospect, he might ask whether he had been at his grandmother's funeral, and if not, why not. And anyway, Ana had wanted him there, for support. Was that so wrong? So she gently asserted herself with Serena, watched as her friend bit back her disagreement, and simply found some good clothes for Finn.

'Are you angry?' Ana asked.

Serena shook her head, resignedly. 'I don't agree. You know how I feel about children and funerals. But then, I don't agree with Cate about not vaccinating Matty. I wouldn't get a baby's ears pierced, like Sharon in my mums' group.' She shrugged. 'Your children are your own country. You set your own laws.'

Then there was the *Morning Star*. Ana took maternity leave, so she could set up home with Finn. There was some debate underway about whether she was entitled to it, and if she didn't get it she knew that was another fight she would have to wage. Although as it was, she found it hard to imagine returning to work at the *Star*.

She flicked through one of the child development books. She looked up 'single parent' in the index. Nothing. There never was. Well, her mother had done it alone, hadn't she?

Ana shuddered and pushed the thought away.

She had just given up on the day's packing and was getting ready for bed when her phone rang.

It was Dave. 'Is Serena with you?'

Ana sat on her couch.

'No. Why?'

He sighed, a sound of despair. 'We had a fight and she's taken off in the car. I thought she might have gone to your place.'

'Oh.' She glanced at the clock. Twenty past eleven. 'Well, sorry, I haven't heard from her.'

'Really?' His voice pleading. 'She's nearly eight months pregnant, Ana. If she's not with you, then I'll be seriously worried about her out driving so late. If she is with you, I won't come over, I just need to know. Could you just say something to indicate, just a word, and I'll never tell . . .'

'Really, Dave, I swear to God, she's not here. I've been packing all day. I wonder where she's gone?' Ana's stomach lurched. No more bad news, she could stand no more harm coming to those she loved. And if Serena had stormed out from Dave, why hadn't she come to Ana? 'Have you tried Cate?'

'No. I'll try her next. Is there anyone else . . . you can think of? Maybe . . .' he hesitated. 'Maybe someone I don't know about?'

The meaning of his question was clear, and hit Ana with its sadness. Poor Dave.

'I don't know of anyone you don't,' she said. 'Really, I don't. How bad was the fight?'

'Bad enough.'

'I'm sorry.'

'I'm so worried about her. I just need to know where she's gone.'

'I know. Let me have a think, Dave. And ring me if you hear anything.'

She was flicking through her address book, try-ing to think of all the people in her friend's life, when her phone rang again. She answered it, hoping to hear Serena's voice.

But it was Elijah.

'Dave called me, told me Serena's gone missing,' he said. Ana glanced at the clock again. It was now almost midnight. Dave must be beside himself. But *Elijah*?

'Why would he call you?'

'He's calling everyone who appears in Serena's diary for the past few months, or who she's been in contact with. He's called the police now too.'

'Oh.' The poor man. Ana was already pulling on clothes. 'I must get over there, help him with the kids. I'd better go.'

'No, it's okay, he's got Serena's friend Cate there with

him.' Elijah paused. 'Dave asked me if I knew of any-where she might have gone . . .'

Ana's body was faintly aroused by the sound of Elijah's voice, even as she registered irritation at his words. What on earth would Elijah know of Serena? Why was he even calling at such a time?

'And of course you don't.'

'Well, that's what I told Dave. Said I had no idea. But in actual fact, I do. She called me a little while ago.'

'You!' Ana dropped her keys and gripped the phone. 'She called you? Why didn't you tell Dave?' Why hadn't Serena called *her*? Her stomach lurched the way it did the night she had found Priya's toilet bag.

'I didn't tell Dave because she rang me in confidence. She asked me not to tell anyone. I shouldn't be telling you, but . . .'

'Tell me, Elijah.' Ana sat down hard on a kitchen chair. 'It's the middle of the night. She's heavily preg-nant. Dave is beside himself. She's carrying twins, she could go into early labour or anything. It's not the time to keep —'

'I know, I know, that's why I'm calling you. But I don't know for sure where she is. It's just a hunch. So I'll only tell you if you promise not to tell Dave, not just yet anyway.'

'Yes! Whatever. Just tell me.'

Elijah cleared his throat. 'She rang to say she had left Dave, and wanted a divorce. She wanted to make a time to meet with me; Friday, she suggested. She said she was going to stay with a friend in the coun-try for a few days. And she said something about a property she owned, a flat, which she's selling without Dave knowing. She wanted me to contact the real-estate agent and act on her behalf; arrange contracts and transfer of money, all that sort of stuff.'

'Oh!' Ana felt her stomach plummeting. She had known things were bad with Serena and Dave, but not *this* bad. Why hadn't Serena come to her? What had triggered this? Had Ana become so self-obsessed that she had failed to notice Serena's growing desperation? 'A friend in the country? And you think you know . . .'

'It's just a guess. It's an old colleague of hers. He lives at Mount Misstep, about ninety minutes north of Melbourne.'

'That Possum guy.' Ana remembered Elijah asking her about him. 'Are you saying . . .' She struggled to breathe for a moment. Was Serena having an affair? Had the two women she considered to be her closest friends in fact revealed *anything* of their private lives to her at all? Or had she simply not been listening?

'I'm not saying that. I don't know, I've got no reason to think that. It's just . . . I know Serena's been there to visit him before.' He sounded embarrassed. 'She's *seen* him, and without Dave. I'm not saying anything at all, only that this is one place where she might be.'

'So, what do we do?'

'Well. What do you think about driving with me up to Mount Misstep now, and we'll see for ourselves? If we find her and she's okay, then at least we know that and we can tell Dave. If she doesn't want him to know where she is, then I guess we have to respect that too.'

Ana made a choking sound. 'Not tell Dave?'

'Who's your best friend, Ana? Serena or Dave? Because sometimes you have to choose.'

'I know. I know.'

'Can you be ready in half an hour, if I swing by and pick you up?'

Ana pushed aside her drapes and stared out at the night. Rain blurred her view of the city's lights, and she could hear the faint roar of the wind. She nodded. 'I'll watch from the balcony. Just pull up and flash your lights and I'll race down.'

She hung up and pulled on a jacket, scarf and hat, before she returned to the window and pressed her nose to the cold glass, staring north. There was the spread of the northern suburbs, street lights and traffic lights and a trickle of cars heading home late. Then the dull glow of the suburbs faded to black, to the single line of long free-ways and the deep dark of the country. Somewhere out there was Serena, running away from her life even as it held onto her with four tiny, unborn hands. Ana pushed her gloved fingers into her coat pockets and watched the rain slide down the glass, and the occasional blur of late-night cars. When one set of headlights paused opposite her apartment block and flashed, she grabbed her bag and ran down the stairs.

34

Serena was driving north on the Calder Freeway when she felt the first pains. She turned the wheel and winced. Maybe she had pulled a muscle. Then the pain was upon her, so hard she cried out, geared down and pulled into an empty truck stop. She threw open the car door and fell on her knees in wet gum leaves, groaning through gritted teeth. The pain moved through her and passed away, like an early roll of thunder on an airless night. She rested her head on her forearms and panted, the rain gentle on her shoulders, until her breath slowed.

It couldn't be labour. She had four weeks to go and she had been late with Cooper and Angus. Poss. He had called regularly over the past weeks, asking in a smaller and smaller voice if she wanted to go out for a coffee, bring the kids up to his property again, read another geology paper. And her bushfire of indignation and humiliation had finally burnt out under the cool balm of his concern. She had got it wrong with him, but they could still be friends. She wasn't in love with Poss, she realised, she'd just been momentarily taken by the idea that *he* was in love with *her*. And now, he was the friend she wanted. Not Ana, the first person Dave would call. No. And anyway, Serena wanted to drive *far*. Wanted to drive into the past, to a time when *she* was the one leaving and coming home, when marriage was a series of delicious intervals between field trips, not endless disappointments and an eternal wait in the lounge room amidst the clutter of childhood.

Serena got to her feet, drenched, and returned to the car. The road stretched empty in either direction, white lines shivering in the rain and stitching their way through dripping trees. A sign informed her she was ten minutes drive from the turn-off to Mount Misstep.

She shivered, and drove off. She felt pleasantly fragile, deliciously pain-free. She ate two pieces of chocolate. The pain became a memory, its only residue her limp limbs. Maybe just a Braxton Hicks. The Jackson Browne tape she had been listening to came back on, and she geared up, relaxing again into the cocoon of speed. Took the turn-off to Mount Misstep and barrelled down the smaller road, through a dark tunnel of trees. Thinking, planning as she drove. She would call the real-estate agent. Ask him to find her a rental property. She would do it tomorrow, she could get a lot done by phone . . .

The pain hit her again. It was big, a thing bigger than herself, and for a moment she thought she had run over something. I'm – In – A – Car. She said it between gritted teeth, to keep focused. She would pull off the road, head into the trees. But then she saw headlights behind her, getting larger, brighter, quickly, and she panicked. No time now to get off the road. An engine roared and lights flashed into her rear-vision mirror and blinded her. The rain came at an angle, dangerously pulling her focus toward it. A truck air grille filled her back window, and spilled over into her side mirrors. She pressed harder on the accelerator. Her steering wheel juddered and she knew she had never been in so much danger in her life, with this semitrailer all but mounting her bumper bar like a dog on heat, both of them thundering along at one hundred and thirty ks on narrow wet road. The beating inside her grew louder, and Cooper and Angus's faces floated somewhere through the waves of pain. She held on for them, gripped the steering wheel, and focused on the white lines as they merged into one, unrolling under her front right wheel like a piece of ribbon. With more flashing of lights, the semi pulled out and overtook in a howl of grinding and gears. Then gone. The relief of it pushed her to tears, loosened her hands, and the car started to jitter wildly until she remembered she could lift her foot off the pedal, she could pull over into the trees.

The pain went out like the tide and she was left with just the horror of it. This was it. The babies were coming and it was too soon. Little hairless limbs, translucent skin, organs unfinished. She was insane to have left her home, the victim of some wild pregnancy hormone that had led her astray, she could see it now. She should have been under lock and key, but she was an adult, she was meant to be looking after herself. What a miserable job she was doing of it. And the babies, two of them, her sacred trust, her gift from the universe. She knew now she would fight for them, whatever fears and doubts she had had. She put her head on the steering wheel again and panted. She had to think quickly, had to be mother for when the pain came back and made a child of her.

How far was it to Possum's? Probably more than an hour's walk. She could abandon the car, but the two contractions had been so strong, and so close, that she could find herself giving birth alone in the trees. She would wait, see if there were more contractions, and how far apart they were.

The contraction came, and she remembered to breathe out the whole way, breathe out the pain. She waited, and another came. Now she was calmer, they were eight minutes apart by the car clock. As soon as the pain left, she started the engine. She would drive for five minutes and then stop to prepare herself for the next contraction. Maybe in this fashion she could inch her way to Possum's.

After almost an hour of this, she stopped in a place where the road gently dipped, and the trees grew high, blotting out the night sky and filtering the rain. She was leaning straight-armed on the bonnet when she heard a growing roar behind her and the semi was back, from the other direction, flooding her with light, the blunt-jawed face of its cabin twice her height.

The engine stopped and she groaned through a contraction, trying to strangle her own sound even as it leached out of her throat. Two men cantered across the road; blueys, bare legs, Blundstones. The pain left her and she wanted to fall to her knees and weep. She held onto the car and felt the sweat run over her, mingling with the rain.

'You right, love?'

She raised her face, her hair clinging to her cheeks. 'Do you know Possum Davies? Mount Misstep?'

'Shit. She's in labour.'

'Up in the church? Want me to go get him?'

'Please. Quickly.'

One man stayed with her, mute and embarrassed through her next contraction, as she rested clenched fists on the boot and screamed through clenched teeth. He held a raincoat over her head until she swatted it away, desperate for the cold water on her burning skin. Finally the truck thundered back down the road, its brakes moaning, followed by a ute.

Possum swung out, in a flannel shirt, khakis and big boots.

'Serena, what the hell are you doing here?' He looked her up and down, his face thin with shock, eyes big. 'Dave called. He's worried sick about you.'

'Having a baby,' she said weakly. Close to weeping at the sight of him, so grateful was she for a friendly face. But strangely longing for her husband, irrationally angry that he wasn't with her. Dave would know, in his very bones, that she was in labour, she told herself. No matter how far away he was, he knew.

Poss bent over her, his body a question mark of anxiety. 'I'll take you to Bendigo Hospital. It's less than an hour away.'

She gasped. 'No time. Can't move. Having them here.' She yearned for the sterile security of hospital, for doctors to catch her tiny undercooked babies as they fell.

'No, you're not! Can you get in the ute? My place is only five minutes.'

'*Nooo . . .*'

'Get her in the ute.'

At Poss's, the two of them staggered slowly down the path to the church, stopping once for a contraction, she flopping on him like a drunk on a bar, looking down at her feet while the pain filled her with noise. For those minutes he didn't exist, he was just something to lean on. Gradually she could hear herself moaning, grinding the pain out of her vocal chords, and soon she felt the texture of his shirt, and his arms holding her up.

'Okay to go?' he murmured.

He held her around the shoulders, guided her through the front doors.

'You need to wash your hands,' she said. At least he had been at the birth of his own child; this would not be his first.

He went away and came back with scalding hot towels. She flinched at them on her lower back, and then felt the kindness of them spread through her muscles. She put her hands on her bulge, now so hot and sore, and could not believe babies were coming. Every labour, it seemed impossible. This one, so much more so.

He offered her a plate with small white triangles on it. She stared at them in confusion. Cotton balls?

'Apple,' he whispered.

'Ugh!' She imagined the tart taste of it, its floury texture in her mouth and she turned away and vomited, thin sticky strings of mucus. It revived her.

She felt the pain rising in her again like something that wanted out from the limits of her skin. She rolled over, on all fours, and she bore it. She fixed her gaze on the mottled green cover of a book that lay on Poss's floor, unable to read the cover. But look at it, how had they laid Gatum ignimbrite on a book cover, how beautiful, maybe they had done it just for her, so she could rest her bulging eyes on the patterns and shapings of history, the rheomorphism around phencrysts of feldspar and look, there was the quartz, puddles of white against the jade. She reached out to touch it and started when her fingers made contact. It was just paper, cardboard, nothing more, and then the pain came back over her in floods.

She could see in her mind's eye the first baby's head, face following the simple curve of her backbone, inching down her vagina, the coiled body starting to elongate, the umbilical cord starting to unwind, the soles of tiny feet finally leaving the upside down floor of the uterus where they had danced. Maybe those toes stretched to brush lightly one last time against the wet floor of the womb, as if to say goodbye. Goodbye. She got the urge to push, and she shouted with fear and relief.

She was stretching, she was tearing, but then she reached down with her fingers and she could feel no tear, just a little acorn that grew bigger and bigger. She pushed back the skin of her own perineum, as if it were cuticles on a fingernail. Then Poss's face was a gawp of fright and wonder and hope, and the baby's head slipped out. She could see the top of it there between her legs. She felt around the neck, a slick of blood and amniotic fluid. No loops of cord. She pushed and the slippery bundle of arms and legs passed out of her with little pain. Poss caught it in his large nervous hands and laid it on the towels between her legs. She took another towel and wiped at the little face, skin translucent, still a creature of water. She gently lifted one leg, like a chicken wing, and saw the little peanut of flesh. So perfect. She lifted him up, the veined cord from his belly still trailing down between her legs, and his squashed eyelids parted a fraction, showing a dark glimmer. He opened his mouth and made a little *hack, hack* sound, and then he launched into a thin wail. Serena felt tears flood her eyes, nose, mouth and she held him to her chest and leaned back on the couch. She stared at Poss and smiled weakly.

He exhaled and shook his head. 'He's all right?'

'I think so.' She tilted the baby towards her right nipple, always her better one for feeding, and watched as he turned his head and gaped like a goldfish.

Poss sat back and put his fist to his forehead, his body slumped. A nest of bloody towels lay at his feet. He dragged himself up and went to the kitchen. She could see him talking on the phone, but couldn't hear him.

Then she felt the pressure again and she cried out. Poss strode back, startled, and she looked at his clear brown eyes, thrust the baby into his arms.

'Take him, wrap him. Keep him warm.'

And she howled.

35

'Here. Take this blanket.'

'What about you? You don't even have a jacket.'

'I'm fine. Put it over yourself.'

Rain beat on the car's roof. Ana tugged the blanket around her shoulders and pulled her hat lower on her head. She squeezed her folded arms and stole a glance at the dark figure beside her. The blue light of a mobile phone screen lit up Elijah's handsome, frowning face.

'Still no signal,' he said.

'How long do you think until someone finds us?'

'It might not be until morning. Are you sure you don't want me to walk out and get some help?'

'Not in this rain.'

They had driven for over an hour, and found Mount Misstep, a dark ghost town in these early hours. But then, somewhere along the turn-off to Possum's house, climbing the hill through dense bush, they had become disoriented. They had pulled off the muddy dirt track to check a map of the area by the light of Eli's phone, only to find these dirt trails were unmarked. When they went to start the car again, the back wheels just spun deeper and deeper in the track's wet shoulder. Bogged.

Ana heard him rustling around beside her, and then his face appeared again, this time in the glow from the glovebox light.

'Jelly bean?' It went dark again. 'Give me your hand.'

She held out her cupped hand and he fumbled for it, held it as he guided the sweets in. She was instantly aroused, and just as quickly despairing. She was miserable with love and longing for this man, aching with the effort of remaining casual with him. She was also worried about Serena, especially if she had driven on these rough dirt tracks in this rain, in her condition. If the phone was working, Ana would have called Dave. What if something happened to her oldest friend, now the closest remaining thing Ana had, besides Finn, to family? What about her children? And then Elijah felt for her fingers, and closed his hand over hers. She felt the warmth of his skin in the darkness and heard how his breath stilled, the way Finn's did sometimes when you had his full attention.

'I've missed you,' he whispered. Not letting go of her hand.

She waited, her heart racing, her head calculating his words. Just friends, she reminded herself.

'I've missed you too.'

'I was pretty shocked when you called. And said sorry.' His voice trembled. He kept hold of her hand.

She said nothing, just felt the warmth of him, and wondered what was happening.

He stroked her hand. 'It was big of you to ring and apologise. It was me who should have said sorry.'

'You?'

'Yes. I was gutless, about the whole thing. I lacked . . . courage. Scared of getting hurt. Even yesterday, when

348

you called, I was so shocked.'

She felt his hand stroking her fingers, still didn't dare touch him back. Her heart raced. 'That's funny. When Mum died, it made me think about how timid I'd been. How frightened.'

'You don't seem frightened of anything.'

'I was frightened of us. Frightened about how good it was, about getting hurt. When I found Priya's toilet bag I shouldn't have pushed you to answer my questions. You had the right to refuse. But I was so scared, I think I used it as an excuse to run away. To leave you before you could leave me.'

When he spoke, she heard the smile in his words. 'I wasn't going to leave you. You were all I could think about.' He paused, spoke gently. 'You still are.'

The darkness hugged them and Ana was glad that all she could see was shadow, so bright and glowing did her heart feel. She finally moved her fingers, let herself take the risk and stroke his hand. She could feel the sweet warmth of his breath as he leant close and spoke again.

'But I was scared of more than us. I was scared I could be Finn's father. I still am, I guess. You made me consider that seriously, and up until then I'd been trying not to think about it. Although I might *not* be, too. You should keep that in mind.'

Ana felt the jolt at the words. Of course, she already knew he had slept with Priya, but to hear it from his own mouth . . . 'Well, yes, there's a chance it could have been Richard.'

'Not just Richard. You see, I don't think I was the only one.'

Ana frowned. 'Priya slept with other men too?'

'One other that I know of. Within days of me. But who knows, maybe there were more.'

'You never said *when* you slept with Priya.'

He sighed and laughed ruefully. 'Well. Yes.'

'Let me guess. Nine months before Finn was born.'

'Yes. About that. But as I say, I wasn't the only one.'

'Can I ask you who the other guy is?'

He paused. 'Could you ask Serena?'

'*She* knows?'

'Ask her.'

Ana sat in wonder, stared out her window at the raindrops racing down the glass. Priya, so private, so reserved, had wanted this child so much. This much. Enough to step outside the comfort zone of her marriage and into the beds of other men, linking her star to theirs in a secret marriage of flesh that would last a lifetime. How many women, desperate for a child, had done such a thing? How many otherwise faithful women had quietly bookmarked their happy, infertile marriages and polished up all their old charms to lure a stranger into this unwitting act of alchemy?

She mused. 'We could do DNA testing.'

They listened to the rain for a few minutes before Elijah replied, sounding thoughtful. 'Maybe it's just me, but I don't think it's that important, not at this stage anyway. What's important is that Richard was Finn's dad for the first eighteen months of his life, and Priya didn't invite anyone else to be Finn's dad, not in that way.' He paused. 'Which is really the most important way, in my opinion.'

'But now Richard's gone, surely . . .' she trailed off.

'Well, you could. It's up to you. I'll do it if you want.'

Ana considered it. It might be Elijah, or it might not be. There was something about the possibility that she liked, didn't want to lose to some scientific procedure. They were clasping both hands now, drawing close for warmth. They finished the jelly beans before he spoke again, his voice low.

'Ana, could we try again?'

She felt herself grinning in the darkness, was glad he couldn't see her. Felt all the world's fabulous potential for happiness rushing at her again, filling up her future.

'Okay.' The broadness of her smile was audible in her voice and they both laughed at it, and for sheer joy.

'And can we never go househunting again?'

'I knew you hated it. I kept telling you you didn't have to come.'

'I didn't hate it. It's just you were so fussy.'

She laughed. 'Well, no more househunting. Instead you can come visit me and Finn in a spectacularly ugly green weatherboard home.'

'Sensational.' He slipped his hand behind her neck and kissed her.

She felt her body melting. Through the rain and wind she heard a thin wail; a far-off sound that could have been an animal, could have been an ambulance siren, and then it was gone, buried in the noise of the elements and their beating hearts.

'So what will we do on weekends if we're not

househunting?' She spoke playfully, slipping a hand under his shirt, but he sat back and considered it seriously.

'We can take Finn to the miniature trains. My nephews like them.'

'We can show him how to fly a kite.'

'I could build him a cubby. That's a bloke's job.'

'We could buy him a puppy. There's all this great parkland behind the house.'

'Maybe we could go back to Serena's beach house sometime . . .'

'Camp in the bush . . .'

'Cook dinner on a campfire . . .'

'Sleep in a tent, with Finn between us . . .'

'But not always between us . . .' She kissed him again, her heart full of joy. Was this her destiny, finally, to be so content with the ordinary and everyday – a child, a man, a home? 'My mother would be disappointed in me,' she murmured.

'Don't women live to disappoint their mothers?'

'Maybe.'

'What about me? How could I disappoint you?'

She laughed, a little anxiously. 'You sound like you're looking for ways!'

He was serious. 'I just never want to do it, ever again.'

'Never ever? That's a big call.'

He stroked her face in the darkness, cupped her jaw in his hands. 'Well, big calls are what I'm making here, Ana. Big calls are what you make when you're really in love.'

She felt her face flush, her body giddy at so much joy. He spoke again. 'You know, when I first met you, I really didn't think you'd take Finn. I underestimated you. And I could see your life was pretty good without a child.'

'It was okay.'

'Just okay?'

'I thought it was pretty good. But I had no idea how good it could be, until it got so much better there, for a while.'

'How?'

'Well, I fell in love with you. And with Finn. And Finn started . . . liking me.'

'You could lash out and say he loves you, you know.'

'He will, one day. But you can't rush these things.'

'Of course you can . . .'

They kissed again, and Ana reflected later that the ambulance could have driven right past them and they wouldn't have even noticed. All she could feel was the farewell touch of the old ghosts as they lost their grip on her forever; as she shot like a train towards Finn, Elijah, and a new spring. Towards a green house and a future that was hers to create, from scratch.

36

Dave put another pillow behind Serena's head and swivelled the breakfast tray towards her.

'Are you warm enough?'

She nodded.

They both looked at the baby in the humidicrib beside them. He had Serena's rosebud mouth and Dave's frown. Long feet and a jaundice tan. The skin on his limbs was loose and downy, and he slept, head turned to one side.

'We need to think about a name,' Serena whispered, still shaky and weak. In the past twenty-four hours she had wept on and off, tears in the shower, while eating, while expressing milk. Her tears came in surges, like the blood. So much liquid after a baby: tears, and blood and milky breasts. A heart runny with love.

'Names,' said Dave, emphatically.

'That's right.' She nodded. 'Is it time to go back to Special Care?'

'Not yet.'

'I'm just so glad she's going to be all right.'

'Our daughter.'

She glanced at Dave, at the side of his face, secretly studied it while he watched his son. Some time during the chaos of the day before, she had become aware of her husband, his hands plunged into first one humidicrib and then the other, talking to the paediatrician, brushing away his own tears with the rough sleeve of his jacket. She hadn't asked what he was doing there, or when he had arrived, or how he had found her.

The little boy was tiny but strong, but for a day, there had been nothing but the enormous question of whether their little girl would make it. She had been born not breathing, and was resuscitated by paramedics as the ambulance staggered down dirt tracks on its way to the main road and to hospital. Once in hospital she stopped breathing again and was placed on a monitor in the neonatal Special Care Nursery, where she stopped breathing again twice in the first few hours of her life, and was each time quickly resuscitated. Duskies, the doctors called the terrifying non-breathing incidents, with little explanation for how or why they occurred. Serena and Dave watched, waited, during hours that seemed in a universe of time all of their own. One, two, three hours went by and the girl simply slept. Four, five, six hours, and then it was night and somewhere in the early hours, Serena had sunk into sleep, exhausted.

But that morning the paediatrician told them the baby would be moved out of Special Care, and in with Serena. Another week in a humidicrib and if she could make it to two kilos, they could all transfer to a Melbourne hospital, and then back home. She would be all right. The nurses helped Serena start feeding the little boy, and express precious drops of colostrum for the girl. There were obstetricians and paediatricians and midwives in and out of the room and the murmur in the corridors . . . *had twins out in the bush, no medical help, lucky she didn't . . .*

In those mad early hours Serena had felt neither grateful nor awkward to have Dave there; he was like a part of herself. But now she looked at him and his hair was wet and combed; he was red-eyed but freshly shaven. Their last parting passed across her mind like a cloud.

'Where did you sleep?' she asked.

He nodded towards the door. 'They let me doss down in an empty room, on a folding bed. Then I nicked a towel and snuck into one of the patient bathrooms.'

She smiled. It was too long since she had seen the rebellious side of her husband, the part of him that had once broken rules with glee. His cast-iron backbone, a stubbornness that had steamrolled through every obstacle on projects, and given him his reputation at work as someone who could get things done. She hoped he never lost that, even if she wasn't around to see it. Her children would come to know it well, she would make sure of that. Access visits, all that stuff, it could be worked out later.

'How did you know where I was?'

'Poss rang. He said, mate, you're about to have your second new baby. Said the ambulance was on its way. I could hear you screaming in the background, and I was pretty wild.'

'With Poss?'

He nodded. 'I called him an arsehole. Asked why you had gone to him.' He watched her.

She stared back, unblinkingly. Didn't answer. She

wasn't sure he expected an answer. Knew he didn't deserve one. He nodded slowly, accepting it, and went on.

'I already had the police out looking for you, so I rang them first. Then I got your mum lined up to take over from Cate, with the kids. As soon as I could, I jumped in the car and broke every speed limit getting here.'

'Were you at Poss's?' She didn't remember seeing him, but then she had been transfixed, terrified, when her daughter's body began to emerge. The head blue, rubbery in a slick of liquid between her thighs. The abrupt shut-off of a siren, the clattering and lights and people, the cord cut and baby whisked into an ambulance. A second ambulance for herself and the first baby; shutting her eyes and willing her tiny daughter to live.

'No. He rang me while I was on the road, said you were en route to Bendigo Hospital.' He shook his head. 'I got to the hospital before you, and I was waiting at the front doors when the ambulances pulled in. They wouldn't believe I was the father at first. Wouldn't let me come with you.'

'How did you convince them?'

'You don't remember?' He looked gaunt, eyes too large above his cheekbones. 'You told them. You said, that's my husband.'

'Did I?'

They stared at each other, back where they had been two days ago. He spoke, his voice quavering.

'Serena, you didn't mean what you said, did you? Because I've got a proposal to put to you . . .'

'I did mean it, Dave. It's too late for proposals.' She

felt sad and exhausted, and pushed the dinner tray away. 'I've sold Butterworth Street.'

'You've . . .'

'I sold it. It was in my name, I didn't have to tell you. I'll pay you back what you put into it. But I'll use that money to get me and the kids set up on our own. I don't want the house. There's too many sad memories there. We'll find somewhere else . . .'

'Wait. Stop.' He reached out his hands, as if to push her back. 'Please just listen to me. You got it all wrong back there at home. When you stormed out.'

'I don't think I got anything wrong. The past year —'

'I'm not going to do a PhD. I've been asking about applying to do a Dip Ed at La Trobe Uni.'

'What, in your spare time?'

'No, you see, this is my plan for getting out of engineering. I just wanted to talk to you about it first. Just listen.' He leaned forward. 'I'll quit Hodson's —'

'You'll what?'

'Shush. This is what I'm proposing. That I quit Hodson's, here and now, and take the rest of the year off. I've talked to the bank, we can get the house revalued and borrow against it. Then next year, I do a Dip Ed, and then the year after I can start work as a high-school teacher.'

She stared at him. 'Are you serious?'

'Completely.'

'You wouldn't be happy as a teacher.'

'Well, it can only be better than being stressed out of my mind as an engineer, and missing out on my children growing up, and losing my marriage.'

'You'd miss engineering.'

He shrugged. 'I'll get over it.'

'You'll halve your salary. Less.'

'I don't mind, if you don't.'

'Well, of course I don't. But . . .'

'What do you think?'

She mused. 'Why did you get a message from Melbourne Uni, not La Trobe? And it was about doing a PhD.'

'I rang them to ask about geology PhDs. I heard there were some scholarships going in minerals geology, and I thought it might be something you'd like to do. Something you could do part time.'

She blinked. 'It's too late.'

'Well, I'm going to resign anyway.'

'Bullshit.'

He reached into his shirt pocket and unfolded a piece of paper before her. She read it. A politely worded letter to Hodson's, announcing his resignation from the company, effective immediately. Asking to be excused from serving out the full notice required by his contract. Thanking them for the opportunities, and citing the needs of his young and growing family for leaving not just the company, but the industry.

She read it three times, and then she laid it on the sheet. Not since he handed her an engagement ring, years ago, had she felt her life change direction like this; with a thump in her heart.

'Can you walk to the nurses' station?' He stood up and reached out to her.

She leaned on him, and together they shuffled out of

the room and down the hall to the midwives' reception desk. It was empty; lights up and down the hall indicating which rooms the nurses were in. Dave walked around the desk, found the fax machine and loaded his resignation letter. She watched while he dialled, and they stood there together while the sheet of paper slid through the machine, and fluttered out onto the floor.

She looked at him. 'I really did sell Butterworth Street.'

He shrugged. 'Well. It was yours.'

'I got a great price for it.'

He smiled at her appealingly. 'Enough for us to live on for the next couple of years?'

She frowned. She suddenly felt weak and uncertain, and wanted to be close to her babies again. 'I don't know. Is it time to go to Special Care yet?'

His expression softened. 'Sure.'

Back in her room, they gazed into the humidicrib. The baby boy, still unnamed, raised tiny fists to his temples and made a baa-ing sound. Streaks of white vernix sat in the crease of his eyelids.

Dave spoke. 'Mum called me after her visit. She thoroughly told me off. Said she'd left my dad for all the same reasons that I was about to lose you.'

'I've always liked Jo.'

'And I've been having this recurring nightmare about Cooper. This dream where I get up one morning and Cooper doesn't know who I am.'

Serena smiled wryly. 'Well, you deserve it, but it'll never happen. He adores you.'

'My mum hinted I might have lost you already. That

there might be another man.' His expression sobered. 'Would you tell me if there was?'

Serena thought guiltily of Poss. Felt suddenly grateful he had knocked her back. 'No,' she said quietly. 'I mean no, there isn't.'

Relief flooded Dave's face, and he picked up both of her hands.

'Serena, I'm so sorry.' Tears filled his eyes, he held her hands so hard her joints hurt. 'I never wanted to be this person. Never wanted to be like my dad. Give me another chance.'

She shook her head doubtfully. 'Would you be fulfilled? Would you eventually resent me for it?'

He stroked her cheek. 'I want a life, Sreny. I want a family, and I don't want to ring home to say goodnight to my kids. I want to know them before they grow up.'

'What will you teach?'

'Maths and science. There's a shortage of male teachers, so it shouldn't be hard to get a job. Do you think I'd be okay at it?'

She nodded slowly, trying to imagine it. 'Yes. Maybe. I don't know.'

He took a deep breath. 'It's been hell, this year, absolute hell. I can understand why you've been so angry with me. I haven't liked myself for a long time.' He shook her hands impatiently. 'What do you say, Serena?'

She nodded slowly. She was trying to re-imagine her life, was suddenly frightened at the thought of how different it might be. 'So, you'd be home for the next six months . . .'

'And next year I'd be at uni, so still at home a lot. You

know what uni's like. And maybe when I finish, and the babies are settled in, you could start doing the PhD as well, part time?'

'So then you'd be a teacher . . .'

'And I'd qualify in time for when Coop starts school. I'd have the same holidays as him. We could go on trips together, Sreny. Caravan holidays down the coast . . .'

'Breakfasts and dinners together . . .'

'Build them a shit-hot cubby . . .'

'Watch bad telly at night together . . .'

'Four children! We could start our own band . . .'

'You might drive me crazy . . .' She was thinking of the last long weekend he had stayed home.

He smiled. 'It would be nice if you let me do things my way. Not tell me how to do everything. Let me make my own mistakes.' He threaded his fingers through hers. 'Remember when we met, what it was like working together? Being in a team? I want it to feel like that again.'

'Only now it's babies instead of rocks.'

'Far more profitable.' He smiled. 'Are you happy to have a girl?'

She thought about it, cautious of the joy welling up in her heart. 'I'll be happy to have a husband,' she said quietly, and then she was being wrapped in his arms, squeezed in folds of his coat, his tears on her neck.

'Thank you.'

For the first time in a long time, she could imagine them as a real family. Life could, just maybe, be fun again.

'I still think the two-storey cubby is a goer,' he murmured into her neck.

She groaned. 'Oh God. The man who's been managing a billion-dollar construction job turns his skills to a backyard cubby.'

They laughed, clutching each other.

She wiped away her own tears, and then his. 'I wanted you so much when I was in labour.'

He held her face in his hands. 'I was going insane. So relieved to get Poss's call, and so angry and so scared.'

She smiled. 'Not as scared as Poss was, I think.'

He laughed. 'I spoke to him this morning. He was very glad to hear both the babies were doing well. Sent you his love. And you'll never guess what happened yesterday morning. After you were taken to hospital, he crashed out on his couch for a few hours, exhausted, and then he got up at the crack of dawn and went outside to take a leak, and guess who stumbled out of the bushes at the back of his property . . .'

'Who?'

'. . . Ana! And that lawyer guy she was seeing a few months ago, Elijah! Poss said he thought he was seeing things. They staggered out of the gum trees hand in hand and looking blissfully happy. Said they had driven up here looking for you, and were amazed to hear you were in the nearby hospital with two new babies.'

'Ana and Elijah?'

'Their car got bogged just half a k away. Poss said it seemed like they couldn't care less about it, they were just ecstatic to hear you were okay. Couldn't stop kissing each other. Trotted off to wake up the publican at the hotel for a champagne breakfast and came back with more champagne and had a steaming bath in Poss's outdoor tub. Arranged for the car to be towed back to Melbourne for an exorbitant price, and then Poss took them to the train and they got on, giggling like a couple of kids . . .'

Serena laughed. 'Priya knew what she was doing.'

'She always did, didn't she?'

Yes, Serena mused, Priya always knew precisely what she was doing, even when she was confusing other people. She sat back on the pillow and thought about beautiful, dark-eyed Finn, always holding his Jarmy and trailing after Cooper. He would go to Ana now, but this sliver of his babyhood would always live in Serena's heart, along with those of her own children. She had watched Ana change, watched her love for Finn spark, and spread through her like a bushfire that would burn forever. And as for working out who was Finn's real father, that was all up to Ana.

But what was a real father, anyway? It took so much more than contributing a sperm to father a child. So much more than earning the money to pay the mortgage and fill the fridge. Whoever Finn ended up calling Dad, if anyone, would earn the privilege the long, slow way. With reading of stories and kicking of footies and cooking of dinners. Just like Dave would do now.

Her last waking thought was that if Dave was a better father, she wouldn't have to be a perfect mother. And with her heart lighter, she turned her cheek into the white pillow and drifted into a healing sleep.

37

'When is it *my* birthday?' Cooper wept as his mother shook a box of sausage rolls out onto an oven tray.

'It's nobody's birthday, it's a christening. For Irie and Joe and Finn.' Serena put the sausage rolls on top of the fridge, to be heated later.

'What about *me*?'

'You were christened when you were a baby. You know, the picture in the lounge room.'

'Finn's not a baby.'

'No. But Finn has a new mummy, hasn't he? So she can christen him if she wants to.'

She nudged her son out the back door and leaned in the door frame to watch as he disconsolately meandered over the deck and down into the garden. She stroked the baby in the sling against her chest, but little Iris Priya slept on. After her frightening start in life, Irie grew stronger and stronger. She and her brother, Joseph David, began filling out, their little arms and legs starting to develop comforting layers of fat. At two months old, they were feeding every four hours, a mixture of breastmilk from their mother, and bottles carefully sterilised and mixed by their father. Irie's waking expression was a coolly confronting stare that made her adoring grandmother Iris declare she was going to be a handful. Joey was a cheery soul who slept well and smiled at anyone.

It was now late October, the sky was clear and the sun was already edging over next door's trees. Within half an hour, Serena's own garden would be bathed in spring sunshine. She could see Dave's hat bobbing as he pulled up old corn stalks and stacked them in a corner, baby Joe asleep in the pram under a shady tree. Dave had worked hard in the garden the last couple of weeks, preparing it for the christening. The circular bed where the vegetables grew had been trimmed and replanted in parts, restored to order in others. The archway into the circle was draped with pumpkin vines and Dave had erected pyramids for climbing beans, and planted strawberries. The ceremony would be in the middle of the circle.

Iris came in and dropped her handbag on the kitchen table. 'Give my girlie to Nana.'

'She's asleep, Mum. Well, she was.' Iris junior opened her eyes and frowned appraisingly at her grandmother.

'Nanna's going to teach you all sorts of things, angel. All about the sisterhood, and the movement and the proud history she's a part of . . .'

'Mum, she's only eight weeks. Can you wait a bit?'

'Well, with three brothers, she'll need to learn how to be a strong girl! How to assert herself . . .'

Serena stroked her daughter's soft cheek. 'I have a feeling this one will be able to stand up for herself quite well . . .'

Iris shook her head, her eyes distant. 'Can you imagine, Sreny? What the world will be like for women when she's your age? My age?'

'No, I can't,' said Serena firmly, tugging her baby out of the sling. Mel had given her a Slingshot! as a birth present.

'Now you've gone and woken her up, you can take her and change her into something nice for the party.'

'And where's Joanne today?' Iris sniffed as she swept the baby into her arms. She had been miffed about Jo coming to stay again this time, to help with the children after the birth. 'I don't want to get in her way, I'm sure.'

'She's gone up the street to pick up some pastries.' Serena hastily spread icing on cupcakes. 'She's going home tomorrow. So plenty of chance for you to come and help if you want to, Mum. It's all hands on deck around here. You'd be very welcome.'

'Oh, yes.' Iris retreated nervously to the nursery, murmuring as she went, '. . . see what I can fit in . . . needs of the Centre very high at the moment . . .'

Serena rolled her eyes. She stood by the window and watched Dave load Cooper up with dry corn stalks and point him towards the far end of the garden. Cooper staggered off obediently, trailed by Angus. Serena would miss Jo when she left tomorrow, but not desperately. It would be good for her and Dave to have the house to themselves again; to feel like a family. And Ana and Elijah were clamouring to have the boys over at the green house, just a short drive away.

The members of Serena's mothers' group had, one after another, arrived with presents and hot meals when the babies came home from hospital. Cate revealed that Mel had set up a roster for them all to cook and offer help, and even Sharon dropped over a couple of bags of McDonalds, which were gratefully scoffed by Dave and the boys. Cate mixed up a variety of foul-tasting tonics, which were meant to aid recovery and boost milk production after giving birth, and Serena dutifully took them for a few days, gagging every time, before she guiltily pushed them to the back of the cupboard and tried to forget them. The bags of chocolate dropped in by Ana's friend Marnie – who had dumped her old mothers' group and joined Serena's – were somehow much more healing.

Her mother returned with Irie dressed in a green growsuit.

'Now, tell me again why Finn is being christened? Hasn't he been christened already?'

'No. Priya wanted to do it but she and Richard couldn't agree on what style, what religion, what words.'

'So *Ana's* going to do it?' Iris sounded doubtful as she buried her face in her granddaughter's milky neck.

Serena put the coffee, milk and sugar out on the table and counted spoons. 'Yes. I think it's a great idea. She said she would have wanted to christen a child of her own and I said well, that's how you've got to think of Finn, and she thought about it and decided she would. The papers came through last week and Finn is now her legally adopted son, so this is a way of celebrating.'

Iris sniffed. 'Well. I hope she's not going to quit that wonderful job of hers.'

Serena laughed. She would leave Ana to deal with that question herself.

'Kiss for Ana?' Ana said hopefully, bending down beside the little boy as he crouched, studying, she could now see, an anthill. 'Cuddle?'

She had become a beggar, addicted to the little arms around her neck, the weight of him on her hip. Little lips on hers. But Finn held his toy phone to his ear and burbled away conversationally. 'Lijah? Lijah?' Ana touched his black curls and perched herself on the edge of her back deck, still so new there were tendrils of wood shavings at her feet. Banksias and wattles and eucalypts shook their branches at her, over her back fence with its gate leading out to the small wilderness of creek and bush. Since moving in, they had gone there every day to explore, and when Elijah brought home the labrador puppy, their daily walks became even more delightful. It was also an escape from the flow of tradesmen coming through the house – plasterers, then painters, then carpet layers, then the men who polished the floorboards. Ana had left the quaint old kitchen as it was, just installing a dishwasher and a new fridge. Anything else could wait a few years. She and Finn planted a dozen trees, and the dustbowl of a backyard was dotted with tiny saplings and tree guards. Now that it was spring, they could catch some sun sitting on the deck.

She left Finn and wandered inside to pack a bag. Tiger the puppy was asleep on Finn's bed. For the first few weeks after the move, Finn woke in the night crying for Serena, and every time, Ana took him back to her bed, secretly gleeful to be breaking one of the rules that everyone had hectored her about. *Don't let him sleep with you, or you'll never get rid of him*. Go to hell, she thought, nestling down with the little boy, he in the creamy flannel pjs she had bought from the expensive babywear store, with embroidered pockets and hems and little hand-sewn decals of Winnie-the-Pooh on each collar. *Don't spend lots of money on clothes, he'll grow out of them in five minutes*, was another parenting rule thrust on her by various helpful souls. She nodded gravely, and then spent a week's pay in half an hour on pretty little boy-things at the British export boutique in the city. *Don't give him milk if he wakes at night*. But on the first night Finn had woken, crying, and as she stood at his door and hesitated, she saw a shadow near the bed, one which could have been moonlight on the wall, or it could have been Priya, standing tall and still and watchful, close to her child as he sat in his bed and wailed. It was then that Ana got the warm milk to calm Finn down, and took him back to bed with her. She would lie sandwiched between Elijah and the little boy, wondering how so much love had come into her life. She thought of her mother, and wondered how long it would hurt for. Was it coincidence that this year of deaths had also been the year she had fallen so resoundingly in love? Did love need a chink in your armour before it could get in? She wasn't sure, but she felt Elijah at her back and Finn curled into her front, and she let the tears fall silently, safely.

After a few weeks, Finn went for one night without waking, and then two, and then he rarely woke before dawn. Then it was Ana who woke sometimes and wandered the house, watching the moon over the banksias, listening to the even breathing of the child in his bed, the man in hers.

Elijah had helped her move in, and then they joked that he had forgotten to go home. After a few weeks they put up flat-for-rent notices, and she dropped in at the *Morning Star* office and pinned one up. Elijah called the same night to say he had leased his flat to someone from her work, a guy called Zac, who had split up from his wife.

'He said he knew you. Seemed a bit grumpy about something, but he said you would vouch for his character?'

Ana laughed. She had gone into work with Finn just the week before. Zac spotted her and hauled her into the editor's office, where he was now permanently ensconced.

'Take as long off as you want, Ana. One month, two . . .'

'I want a year.'

He looked aghast. 'Ana, we have a vacancy here as senior columnist. Replacing me. It's yours for the taking.'

She smiled, and shook her head. Firmly removed Finn from the filing cabinet drawer that he was proceeding to empty. 'A year, Zac. At least. And then I'll think about what I do next.'

He groaned and slumped on the desk. 'Jesus, Ana. We need you. All these bloody reporters are so young. They're all into health food, all rushing off at lunch time to go jogging.'

'Oh thanks, and you want an old bag like me to balance the team?' She sat back and laughed, and tried to remember if she had ever done such a thing in this office before.

He studied her. 'You'll never come back.'

'You never know.' She had met with Parker Publishing

just that morning about ideas for a book, but decided not to mention it.

'No, I know.' He pulled out a leave form and picked up a pen. 'Here you go. Take this to HR. If I can ever do anything for you . . .'

'Thanks, Zac. You'll be a good editor.'

'Yeah, yeah. Maybe. And if that jammy lawyer bastard ever lets you down and you, er, want another game of Scrabble, well . . .' He watched her with warm eyes, his voice trailing off awkwardly, '. . . you know who to call.'

She dropped in on Pete Pryor's office on the way out, sheepishly crouching to Finn's height to introduce him to the gossip writer. Pryor proved to have quite a way with children, and soon had Finn sitting on his desk, shaking a snow globe.

'You enjoying motherhood?'

'I am,' said Ana.

'Quite a gift your friend left you.'

She nodded, aware of his curiosity, his appraisal. 'One of the best. Hey, thanks for the flowers at my mother's funeral.'

'No worries. Zac's idea, actually. Unusually New Age for him, I did think at the time.' He raised his eyebrows and tilted his head questioningly. Ana let it pass. 'And I hear you're back with the boyfriend? Love is in the air?'

'Spring. You know how it is.'

'Ah yes.' He turned his gaze to Finn again. 'Well, we'll be sorry to lose you for a while, Ana. But I think you're making a good move. My children made a human being out of me. Yours will do the same.'

'Surely not.'

'Ah. You never know.'

Ana smiled at the memory as she stuffed small jeans into a backpack and watched, through the front window, Elijah taking shopping bags from his car and crossing the garden to the front door. She heard Finn come clattering back into the house. She paused, waiting for the whoops of joy as the small boy and the man met outside in the hallway, and then she clipped the leash onto the puppy and lowered her to the ground. It was time for them to go.

In the sun-bathed green of Serena and Dave's backyard, the twins, newly christened, were carried out of the circular garden bed by their parents. Ana moved forward with Finn on her hip as the minister called up the little boy and his godparents.

Serena stepped back up with Elijah and they murmured replies of assent, and then she left the circle again, to watch from outside as the minister continued. Baby Joseph was grizzling, and Serena slipped him into the sling, warm on her chest. Irie rested along Dave's right arm.

Serena slid her eyes over the crowd. Romeo and Katrina, with their children; Iris holding Angus's hand as he strained to escape; Ana holding Finn close; Elijah in a suit beside her. Poss, in khakis; Ana's friend Marnie; Sharon and Mel. Cate, who earlier that day had pulled Serena aside and told her she was pregnant.

And then she saw Jo, resplendent in a tie-dyed dress, at the edge of the crowd, a sprig of fresh jasmine pinned in her grey hair. Jo caught her eye, and the affection and nostalgia in the older woman's face halted Serena from across the garden, like a cool hand laid on her cheek. Their old conversation echoed in Serena's mind. *They grow up so fast. Make the most of it.* And Serena said silently to herself, *I will.* Dave laid one arm around her shoulders, glancing down at Irie in his other arm as he did. Cooper stood in front, his small hand in Serena's, and she looked down at the top of his head and squeezed her firstborn's fingers gently.

I will.

Acknowledgements

I would like to thank the Centre for Grief Education; also Liz McMillan, Carolyn Beckett, Richard Birkett, Olga Lorenzo, and fellow students at RMIT. Thanks to Curtis Brown literary agent Tara Wynne and Penguin publisher Clare Forster for backing a debut novel, and to publisher Kirsten Abbott. I'm very grateful to this book's editor Belinda Byrne, for her hard work and guidance.

Thanks to Joan and George Cusworth for their support, and to my boys, Ewen and Red.

And thanks to Simon Maher for sharing the juggle between book and babies, and for teaching me about geology.